OLWEN AND EISA

Book Three of The Ravenstones

C.S. WATTS

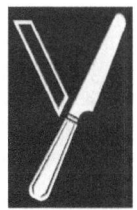

Watts, C.S./The Yellowknife Press, Vancouver, B.C.
www.theravenstones.ca

Publisher's Note: This is a work of fiction. Names, characters, places and incidents are a product of the author's imagination. Locales and public names are sometimes used for atmospheric purposes. Any resemblance to actual people, living or dead, or to businesses, companies, events, institutions or locales is completely coincidental.

The Ravenstones: Olwen and Eisa / C.S. Watts. -- 1st ed.
ISBN 978-1-7750777-8-7 (print)
ISBN 978-1-7750777-9-4 (ePub)

Success is not final, failure is not fatal:
it is the courage to continue that counts.

— Winston S. Churchill

DRAMATIS ANIMALIUM

INTREPID ADVENTURERS IN A NEW WORLD
Eirwen, a polar bear, former supreme commander of Vigmar's forces, now leader of the bear clans
Fridis, a feisty eider duck, adventurer and amateur detective

THE BIG CATS OF AERONBED
THE LIONS
Albiorix, King of Aeronbed
Olwen, his daughter
Temorwig, his oldest friend, Olwen's "uncle"
Aedelbur, his chamberlain
Mirati, chief wizard

THE PANTHERS
Anishger, leader of the Grand Council of Panthers
Rithild, member of the Grand Council; representative of the panthers in the capital
Eisa, Rithild's lieutenant
Kalishin of Dariah, Eisa's father (deceased)
Rashtad, senior member of the Grand Council

Zlatan, newest member of the Grand Council
Dughyl, Grand Council member
Antakama, Grand Council member

THE BLACK LEGION OF PANTHERS
Parthanyx, Rithild's nephew, chief commander in Heimborn
Heimdell, squad commander
Hildric, squad commander, acquaintance of Eisa
Segomo, squad commander
Geifu, Segomo's second-in-command
Samirxun, squad commander, friend of Eisa
Todog, sergeant
Estrog, corporal
Vlad, corporal
Draco, soldier
Labros, soldier

BLAKFEL, CAPITAL OF VIGMAR
Don Grimezel, a donkey, Emperor of Vigmar
Dona Morana, a donkey, Empress of Vigmar
Gulbren, Don Grimezel's son

THE IMPERIAL HOUSEHOLD
Gloton, a wolverine, First Secretary
Guntram, a raven, Gloton's predecessor (now missing)
Vulpé, a red fox, chief of Vigmar's security
Don Baaldulce, a donkey, Vulpé's predecessor (now missing)
Seanan, an owl, court doctor
Haidar, a mountain goat, head of the palace kitchen
Parvash, Haidar's father (deceased)
Alsvid, a pony, assistant to Haidar

VIGMAR'S MILITARY FORCES
THE TASANDIK WOLF CLAN
Adarix, field marshal, leader of the pack
Ammarich, eldest of the brothers

Alberic, youngest of the brothers, former aide to Eirwen
Asteel, senior member of the pack
Amlich, newest, youngest member of the pack
Amrin, member of the pack
Amteil, member of the pack
Albelin, young member of the pack
Emrin-Can, a wolfhound, member of the Imperial Household seconded to the pack

THE ARMY

Aravat, an elephant, supreme commander
Nashorn, a white rhinoceros, field commander, Army of the North
Dorkal, a mountain dog, field commander, Army of the North
Grishon, a mountain dog, field commander, Army of the North
Emer-Sigr, a black mare, field commander, Army of the South
Harclan, a mountain dog, field commander, Army of the South

THE AIR FORCE

An-Mot, a golden eagle, commander of the eagles
Rad-Alya, a golden eagle, An-Mot's predecessor (now missing)
Aeron-Urd, a gyrfalcon, air marshal in charge of air defense (hawks and falcons), friend of Fridis
Raicho, a peregrine falcon, aide to Aeron-Urd, Fridis's companion in exile
Garfreg, a gray falcon, colonel and junior member of high command
Corvus, a black falcon, squadron leader in Aeronbed
Lorcan, a northern harrier, squadron leader in Aeronbed
Tulkinar, a red-shouldered hawk, lieutenant in Aeronbed

THE BEARS OF HEIMBORN

Hunspek, a.k.a. Raven, a mysterious, self-important bird
Anat, leader of the Ethanead clan
Goran-Art, Anat's brother and former clan chief (killed by Parthanyx)
Somerled, a wise elder
Haefan, leader of the Adelgrid clan
Vidar, leader of the Sethadi clan

Bakman, leader of the Alciburg clan, Eirwen's second-in-command
Aedelborn, leader of the Kantavlast clan
Gullhinder, leader of the Sethana clan

THE MISKEN MOUNTAINS
Señor Piro, a badger, retired senior manager of the mines
THE AKOM PARTNERSHIP
Achimi, a badger
Kelnek, a falcon
Obtala, a snow leopard
Merithu, a brown bear

THE PEREGRINE FALCON COLONY
Lord and Lady Sesteros and their chicks

LIONS'
REDOUBT

BLAKVUL

VIGMAR

Valley of Ethnot

Battle of
the Antern Mountains

Sestoros Sanctuary

BLAKFEL

MANARIS

Arrival point of
Eirwen and Fridis

AERONBEL

Ethanead

HEIMBORN

N

W   E

Najara

Forest of Utgard

S

ARUNDATI

Misken Mountains

Mt Ari

Fridis'
Retreat

SOUTHERN SEA

I

AERONBED

THE COURT OF AERONBED

"Have you seen Lord Temorwig this morning?" the King of Aeronbed asked of his chamberlain, and not for the first time that day.

"No, I have not, Your Highness," the ever-patient retainer replied.

"You're sure about that, Aedelbur?" Albiorix persisted.

"Let me assure you, Majesty, I have not seen him. However, that doesn't mean his lordship is not about. It's still early and many have yet to return from their sport. I can, of course, have someone summon him. That is, if you deem the matter pressing."

"Please do so, and send him in as soon as he arrives."

Aedelbur nodded and turned to go. The elderly lion hobbled out, limping painfully.

The king sat back on his ornate wooden chair, watching the old retainer totter away. "Poor fellow," Albiorix sighed. "He's not long for it."

His Majesty was enjoying a hearty breakfast, dining alone in his private chambers. These rooms were set on the topmost floor of a rather austere but well-fortified castle, completed many years ago by the king's predecessors.

At one point in its venerable life the stronghold had been large enough to hold every inhabitant of Aeronbed's capital. Back then, it stood alone, high on a well-chosen promontory, overlooking the great sea beyond. However, over several generations, the kingdom grew and prospered, and Manaris along with it.

Eventually, the city's burgeoning population, their security and ambition increasing in tandem, spilled out from the castle's confines into the surrounding countryside. Nearby forests were cut down, creating new fertile farmland; existing farmsteads, meanwhile, became residential neighborhoods; modest homes grew larger and grander; crude stalls and shacks were transformed into rows of shops.

Ultimately a crowded, busy harbor town took shape, although in a most haphazard manner, defying any attempt at planning. The castle's walls were extended to encompass the farthest reaches of the town, which now stretched down to the very edge of the sea, thereby ensuring that every inhabitant remained safe from outside attack. Only the harbor gates and docks remained open to the dangers lurking in the mysterious waters beyond the horizon.

High, rounded turrets stood at the four corners of the castle, each one providing an unrestricted view of the adjacent ocean, for if any villains were to attack, they would surely not come by land. Indeed, thanks to the sheer cliffs and high rocky outcroppings on one side and forbidding stone block fortifications on the other, the capital was well-protected from such assault.

The eyes of the capital's defenders, therefore, were always directed outward, to the sea, keeping watch for marauding pirates and enemy ships. Despite (or perhaps because of) these safeguards, neither pirate nor pillager had ever dared trouble Manaris, at least within living memory. The inhabitants went about their daily lives undisturbed, confident about what the future held in store for them.

With another sigh, the King left his comfortable chair and strolled onto to the magnificent balcony, his eyes fixed on the commanding view. The early morning sun warmed his back and fragrant breezes wafted up from below. Although they heralded a good year to come, it was still early in the spring, far too soon for such benevolence from the spirits.

On this pristine morning, His Majesty's thoughts immediately strayed from the regular strategic maneuvers, diplomacy and politics. Rather, they were taken up by something both mundane and exquisite — the ever-pleasing scene. The lion purred with delight, as he always did when he looked out towards the west, to the point where the calm azure sea and the cloudless aquamarine sky met in a thin line far, far away — so far that no one had ever travelled to that distant uncharted point.

The King's imagination wandered off to those unfamiliar lands he was certain lay just beyond the horizon. What kinds of creatures were to be found there? What discoveries, what riches, what surprises lay in store for the daring explorer? But although he had often fancied he'd be the one to visit the unknown places beyond the ken of Aeronbed's inhabitants, he knew his destiny lay on earth, not water. And as the years had surreptitiously crept up on the old lion, Albiorix had been forced to accept the truth of his situation: he no longer had the stamina for a sea-bound adventure. He'd never find out the answers to those questions, at least, not in this lifetime.

Standing on his back legs, he leaned over the parapet, examining the townscape below. Although the narrow laneways and empty squares matched the sea's tranquility, the absence of activity failed to trouble the lion. It was not market day and most of the able-bodied had already left for the front lines. The fighting season up north would soon begin, once winter released its awesome grip and gave way to spring.

Retreating inside, the King sat back down, waiting impatiently for Temorwig's arrival. It wasn't long, however, before the warmth of the room's massive fireplace overcame the lion.

He awoke with a start. Aedelbur was in the midst of announcing his old friend.

Albiorix jumped out of the chair and embraced the other cat. "How are you keeping, Temorwig?" the King said, dispensing with formalities. "What news do you bring us?"

"Well enough, your Grace. That is, for a graybeard like me. The aging joints, you know — they throb mightily in the winter season."

"Say no more, cousin. Say no more. Don't forget, you're speaking to the oldest cat around here. No one knows aches and pains better than my poor bones."

Instinctively, the two lions moved closer to the fireplace, basking in its heat. "Our fighting days are well behind us now," Temorwig said. "We happily let others go to battle in our stead."

"True enough, cousin. Still, someone must provide wise counsel and give the orders of the day. That's why the young ones are content to keep us around and leave us in peace."

They both laughed, for that picture was far from accurate. The King may have slowed down, but his wisdom and savvy had suffered little. His authority was as great as when he was young and spry.

"And young Temorwig?" Albiorix asked. He gestured towards the dining table, indicating his friend should indulge himself. "How is the cub?"

"No longer a cub, sire, that's for sure," Temorwig said. "I miss him dearly, although that's neither here nor there. As to his wellbeing, I haven't the slightest idea." The lion shrugged and sat down at the table. "You know how it is," he added. "Reports of troop movements in the hinterland take an age and a half to reach Manaris. As for the latest skirmishes — nothing at all."

"Wasn't he on his way south?" Albiorix asked. "Just when those accursed wolves showed up?"

"Indeed he was. Ordered to change course and take charge of a couple of local units. Temorwig saw a few battles against those fiends, but — the spirits be praised — he came out unscathed. And since the close of autumn, that region's been quieter then a dead hyena."

"He's still guarding Heimborn?"

"Over winter he was stationed in the mountains, but his company's moved on now. Already in the far south, I expect. No doubt he'll see action as soon as the fighting picks up."

"Well, that's all to the good," His Majesty said. "He should have an easier time down there." He paused to tackle some of his unfinished breakfast, passing some choice pieces over to his friend. "Tell me, how did his first command go? Those wolves are tough customers — it couldn't have been easy."

"You know how these young ones are, Majesty." He grinned

broadly and grabbed the offered joint of meat. "Temorwig's told me very little about the actual fighting. I'm sure he doesn't want to worry me. And for my part, I've no desire to pester him. He's grown up now, far too old for my counsel."

"One's never too old to hear — and accept — good advice."

"True enough, my lord. But offspring are quick to close their ears to direction from their elders."

Albiorix laughed. "Wasn't it the same when we were young?" The two lions had been comrades for many years, and the memories of the mistakes of that era resonated still.

"So young Temorwig's off to help our southern allies," Albiorix said.

"Astakume's lot needed some toughening up," his friend said by way of agreement. "Odd allies if you ask me." He spat out a piece of tough gristle. "Hardly trustworthy. Hah! I've seen more backbone in a dead fish."

"We can't get to choose all our friends. Some of these alliances have long antecedents. Surely you've not forgotten that it was the falling out between the donkeys and antelopes that precipitated the war between Vigmar and Aeronbed."

"Ancient history." Temorwig sniffed. "I've no mind for it."

"Well, my old friend, get a mind for it," growled the King. "We may well need the antelope to legitimize our claim over Vigmar — that is, once this wretched conflict is finally over."

"I suppose they're better than some of the villains we've come across over the years."

"Aye, there's a long list." Albiorix sighed. "And by my reckoning, every week I come across one or two more I'd happily throw on that dung heap."

"Couldn't agree more, sire. Just imagine sharing power with the donkeys!" They both laughed at such an absurd thought.

"You pass on my regards to your son the next time you're in contact with him," the King said, changing the subject. "He'll do you proud, I know it."

"Thank you, Majesty. I will."

"I hold you both close to my heart. I remember him as a young 'un, running and tumbling about underfoot. Full of good spirits he was."

"And still is, sire. He'll make great sport of the campaign, whatever comes about. And, if I may ask, what of your son?"

"You may, cousin, and of my daughter as well. Both are in excellent health and, as we speak, heading back to the front lines. I saw them recently, you know. Brief visits." The lion frowned. "Of course, too brief for my liking. Naturally they were in a hurry to return to their commands. What can I say? Their home is not with me anymore but with their troops. That's where their hearts and minds lie now. So be it. It's the way of life."

The old lion had spoken with more than a trace of regret. But Albiorix's tone changed abruptly as he turned to another subject. "What news do you hear of Heimborn, as those creatures like to call the place?"

"The bears' homeland?" the other lion replied, his eyes widening in surprise. "Why, nothing much. Although I must confess I don't follow developments there on a regular basis."

"Really?" Albiorix countered. "What I'm picking up is completely different. Even talk of rebellion. Well, at least some sort of trouble."

"I doubt that, sire. Things have been peaceful in Heimborn for as far back as I can recall. Of course the panthers keep a tight enough rein on the situation. Hah! So tight we lions don't even think about the place anymore." He leaned back in the chair, gesturing with his front paws. "Haven't I always said, Albiorix, those creatures are a spent force and a dissolute species. They've neither the will nor the means to stand up to the worst of our troops. It's been like that for years."

"Still, if the bears ever sought an opportunity to test us, it's right now, when we're preoccupied with Vigmar. Aeronbed can ill afford an internal struggle at the same time as open combat with the enemy."

"True enough," Temorwig agreed, helping himself to another offering of meat.

"Really, I don't understand this latest attack from Vigmar," he went on. "What's given Grimezel the hope he might gain a foothold now, when every previous effort has produced nothing but wrack and ruin?

All those years of war and so little to show for it — the whole thing beats me."

"Grimezel, that fool!" the King ranted. "He gets to call himself emperor just because he rules two kingdoms."

Overcome with anger, Albiorix leapt out of his chair and began to stalk back and forth. "Hah! Aeronbed is larger — and wealthier — than the two put together. Perhaps I should divide our dear country in half and create a brand new title. That'd teach him!"

"No one's fooled by his pretensions. At least no one in Aeronbed."

"I remember Morana's grandfather," Albiorix carried on. "The old donkey wasn't so bad for a hoofed creature. A credit to his species, even. At least *he* showed a bit of gumption. *And* he certainly had brains. A tough old bird when it came down to negotiations, but at least he and I could carry on a civil conversation ... now and then. As for Grimezel, hah! That donkey is just an ass! And don't get me started on the Empress."

"You heard about Grimezel's son, no doubt," Temorwig interjected, ignoring the joke.

"I have indeed. I'm very well informed on these matters, you know," the King replied, sitting down again. "It's a shame. Despite everything, I do feel for Grimezel. No offspring — pup, cub or foal — should die before his parent. But such is war, and the donkey did bring it upon himself. Now that the Empire has no true heir, the cat will be among the pigeons, so to speak."

Temorwig said nothing, having no head for such matters.

"I digress," Albiorix continued. "We were speaking of the bears."

"Trust me, sire. As I said earlier, there's nothing to worry about."

"I do trust you. But experience tells me I'd prefer proof."

"I can have a closer look, if you wish. Rithild and I are traveling together later today. I'll push him on the matter. Knowing our cousin, you'll have your answer faster than a cat can pounce on her prey."

"Excellent. I appreciate your personal attention to this matter. You are my oldest and dearest friend, Temorwig. I rely upon you for unvarnished counsel — those things I welcome *and* those I don't."

"At your service, as always, my lord."

"It may be nothing at all," the King continued, "but I do need to know what's going on. I've not forgotten that prophecy."

"Bah! Give it no heed, Majesty. An old cat's tale, or, worse yet, an old bear's mad ravings."

"Still — "

"If I've said it once, I've said it a thousand times: don't give it any thought. The story lives only through your thinking about it."

"And yet, and yet ... I tell you, Temorwig, my whiskers are all on edge."

At that very moment, old Aedelbur knocked on the door and opened it. The two lions watched as he limped slowly into the room.

"Your Maj— " the chamberlain began, in a vain attempt to indicate the arrival of a visitor.

An attractive young lioness, pale blond in color, rushed into the room, brushing him aside. "Father!" the lioness cried out. She ignored the aged retainer and hurried forward to embrace the King.

"Olwen! Daughter! My treasure and delight!" Albiorix responded. "I thought you'd left for the north."

They hugged each other while the chamberlain shuffled off, muttering about the terrible manners of the young.

"Perhaps my mind is failing me," Albiorix continued. "Did I not bid you farewell mere days ago? If so, what brings you back, so soon and unannounced? Has anything gone wrong? Does Vigmar's advance already threaten us, so early in the season?"

The lioness, out of breath from her hurried return, struggled to regain her poise.

"I know my return comes as a great surprise, Father," Olwen said at last. "And no, we've not caught sight of the enemy's forces. The point is, I hardly know where to begin. Please, do sit down. Both of you. This strange tale may take quite a while."

2

A CURIOUS TALE

Albiorix ushered Olwen and Temorwig into a small antechamber where the three lions could speak undisturbed.

"You're right, I did leave the capital three days ago," Olwen began, sitting down. "As you say, I was on my way north with my company, alongside many other troops. The winds were warm and at our backs, our spirits excellent and the pace measured. Everything was as we would have wished, and no danger loomed on the horizon.

"At the end of a second day's long march, we encamped for the night in a dense wooded area right next to the trail. I'm sure you know it, Father, since you've often traveled that route. At the end of a full day of sun, the evening had clouded over and the night was mild and calm.

"The evening began well enough. The sentry posts reported no disturbances, and since we were still far from the enemy, we felt quite relaxed. Yet despite this seeming perfection, something I could not explain was troubling me. I slept restlessly, turning frequently, as if I were lying on jagged rock and could not find a comfortable position. Several times I woke up completely, and on each occasion found it difficult to return to sleep. It was between one of those episodes of fitful sleep and wakefulness that I heard my name being called."

"Someone was calling for you?" Temorwig asked. "In the middle of the night? A guard?"

"No, not a guard. Not anyone I could see."

"A dream?" Albiorix suggested.

The lioness hesitated. "Truly, I wasn't certain. Not at that point, anyway."

"Most curious," said Temorwig.

"You should have seen the fur on the back of my neck. It was standing straight up, let me tell you! But I looked all around and I could see nothing at all. That is, nothing but trees and darkness. After a while, concluding that it must have been my imagination at work, I began to calm down.

"But then, just as my eyes were beginning to close, I heard the voice again, more distinctly this time. My name was being called very, very quietly. It was a strange voice, unlike anything I've ever heard before, a deep-throated whisper speaking the words very calmly, very seriously, like a command."

"Your name was being called?" the King said. "Just that?"

"No, more than that. The exact words were 'Olwen, arise and follow.'"

The two old lions looked at each other. "Follow what?" Albiorix asked.

"Whatever or whoever was the source of the voice, it remained out of sight, too far away for me to see. I turned my head in every direction and finally determined that the call was coming from the very depths of the forest.

"I stood up. No one else was awake, apart from the guards. But I could see they were sitting quietly, utterly undisturbed. They paid me no heed and they paid no heed to the voice. It seemed as if no other member of the company but myself could hear it."

"So you alone could hear the call," the King said.

"No one else even bothered to look up — not a single head moved or ear twitched. I continued to hold back, still thinking I was hearing nothing more than the call of some night creature or a tree branch rasping in the breeze. But the voice beckoned me again, and this time I could not refuse it. You know what they say about curiosity and cats? Well, in spite of that, my curiosity overcame any caution I had left."

"But Olwen, it could have been an evil spirit," Albiorix protested with increasing anxiety. "Some creature trying to deceive you. Did you consider that possibility?"

"Hush, Father, of course I did. Well, at least at first. But then I realized I felt no fear at all. It was not a frightening or menacing voice, but rather imploring, even reassuring."

"What happened then," Temorwig asked.

"As carefully as I could, I crept around the sleeping troops and then through the underbrush in the direction of the sound, until I was completely outside the encampment. I hunted around for a while until I found myself standing before an abaster tree."

"Really?" Temorwig said. "An abaster?"

"A rare find," said the King. "Most telling."

"I've heard my teachers speak of such trees but have never actually seen one," Olwen added.

"I've never seen one," Temorwig said, "in all my years."

"How was it placed?" Albiorix asked.

"It stood tall and straight, all alone but surrounded by the usual green conifers, budding willows and great old oaks that grow in that region."

Her listeners marveled at the picture that was unfolding in their imaginations.

"When I finally took my eyes off that magnificent tree," Olwen went on, "I noticed off to my left a large pool of water."

The King's eyes opened wide. "A pool, you say? Describe it."

"Really nothing out of the ordinary in size, about as big as three sleeping lions placed end to end. I could have leapt over it easily if I'd tried. But the water itself — that was special."

"How so?"

"For one thing, the water was completely still, undisturbed by the breeze. For another, the surface was impenetrable. No reeds or rocks broke its surface, and it seemed to give back no reflection. I found myself being drawn irresistibly toward it, and I crouched down to touch the water with my paw."

"You didn't drink from it, did you?" Albiorix interjected.

"I was tempted, but no, I did not."

"Good."

"In fact, just before I could touch the water, I heard the voice again, very near to me. I pulled back and glanced up, and there, on a low branch of the abaster, I saw a large, coal-black raven. Neither of us said a word; we just stared at each other, until finally I asked the bird if he had been the one who called me. He did not respond; rather, he unfolded one of his wings and pointed at the water. I took his gesture to mean that the answer to my question lay there, in the dark depths of the pool, so I turned back to inspect it — that is, as carefully as I could in the darkness."

"A raven! Of all birds, Olwen," interrupted the King, "you know what they say about those creatures. They can't be trusted. They're sent to make mischief and confuse our minds. I've never told you my own experience with those creatures, but let me assure you — "

"Pssh, Father, those are just old superstitions," Olwen purred in response, smiling brightly. "No one believes that anymore."

"Daughter — " Albiorix growled, about to voice an objection.

Temorwig interceded. "Olwen, please go on with your story. You know how your father is." He put a large paw on the King's shoulder in an attempt to pacify his old friend.

"I will, Uncle, I will," Olwen replied. "So, as I was saying, the raven pointed to the water. At first, since the surface was as murky as the night, I could make out nothing at all. But soon, by some force of magic, or maybe sheer will, it cleared up, and suddenly I could see myself in it, as if I were gazing into a mirror in broad daylight. As I stared into the water, behind me in the reflection I could see the stars and a brilliant full moon shining in the sky. It was a glorious sight. The moon seemed so near that I wouldn't have been surprised if it had touched my shoulders.

"But then I suddenly remembered that the evening sky had been completely overcast; neither moon nor stars were to be seen at all that night. Just to make sure, I turned my head and looked upward. I was correct; the sky was as dark and dull as a tomb, entirely swathed in dense clouds. Then I looked back toward the pool, but the vision had disappeared as quickly as it appeared. The water was murky once again.

"It seemed that I'd broken some kind of spell by looking away. You can't imagine how I felt — as if I'd lost something truly important. 'Friend Raven,' I implored, looking at the bird again, 'what do you wish me to understand? Now I see nothing at all.'

"The bird merely raised its wing and pointed again to the dark pool. Although I was skeptical about seeing anything more, I couldn't help but obey. This time the picture came instantly. However, it was totally different — not a fixed image as I had previously seen, but one that changed as I looked at it. It was like watching a story in progress.

"It began with a scene of a ridge high in the mountains, a place unfamiliar to me. Although I could see an animal walking along the ridge, the creature was too distant for me to make it out clearly. At first I thought it was a panther, for it was jet black and moved gracefully, like one of us. But then, to my astonishment, I realized the creature was not a cat but a great black bear walking very slowly. Deliberately, even. Not lumbering awkwardly as they usually do, but moving nimbly and with dignity. From time to time I'd lose sight of the bear as it moved through thick woods. Finally it came into view again, much closer to me, and then it stood up on its hind legs.

"As it stood, the bear changed color. It became pure white and then grew even larger. And then, as if this were not enough, a light seemed to radiate from within it. I'm sorry, Father, but it's difficult to describe. It was as if the bear was light itself. Its radiance illuminated the entire scene I gazed upon. The bear then looked right at me — or at least it seemed to."

"It looked right at you?" Albiorix asked. "You're sure about that?"

"Yes, and then it spoke to me."

"To you? Really?" The King rose and began to pace back and forth. "You need to be precise now."

"The bear's mouth never moved, or at least not I could see. But I could hear his words, coming from somewhere."

"What did the creature say?"

"He said: *Even the darkness will be driven out and the night will be clear as day.*"

Albiorix stopped pacing, and Olwen paused briefly to let the words sink in.

"You're certain?" the King asked.

The lioness hesitated before replying. "I think that's what the bear said. You realize I've never experienced anything like this before — something both amazing and impossible to comprehend. I turned back to the raven to ask what I should take from it. But the bird was gone; it had flown away without a signal or a sound. And when I looked back at the pool, the moving picture had vanished."

"What happened then?" Temorwig asked.

"I felt so disappointed! I'd been given a gift and then I'd wasted the opportunity. I wanted more; I wanted to understand what I'd seen. I wanted the bird to come back. If only I'd kept my focus on the image, the whole story might have been revealed and explained. I sat for the longest time, hoping the raven would return or the vision would reappear."

"But it didn't," the King said.

"Alas, no," Olwen confirmed. "Everything was back to normal, and nothing else out of the ordinary occurred. Then, as I sat there trying to make sense of it all, something told me I must return immediately to Manaris and tell you what I'd seen."

The lioness paused again and added, "And so, here I am." She looked back and forth between the two older lions, hoping for, even expecting some sort of guidance. But for the longest while neither spoke as they considered what they had just heard.

Finally Temorwig opened his mouth as if to say something. The King, however, quickly held up a paw to silence him. "Say nothing just yet, my old friend. We must not jump to conclusions."

"And yet it does seem to fit," Temorwig pursued, ignoring the caution. "The stories we heard from the troops fighting the wolves — no one wanted to believe them; it made no sense. And then we received word the mighty creature had been killed in battle."

Olwen's eyes opened wide at these hints of extraordinary events, but she said nothing.

"Perhaps," Albiorix suggested, "the creature was indeed killed and Olwen's vision a sign of its fate. It has gone to wherever dead bears go.

As for me, I think not. This was a revelation not of the past but of the future. It was intended to instruct or perhaps warn us."

"Visions, bah!" Temorwig declared. "A dream, more likely."

"Not a dream," Olwen protested. "It was all quite real."

"Are you sure, Princess?"

"As sure, Uncle, as I'm sitting here in Manaris talking with you," the lioness declared, more than a little annoyed by the question. "And let me remind both of you that I'm no longer a cub. I fight alongside Aeronbed's very best — "

"Forgive me, Princess, I meant no offense," Temorwig interjected kindly, holding up his front paws to stop her budding tirade. "In my eyes, dear Olwen, you will never age."

The lioness ignored his apology. "What's this tale about the wolves and a bear?" she demanded. "I've heard nothing of it."

"But what does it tell us?" said the King, staring off into space and ignoring his daughter's question. "You saw or heard nothing else? Are you completely certain? When the picture and bird disappeared, what did you do then?"

"I returned back to the campsite, where I tried to revisit the land of sleep. Without success, as you can well imagine. At the earliest light I asked leave of my commanding officer, hastened to bid my company farewell, and returned here by the high road."

His expression grave, Albiorix closed his eyes, meditating upon the words of the lioness. The other two watched him in silence.

Finally the King broke his reverie. "Olwen, you were wise to return," he said. "You must be exhausted from your journey. Go to your chambers and get some rest. I will explain everything to you later. Temorwig, I feel even more strongly that you need to meet with Rithild. Seek him out right away. I have to know more — everything, any news from Heimborn — and as soon as possible.

"In the meantime, I will consult with my wizards. Perhaps there is mischief afoot here or, if the spirits are with us, we've been given a gift of insight. But we must know what it all signifies. Go now, both of you. We shall speak again soon."

3

MEANINGS, CONFUSIONS, OBFUSCATIONS

"Well?" Albiorix demanded brusquely. "What do you think?"

The lion was speaking to, or rather at, his three chief wizards, demanding their immediate response to his inquiry — what to make of Olwen's mysterious tale.

"Your grace," replied the most senior of the wizards, "you, among all creatures of this noble land, know these are not easy matters to sort out, let alone explain. It is why the science of foretelling is a life's study. We investigate closely, we think about every factor, we do not jump to conclusions; we must consider every aspect carefully before pronouncing a verdict. We may even need to speak further with the Princess to ensure that we are aware of every minute detail, for everything is important in such divinations."

"Time is of the essence, Mirati," Albiorix urged. "When can I expect a completed prediction or, failing that, at very least a well-crafted understanding from you three?"

"Majesty," the chief wizard replied cautiously, "we must also look into the matter of the most auspicious days for providing answers to such questions. You know as well as I do that answers can come only at their own due time."

What Albiorix did know was that the wizarding profession liked to take its own sweet time and then cover itself by providing for every possible eventuality. That way, later on they could avoid any possible accusation of making a mistake. To be accused of error, let alone to be found in error, was unacceptable. Because their reputations, their careers and sometimes even their lives might depend on the answers they provided, they tended to take few, if any, real chances. But the King was wise to their tricks and convoluted ways. No matter how hard Mirati might try to escape Albiorix's net and postpone the inevitable, His Majesty would not allow it.

"When?" the King snarled at the wizard, who, despite his lord's displeasure, was taking it all in stride. Mirati understood that rulers of every sort seek simple, clear-cut answers to complex problems. It was an ongoing tussle between the needs of kings and the abilities of wizards, complicated by the imprecision of the omens and the confusion of the witnesses. Those in charge never really understood how challenging it was. The chief wizard had become chief for good reason — Mirati was skilled not just in the science of prophecy but also in the arts of politics and negotiating.

The wizard picked up a scroll from a nearby table, studied it closely, muttered to himself, closed his eyes as if to meditate, opened them again, reached for a pocket-sized globe and then studied it assiduously. The impatient Albiorix paced back and forth, his tail swishing furiously. Mirati then placed the two objects on the table side by side and his eyes darted back and forth between the scroll and the globe. Every now and then he placed a claw on a specific part of the scroll and gave the globe a quarter-turn. Sometimes he seemed almost ready to render a verdict, but then he quickly relented and went back to work. Finally the lion turned to his two colleagues; they huddled together in a corner of the room, speaking quietly among themselves. After a few minutes the chief wizard came back to face his king.

"In three days, Your Majesty," Mirati declared, "the alignment of the stars and moon will be rather promising. Although I must admit, the moment will be even more auspicious in three weeks. If Your Highness would care to delay —"

"Never!" roared the King, his irritation growing. "I must have an answer this week. In fact, even three days is excessive. Nevertheless, I will hold myself in check — that is, if I must. Go now, Mirati. Not one more moment's hesitation; begin your work at once."

The wizards bowed low and moved to depart from the chamber. As they were leaving, the King roared after them, "And when you return, don't give me vague theories or generalizations. Remember, Mirati, I shall expect clear answers from you three."

The chief wizard smiled to himself as he went through the door, leaving the King muttering aloud in evident frustration.

⚜

THREE HUGE CATS, TWO OF WHICH WERE JET-BLACK PANTHERS AND ONE A tawny golden lion, were heading south from Manaris, moving at an appropriately slow pace in the midday sun. Temorwig, the lion, and the panthers, Rithild and his lieutenant, Eisa, were marching along a dusty hard-baked earthen trail, set almost dead center amid flat, greening fields in every direction. The three had just descended from the cooler mountainous heights surrounding Aeronbed's capital. In these neighboring lowlands, which lacked the sea's moist and cooling breezes, the earth would become parched in summer and the still air claustrophobic.

Today, however, in early spring, the lowlands offered the cats a pleasing and hospitable escape from the damp coastal chill. Like all the preceding days of late, it was unseasonably warm and ferociously sunny, and it was not long before the three cats, tired and panting as they plodded along, were searching for a shady spot where they could confer in comfort. At last they came across an ancient fortification, long since abandoned, where they could rest and talk more comfortably.

Temorwig looked around and groaned loudly. "I had hoped to have this conversation completed long before we reached this miserable outpost," the lion complained. "And now I must return over the same hard ground, all the way back to Manaris. Surely, cousin, we didn't need all that small talk."

Baron Rithild merely laughed by way of reply.

"I tell you truly, Rithild, this march has been a waste of my time," Temorwig continued. "At my age it does me no good, no good at all."

"Come now, my lord, think of it as a useful stretching of those old limbs. Keeps you limber, it does," the Baron replied jovially, giving his cousin a playful push. "And with this magnificent weather? Well, what could be better?"

"Easy for you to say — you're still young. Well, compared to me, anyway. I'll wager there are plenty more lives in you yet, Rithild."

The Baron laughed. "Not that much younger."

Temorwig grunted and stopped outside the ruins.

"I regret it had to be so," the panther went on. "The Lieutenant and I would never be able to reach our destination on schedule if we'd delayed our departure. Also, these matters need to be spoken of carefully and in private. We must be on guard at all times; even out in the open country there are unseen ears and eyes. Here, at least, we can speak in complete secrecy. And Eisa must be party to our conversation; the subject concerns him as well."

"So be it, Rithild," Temorwig replied, hardly convinced. "And here we are at last, so let's get on with it."

The lion walked under a stone archway and into a courtyard. The two panthers quickly followed. Although the old fortification was in a state of disrepair, there was little danger of being overhead by potential spies.

"If I understand you correctly," Rithild said, "the King is concerned about news he's been receiving. It's the Heimborn bears — something about an uprising, I gather."

"Exactly. But you know as well as I do, while the King's manner may be restrained, much lies behind his words. Do not take the word *concerned* lightly."

"Hah! That's a mistake I'd never make."

"Good."

"Do you know the source of his information?" the panther asked.

"No, I do not. Albiorix has always had recourse to his own sources, and since he heard that confounded yarn from Olwen he's even more troubled about the reports. Now he's convinced something is amiss."

"Yarn? The Princess?" Rithild asked quickly. "I've heard nothing of this."

"I cannot say anything more at present. The King has yet to receive a satisfactory explanation from his wizards as to its meaning. My word, who knows where this absurd story will take us." The old lion made that last observation more to himself than to the others, then shook his great mane in some disbelief at what he was saying.

"And yet, whatever the truth of the account," Rithild pursued, "it has already heightened His Majesty's anxiety?"

"Albiorix is a great king and leader, but you know how he is, always putting faith in such things. And of late he's become more and more superstitious, looking for signs and omens everywhere. Sometimes I think — But no matter. It's better left unsaid."

The panther alert to every nuance of the lion's words, quickly put two and two together. "Don't forget, Temorwig, you and I have encountered dark forces before. A long time ago, certainly, but ... "

The Baron didn't need to complete his thought. As for the lion, his expression indicated that his memory of the event was still fresh. With a dismissive wave of his paw, Temorwig said, "Let's leave that tale for another day, old friend." He glanced over at Eisa, who'd been paying close attention.

"It would help me if I knew the source of these rumors," Rithild persisted. "I needn't remind you that news of troubles in Heimborn is of equal — maybe even greater — concern to us panthers."

"Aye, I grant you it would be. But as I've said, His Majesty did not care to share that detail with me. He would only say how well informed he was, which — as we both know only too well — usually turns out to be true. That's how Albiorix has met with such success over the years: he's always one jump ahead of the rest of us."

"Well, in this case, I regret to say, his sources — whoever they are — are misinformed. I can assure you, all is well in those parts."

"That's exactly what I said to him. I relayed what you told me previously, that you and your forces on the ground outside Heimborn have matters well under control, and that you've received no recent reports of trouble. As you well know, I've always felt those bears are a spent force. Their best days — if you can even call them that — are long gone. If you ask me, the creatures are more of a curiosity than a threat."

"I'm glad to hear your trust in our efforts remains unaltered. I can only repeat that nothing has changed since we spoke last. I'm afraid to say, your trip with us has been of little value. Except, of course, to confirm the current state of affairs."

"Albiorix did ask me to check again with you, since he was so upset, and I pledged to do as he bade me. And so here we are, Baron, sitting in an old, abandoned fortress along a dusty trail in the middle of an open field. It's a far cry from my comfortable bed, let me tell you."

"Here we are indeed." The panther smiled. "Well, no harm done."

"Except to my sore knees."

Rithild laughed.

"And you can assure me your grip on affairs remains as firm as ever?" the lion insisted.

"I can. A few days ago I received an update from my nephew Parthanyx. There was a spot of bother with one of the bear clans and he had to dispose of their leader, a troublemaker no one will miss. Of course these things happen from time to time. To call such an incident trouble — let alone an 'uprising' — would be a vast overstatement. We both know that a show of force is necessary from time to time to keep the bears in check. Fortunately those creatures are a craven race and easily quelled. I guarantee you, we'll hear no more from that clan, or from any of the others. And even in the unlikely event that we do, the bears can be brought to heel without much effort."

The lion thanked the panther, but Rithild was not yet done. "Having said that, Lord Temorwig, I do understand how anxious the king can become when he gets the wind up. It's for this very reason I've asked young Eisa to sit in with us. After we finish here, I'm sending him on to meet with Parthanyx and the other commanders. Where the King is concerned, there can be no mistakes. In a few days' time I'll be able to reconfirm everything I've told you. Naturally we'll come down hard on any more troublemakers, should there be any."

"Excellent. I want to assure you that the King has every confidence in you, in the panthers' Grand Council and all the panther commanders. You've never failed us — never. Albiorix does not doubt you now; he just needs reassuring."

"Thank you, Temorwig. I appreciate your words of praise. And please keep my last comments in proper context. There was a disturbance, but nothing out of the ordinary, nothing any of us would remotely consider a rebellion. And, like a tiny flame, it's already been extinguished. Indeed, I'm almost embarrassed to mention it. If the King's mind had not needed easing, I wouldn't have brought attention to the report."

"That's what I wished and expected to hear. I will report your comforting words to His Majesty, exactly as you've relayed them to me. I apologize for harping on it."

"Merely doing what you must, my lord, which is required of all those who support the King. And now we must leave you. Lieutenant Eisa and I still have a long road ahead of us. It will be a while before we can rest again."

"May the spirits of the trail speed you on your way. Until we meet again. And, if there should be an unexpected development, I presume you will advise me. Without delay?" The lion raised his eyebrows and waved his long tail pointedly.

"You can rely on me completely."

The three cats parted, the lion heading back toward the castle of Manaris. After watching Temorwig until he'd disappeared from view, Rithild and Eisa resumed their southward trek toward Heimborn.

"Well, Eisa, you know what you have to do," the older panther said after a few moments of sober reflection.

"Yes, my lord — bring that stupid Parthanyx to heel."

"I'm embarrassed to call the cat a relative. Parthanyx causes me — all of us — more problems than he's worth. And now the idiot's gone too far."

"Yes, sir."

"We must stop things before they get out of control. Hmph. Let's hope it's not too late already."

Eisa nodded. "By all the spirits of the woods, if only we knew who's feeding information to the King!" The panther looked around as if half-expecting the traitor to stand up and show his face.

"Little chance we'll ever find the villain," the Baron lamented, coming to an abrupt halt. Rithild grabbed his assistant's shoulders and looked him right in the eye. "It's crucial that matters get resolved quickly, Lieutenant," he said. "Otherwise the council won't be able to keep a lid on the situation. Time is not on our side. And you know what will happen if we lose the trust of the lions."

"I shudder to think, my lord."

Rithild's expression said it all.

"I'll get going immediately, my lord," Eisa responded.

"The spirits go with you. Be strong, Eisa, be merciless. You have my full authority to act, and I know you'll do the right thing. I'll join you within days. You know the rendezvous point."

"My lord, I'm gone like the wind."

The young panther was as good as his word. Rithild watched him race away.

⊗

"YOUR MAJESTY, I HAVE JUST RETURNED FROM SPEAKING TO RITHILD."

Temorwig and Albiorix were once again standing together in the King's chambers overlooking the sea beyond Aeronbed; it was late that same day. The night was clear and calm, the stars and moon reflected in the mirror-like surface of the pristine waters. However, this time their minds were not on the view.

"By all appearances you've had a long day, Temorwig. The dust of the road hangs on you like a second coat."

"It was as hot and dry as I've ever seen this time of year, Majesty. I'm as thirsty as a stranded fish."

The king ordered some refreshment for his friend and Temorwig began his rendition of what he had heard.

"As I told you earlier, Albiorix, there's nothing to your information. In this rare case your informants must be wrong, or they have overstated recent events." The old lion licked a paw and brushed his face clean. "Rithild mentioned one minor incident, an altercation that left a bear dead, as he richly deserved. Nothing more than that."

"Nothing more than that," repeated the king slowly.

"Nothing. At least, according to Rithild. Naturally I cannot swear to it myself; I am relying on his good account."

"And you trust his word?"

"How could you even ask such a question? We've a long-standing arrangement with the panthers and the Baron has been our trusted ally these many years. He's given us no reason to think otherwise."

"Not yet, anyway."

"If I may speak frankly, my liege, your suspicions are beginning to verge on paranoia. What causes you to doubt so?"

"My informants have never been wrong. And now I have Olwen's prophecy."

"Bah! In my opinion that was nothing but a bad dream. She may be your cub, but she's still young and impressionable."

"Olwen is wise beyond her years."

"So what have your wizards told you?"

"They're still considering the matter."

"Hah! Not in any hurry, I'm sure. And when they return with their learned judgment, you know as well as I do what they'll say. First they'll hem and haw and then, to save their own necks, they'll give you so many choices the result will be as meaningless as searching for raindrops in a fog."

"I did command the wizards to be clear, with no shilly-shallying. I will not stand for their usual tricks."

"Well, Your Majesty, I shall await their results with bated breath," Temorwig replied, his words heavy with sarcasm. "So, when will you hear something?"

"In three more days. Mirati sees it as the most promising of dates available. Of course, he argued for more time to study the details."

Temorwig rolled his eyes skyward. "I'll bet he did."

"Enough! You go too far, Temorwig. At least hold your views until we hear back from them. I know you don't share my confidence in prophecy, but you also know my impeccable record as king. I have ruled with greater success and for a lot longer than anyone before me. And I have done so through trusting my instincts."

"I'll give you that, my old friend. I can never forget the many times I owed my life to your quick thinking."

"Well, then, leave off."

"So be it, Your Majesty. If I've spoken unwisely, it's only because we have no reason to doubt Rithild. The panthers have been most effective at keeping a firm grip on Heimborn for many a year, and I don't want to interfere in their running of things. When one has delegated matters to those whom one trusts, it's good business not to meddle."

"As long as the trust is there, of course. Of course."

"You frustrate me, Albiorix. I can hear the suspicion in your voice. You know you've nothing firm to go on."

"True enough, and I promise to keep an open mind on the matter. I thank you, as always, for your honest opinion."

"That's why we two have survived into old age and still remain friends."

They embraced, as old friends do, and parted for the night.

4

ALL IS NOT WELL IN THE BORDERLANDS

"I tell you, Eisa, it's a fool's paradise we're living in," Parthanyx declared, pacing back and forth.

Eisa tried to respond, but Parthanyx was just getting started. "I know you must do your duty by old Rithild — he's a respected elder and all that. But let's face facts. The Council represents the past, not the future. We here on the front lines are the future, tested every day, holding the line against corruption and pestilence.

"My uncle tells us to mind our manners and not offend the royal family. Bah! I'm tired of these petty edicts coming out of Manaris. And I'm not alone. Such rules and regulations mean nothing to us. Those elders recognize only the old ways of doing things. Life has changed. You see it, Eisa; at least, I trust you do. If not, look around.

"What do the lions know of the problems we face on the front lines? It's been a long time since we've seen Albiorix out here. Can you even recall when the King was last in the field? I, for one, cannot. And the old fool rules us still. I ask you, what has that family done to deserve such loyalty from the panthers?"

Parthanyx was jumping from complaint to complaint as he lectured Eisa. They were in a large field tent at the panthers' encampment, just outside Heimborn's borderlands. The lieutenant had arrived moments before. Although the younger panther was tired, thirsty and footsore, he knew time was of the essence, so he'd not hesitated to enter into this necessary discussion with his old compatriot. However, Parthanyx continued to stalk back and forth during his harangue.

"Calm down, cousin," Eisa responded. "Don't forget that Albiorix has brought us much wealth. Before you or I were even born he was leading Aeronbed to victory after victory."

"My point exactly. Albiorix is well past his prime. He's tired out and too accepting of the status quo; the lion hasn't had a new idea in years. There's no fight left in him. I tell you, Aeronbed needs new blood and new energy."

"Be careful what you say, Parthanyx. That's treasonous talk."

"I call things as I see them. I've no time for this regime's dithering and naysaying."

Eisa laughed uneasily. "Easy to claim, this far from Manaris. I'd like to see you say the same to the King's face."

"Would you now. Well, one day you may have that pleasure. Just make sure you're present for the grand event."

"I don't understand you. What's the cause of this bitterness? You've changed."

"It's living out here that's changed me. You've become soft, Eisa, soft from all that high living back in Manaris. Here life is hard, and so are we. While you luxuriate in comfort, we have to deal with those repugnant creatures. Stay out here long enough and you'll see for yourself — the bears are vile. They'd slit our throats as soon as look at us. We can't afford to let down our guard for one moment. Let me tell you, Eisa, we'd all be dead by now if we lived by the lions' absurd accords. So my brothers and I have created our own set of rules."

"Are you telling me that the decrees permitting the bears certain rights and liberties are being ignored?"

"Listen to yourself! Are you mad? If we provide the bears with any privileges, they take advantage of them. Give them a break and they do nothing but subvert our authority. They're nothing but whiners, cheats and thieves. Nothing good can come from living side-by-side with them!"

Parthanyx's rage had grown with each accusation. "If you gave the bears any kind of freedom, you'd have nothing but chaos. What do those bureaucrats in Manaris know of the reality of life out here? They romanticize the bears. They see them as simple, easygoing creatures that pose no risk. Bah! We alone see the truth. Living with those beasts day in and day out, we understand them. They'd kill us without a second thought. Extermination — it's the only answer. Before it's too late!"

Eisa was horrified. "What are you saying?"

"You understand me well enough."

Too shocked, too dismayed by what he was hearing, the lieutenant couldn't manage to argue the point.

"Are all of you as one on this matter? The entire force of panthers?"

"We are. Ask any of the others."

"Don't worry, I shall," Eisa responded. "But before I go, listen to me. Rithild is protecting your hide back in Manaris. If it weren't for him covering up for you, you'd have been cashiered long ago. Remember, we panthers stick together. It's not soldiers in the field against those of us back in Manaris. We're all brothers in arms, no matter what you may think."

Parthanyx sneered. "You and Rithild are no better than the rest of them. The Council and the lions are in bed together — you're all the same to us. Frankly, I don't give a fig for your opinion, nor do I care whether Rithild condemns me to Albiorix. Your pitiful ideas have no meaning out here. The world's a jungle, where only the strong and the ruthless survive. The bears are out of control and we have to destroy them."

"That's not what I've heard."

"What would you know about it?" growled Parthanyx.

"You're not the only source of information about what's going on out here," Eisa said. "Rithild has his own informants." It was a pathetic riposte and he knew it.

Parthanyx's scornful expression spoke volumes. "You may have time to waste," he said, "but I've got work to do: loyal panthers to lead and stupid bears to humiliate. This meeting is over. Give my regards to my dear uncle."

"You can't treat me like this, Parthanyx. Today I speak for Rithild.

He'll hear about your treachery." Eisa, furious, turned to storm out of the tent.

He'd taken barely two steps before Parthanyx was on top of him. The unsuspecting lieutenant was pinned down by his well-muscled, more powerful cousin. Eisa was too astonished, too horrified even to struggle.

The fierce panther brought his head down close to Eisa's. Then his eyes were distracted by the red amulet tied around Eisa's neck. "What's this?" he said. "Oh yes, I remember now. Your father's little decoration. He used to wear it when — " The panther snorted. "It didn't do *him* much good, lieutenant, did it."

Eisa tried to struggle out of the other's grasp, but to no avail.

"Remember this moment," Parthanyx hissed into the other's ear. "I could kill you as easily as I might snap at a fly, and it wouldn't bother me one bit. I wouldn't think about it longer than it would take to do the deed. You're weak, Eisa, and I'm strong. You are no longer one of us. You're nothing out here. Take your pitiful ideas and slink back to Manaris, where you belong.

"And one more warning before you go. When we finish with those stinking bears, we'll turn our minds and claws to the degenerates back home — you included. Hah! You can take that message back to Rithild as well. The next time — the only time — I want to see your face again is the day I spit in Albiorix's face, and not before."

Eisa said nothing and did not resist, trying to remain cool while Parthanyx glowered over him. Finally the cat relaxed his cruel grip and let his fellow panther scramble to his feet. Then he shoved him through the entrance of the tent.

The lieutenant ran off as fast as his legs could carry him, past the sentries, past the outposts and past the companies stationed along the way, not daring to look sideways or backwards. He did not stop until he was some distance from the panthers' encampment. Eisa was aghast at what had just happened. In his wildest imaginings he had never expected such venom and violence from his own kind.

The panther's thoughts jumbled together into one huge morass. *He's gone mad. It's far worse than anyone could have imagined. Surely the rest of them haven't adopted a similar position. Surely such an attitude can't be so widely entrenched. But I fear it is, and, if so, Parthanyx and the others will bring us all down. How could the Council have missed this spiral into insanity? Wasn't anyone paying attention? And what can I — what can the Baron possibly do about it?*

Fear and despair overwhelmed him. His efforts to bring Parthanyx to heel had failed miserably, his meeting a total fiasco. How could he go back to Rithild with such a catastrophe weighing upon him? But then, what else could he do?

The Baron was still en route to their meeting place, as Rithild had not been able to keep pace with his much younger assistant. This delay would give Eisa a few days' grace before they were to meet up, time to canvass some of the other panthers stationed nearby. He needed to make sure Parthanyx was speaking the truth about how the local commanders felt.

Eisa allowed himself a grim smile at that thought. It was no longer a rebellion of the bears that was the concern. Rather, it was now a revolt by the panthers in the field. What a bloody mess!

Eisa trusted that Rithild would know what to do. The Baron had stature and prestige as a respected elder, and as Parthanyx's closest relative, he could call on family ties to resolve the matter. Perhaps a disaster could still be averted. However, Eisa had his doubts.

5

PAINFUL CHOICES

E isa's subsequent investigations — awkward interviews with many former friends and comrades — bore out the horrible truth of his discovery. While few shared Parthanyx's manic behavior and extreme hatred, most were of a similar mindset. Eisa could only conclude that the panthers of Aeronbed were now a divided camp, with the majority — and the accompanying power base — now siding with Parthanyx and his fellow commanders.

To add to Eisa's woes, it was also clear that he himself, as a representative of the establishment in Manaris, had become an object of distrust and distaste, not as suspect as the bears of Heimborn, but definitely not far off. He saw only two horrible choices before him: join in the local rebellion or return to the capital in shame. Both options were too awful to contemplate for a cat as loyal to Aeronbed as Eisa felt himself to be. Having no idea what to do, he simply agonized over the situation, hoping against hope that wise Rithild would have some well-considered answer.

The Baron took longer to show up than Eisa had expected. Indeed, by the time the older panther arrived at the rendezvous, tired and limping from the long march, Eisa was as morose as a big cat could get. He almost wept when Rithild appeared. Quickly the young panther blurted out what he had found: Parthanyx's disloyalty, his aim to crush the bears, his disdain for the powers in Manaris, the overwhelming support he enjoyed from the other commanders and the stark choice Eisa saw before them.

After a short period of somber and silent reflection, Rithild's first question, surprisingly (at least to Eisa), was not about the panthers but about the bears. What had Eisa found out about their activities?

"The rumors appear to be true. Something happened when Parthanyx was meeting with one of the clans. The word is that he killed one of the leaders after being provoked, and then everything went crazy. A short altercation ensued, after which the panthers decided that withdrawal was the best course of action. However, I could find out no details of what actually happened.

"That wasn't the end of the matter. It appears the bears have begun to organize. And it hasn't stopped there, which may be the reason why everyone is so worked up. From what I've seen, the commanders have stepped up their vigilance and counterintelligence. I wouldn't call it harassment or persecution — after all, we're only talking about bears. Everyone agrees those creatures must be kept in their place."

"Is it open rebellion?"

"If it had come to that, I think the commanders would have instituted far harsher measures. I haven't come across any evidence of that on my travels, although I confess I haven't been anywhere near the bears' dwelling places. However, my whiskers tell me something is amiss; I'm just not close enough to the situation to figure it out. Of course, I only had so much time to investigate before I had to leave to come here."

The young panther expected Rithild to have some clear strategies mapped out, or at least an idea or two. Instead, the Baron surprised Eisa by asking what he would suggest.

"The situation is so different from what I expected," replied his lieutenant. "Honestly, I have no ideas to put forward. It's you and I, sir, who are now in the minority. Naturally, some cats here hold less extreme views and, in a pinch, may be prepared to support us. And, to the best of my knowledge, those in command at Manaris would never hold with Parthanyx's position." Eisa jumped up and moved about anxiously as he completed his report. "I'd say the vast majority of panthers in Aeronbed would agree with their comrades in the field. Although the alliance with the lions has been profitable for us, many have never found it easy to accept their ongoing leadership. Something like this uprising presents an opportunity for every malcontent and complainer.

"I don't need to tell you how dangerous the situation has become. Albiorix was worried about the bears, but now he must worry about both the bears and the panthers. Not to mention Vigmar, with whom we shall engage again as soon as the fighting season is upon us, and that day cannot be far off. At this rate Aeronbed will be fighting on several fronts. We could be looking at civil war here. What a disaster, what a bloody disaster!"

"Eisa, calm yourself. This is no time to panic. We need to think through this situation very carefully. Our fates depend upon what we decide today."

Eisa took a deep breath. "Of course, my lord, but I see no easy choice ahead of us. Do you think you could intercede? Can you speak directly to Parthanyx, make him see reason?"

The thoughtful Rithild took his time before he spoke again. "From what you've told me, I see no point in meeting with Parthanyx. He's out of control — completely. He has always been impetuous and undisciplined, but I thought, or hoped, that his natural leadership abilities and sense of duty would help keep his flaws in check. Unfortunately the reverse has occurred and he's become a danger to us all.

"It may well be that we've come to the end of an era. These are troubled and unpredictable times, Eisa. Every creature has its day, and the big cats' day of rule may finally be approaching its sunset. I know, I know, it's easy for me to say, for I am older and the best part of my life is behind me, while you are just entering the fullness of youth. But don't despair, Lieutenant. My words are only conjecture, and we may yet find a way out of this situation. I'm not without hope and not without my trusty bag of tricks. At least for the time being, we may not have to pick sides. You and I may have the luxury of seeing which way the cat will jump before we decide our course.

And so, if one side should prevail, we will not have alienated the other."

After pausing briefly to gather his thoughts, Rithild carried on. "I'm going to suggest an approach to you, Eisa, something that may yet keep us both safe. I shall return to Manaris to alert them to what has occurred in Heimborn. I will play for time. However, to make this plan work, I'm afraid you'll need to remain here."

"Here, my lord?" Eisa gulped visibly.

"It's the only way I can see out of this mess, the only way the two of us can keep our heads," Rithild repeated. "You must stay here."

"Stay here?"

"Yes. Remain on site, as part of the local forces."

"If I may be so bold, sir, I can certainly see how your head might be saved. As for me, however, if I stick around here, my head will certainly be rolling around on the ground before too long. You didn't have to face Parthanyx; I did, and that's an experience I've no desire to repeat."

Rithild grabbed the younger panther by the shoulders. As his claws dug in, Eisa winced. The older cat's piercing eyes bored into those of his lieutenant. "Don't underestimate your abilities in this matter. There's power in all of us. Trust in yourself; everything will work out.

"Now listen to me. Here's what I want you to do. You must appear to have changed sides. Befriend and join up with the local commanders. It doesn't need to be with Parthanyx. In fact, it's probably best that you stay as far from him as possible. Play up to their vanity. Tell them that, once you had time to think things through, you saw the wisdom of their position — a change of heart, that kind of thing. Don't forget, you have old friends among this group; you also have seniority, training, skills and authority. You are their equal and you can be of use to them. You're a prize catch, in fact. Make use of that.

"Your performance, I'm afraid to say, will be the easy part. The second is much more dangerous. You are to keep your eyes and ears open. Find out the exact details of what's going on, with both the panthers and the bears. Report back to me as often as you can; for the present we'll use this spot as a meeting place. Later we can arrange an alternative way to communicate."

"With all due respect, my lord, you don't have the time or the strength to keep going back and forth between here and Manaris. Meeting here will be impossible."

"Of course not, Eisa. I'll find someone else, someone I can rely on, to meet with you. We can establish regular times to meet and ways to pass on messages. Don't worry, it'll be someone appropriate, someone we both can trust, so you'll be safe from discovery. Well, as safe as we can make things, given the circumstances. In this way I'll be able to protect you, and you me. We'll play both sides against one another, and only you and I will know of this plan. Is that clear?"

"Yes, my lord, I think I see where you're going. It might just work."

"Excellent. That's the spirit! There's one more thing, and this is the greatest challenge I will give to you — one final path, one that you must take if, and only if, you've no other choice and are absolutely certain it has a chance of success. Do you understand me?"

"If you tell me what it is I may understand."

"If the tide of affairs turns here and the opportunity presents itself, or if you find yourself at the mercy of the bears — I know you will think that's impossible, but believe me, Eisa, in war we must be open to every eventuality, so hear me out — you must switch sides. You must join with the bears."

"What?" Eisa cried out in horror. Was Rithild losing his mind? "I could never do that. Turn traitor? The very idea is unthinkable; it goes against everything I hold dear. It's true I don't hold with the extreme views of Parthanyx — our cousin goes much too far — but the bears are not at all like us. They're of a lower order; there's no way one can associate with them. Anyway, even if I could, would they not kill me first?"

"Use your wits, Eisa, and listen carefully. I said you'd consider it an impossible task, but think it through. You're a smart young panther. You could be valuable to the bears as an interpreter or go-between, even as a prized turncoat. Believe me, stranger things have happened in war. You remember last year, when the apes abandoned Vigmar to join Aeronbed? Who would have believed that turnabout before it happened?"

"But that's not the same; the apes are equals. Vigmar's rulers, those donkeys, did not control them. Here in Aeronbed it is we, the panthers, who keep the bears in check. While we treat them fairly, even appropriately — as subservient creatures deserve — they doubtless see us as oppressors. They will surely — "

Rithild cut him off in midstream. "Listen to me. Just as you'd be a valuable catch in the eyes of Parthanyx, you'd also be one to the bears, and probably an even greater one. Who knows, with your brains you should be able to run rings around those poor, simple creatures. Just imagine, Lieutenant. In that way you'd be playing not two but three sides against one another. Thus your position would become even safer. If caught, you could always claim to be working for the other side. No one would be the wiser and no one could check on your story to disprove it. And let me repeat — only you and I would know."

"And whoever you choose to be the messenger," added Eisa.

"Naturally." The Baron waved a paw dismissively. "The cat will have to be well chosen and absolutely loyal to me — ah, that is, to both of us. I will give the matter careful thought on my return to Manaris. Eisa, I know this will not be an easy choice for you. However, I'm convinced it's the most logical and, ironically, the most secure option available to you. And for me too, of course."

Eisa remained doubtful. It wasn't difficult to see how the Baron could benefit from that arrangement. However, he was less certain about his own future. The more the young panther thought about it, the path Rithild proposed seemed downright suicidal. Nevertheless, he could come up with no alternative solution, other than simply returning to the capital with his patron. And Eisa was not looking forward to that eventuality. As soon as word got out that both the bears and the local panther forces were out of control, the loyal panthers who remained in Aeronbed would become objects of derision and scorn. Eventually they'd be distrusted and then ostracized by the majority lion population for their incompetence and failure. Ultimately their favored place among the nobles and powerbrokers of Aeronbed would be lost.

The game Rithild was proposing was a high-stakes gamble. Yes, Eisa could lose, but he could also be a big winner. If the fates proved sympathetic to his plight and he kept his wits about him, he might just pull through unscathed. Certainly the first step should not be difficult, and he could minimize the risks involved in the second by taking great care. As for the third, however, Eisa trusted he'd never find himself in such a position. To take such a drastic step was still unthinkable.

Somehow the die had been cast. Eisa sat silently pondering his fate. While the panther could not personally stomach an outcome that Rithild clearly could — with the likes of Parthanyx ruling the day or, even worse, the bears in ascendency over the cats — Eisa realized there was now no going back.

6

THE WIZARDS'
PRONOUNCEMENT

On the third day Albiorix rose early from his sleep, excited and eager to hear the words of wisdom from his wizards. The lion asked Temorwig and Olwen to join him for the announcement of the results. While the former remained skeptical, the latter's curiosity to learn what Mirati and his brethren would declare about her strange experience in the forest knew no bounds.

The three cats waited impatiently in the King's chambers for the precise hour that Mirati had declared the most auspicious time of day to reveal the results of the wizards' divination. The King paced back and forth while the other two tried without success to engage him in diverting conversation. But the appointed hour finally arrived and then passed, and still no wizard had appeared.

Fuming, Albiorix sent a pair of burly guards to round up the missing scholars. While they waited, the volume of his growls grew markedly, only to increase yet further when the two emissaries finally returned, anxious and unaccompanied. As the guards had expected, instruments of divination lay scattered about, along with many books and manuscripts, but they could find no sign of the three wise lions or what might have happened to them.

"Do you think they've been kidnapped?" Olwen asked.

"More likely they just ran away after hearing the King's threat — I mean order, that they be clear and straightforward," a rather amused Temorwig suggested. "Hah! That would've been a first for this lot. I hate to say it, Albiorix, but — "

"So don't!" the furious king roared. "Follow me, all of you!"

As they marched along at a frantic pace in the direction of the wizards' quarters, the King was heard to mutter, "I'll have their heads cut off and put on spikes, as a warning to any other pretenders!" and "When I find them, they're going to be a sorry lot!" and suchlike. When they arrived in the part of the castle where the wizards worked and lived, he instructed the two guards to search their private chambers while he, Temorwig and Olwen explored the enclave where Mirati directed the trio's scientific examinations and experiments.

Since Olwen had never ventured there before, everything was a surprise. The room felt confusing, both spacious and claustrophobic, perhaps because of the almost utter darkness in which the three found it. For a place where a great deal of work and thought must go on, it seemed to the lioness particularly dusty and gloomy, rife with strange and disagreeable odors. It was as if an evil spirit ruled the place.

Heading directly to the windows, Albiorix threw open the shutters and the grimy panes that had been blocking the sun's precious rays and keeping out the fresh air. Once their eyes had adjusted to the welcome light, the three lions found an array of scientific tools and extraordinary objects that Olwen assumed were typical of the wizards' work: a bubbling beaker filled with a gelatinous turquoise substance; a cage containing several green and orange striped lizards, each with two heads; a massive globe picturing the night sky with its stars and moons.

Large blackboards were filled with scribbled writing in languages unknown to the three newcomers and calculations that made no sense at all. Three tall, pointed hats were neatly arrayed on wooden pegs along one wall, which also held an ancient map of Aeronbed with place names none of them recognized. There was also a set of curiously shaped ceramic jars containing some foul-smelling plants and herbs; a weird-looking winged insect pinned to a wooden tablet, half dissected and carefully labeled; and finally, on a large circular wooden tablet, a massive leather-bound book of instruction, charms and incantations, finely lettered and beautifully illustrated.

"Your wizards have availed themselves of all the latest techniques and gadgets," Temorwig observed. "I'll give them that much."

"They do seem to have been hard at work," added Olwen, glancing down at some scrolls on the table. "I see references to my meeting with the raven."

"This is most strange," the King said. "They've left all the tools of their trade here — everything, even their hats! Perhaps you are correct, daughter. A kidnapping would explain their disappearance. Perhaps by someone who seeks to conceal the true meaning of the prophecy."

Albiorix called to the guards, demanding to know if they'd found anything. In contrast to the chaos of the laboratory, the wizards' personal chambers were found to be as neat as pins, revealing no clues of any kind. Each held an assortment of modest tunics, limited possessions and books of the trade. No conclusions could be drawn from what was found there.

Having sent off the guards to conduct a search of the castle, the King began to pace up and down the room. Albiorix was all business now, focused on solving the puzzle facing them. "What can we deduce from this sight?" the lion asked, indicating the disarray of the room.

"Obviously they were trying to reach an understanding of Olwen's dream — " Temorwig replied. "Sorry, I meant to say the *visions* she witnessed in her visit with the great black bird."

"And they left without their hats," Albiorix added. "So either they were forced to leave in a hurry or were trying to disguise themselves when they left."

"Unless they have a second set of hats," suggested Olwen.

"No. When they become full-fledged wizards, they're given only one wizarding hat to wear," her father replied. "They can have no other. They must have left their hats on purpose. Perhaps to give us some kind of message."

"Or a warning?" Temorwig guessed. No one spoke for a minute while they thought about that possibility, but no brilliant — or even less than brilliant — ideas came to mind.

"I hate to say this, Majesty, truly I do," Temorwig said finally, "but I fear I must. Is it possible you frightened them with your demand for a clear-cut prophecy? You know how difficult that is to achieve. In all my years I've never once seen it accomplished."

"I would not like to admit it," replied Albiorix, getting up and walking around the room, "but a king must concede error as much as any commoner. Possibly — though I'll say only *possibly* — I was a trifle harsh with the chief wizard. Maybe the three of them found it easier to disappear than to face my wrath when they failed to comply."

"There is another possibility," Olwen ventured. "Perhaps they did uncover something, something so terrifying they were left in great fear — afraid for their lives, afraid to wait a single moment longer, too afraid even to stay and tell you."

The trio contemplated this frightening prospect. As Olwen thought about what the wizards might have uncovered, the lioness found that her every sense was sharpened. She could smell the sea air blowing in through the open window, slowly pushing aside the dankness inside the room. She could hear the wind whistling outside, the distant waves breaking on the shoreline and the odd seagull crying offshore. She could sense the texture of every object arrayed before her. And then, much, much closer, Olwen could feel her own heart beating wildly.

Albiorix interrupted her reverie. "If they have been kidnapped or forced to flee so unceremoniously," he declared, "there's still a chance they can be found. But if they have run away of their own accord and do not wish to be discovered, we cannot expect to unearth them. They are wizards, after all; they have powers we do not share. They can secrete themselves away where we will never uncover them."

"Perhaps we'll never see those three again," added the King after a brief pause, sighing mightily. "And they were the last of their breed. How can I possibly find replacements?"

The question was unanswerable. "Surely there's someone else who can decipher what Olwen has seen," Temorwig said finally. "Are there no junior wizards or schools of divination with promising young students waiting to take their place?"

"I fear not, Temorwig. We both know that prophecy is a dying art, and its prospects for the young are dim indeed. They look elsewhere for their rewards, and who can blame them? Frankly, even if there were others, what hope would we have of finding out what the vision means in time to act? These three were the best, the most talented I could command. I doubt we could trust any student to come up with the correct divination."

"There must be some learned ones among us."

"Perhaps there are one or two. The problem is we'd have to start all over again, and I fear we've little time left. I wanted a speedy answer from the wizards — I have always been impatient, a cat in a hurry — and perhaps I simply pushed them too hard." The king growled in dismay and frustration.

"Although I've been anxious to return to the front lines to rejoin my comrades," the lioness interjected, "I could delay my departure and try to work out the puzzle myself."

"You, Olwen?" the surprised king replied. "You've no training in such arts. It takes years to learn the ins and outs of prophesying."

"That may well be, but it was I who met the black bird. Those were my visions and my recollection of what occurred. No creature is better placed than I am to interpret my own thoughts, memories and words. Also, don't forget that I've learned many things over the years from my teachers. You might be surprised how much I know."

"Naturally I've great confidence in your ability. However, our wizards study and work their whole lives to achieve the knowledge necessary to decipher such events. At best you have only an amateur's familiarity with the subject. How could you — "

"Let Olwen have a crack at it," Temorwig interrupted. "Sometimes real comprehension lies in a surprising place, in the very last place you'd think of looking. You speak of prophecies, Albiorix, but let me speak of signs. I believe there's something about the chain of events here, something that requires Olwen to play a direct role in working through this mystery."

"Still — "

But Temorwig would not let up. "It's exactly as Olwen says. She will not have to describe her innermost thoughts to someone else."

Albiorix considered his friend's argument, for he believed in such things even more than his fellow lion did. He turned to his daughter. "Uncle Temorwig speaks most wisely. Truly it seems fitting that you should try your luck. You brought this puzzling vision into our lives; therefore you shall be the one to figure it out."

"Well, I can't promise anything. I can only try my best."

"No one can ask more of you, Princess," Temorwig declared.

"I have complete faith in you, my daughter," the king added. "You must start work immediately. We've no time to lose."

7

RITHILD DISSEMBLES

"Well, my lord, what did you learn on your trip to Heimborn?" Temorwig asked brusquely. "Good news, I trust."

Rithild's brow furrowed and his eyes darkened. He did not bother to reply.

"Your silence betrays your mood," the lion continued. "I gather you were less than pleased by your discoveries."

The two were walking carefully along the sturdy but slippery sea wall that sheltered the harbor of Aeronbed from occasional rough seas and winter storms. The lion and panther were alone, as Rithild had requested, for the latter wanted no witnesses to their conversation. Today, although the wind from the west was strong, the seas remained surprisingly calm; only small waves lapped against the stones holding back the water several feet below them.

Looking back from the wall toward the small harbor, they could see a great deal of activity, both offshore and onshore. Little boats were coming and going and the town's inhabitants were preparing for market, setting up their wares in various tented stalls. Some early morning buyers were getting a leg up on the competition while a few elderly loungers chatted together in shady corners. The great castle rose majestically behind it all. It was a typical market day in the capital, its ordinariness standing in stark contrast to the tenor of their conversation.

"Speak up, Baron. We haven't got all day," Temorwig said when his comrade again failed to respond. "Cat got your tongue?" The lion always enjoyed making this little witticism and laughed accordingly.

Rithild continued to hesitate as he attempted to find the best way to phrase what he knew would be unwelcome news. "Pardon me for my slowness in replying," the Baron said at last. "These are difficult, even painful, matters for me to acknowledge. I met last evening with the Grand Council of Panthers as soon as I returned from Heimborn, to apprise them of the most recent developments in the borderlands. It is important that they — all of us — be as one on this, er, this problem."

"Problem?" said Temorwig. "You gave me to understand there are no problems."

Rithild, ignoring the interruption, looked out to sea and carried on. "We met at length last night," the panther went on, "and are in complete accord. The Council has deputized me to speak to you on its behalf, since you and I are already in communication on the matter."

"Now you worry me; the Grand Council rarely meets these days. Things must be serious indeed!"

"They are, my lord."

"Well, then, best jump into it. We've no time to waste."

The panther stopped in his tracks, swallowed deeply and looked directly at the lion. "First of all, Temorwig, I must confirm to you that there is indeed a rebellion."

"What?" roared the lion. "You assured me — and I assured His Majesty — that nothing was afoot. How — "

"I deeply regret placing you in such an awkward position, and freely admit to misjudging the situation. I won't make excuses and I take full responsibility. Naturally I offered my resignation to the Grand Council, but they refused to accept it. In their view, this is my doing and I must undo it. So be it."

"You know I'll have to advise the King. He'll be livid."

"If I can be of any service toward mollifying His Majesty, just say the word."

Temorwig let out a huge *harrumph*. "It may well be necessary, but let me hear the tale first. If I need anything further, I will certainly call upon you. For the present, just give me as much detail as you can."

"I'll be brief. You'll recall that when we last spoke, I mentioned there had been one small incident in Heimborn. I took it to be — so did we all — an isolated matter, one which we could resolve easily and quickly. But it has not turned out to be so. The rebellion started with that one incident and has grown rapidly. That's the reason I didn't know more when I spoke with you last. When I conferred with the local forces about the uprising, I was told it was under control. But to everyone's surprise it has spread rapidly, like a forest fire we cannot contain. Indeed, the situation changed dramatically over that brief period of time."

"I'm sure I've no need to remind you that the King will see this as gross mismanagement on the part of the Council. It's long been the panthers' job to keep those bears in check; we leave all that business to you."

"I know that only too well, my lord. I'm at a loss for words. This failure shames us — the entire Council and me personally."

"It's unlike the bears. They've been passive for so many years," Temorwig mused. "What started it, then? And who is their leader?"

"The answer to that question is unclear. Rumors and stories abound but nothing is confirmed. It's possible that only one bear was behind the original uprising. Still, it's a moot point now, since many others have joined in."

"That's the best you can do?"

"I regret to say it is."

"What are the commanders in the field doing?"

"They're cracking down, as they should. However — "

"However what?"

"The commanders need more resources to deal with the bears. They were well equipped to manage a conquered and docile group of animals, but a state of open rebellion is another matter."

Temorwig groaned loudly. "I trust the Council realizes that one war is already in play, and that our forces are completely taken up in fighting Vigmar."

"I am well aware of it, Temorwig. The Council is as well."

"But you're still asking for help?"

"Yes. The Grand Council cannot be answerable for the results if our commanders in the field do not receive more troops and supplies."

"This is absurd. We've subsidized you panthers for many years now. You've had an easy time of it — the easiest role in Aeronbed, in fact: keeping your feet on the necks of that pathetic race while we lions and tigers fight off the incursions from Vigmar. You've had years to perfect managing that territory."

Temorwig paused briefly before adding, in a particularly bitter tone, "No doubt your local commanders have also benefited from the spoils that Heimborn has to offer. And now, at the slightest provocation, your forces fall apart and come asking us for help. Now I know His Majesty will be livid. *I'm* furious — and I never get furious!"

The panther hung his head.

"You know what Albiorix will say, don't you," the lion continued. *"Send them all to the northern front, where they can enjoy the never-ending daily slaughter*. That's what he'll say. Are you sure you want me to tell him the Council can't manage the situation? Because there's plenty of lions who'd be happy to change places with your forces."

Rithild looked appropriately shamefaced. "I know how this state of affairs must appear to you," the panther said. "It embarrasses me no end to bring such a request to an old comrade like you. I told the Grand Council we'd look like fools or, even worse, like cowards. But they insisted. Listen, Temorwig, as I think more on the matter, I ask you not to pass on this request to Albiorix, not under any circumstances. We shall try to — no, no, I say unequivocally, we *will* take care of the matter, and on our own. I will steel the resolve of the Council. Trust me, it will be done. You'll hear no more of such requests, or of this rebellion."

"Excellent. That's the kind of fortitude we need. I'll tell the King he was correct after all. Albiorix loves it when he's proved to be better informed than the rest of us. But I will also assure him that the panthers, our staunchest, longest-standing allies, will deal with the situation. He will also appreciate hearing that news. I will leave you completely free to rectify the mess, but you must keep me abreast of developments at all times. This fiasco cannot be repeated, Rithild. You understand me? No more surprises. My own credibility is also at stake. If you fail me, or if the Council fails the King, I cannot spare you a second time."

"Temorwig, I understand fully. It will not happen again," the panther declared firmly. "We — the Council — will make things right."

"You don't have long, Rithild. I'll expect to hear from you soon."

"Absolutely, my lord, without question. ... Before you go, one more thing. I should tell you that I left young Eisa behind."

"Your assistant? In the borderlands?"

"My lieutenant. Yes, the same."

"Whatever for, Rithild?"

"The results of my enquiries speak for themselves. It's clear to me now — to my utter shame — that we senior-ranking panthers here in Manaris have not kept adequately informed about what's been going on in Heimborn. To realize that Albiorix is better informed than I was about our own affairs doubles my embarrassment. I've decided that an ear on the ground is the only way to assure myself — and, therefore, you and Albiorix — that no further surprises lie in wait for us in the days to come. I'm trying to establish a secure means to communicate with him."

Temorwig nodded. It seemed a sensible approach, given what had occurred. "That's your business, Rithild; I won't tell you how to run your affairs. As long as I can assure the King that all is now under control and this rebellion is being put down ... "

"Lord Temorwig, I can assure you of both."

The lion left the panther standing far out along the sea wall. As Rithild watched his shaken comrade depart, the winds and seas behind him increased in ferocity, as if to mimic the beleaguered state of the kingdom. He knew Temorwig would be hastening to meet with Albiorix. He imagined with grim amusement how the conversation would go and what its outcome might be. The panther was rather pleased that he would not have to be present to bear the King's wrath.

However, Rithild was even more pleased that he'd met his real objectives in speaking to Temorwig. First, he'd avoided having to reveal the true extent of the problems and the greater danger now existing in Heimborn. Second, the simple step of asking for help — a request he had known would be rejected — had ensured a paws-off approach on the part of the lions. The panthers and no one else would have the authority to deal with the dismal state of affairs in Heimborn.

Rithild had been able to keep all kinds of information to himself, buying crucial time for the panthers to resolve the matter. Now he had to bring the Grand Council around to his way of thinking. Despite his assurances to the contrary, he had yet to speak with them. Who knew the direction events would take, let alone how the rebellion would sort itself out? Although Parthanyx was unpredictable and dangerous, he was also a risk-taker who might yet turn out to be a brilliant general. And should his nephew win out, Rithild considered, he'd clearly need a skilled politician around to manage the kingdom.

And if Parthanyx did not succeed, the Baron could claim he'd always been opposed to the upstart. With Eisa's eyes and ears to keep him better informed, plenty of time remained for further maneuvering. Now all Rithild needed was a trustworthy go-between.

8

DECIPHERING THE PROPHECY

Olwen would never have given prophecy a moment's thought if she hadn't encountered the raven. Although she was not learned by any means, she was practical and sensible and imbued with excellent instincts. The Princess had always considered that the advocates of divination, including her father, exaggerated the science (or art) involved in its practice. Something told her that not only could she not ignore the incident, it was also truly important, and in ways she could yet barely fathom. She was more than prepared to give it her all.

To start with, Olwen was aware that there was an essential logic to interpreting what each aspect of the vision meant. That reality, when combined with her own common sense, would, she trusted, lead her to the answers she sought. All she had to do was break down the sequence of events into its component parts and then put it back together again. How difficult could that be?

The Princess decided to start with examining the various creatures involved. That seemed to be the easiest and most concrete way to begin: the raven was the host of the vision, which had revealed in turn what she took to be a panther, a black bear and finally the white bear.

Following that, she would turn to investigating the background of each picture: the clear, still night sky with its stars and moon, then the moving picture of the mountain ridge and forest. Finally she would study the time of day and the colors: essentially black and white. Was that it? Had she missed anything? No. Olwen concluded that she had captured everything in retelling the tale to her father.

Looking at it from another vantage point, however, the lioness wondered whether anything was absent from the picture, something that should have been present but wasn't. That was a more difficult question, like a guard dog that didn't bark when it should have. However, after working her memory cells to their utmost capacity, nothing untoward occurred to her, and she let it be. Then Olwen considered the opposite: was there anything that shouldn't have been there but in fact was present? Well, the stars and moon were wrong. That she knew already, but what of it? She had no ideas as yet to explain any of it.

Her father would want to know if the message was a promise or a threat, something to welcome or something to fear. What, she asked herself, had she felt during the meeting with the raven? What sensation had she come away with in the end? Albiorix would want something concrete from her, not something vague or several possible suggested outcomes. The lioness was aware that their imprecision was one of his biggest complaints about the wizards, and she also knew that coming up with a specific answer would be the most difficult challenge for her. The whole thing was a guessing game at best. If she took one wrong turn at the beginning she would likely end up far from where the prophecy was really heading, misleading the King and potentially jeopardizing the entire existence of Aeronbed — that is, of course, if there was any real science involved.

As Olwen thought through the awesome responsibility she had taken on, she found herself gaining new respect for the wizards. She was beginning to understand the immense difficulties they faced in their job. No wonder they had run away, if indeed they had. They'd still not been found; in fact, there were no traces of the trio anywhere. Mirati and his two associates had simply vanished into thin air.

Perhaps, Olwen mused, the wizards had powers of invisibility that no one was aware of; perhaps they were still lurking about in their midst. If so, she hoped they could find a way to provide her with some helpful clues for what looked more and more like an impossible task for anyone, scholar or amateur.

Olwen began to regret she'd volunteered to solve the riddle. Nevertheless, the lioness reminded herself, it was her vision and she had as much chance as any other creature to figure it out, if not better. At least she had witnessed it and could remember everything about it; she'd no need to rely on anyone else's interpretation or faulty memory. So, burdened with troubling and conflicting thoughts, Olwen began the arduous task of sorting the whole thing out.

⚜

"YOUR MAJESTY, I COME FROM MEETING WITH LORD RITHILD," TEMORWIG said.

"And did he bring you a report from Heimborn?"

"Yes, he did, and the news is not good."

Albiorix sighed. "Why am I not surprised. How bad is the situation?"

"The bears are in open revolt, although how widely the rebellion has spread, Rithild could not — or would not — say."

"Did the Baron ask for our help in putting down the revolt?"

Temorwig was astonished. The King's knowledge of events — or his astuteness at guessing what had happened — continued to surpass anyone else's. "Albiorix, do you have spies everywhere? How did you know he made such a request?"

The King chuckled and shifted his tail. "In this case I put two and two together. It's true I'm well informed, but more than that, I know the nature of my fellow cats. So what did you tell him?"

"I told him we've provided the panthers with ample support over the years. Also that they've enjoyed the easiest assignment in the kingdom, with the greatest opportunity for self-enrichment. In other words, I rejected his request."

"Stout fellow. And what did Rithild say then?"

"He was embarrassed. After hearing my reaction, he maintained that they would break the revolt on their own, without any assistance from us."

"Did he now. The Baron didn't try to argue the point?"

"No, Rithild seemed easily cowed by the force of my arguments. In fact, he even asked me not to mention his request to you."

"Really? Very interesting."

"Do you take anything from all this, Albiorix? Beyond the obvious, of course."

"Possibly. I will think on it in due course."

"So you're not surprised?"

"It does conform to the information I've been receiving for some time. I just needed confirmation."

"Do we need to take any action?"

"Yes, but not in any way you might think. Things may unravel yet further. There's no need to act in haste."

Although Temorwig was puzzled by the King's calm manner and circumspect attitude, he knew better than to push Albiorix farther than he was prepared to go. He had expected the King to go on the warpath about being deceived — or at least misinformed — by Rithild. The lion was rather relieved to be spared from experiencing his cousin's usual wrath, but he felt uncertain and troubled by both the lay of the land and Albiorix's response. How much more did the King know that he was not revealing?

"Any words of wisdom from Olwen?" Temorwig asked, changing the subject.

"Not as yet," replied the King with a sigh. "She may be coming face to face with the reality of the challenge she's taken on. I know from personal experience that it's much more difficult than one might think. In truth, Temorwig, I hold out little hope for an accurate prediction. But let her try. Olwen's determination is her greatest attribute. She may yet surprise us."

AT THAT PRECISE MOMENT OLWEN WAS SURVEYING THE ARRAY OF STRANGE tools, devices and reference materials strewn around the wizards' musty chamber, which was once more shuttered to preserve secrecy. What to do with the various implements? Where to start? Having no idea how they worked or what to do with anything, she began to pore over the books in hopes of finding some useful descriptions or diagrams or words of wisdom.

Unfortunately the lioness could barely understand what was written in the manuals. The texts tended to be in a foreign tongue, written in an indecipherable scrawl or simply too difficult for her to comprehend. In many cases she didn't even recognize the words. Soon enough Olwen discovered that she had no patience for such work. Desperately frustrated, she tossed aside the documents and began to pace around the room, hoping for some sort of inspiration.

As her father had done a few days earlier, she went over to the windows to throw them open and let the warming daylight brighten her mood, if not the room itself. It was now late in the day and the sun was beginning its slow descent into the sea. Its rays shone horizontally into the room; all the nooks, crannies and corners on the other side were lit up, revealing things Olwen had never before noticed. Golden particles of dust danced in the gorgeous glow now flooding the space. In this shimmering, almost liquid light the chamber seemed an entirely different and thoroughly magical place.

As the sun continued its descent, revealing more with each passing minute, Olwen found herself momentarily blinded by some object on the other side of the room reflecting the intense rays into her eyes. She stepped aside to regain her sight, searching out the object she'd not noticed before. On closer inspection, the lioness saw that the reflection originated from a small wooden box sitting on an upper shelf, the sides of which were decorated with an array of striking jewels.

As Olwen looked around her, she saw that the jewels were casting a splendid rainbow across the walls of the room. The colors echoed the stones: purple amethyst, rose quartz, yellow beryl, green emerald, blue sapphire and piercing white diamond. The box itself was barely visible, almost hidden by the mundane objects surrounding it. Only with that precise angle of light at that particular time of day would anyone even notice it. Already the sun was beginning to meet the horizon and the reflections were losing their intensity.

Intrigued, Olwen moved forward to pick up the box. However, when she got close enough to take hold of it, the box inexplicably vanished. She backed up, and as she did so, it could be seen again, though just barely. The lioness realized that, as the sun continued to sink into the sea, the box was effectively disappearing from view. With each passing minute it was becoming more and more difficult to detect. Was it a trick of the light or was it magic?

Mystified, she again moved toward the box. This time she put out both paws to seize it, even though she could no longer make out its exact location. The lioness would be able to feel the box and pull it toward her, even though it remained invisible to the naked eye. Gingerly her paws closed over what appeared to be open air on an empty shelf. However, she could easily feel its firm surfaces against her pads, their flatness broken only by the occasional gemstone.

Almost with reverence, Olwen took the box over to the heavy round table. After pushing away the ancient book with her muzzle, she placed the box carefully at dead center, all by itself. She knew the box was there, but still, by some strange force, she could not see it.

Most wondrous and mystifying, Olwen thought. The lioness had never come across anything like it. She wondered whether the box could be opened. Was there anything inside? And how could she open something she could not see? *Well*, Olwen decided, *it's not so different from operating blind in the deepest dark of night. You simply work by feeling with your pads and using your claws.*

So that's what the lioness attempted to do. She scratched to find an opening, any narrow joint where she could insert her razor-like claws and pull two pieces apart. But the box appeared to have no lid, no top or bottom, no front or sides — it was just a block of wood scattered with precious stones. But Olwen could feel that the box was too light to be solid all the way through. She picked it up once more and shook it. Yes, she got a definite sense that it was hollow and contained something. Was it just so well made that the opening — like the box itself — remained invisible to all but the initiated?

Olwen pondered other ways to open the box. Could there be a

secret word or expression — likely known only to the wizards — that one had to recite? Or did the top twist off in some fashion rather than being pulled apart? What about a secret spring, released by pushing one or a combination of the jewels, or even a magic spell? Perhaps, under duress, it could be forced or broken open.

While working through the possibilities, Olwen wondered whether she was being led astray. Perhaps the box was simply a diversion, keeping her from completing her far more important task. She'd become totally sidetracked, engrossed in solving this new, more entertaining puzzle rather than getting down to the more mundane chore of figuring out the meaning of the prophecy. Olwen knew she could spend hours on the box and possibly never succeed in opening it. And if by chance she did manage to crack it open, would the box contain yet another indecipherable text, a clue to a new wild-goose chase, or simply nothing at all? Meanwhile, the precious hours would have slipped away.

Despite these contrary thoughts, Olwen was certain the box was important, maybe not on this day, but someday. The way things had unfolded — the visit from the raven, the disappearance of the wizards, her decision to unravel the meaning of her vision — everything had been meant to happen, and for a purpose. Even her opening of the shutters and then turning around, only to be blinded by the reflection from the box at that precise moment — it had to mean something, it had to lead somewhere. But what, and where?

After making several more fruitless attempts to open it, Olwen put aside the box to focus on the more pressing problem: the meaning of the message relayed to her by the raven. Although the effort did not come easily, she persevered. But the lioness could not forget about the box. More than once she stopped to pick it up and try out a fresh idea, all to no avail.

At last, after many hours of considered thought, referring to texts, logic, inspiration, pacing back and forth, staring blankly through the windows at the sea or the evening sky, chewing on her tail and even pulling at her whiskers, Olwen arrived at what she thought was the definitive meaning of her experience in the forest. As soon as she was satisfied with her conclusions, she decided to call upon Albiorix and Temorwig.

Although the hour was quite late, she found the pair exactly where she'd left them, in close conversation in the King's private chambers. The older lions welcomed her effusively.

9

NOT SO FAST

"Father, Uncle, it's taken hours and hours of thought and work," Olwen declared excitedly, "but I'm sure I've come up with the answer."

The surprised king had doubted that any animal, trained or not, could come up with the meaning of the raven's prophecy in just one day. Nevertheless, Albiorix gave his daughter leave to continue.

"Let me begin by going through the individual parts. After that, I'll piece together the whole picture. First, I looked at all the creatures. The raven — he was the first one I saw. You know better than I, Father, that the raven is an animal that inhabits all parts of this world; he goes where he pleases and according to his own whims. He's one of those few birds who owe allegiance to no other creature, but at the same time he serves all of us, by bringing wisdom and guidance to the rest of the animal world. I understand from my reading that the raven represents truth and ideas, but only if he talks. My bird did not talk; he only pointed his wing.

"So what do I take from all that? If ever there was a creature to introduce a prophecy, the raven would be the most appropriate. As well, because the raven is so independent, I know I can trust that he was not sent by the enemy to trick me. Thus, the first conclusion I draw is that this meeting was not an accident or simply an aimless dream. It was meant to provide some important message or crucial intelligence. However, it was also no more than that; it wasn't meant to make some deep philosophical point or argument."

Her father signaled his agreement. Temorwig acknowledged her logic with a small smile and added, "What you say makes sense, Olwen. But even I know the raven can also represent evil. Could it be that the bird, while not sent by another force, came of his own free will like some trickster, just to torment you or, even worse, to destroy us with false information?"

"What you say is quite true, Uncle. The raven has often been considered harmful, even a herald of wickedness. But I believe that view comes from our more superstitious ancestors, who considered all things black to be bad. No offense, but look at our staunch allies the panthers, who are as black as — well, as black as a raven. The more recent interpretation of the color is that it represents permission, judgment or potential. That would argue even more strongly for my conclusion that this bird was the logical host of the foretelling."

"Well said, daughter," interjected the King.

"I don't understand," Temorwig said. "You said your raven did not speak but only gestured. What of that?"

"If he had spoken, he would have been bringing me some kind of higher knowledge, just as a professor would instruct me. However, because he did not speak but only pointed, I conclude that he was simply guiding me toward a truth or a piece of crucial information. You see the distinction?"

"I guess so," replied Temorwig, not really seeing the difference. "Still, it seems like splitting hairs to me."

"Let's continue," Albiorix interrupted, "and not get sidetracked on this particular point."

"Thank you, Father, I shall. So the next creature I encountered was a panther. At least, I took it to be one of our many cousins. You know better than I that in prophecy the cats, especially we lions, epitomize strength, courage and refinement. It makes perfect sense, given our nature, and can only be seen as a good thing. However, if so, why was the panther supplanted by a bear? The bear can be seen only as a dangerous and destructive force."

"Indeed, that particular aspect is something that worries me," the King said. "It's why I really need to understand what the prophecy means. The wild bear — I won't say he is evil, but the creature is threatening to us, particularly now that we know the bears are in open revolt. Yes, daughter, I can see your surprise. Temorwig confirmed the news to me only this morning."

"Could not the transformation of one creature to another signify the potential for change?" Temorwig asked, getting back to the issue.

"Yes, but into what?" pursued the King. "And why would anyone want change? Are not things in Aeronbed just as we like them?"

"Who could disagree with that, Your Majesty?" Temorwig replied, shrugging. "Although, since we seem to be continually at war with our neighbors, one could easily argue that perfection has yet to reign over the realm."

The King opened his mouth to respond but quickly shut it again and shook his head.

"Whatever the case," Temorwig continued, "ignorant as I am about the workings of prophecy, I can only ask questions, not answer them."

Olwen interceded by posing a new line of inquiry. "If these animals do signify change, then what about the second change, into the white bear? The color white represents purity and spirit, even wisdom. So the panther is replaced first by a dark bear and then by another, ivory-colored one. The second bear could be considered superior to the first, so that's an auspicious transformation, is it not?"

"I suppose so," noted the King morosely. "Still, it's a bear you saw, not a cat."

"Hold on," Temorwig said. "I thought you said the notion of black as evil is outdated, so going from dark to light doesn't necessarily mean anything. Or does it? The more I hear, the more perplexed I'm getting."

"I said black represents permission and potential," Olwen replied. "In this case, seeing the transition to white as a good thing makes some sense, as possibly fulfilling something that was meant to happen."

By then the trio were at a loss as to what more to make of Olwen's summation. Or possibly, since the implications of any conclusions they might arrive at were far too awesome, they were simply afraid to admit what they really thought.

After a few moments of silent reflection, the King raised a new point. "Did you consider the number of animals you saw?" he asked.

"The number?"

"Yes, how many creatures there were. First one, then two, then three in total."

"I had no idea it was important."

"Ah well, you'll soon learn that everything is important in matters of divination. As I recall from prophecies I've been guided through in past years, the number one indicates single-mindedness, intolerance and stubbornness. Two stands for indecision and lack of responsibility, or, if one looks at it more positively, unselfishness. And three is bravery and enthusiasm, if not even brilliance."

"I was not aware of those distinctions. Still, if so, am I not correct in concluding this vision represents a good omen? What starts out as an unworthy set of traits ends up as something worthy."

"Quite possibly, although — "

"Excuse me," interjected Temorwig, who didn't like the way this was heading, "Are they not three individual creatures? They appeared not as a group of three but each one separately. Thus I would argue that we should be looking not at number three but at number one. My word, Albiorix, this is becoming far too confusing for me."

"Precisely the problem we always face. It's why the task is so difficult. Without our wizards to interpret, we're merely guessing in the dark. And to make matters worse, let me now add to the confusion. Did you take care, daughter, to analyze the position of your vision?"

"What?"

"The position, Olwen," the old lion repeated more loudly.

"I, I don't understand. What do you mean by position?" The lioness glanced toward Temorwig, but the old lion looked more befuddled than ever.

"Let me explain to both of you. Did you seem to be looking up or down at the creatures, Olwen, as the images moved across the surface of the pond? Were they coming toward you or going away from you?

Did they appear close to you or far away? Were they on the left or right or in the center of the picture, and how about the top or bottom?"

"I'm sorry, this is just too much!" Temorwig interjected. "How can any ordinary lion figure all this out?"

Olwen was crestfallen. "I'm sorry, I had no idea those aspects were also important. I'm beginning to agree with Uncle Temorwig that it's almost beyond comprehension."

"How could you have known," responded the King more kindly. "You're very young and you're not a wizard; you've certainly not made the study of prophecy your whole life's work. But I can assure you, the answers to my questions will indicate whether the events will happen sooner or later, how dark the future will be, how much effort will be required to overcome whatever challenges are put in our way, whether we are looking at birth or death ... and so on."

"So there's a lot more to be worked out," Olwen conceded. "That is, before we can even hope to arrive at the right conclusion."

"If we ever get there," the always skeptical Temorwig added.

"Now, don't be too hard on our dear Olwen."

"I'd be the last creature to criticize Olwen's efforts, far from it. It's the blasted profession and the 'science' as a whole that I question!"

They both ignored him. "Is there anything else, Father?"

"I'm afraid to say it, but yes, there is. Let's look at two more things. I think you said the panther — which then became the bear — was walking on a mountain ridge. The mountain indicates that it has a high obstacle to overcome, to reach the top, as it were, and it has yet to reach that pinnacle. However, the fact that the creature is walking means that it is capable of completing that journey on its own. The second important aspect is the nature of the scene you witnessed. You said it appeared to be a wide-open landscape rather than a confined or closed-in place. Do I remember that part correctly? If so, it means the scene evokes happiness and potential. Thus, for the bear this situation is most welcome, for the creature can achieve what he seeks."

"How do you know all this?"

"Oh, I've picked up a few things over the years." Albiorix laughed.

"But hold on," interjected Temorwig. "I still don't understand. Are we talking about the bear, about us, or about the future of Aeronbed?"

"Temorwig, you always leap to the nub of the matter. That is indeed the key question. But before we get there, let's turn to Olwen's earlier vision, the reflection of herself and the stars and moon instead of a clouded night sky."

"But how important is that view in the whole scheme of things?" Olwen asked. "It was just a reflection of me, or at least so I thought. I didn't imagine it could compare in importance to the second picture."

"Remember, everything you witnessed is important. It's up to us, in the absence of the wizards, to determine how important."

"So what does it tell you?"

"Ah well, I can interpret some of what you perceived, but not everything. I'm guessing there are two visions here — one referring to you, Olwen, and one to the future of Aeronbed. This first one deals with you. I know that an overcast sky signifies difficulty, so I assume that a clear sky indicates the opposite, that whatever challenges lie before you will be surmountable. The moon represents the emotional, darker and more unapproachable side of yourself. I would say that romance is on the horizon for you."

"Father!" the lioness exclaimed, horrified at the prospect.

"It's not me who makes this claim. It's what you saw."

"Well, at least that's a bit more cheerful," Temorwig added, winking. "But what of the stars?"

"I must confess I don't know what they mean," the King replied. "I'm afraid we've reached the limit of my knowledge on that score."

"Perhaps they mean nothing at all."

"I doubt it, Olwen. In my limited experience, I've found that everything is significant."

Temorwig looked doubtful but said nothing more.

"Finally," said the King, "what about the tree in which the raven sat?"

Temorwig groaned. "Not the trees as well. Is there no end to the questions?"

"Is that also important?" Olwen asked, sighing. "The tree was not in my vision."

"Olwen, I repeat, everything is important, even those aspects that appear trivial. The point is, we do not really know where the vision began or ended."

The lioness groaned. "I recall that it was an abaster tree, but I don't know much about such things."

"Is there not something called the tree of life?" Temorwig asked.

"Indeed there is, my old friend. If this was such, and if I had to reach a conclusion on that basis, I would see the tree as representing the end of things," the King replied. "The afterlife, as it were, where a cycle of life comes to an end and all things are reconciled."

"Well, I never," said Temorwig.

For a while Olwen was silent. Then she said, "It's almost too much to take in. Just to get this far has taken every piece of our knowledge and exhausted every brain cell. Now I see we've much more ground to cover. I had more to say; I'd even come to some conclusions. However, now I see they are irrelevant. I don't even know how to put it all together."

"Do not despair," said the King, laughing. "Let's not say *irrelevant*, perhaps merely premature. This is usually how I feel after listening to the wizards. It's why I gave them specific orders to be clear and precise in their assessment. And it's perhaps the reason why they ran off as they did — simply because they knew it was beyond their capacity. We three must think some more about what we've discussed this evening. I know I will, well into the morning hours. We'll speak of the vision again tomorrow, after a good sleep. In the meantime, I thank you, Princess, for all your splendid work."

"I'd say I'm owed few thanks. I'm more bewildered now than when I began, and I don't even know where to go from here."

The King laughed again, spoke more reassuring words and embraced her. As night was now well upon the three lions, they took their leave of each other, each deep in thought.

❧ II ❧

VIGMAR AND ARUNDATI

10

HOW IS HE?

The Empress of Vigmar swept into the room, catching Seanan by surprise. "Well, Doctor," Dona Morana demanded, "how is he?"

"Would Your Highness prefer a medical opinion or a political one?" the owl asked in return. He tried to stifle a yawn, unsuccessfully. The bird was awfully tired, for he'd been up many hours now assisting a whole host of patients, not just his most important one. Seanan was a night bird, but even owls had their limits.

Dona Morana, ignoring the bird's fatigue, sighed perceptibly and rolled her eyes skyward. What would it take to get a straight answer from these medical quacks? Still, on this rare occasion the imperious donkey restrained her usual impulse to bray and complain. "I suppose you're going to give me both answers," she responded, more evenly than anyone might have expected. "Whether I like it or not."

Coming from the normally humorless Empress, this retort was rather amusing. Still, she barely cracked a smile; in fact her look was cold and her tone even more chilling. The owl had rather hoped Dona Morana would go a little easy on him, for he'd been ministering to her husband around the clock for days — and nights — on end. Seanan knew better than to expect sympathy from those quarters, but that hadn't stopped him from hoping.

Unfortunately the doctor had few results to show for all his efforts, only his own sore eyes and bowed shoulders. While the owl was an optimist by nature, his medicines had proven useless. How could one heal a broken heart, after all? Certainly not with the herbs, pills, solutions and potions an enlightened doctor in those sophisticated times had at his disposal. Seanan had consulted his great tomes, both new and ancient, and his learned colleagues from the farthest reaches of the Empire, just in case someone knew of some mystical balm, and he had even pursued less legitimate sources that many would have considered heretical. In the case of a mortally ill emperor, no expedient, whether fair or foul, could be ruled out.

Seanan knew of only one sure healing resource, but that resource, that one individual, was no longer in the capital. Indeed, no one was certain where Grand Duchess Fridis was keeping herself lately. Word had it (if such word could be relied on) that the pretty duck was hiding out in the far south of Arundati, far from Vigmar's centers of power and intrigue, far from the long reach of those who would do her harm. Clearly Fridis knew enough not to return, let alone to reveal her exact whereabouts; only a crazed or foolhardy animal would have done so.

A dark, sour voice interrupted the bird's internal meanderings. "Well, I'm waiting. What have you got to tell me?"

Seanan gazed up at Dona Morana, whose rear hoof was beating an impatient little tune on the stone floor. The elegant donkey, wrapped in ermine and mink and wearing the symbols of her rank and position, was sitting on the large throne that belonged to the now dying Emperor. The message was clear for all to see. She had been co-ruler of Vigmar, but now she ruled alone while the Emperor could or would not speak for himself. If and when Don Grimezel died, all power would then reside with her.

"Your Highness, since we spoke last there's been no change in the Emperor's condition," Seanan said. "His Majesty remains weak; he does not eat and we are only able to get him to drink a little. He is unable to communicate with anyone. However, while Don Grimezel has not improved, his condition has also not deteriorated. As such, hope for recovery remains."

"Is that the political report or the medical one?"

Seanan was taken aback. Was it not obvious? "The political one, Your Majesty," the owl replied.

"Well, then," she sneered, "let's hear the unbridled truth. Enough with the comforting platitudes."

Seanan clenched his beak tightly to keep himself from hooting in anger. He was beginning to feel ill himself. The bird already knew that Dona Morana was callous and unfeeling; today, however, her disdain verged on cruelty. The donkey never spoke a kind or gracious word unless it was to her advantage, and even then, such words surfaced most grudgingly. Seanan had already decided not to stay in Blakfel should the Emperor die. No creature of good conscience would be able to bear the bleak era that would surely follow.

"In my professional opinion, the Emperor is dying. It's a matter of mere days or weeks. Perhaps a trifle longer, but without nourishment, his body will begin to decline to a point where it cannot survive." There, he had said it. Would she be satisfied now?

The doctor saw the slightest upward curl of her lips. Was that a smile? If it was, the donkey quickly suppressed it and Dona Morana resumed her impassive imperial stare. "Thank you for your candor," she replied calmly. "However long it took you to spit it out."

It was another slap, but at least he'd received some token gratitude along with it. Seanan bowed.

"You may go. Let me know immediately if there's any change, one way or the other."

The owl bowed again, then backed out as the Empress dismissed him with a careless wave of a hoof, her mind now turning to other matters. Closing the door behind him, Seanan heard Dona Morana call for food and drink.

The owl wondered whether he could find some way to get word to Fridis. Even though the feisty eider duck was merely a grand duchess, many of her loyal fans had taken to calling her Princess in her absence, perhaps as a way to protest her banishment. However, no one knew where she was hiding, and even if someone did, Seanan dared not leave at such a time, with the Emperor in his charge.

Seanan paced through the darkened hallways, lost in thought and weighed down with concern, barely acknowledging the greetings of other members of the court. There was no comfort to be found there, or, for that matter, anywhere in the capital. He considered going off to his quarters for some badly needed rest, but he had one further charge to attend to before he could achieve that blessed state. He must bring General Aravat up-to-date on the Emperor's health.

After some searching, he found the elephant not in the war room but in deep conversation with his colleagues in the square facing the palace. Seanan supposed the members of the high command were enjoying a rare respite from their claustrophobic meeting rooms. It was surprisingly warm for late winter, but the generals displayed little appreciation for the mild weather as they clustered in small groups, talking earnestly.

Aravat noticed the doctor's arrival from afar and signaled with a curt wave of his trunk that Seanan should wait until he had finished his discussions. The owl made his way over to the very center of the square, where a huge statue of Vigmar's founder had been erected many years earlier. After glancing up at the likeness of the venerable donkey, Seanan sat down to wait.

After several minutes Aravat dismissed the others, who strolled off in twos and threes. The elephant lumbered slowly toward the doctor, who by this time had closed his eyes and was leaning ever so slightly against the statue's plinth, enjoying the warmth of the soft air on his feathers. The weather felt almost springlike.

"A rare day is it not, Doctor," Aravat called out as he strode over.

"Indeed it is," replied Seanan, his eyes still closed. "It's just what one needs to restore the soul."

"Ah, if only it were so," Aravat responded somewhat gloomily.

Opening his eyes at last, Seanan looked up at the huge elephant. "Cheer up, General. Have we not much to be thankful for?"

"That depends on what you have to tell me."

Seanan nodded slightly and opened his eyes wider. It was true, the owl admitted ruefully. Whether one should give thanks or hurl curses invariably depended on where one was coming from and where one hoped to go next.

The doctor recounted his current assessment of the Emperor and his latest meeting with the Empress, leaving out his own asides and personal observations. The great elephant sighed deeply. At very least, considered Seanan, they were in agreement: it was definitely news to be sighed over.

"General," Seanan said, "what will happen if — "

"I know what you're going to ask," interrupted Aravat, raising his trunk to stop the owl from speaking further. "It just so happens that my colleagues and I were considering that very question when you arrived. I must tell you, for many of us it's not an easy subject." He stopped there and looked directly at the doctor, as if to ask, *Can I trust you?*

Seanan picked up on the elephant's concern. "I'm a creature of the healing arts, General. I care not for politics or the games that inevitably accompany such things. My job — my only interest, in fact — is to heal the sick, and one poor patient in particular. I am, nonetheless, worried about the state of affairs in Vigmar should Don Grimezel die, and I therefore seek your counsel. What you might say in reply is only for my own information, nothing else. At some point I will have to decide on a course of action — an action related solely to my personal future, I assure you."

"It's not that I don't trust you or doubt your ability to keep silent under pressure. It's only that sometimes even the best-intentioned among us can say things inadvertently. Hah! I've seen heads roll because of a poorly employed adjective or misplaced pronoun."

"I assure you, we owls are the silent ones of the animal kingdom. Nothing untoward ever slips from our discreet beaks."

Aravat considered the bird's claim. Ultimately concluding that he knew of no owl that had gone *awry*, to use his own terminology, the elephant chose to accept it. "Many of the senior officers are much concerned about, er, recent developments," he said carefully. "You will recall that when the Emperor and Empress became co-rulers, each of us was asked to swear an oath of allegiance to both of them. Well, perhaps *asked* misstates the case; it was expected of us if we had any hope of staying in our positions.

"Oaths are a sacred trust, you know, but at the time most of us considered the commitment pro forma and gave it little consideration. As you can well imagine, no one expected this turn of events. Thus, if

Don Grimezel should die, or even remain in his current state, we are by custom and history obliged to support and maintain the current regime. Simply put, it is our duty. Some — I won't say who — are not happy at such a prospect, and they may choose to leave the alliance despite their pledge. Still, for the most part the generals will abide by their oaths, though some more willingly than others. Forgive me, Seanan, if I point out the obvious — I speak frankly here — the world has provided us with very few alternatives to the current regime."

The elephant paused long enough for the owl to begin wondering if he was supposed to provide an answer to the conundrum facing the generals. But as Seanan contemplated proposing a hypothesis, Aravat carried on. "And so, to conclude, better the evil you know than the evil you don't know. Do you catch my drift, Doctor?"

"Indeed I do. I must say there are times when one is happy to be just a simple creature practicing the medical arts."

"Not, I would think, when one is responsible for the health of a dying emperor. I imagine your life can be — probably already is — as challenging as ours."

The owl blinked his huge eyes and shivered noticeably. That reply was not one he'd been expecting. "Ahem, well, I don't really know, er, that is, I — " he managed to utter, and then stopped in mid-sentence. Seanan decided that enough had been said between them. He bowed low to the General to take his leave.

Aravat bowed in return and turned to go back into the palace. However, before the elephant had got far, the doctor called out, "I thank you for your candor, General. Have no fear. I shall not breathe a word of our conversation to anyone."

"Doctor Seanan, you're speaking to the new supreme commander of Vigmar's vast and mighty armies. What have I to fear?" Aravat smiled broadly and blew a mighty blast of air from his trunk.

Puzzling over this last remark, Seanan watched the elephant leave. Was Aravat trying to tell him something? Was he being sarcastic or serious? Was it a warning or a jest? Between them, after all, who really was the most vulnerable?

II

PONDERING HER FATE

F ridis pushed through a clump of tall oat grass and stepped onto the top of the sand dune. The duck's eyes were quick to take in the broad, sandy shore separating her imposing vantage point from the Southern Sea. The beach stretched on as far as the eye could see in both directions, broken only by occasional volcanic outcrops that the earth had chosen to thrust into the turquoise waters.

Waves rolled in relentlessly, flailing against the impervious black rock and white sand. A stiff but unsteady breeze blew in from the south, causing the tall coconut palms to sway back and forth, pushing their delicate fronds this way and that. The hot sun, now almost at its midday point, shone down without respite. Looking out to sea along the entire length of the far-off horizon, Fridis spied a thin line of fluffy clouds. Ever since she'd arrived, the clouds had kept their distance offshore, never coming inland.

It was a place of exquisite harmony, plenty and beauty. Why had no one ever told her of this splendid setting? After being stuck for months in gray and gloomy Blakfel, here she had discovered a paradise of warmth, peace and brilliant color. Why had they kept this region such a secret? Why was it not full of other refugees from Vigmar, equally seeking relief and sanctuary?

In keeping with her daily routine, Fridis flew over to a large, shallow pool lying just offshore. These waters, protected by coral reefs and sheltered by a line of rocks more distant, were teeming with food. Every day at some point, the pretty duck would stop her feeding and gaze about, mesmerized by the richness and vibrancy of the natural world surrounding her, amazed that such a place existed.

Ironically, Fridis's pleasure in her own deeply satisfying plumage and profile had paled in comparison to what her eyes now fell upon on any given day. How could her flecked brown and white plumage compare with the brilliant yellow, limpid aquamarine and coral pinks, just a few of the fantastic colors surrounding her? The duck felt humbled, almost ashamed of her past boasting. How silly and vain she must have appeared!

To top it off, the few creatures Fridis had encountered so far in the southern part of Arundati seemed so relaxed, so unconcerned about themselves and their status, let alone the war up north. *Should this not be how life is?* the duck wondered. Better indeed to mind one's own business and ignore the strife and envy. Here she'd found a land of plenty, with more than enough for everyone.

"If only Eirwen had been able to see this part of the world," Fridis had declared more than once since arriving. Of course, with his heavy fur coat, the polar bear would have been completely unsuited to the climate; the region was simply too hot. Still, at least he'd have the ocean to enjoy. The salty water teemed with fish to eat and friends to replace the ones he'd lost. However, it might also have reminded the bear of what he was missing, causing him to pine for the pure white snows and frigid waters of the Far North to which he was much more accustomed. Fridis sighed deeply. She'd never find out now.

Fridis glanced back inland to where the sandy beach melded into the scrub grass, searching for her aloof but faithful companion, Raicho. The disciplined, ever-vigilant peregrine falcon had taken shelter in an immense banyan tree close to the shore. He caught her eye, waved a wing to signal that he was keeping track, and then flew up into the empty blue skies for one of his frequent scouting forays. The duck watched her companion hover, seemingly motionless, against the stiff breeze, his wings dipping slightly this way and that to maintain his stationary position over the beach.

Finally Raicho broke free to traverse a perfect figure eight over the entire beach area, out to sea and then back overland, flying swiftly above the thick bamboo forest lying just beyond the beach. The falcon did this maneuver at irregular intervals during the day, patrolling the largely empty skies as he kept watch for interlopers. As far as Fridis could tell, no creature, hostile or friendly, ever came to this particular spot. The cove had turned out to be a perfect hiding place. But that was, of course, exactly what Aeron-Urd had intended for her.

Fridis wondered how her good friend was faring back in Blakfel. It had been a long time since she'd last set eyes on the old gyrfalcon. Or so it seemed, for down here in the tropics, time appeared to stand still; each day was so like the day before and the day after that one began to lose track of everything. Everything, that is, but the subtle changes in the refreshing winds and cooling waves. How long had it been since they'd left Blakfel to obtain her precious jewels? Jewels — what a laugh!

The two birds had set off many weeks ago, without any ceremony, in the early morning hours (as suggested by First Secretary Gloton to preserve secrecy), heading for the mountains of southern Arundati. Those ranges, the wolverine had promised, were the best source of the fabulous gems she coveted, the ones she needed for her grand revival meetings. The party of four made an unlikely quartet. Fridis, the eider duck, was accompanied by three members of Vigmar's air force: her friend Aeron-Urd, a gyrfalcon, the commander in charge of air defense; his lieutenant Raicho, a peregrine falcon; and a junior-ranking red-shouldered hawk named Rorbeg. They had left Vigmar's capital in the depths of winter, seen off only by Gloton. It had been, Fridis felt, a lifetime ago.

For Fridis, a duck not given to annual migration, the unusual trip had begun as a great adventure. The birds had flown southeast, away from the mountains surrounding Blakfel and into the lowlands of Vigmar, first passing over the rolling hills and plains where she and Eirwen had first arrived, and then, without a halt, continuing in the direction of Arundati. The trip had taken many days of hard flying against stiff headwinds, and they were forced to stop and rest up several times.

But, after leaving the gloom and despondency of the capital behind them, their hearts and spirits had woken in concert with the clearing skies above. A pure, shimmering blue replaced the dull, muted gray, a change that in itself was a real treat for Fridis. The conditions had improved steadily, and cloudless days became the norm rather than the exception. The welcome sun accompanied them every day, growing more intense the farther south they went. The landscape below also began to change dramatically, becoming ever more green and lush.

When the four birds crossed from Vigmar to the forests, fields and mountains of Arundati, they met with their first surprise. Waiting for them was the black falcon Corvus, one of the Air Marshal's squadron leaders. Fridis remembered meeting the bird earlier in the fall, before he had set off for Aeronbed in search of the missing armies. Was the falcon bringing the news they'd long been waiting for? Their hopes rose, and the quartet quickly landed to hear the emissary's report.

Leaving the red-shouldered hawk to guard the skies above, Corvus, Raicho and Aeron-Urd went off to talk in private. Fridis waited anxiously nearby to hear what intelligence the black falcon had brought to them. When Aeron-Urd slowly returned to her, the desperate look on his face said it all. It was not going to be good news.

"Duchess," the gyrfalcon began, in a quiet, serious tone, "there are times in a commander's life when — " The bird stopped and looked away, unable to complete the sentence.

"Go on, my friend. Best to get it out quickly," the apprehensive duck responded. "Something has happened to Eirwen, hasn't it."

"Never have I more hated being the bearer of such tidings. And to you, Fridis, of all creatures ... "

At those words Fridis felt the pit of her stomach tighten and harden. The duck tried to steel herself for whatever was to come, but she could not — she feared the worst.

Aeron-Urd continued with his account. "Corvus has brought word from the wolf pack. Two messengers who were en route to Vigmar — the wolfhound Emrin-Can and the wolf Amlich — were discovered on the mountain slopes of eastern Aeronbed. Lorcan and his squadron rescued them from an enemy attack. It was a near thing, but that's of little concern to you. The pair had been sent by Adarix to provide Blakfel a status report on the wolf pack's activities since it left Vigmar last year. More important, they had news of the current whereabouts and status of the pack and of Lord Eirwen.

"I will not beat around the bush. I regret to say that your friend — and Vigmar's champion — has been killed in battle with the big cats." Aeron-Urd swallowed hard and stopped to let the dreadful news sink in.

To her surprise, Fridis felt strangely calm. She had already come to terms with the polar bear's absence from her day-to-day life. And now? Somehow she'd been expecting this sad development. Eirwen had gone off to war — a dangerous, bloody business, where death was not the exception but the rule. And so much had happened in her life since then as she carved out a new raison d'être in Blakfel. Although Fridis felt the harsh sting of the words she'd feared for so long, she was not nearly as devastated as she'd expected. Perhaps the grief would come later …

"How — " the duck said. "How did it happen?"

Aeron-Urd described what had occurred, at least, as much as Corvus had been able to relay. Even though the story had been passed along several times from one creature to another, the incredible tale had changed little in the retelling; it was consistent with what Adarix had experienced and then observed from afar. No one had seen a need to embellish the account; it was heroic enough just as it was. Naturally, Gloton's false accusation of Eirwen, which had been passed on by Emrin, had not been repeated. That piece of the story remained known only to the wolves and the dog.

The more details Aeron-Urd provided, the more waves of anguish washed over Fridis. By the end of the story the duck could barely speak. Now, she realized, she was utterly alone in this strange land. Of the short-lived band of three — the bear, the raven and the duck — only one remained. And she was so, so far from home. Fridis began to weep bitter tears.

There was nothing else Aeron-Urd could say. As the pain swept over and through her, the gyrfalcon put his large wing around Fridis's quaking body to comfort her as best he could. He remained outwardly composed, but the sight of the duck's anguish stirred in him an equal measure of sorrow and anger.

Managing at last to composed herself, Fridis asked her friend, "Did they ever find Eirwen's body?"

"His body?" said the surprised Aeron-Urd.

"Yes. Did they go back to recover his body?"

Aeron-Urd tried to frame his answer as gently as possible. "Fridis, we're speaking of a battlefield where the wolf pack was on the run from the enemy. Going back would have been impossible. They could not have risked it at the time; they had to keep moving until they found sanctuary. Perhaps in the springtime — if conditions permit it — they might be able to search the site."

"So — "

"I hope you're not suggesting what I think. Of course, I wasn't there, but from what I understand, no creature could have survived a fall down that mountainside. Your hope is understandable, but don't fool yourself, don't torment yourself with false expectations. There can be no doubt in this matter. You must accept this great loss — as we all do."

"I know, it's just that ... " Fridis could not express it now, so she left off. It was not so much that the duck had doubts or wanted proof. She just wanted Eirwen to have a proper send-off, one befitting his immense sacrifice. Fridis had been angry with Eirwen for going in the first place, and now the duck was equally angry at his being so stubbornly noble that his actions had led to his death. Fine for him, but she was the one left behind.

"If it's of any consolation," Aeron-Urd added, "I have ordered Corvus and Lorcan to return to Aeronbed to assist Adarix in his operations. Perhaps in time they will learn more details about Eirwen's death and his, um, current whereabouts." It was not much, but better than nothing.

Fridis asked Aeron-Urd to leave her alone for a while. The duck needed to come to terms with the dreadful news and with her new reality: being completely on her own in this strange land. She also wanted an opportunity to reminisce to herself about the all-too-brief time she and Eirwen had enjoyed together.

While the falcons and hawk looked on sadly from a respectful distance, Fridis flew over to a nearby stand of tall, stately pine trees. The shadowed, enveloping grove provided Fridis the retreat from reality she needed. The sunlight above barely made its way through the closely overlapping branches; below them, the ground, with its thick cover of dry reddish brown needles, was crackly but soft. As a result, the grove was tomblike, dark and almost devoid of sound. All Fridis could hear was a distant twittering of small birds who had no care for her sorrow, and the occasional swish of a spindly treetop being buffeted by the breeze on high. The trees formed a perfect place to find seclusion and meditate on her fate.

She and Eirwen had packed a great deal of life into their very short time together. Of course, the duck had expected to share many more years and adventures with the polar bear. She imagined that anyone who had lost a dear friend must feel like that: a life cut short so soon — too soon. Fridis was glad she'd made a special effort to send Eirwen off to his war as she had; at least that farewell fly-past had been the semblance of a final goodbye, a visual reminder of their leave-taking.

However, in retrospect, that farewell seemed a far cry from what she wanted out of life. The past months had brought nothing but surprise, adventure (and misadventure), danger and excitement. To assert that things would never be the same without Eirwen was almost laughable. She could never have foreseen all that the past year had brought, and what the future held in store was even further beyond her capacity to imagine.

After wandering for some time among the venerable old trees, Fridis was able to achieve a modicum of solace. Moving slowly, she returned to rejoin her companions.

"Fridis," Aeron-Urd said when the duck was standing before them, "you will know, without my having to say it, that you have my deepest sympathy. Indeed, the sympathy of all Vigmar's loyal subjects. You have but to ask — whatever support you need in the days to come shall be granted to you."

Fridis was grateful for his understanding but said nothing.

"I must ask you, then," the gyrfalcon continued after a short pause, "what is it you wish to do now? You could return to Blakfel, where, I would imagine, the news has already been received. I expect the capital has already instituted an appropriate period of mourning, and your presence will be expected."

As Fridis maintained her silence, Aeron-Urd paused again. "Or perhaps you'd rather continue on our present course, toward the Misken Mountains."

Fridis had already been thinking about her options. The duck had determined that not only was there nothing really to return to — or for — in Blakfel, it would also be far too depressing to have to deal with an endless array of formalities and ceremonies. Far better, she decided, to keep her mind occupied with a change of scenery and her new objective. So, with little further ado, the quartet continued on its chosen path south, leaving Corvus to return to his squadron.

12

THE MISKEN MOUNTAINS

As they flew on toward their destination, the thoughts of Aeron-Urd and Fridis turned to other, far different concerns.

The duck's mind was on Eirwen and his reason for embarking on the quest that had led to discovering Vigmar. It had been all about the polar bear's missing friends. Now, however, Eirwen was dead and she was left high and dry, alone and without any way to return home. So now what? What was she supposed to do? Like the bear, Fridis had taken on a new persona and played an unexpected role in Vigmar, but what of it? Was there anything she wanted to achieve on her own? There was, the duck decided, no easy way to resolve such questions, certainly not yet. She would simply carry on and see what unfolded.

Aeron-Urd, for his part, was thinking about the war. The gyrfalcon knew he had time to accompany Fridis to her destination. The loss of Eirwen, however, meant he would not be able to stay with her indefinitely, should the duck wish to linger there. Planning for the spring offensive in light of what had now been learned would begin in earnest and would inevitably require his participation. Still, Aeron-Urd was prepared to enjoy what little time he had left with Fridis.

Their first destination was the Misken Mountains. They were so named, Fridis had learned, because of their intense black color and scarcity of vegetation. It was there they would find the first source of the rare jewels Fridis was seeking. But was there any point now in gathering them? Previously the duck had seen her future back in the capital as an empty canvas, yet to be filled by her own brushstrokes. Now she could no longer picture herself in Blakfel, not at all. Still, they had flown this far. Why not, at the very least, see the jewels for herself.

By this point the four travelers had left the coniferous forests and open plains far behind them. From here on, the birds would be flying over mist-laden jungles of tall, spindly bamboo, spreading banyan trees and entwining, grasping vines. The dense haze and the thick green rainforest canopy often hid the ground from their view; it was, Fridis thought, like flying over a lush and perfect carpet that extended in every direction as far as one could see.

Eventually, in the distance, their goal became apparent. A range of craggy black mountains rose dramatically before them, jutting through the green tropical valley floor and reaching sharply into the blue sky. The range was awesome from afar, but it was only when the birds reached its outer edges that Fridis began to appreciate their incredible size and height.

The source of the gems, near the center of this challenging domain, was closely guarded, and in more ways than one. First, the location of the mine made it virtually impregnable to all but the most daring of thieves. The overland route was deemed so arduous that the mine's owners didn't even bother worrying about it. The approach by air — the only feasible way in — was a secret known only to a few, carefully kept from prying eyes and inquisitive ears. In addition, great efforts had been made to ensure that interlopers, whether through curiosity or by accident, would never penetrate the Miskens' inner sanctum.

The way in from the jungle and through the mountain passes was watched over by numerous sentinels at constantly varying strategic points. Lookouts were rotated on an irregular basis, only a very small number knew individual passwords, and the codes were never shared between species. Aeron-Urd had no idea who would be guarding the various points of entry; he had been required to memorize several variations of codes — no mean feat even for a brainy falcon.

Hidden warning stations alerted the inner sentries to arrivals, both welcome and not; any animals who arrived unannounced were to be stopped unceremoniously. Should the security guards be overwhelmed by bandits or an enemy force, the deepest caves — where the treasure was kept — could be sealed off. And if any creature did manage to penetrate into the mine, false tunnels had been dug over the years to confuse them; those routes ended in nothing but a blank wall, a circuitous maze or much, much worse. Even if one could get in, getting out alive was quite another matter.

Of course, despite the elaborate defense mechanisms, the riches of the mine meant that its allure could be overpowering for the greedy, the envious or the desperate. Over the years, several attacks had been attempted. None, however, had succeeded in penetrating the confines of the mine, let alone achieving the goal of seizing a portion of its wealth.

The mine and its treasure trove were located midway up one of the highest mountains in the range. The birds' only way in was to fly through several deep, narrow chasms. Fridis couldn't help but notice the silent watchers at almost every juncture, keeping the four under close observation. Occasionally — and, it seemed, arbitrarily — they were stopped, whereupon Aeron-Urd was asked to repeat a specific password.

The birds were buffeted by sudden strong updrafts and downdrafts that made for a grueling flight, better suited for strong raptors than the smaller, less streamlined duck. When the mine entrance finally came into view, Fridis saw that it lay halfway up a sheer rock face. It was just a sizeable cliff ledge and, beyond the ledge, a deep, darker hole cut into the black rock. Clearly no land-based creature but the most determined mountain goat could ever scale that mountainside.

As they landed on the cliff edge, a host of additional lookouts — kestrels and black hawks — and a welcoming party of bighorn sheep and badgers appeared, as if out of nowhere, to greet them. Fortunately Aeron-Urd was well-known there; indeed, a squadron of his hawks was the first point of defense. More to the point, the Air Marshal had begun his career in the region, having grown up in those very mountains. The old gyrfalcon felt very much at home here and was a welcome figure to those who greeted him. Much celebration ensued, both personal and professional, to honor the arrival of both celebrities and inaugurate their brief visit.

The first day was spent acclimatizing. Although Fridis was forced to endure the unavoidable welcoming ceremonies, speeches and feasts, they were cut short because of the sad news from the front and the need to respect Fridis's feelings. Thus it was only on the morning of the second day that Aeron-Urd, Raicho and Fridis were escorted to the jewels.

Employing the utmost care, the keepers of the gemstones led them through a confusing array of tunnels, purposefully chosen so that the visitors would find it impossible ever to recall the correct route. Even Aeron-Urd, who had visited the storehouse of gems more than once in his life, would have been hard-pressed to remember the directions. It was the badgers who escorted the trio, for it was those creatures who did the burrowing essential to uncovering the stones; they considered themselves the true protectors — if not the rightful owners — of the jewels.

After many twists and turns, ups and downs, and even one false turn, the animals reached the treasure trove. In a largish, well-lit chamber, they encountered four sub-chambers placed opposite one another. In the first three they found collections of roughly cut stones of various kinds: in one there were emeralds, topazes, opals and jade; in another, rubies and amethysts; and in the third, sapphires and tourmalines. In the fourth sub-chamber there were two smaller rooms: a cutting and polishing area and a sorting, counting and presentation space. In this last place, the final one they were taken to, an array of particularly beautiful cut stones had been placed in large piles on a pristine and superbly polished rock surface.

There at last, Fridis was permitted to choose whatever she liked from the wide assortment of jewels. It was a fantastic sight, almost overwhelming, and almost impossible for her to make a choice. The badgers were thrilled to have such a distinguished and appreciative (not to mention romantically tragic) visitor. It was a rare opportunity for them to show off all they had to this newcomer whose story had spread throughout the land. In Fridis's eyes, the stones were awesome to behold; gleaming brightly in the flickering candlelight, they seemed alive, as if they each held their own light.

When Fridis had set off on this expedition to the south, she had known only vaguely what she was after. Now, with Eirwen's death overwhelming her sensibilities, gems no longer held the same allure. Certainly they were not as crucial to her future in Vigmar as she'd once thought. Fridis was now inclined to simply enjoy the experience and not accept any of the jewels. But she was equally conscious that a great deal of effort had been put into the trip, and that the badgers were quite excited about her selection. The duck didn't want to disappoint them by refusing to take anything.

Thoughtfully, Fridis ran her soft wingtips over and through the piles of gems, trying to see which ones appealed to her the most. In the end, befitting her new mood, she selected a restrained assortment of ten magnificent stones. Some were as brilliant and clear as the air itself, some milky and deep, and some seemed to have so much personality and character that they might have spoken volumes about their past if so asked. The duck hoped her modest selection would indicate her gratitude for the opportunity and her admiration for the stones' fine quality, at the same time revealing her innate lack of greed. The badgers nodded their approval of her choices and took them away to be wrapped for the trip back to Blakfel.

Fridis couldn't help but notice that, as the three birds were being escorted back to the surface, they were not following the route by which they'd entered. While every chamber, tunnel and turn looked more or less the same, they were clearly being led along a brand-new path. The badgers moved quickly, apparently knowing their way instinctively or through familiarity, and Fridis suspected no one else could ever figure it out. Eventually she began to notice the air was fresher, and at last they made their way to the open space at the opening to the mine. After the close, warm air of the confined tunnel system, it felt good to breathe the cold, crisp mountain air once again.

That evening, their last on the mountain, would see one more feast to mark the visit of such an honored guest. It was held, as before, in a large cave, the ceiling of which rose way above their heads. Long tables were arrayed throughout the space, each holding an abundance of choice offerings. Stories would be told, speeches made, elaborate toasts given and amusing performances presented to delight and amuse them all.

This time Fridis was seated beside the retired senior manager of the mine, a venerable old badger (or so he seemed to the duck, who'd met few such animals in her life) who went by the name of Piro. After copious amounts of food and drink, everyone — even Fridis — had become quite relaxed and more than a little talkative.

"Tell me, Señor Piro," asked Fridis, who, despite everything that had happened, could not stop playing the detective. "I'm very curious. When we arrived here, I would have sworn that no creature but a bird could make it up this precipice. But what do I find when I arrive? Bighorn sheep and badgers! The first creatures I can well understand, even if I still find it hard to believe. But badgers? All the way up here? I don't get it. Don't badgers live in burrows deep underground? I would expect to see you in a forest glade or at a river's edge. But high up in the mountains? It just doesn't make sense."

"Bighorn sheep have always frequented mountain locales," the badger said grandly. "They're well-known to make use of the most meager of ledges, ones that no other creature could stand upon."

"Indeed they do, and that's why I'm not asking you about them. Even if I had to see them way up here to believe it, their presence can be readily explained. It's you and your fellow badgers that I'm asking about."

The badger glanced around and shrugged warily.

"I'm also curious," the duck persisted, "about the arrangement with Vigmar. I'm not really sure what your family gets out of it."

"You ask many questions, Duchess."

"It's one of the things I'm really good at." Fridis laughed. "Asking questions, that is. Getting answers — now that's another matter."

They both laughed good-naturedly. Fridis was pleased to be able to put her mind to other things than the death of Eirwen.

The badger drank deeply. "You know nothing of our history, then?"

"No, I'm afraid not. None of it."

Piro looked around the cavernous space. The others were absorbed in conversation and no one was paying the slightest heed to what the duck and the badger might have to say to each other. Piro picked up his drink and indicated with a discreet nod that they should move off to a quieter table against the far wall of the cave. *Over here*, the badger motioned. He swept ahead, a little unsteadily.

"Sometimes it does no good to dredge up the past," Piro declared when they were settled. "Many painful memories, you know, and some in authority take offense at the very idea of reflecting on loss and sadness. They see attempts to upset the established order of things, when all that is intended, of course, is reminiscence and the spinning of folktales. You understand what I mean, do you not, Duchess?"

Although Fridis was not exactly sure, she certainly didn't want the badger to stop. "I believe so. You want to make certain no one misunderstands your true purpose. Is that it?"

"Exactly. What I will tell you is ancient history — nothing more than a good yarn, perhaps even a myth about our ancestors, told for your amusement. That is all, yes?"

"Yes, certainly, certainly. Nothing more."

"Well, then," the badger started. "Sit back, relax and let me tell you a legend of days gone by." He turned to face the duck squarely and spoke as softly as he could, so that no one nearby might hear him.

13

PIRO'S STORY

"Many years ago," the badger began, "I don't know exactly when, but long before my time, Arundati was a land of peace. All creatures got along well with each other, even though (at least when I think about it today) how they managed to do so seems to me nigh impossible. Naturally, disputes arose and misunderstandings occurred. For example, jackals aren't able to communicate with giraffes as easily as with each other — you know how it is. Still, generally speaking, most animals lived together in harmony.

"At that time we badgers were concentrated in this part of the world. Of course, we had cousins elsewhere and our business required extensive travel, but most of us lived happily enough in the mountains of the south. So too did many others, and in those days it seemed that most creatures roamed about without restriction or concern for borders or safety. Those were the good old days, mark you! Arundati was a land of plenty, a place to live and let live.

"Badgers have always been well-known for their underground explorations; we couldn't stop ourselves from digging even if we tried. It's in our blood, you know. One thing leads to another, as it were. First we dig for food, then we like what we find and build homes; then the homes become larger and grander. Then we begin to spend more time underground and begin to explore and excavate more and more, and we begin to discover things we did not expect. Finally, we begin to realize that what we've found is greatly prized by others.

"By the time we badgers began to develop our expertise in hunting for raw gems, others began to see the opportunities for trade and creating related businesses. There was much profit to be made, don't you know. Inevitably alliances began to be formed, bringing together the skills of several animals. The greatest of those collaborations — at least in these parts — was a foursome: a badger named Achimi, a snow leopard named Obtala, a falcon named Kelnek and a brown bear named Merithu. A curious mixture of creatures, you might think, my lady. Indeed, today such a partnership would be impossible to arrange.

"Achimi was the best of the best. His ability to nose out the finest jewels was renowned far and wide. But naturally there's more to the business of mining than just finding the gems; the others had roles to play in processing, distribution, developing markets, dealing with rivals and warding off what few thieves were about. They developed into a team unlike any other in the land. They trusted each other, all playing their part admirably and avoiding stepping on each other's toes — or claws, as it were. As a result, success followed upon success. Eventually theirs became the wealthiest of all such operations in Arundati, carving out an immense territory and employing many others in the process.

"As the years went on, the four were able to stop working full-time. They began to enjoy the fruits of their labor and became creatures of leisure, simply overseeing the operations. But Achimi's nose for knowing where to dig next was still essential to their continued success. So, while he might enjoy his time off lounging about in the dark or sunning himself on some water's edge down in the valleys below, the demand for their product never let up. That required Achimi to be on the constant hunt for new sources of gems.

"After several years a number of the richer veins of stones had played out, and Achimi took to looking deeper and farther afield in his search for new ones. On the southern side of this mountain — opposite where we are now — are many fantastic caverns, with curious hollows and connecting tunnels created over the eons by decay, the earth's movement and underground rivers. Achimi was exploring this area on his own one day when the floor of the cave he was crossing broke through. Apparently his weight, slight as it was, plus the never-ending forces of erosion below had combined to bring about a collapse at just that moment.

"Now, I can guess what you're thinking. How does old Piro know all this detail, eh? Well, Duchess, what I'm describing to you, of course, I did not personally witness. No creature did. Achimi told the story to his three partners. Naturally I cannot verify any of it, but then again, it has come down to us from more than one source, so I've no reason to doubt it. It just got passed on and on, as these things do.

"So, as I was saying, Achimi fell through the opening in the cave floor. Fortunately for him, the drop was not great; in fact, he fell into a small lake that had been created by the flow of water. He was more shocked than hurt, and awfully surprised to find himself treading water that far underground. Coming to the surface and gasping for air, he found he could just see the edges of the lake in the dim light, and he swam over to one side. Luckily the bank's incline was not too steep and he was able to clamber out without much difficulty. And there, to his amazement, Achimi discovered an entirely new network of caves and tunnels, the like of which had never been seen before.

"However, not everything was going Achimi's way. Unfortunately, the hole he'd fallen through was much too high to crawl back up to, and he could find no claw hold, no place from which he could maneuver his way. As fate would have it, he'd told none of his partners where he was going that day. So Achimi knew right off the bat that no help, no search party would ever arrive. He needed to find another way out or accept his dismal fate.

"And it was his searching for a way out that led to the unearthing of the Miskens' vast, seemingly endless store of precious stones. They were just lying about for the taking. It was a stroke of pure luck, nothing more, nothing less. Of course Achimi eventually did find a route out — well, of course, hah! Otherwise there'd be no story to tell, eh? Where we're now sitting, eating this fine meal, is merely an entrance to the mountains' fabulous riches. And where Achimi fell through is in another spot altogether, known to only a few of us even to this day." Piro winked knowingly at Fridis.

"But what — " the duck started to ask.

"Wait, wait. Hold on to your questions," Piro went on, warming to his tale. "My story has only just begun. Many things happened after that momentous discovery." The badger paused to take a long and clearly satisfying draught of drink from his vessel.

"Now I'm sure you understand," he continued, after carefully wiping some leftover drops from his whiskers, "being the wise duck you are, that the finding of such a treasure trove of gems, of such impeccable quality and so easily mined, could never be the end of the account. If you had found the gems on your own and you could keep the discovery a secret, would you have told anyone else? Perhaps you would, but perhaps you would not, eh?"

Before Fridis could open her beak to venture an opinion, Piro carried on. "I can only speculate as to his motivations, but as I said before, Achimi did tell his partners. Perhaps not right away, but soon enough. I suppose he was an honest enough badger, but truth be told, I imagine he saw that the treasure could not be kept a secret for very long, and he would need the others' support and protection sooner rather than later. So he told his three partners and they soon gathered together to assess their new situation.

"It wouldn't take a genius to see that they were now rich beyond their wildest dreams. Each of the four being an equal partner — well, I'd say they could have bought up the entire Empire with what they had sitting before them. But they had to be careful, for it was the scarcity of the stones that gave them their value. To put them onto the market all at once would devalue the whole hoard. They knew they had to husband this precious resource, and let it out only bit by bit.

"I gather some bickering occurred and there were some legitimate differences among the four about how to oversee and run the business, but they managed to resolve those matters and carry on as before. I imagine you're thinking, my lady, that they had a falling out or a major disagreement about sharing the spoils. But no, it was quite the opposite: things continued to go well — actually very well, in fact — for a number of years. They were successful in keeping the new source of gems a secret from everyone else, even from the rest of their employees, and they prospered mightily.

"However, one day several years later, Achimi made an interesting discovery. In the recesses of one cave, seemingly hidden away, he found three particular jewels. Now, I need to explain to you that these were not raw gemstones as he had found elsewhere; these ones were already cut. Even more striking, they were not hidden among others or wedged into the bedrock, waiting to be pried out by experienced badger claws. No, the three were laid out side by side in a row, already in pouches, as if placed there carefully by some other creature. Well, if that were the case, it must have been a long time ago, for it was clear to Achimi that no one had been in that cavern within living memory.

"You can imagine it, can't you, coming upon such a mysterious find? You'd know you weren't the very first to visit the site, and suddenly you'd sense unseen eyes looking at you. You'd shiver with fear and look around, hoping to find the owners of those eyes, or at least some answers. Aye, it'd be a spooky experience, and Achimi was not immune to a feeling that he'd had a close brush with the spirit world. Every question that would strike you (and me, for that matter) also occurred to Achimi as he sat there staring at the pouches. How did they get there? Why were they placed just so? Why were they wrapped up? How long ago? By whose paw or claw? Was it some kind of trap? What would happen if they were disturbed? Was he being tested? Should he leave them be? And so on.

"Of course, in the end he had to open the pouches — we're all curious creatures, are we not? No animal could have withstood such a lure. And that is how we know what the gems looked like and what properties they held."

Fridis, listening to this long, convoluted story in the warm hall after so much food and drink, had actually begun to doze off. She was at the point of closing her eyes when Piro mentioned the three gemstones in their pouches. Suddenly her mind sprang to full attention and the duck opened her eyes wide. "Three special stones, you say? What —" she started to ask the badger.

Piro waved his paw again to stop her in mid-sentence. "No, hold your questions a while. There's yet more to tell." While Fridis looked on, the badger took another long swig to restore his dry throat and returned once again to his story.

"So Achimi opened the pouches and discovered three of the most unusual gems he'd ever seen. After all those years he was probably the foremost expert in the land for judging the quality of such stones. Achimi knew they were unique, merely from the fact they were already cut and polished. Still, at first blush they didn't appear to be particularly valuable or rare, and he wondered why someone would have gone to the bother of wrapping them up so carefully. Each had its own unique luster and color and each was out of the ordinary in terms of shape, but so were many other gems Achimi had come across. And these ones didn't seem to demonstrate any special clarity or purity.

"I wish I could tell you that Achimi had some badger-like brilliant insight. Alas, no; in fact, no idea came to him at all. So, after a bit, he simply wrapped up the gemstones again and put them aside. Nevertheless, as he carried on with his work, his mind was continually being drawn back to those puzzling stones. He couldn't figure out the mystery, but he couldn't leave it alone either."

The badger stopped briefly to take another swig. The captivated duck said nothing, not wanting to interrupt the story's flow.

"When Achimi had finished his day's exploration," Piro continued, "he gathered the three gems up with the others he had chosen that day and began to make his way back to base camp. It was his regular route, nothing out of the ordinary. But on the way, either fatigue or carelessness overtook him, or perhaps he was thinking too much about the stones. Who's to say after all these years? Maybe all three together. In any event, he slipped, lost his footing and fell from a narrow ledge that he had to cross to get out of the cave. It was a serious drop, and unlike his earlier fall into the underground lake, he tumbled quite a way down onto unforgiving rocks. He was knocked unconscious. What's worse, when Achimi finally regained his senses many hours later, he found he could not move his back legs. In short, he knew he could not get out without help.

"Achimi lay there for a while, stunned by this reversal of fortune. He possessed everything a badger could want — all the prosperity, recognition and success he could have wished for — but now it was meaningless, because he was about to die. No one was aware of his exact location, and because of his secretive ways, it was hardly likely his partners could have found him in time, even if they'd known he'd gone down there."

The badger took a breath and sighed deeply, as if to indicate his fellow feeling for his forebear. Nevertheless, his account was far from finished. "Still, Achimi was not one to quit," Piro went on, more optimistically. "As best he could, he dragged himself forward with his strong front legs. In great pain and with much effort, he was able to reach one side of the cave, but once there he would have to climb the steep rock face. Although with four legs he might just have managed it, with only two it was impossible. Nevertheless, he made several attempts, only to fall back each time. Now Achimi knew the game was up — he would end his days starving to death, all alone amid incredible riches. Irony, that's what they call it."

Piro waved around his drink, spilling several drops in the process. He then took another big swallow from his seemingly bottomless cup before picking up the story once more. "He kept trying to think of a solution, but nothing came to him. He had no tools, no crutch, no other avenue of escape; all appeared to be lost. Achimi lay there, overcome by frustration, despair and, finally, acceptance of his fate. He fell in and out of consciousness. In his pain he began to hallucinate — he thought he heard birds singing and the voices of loved ones. And every time he came to, however so briefly, in the utter silence and gloom, he prayed to the badger spirits, wishing with all his might for someone or something to save him."

Piro paused dramatically, took a quick look around and then drank again. While the badger was wiping his mouth with his paws, Fridis waited for the denouement with bated breath.

"For some time Achimi lay where he was, waiting for death to take hold. But such a fate would not be his that day. After a while he noticed that one of the three pouches was beginning to glow from an inner light. It was a bluish white light that became brighter with every passing second, eventually becoming so powerful that it shone clear through the leather. Overcome by the incredible intensity, Achimi was forced to cover his eyes with his front paws. Can you believe it? It was just like staring into the sun!

"Achimi had no idea what to do. But soon enough he felt an incredible power and strength flowing through his entire body. His pain disappeared and he could feel his broken bones healing. Even more amazing, somehow he found himself out of harm's way, at the mouth of the cave. As I heard tell it, Achimi was never certain whether, in his dazed state, he'd crawled there on his own or he'd somehow flown there or he'd even dreamed the whole thing. When he found himself at the entrance to the cave, it was as if nothing evil had befallen him. There he stood, safe and sound, the picture of health, with the three gems in their pouches beside him. The radiant light from inside the pouch had disappeared and life seemed back to normal."

Once more Fridis, now hanging on to every word of this amazing tale, sought to ask a question. But again Piro signaled to her that his tale was still not finished.

"Can you imagine Achimi sitting there in a daze, having first suffered through his accident and despair and then experiencing such a miraculous rescue? You understand what we're dealing with here — something powerful, something amazing, something enchanted! What would you do? Would you share this story with just anyone? Was the magic (if that's the right word for it) best kept a secret or should it be shared with all the animal kingdom? How would you protect such an incredible gift? Most important of all, could you even comprehend what had just happened and what you now possessed? And if you did, would you be able to explain to any other animal what had just occurred?

"Remember, Kelnek, Obtala and Merithu were Achimi's friends as well as his business partners. They were his family as much as any family can be. Although I don't know how long he thought about it, ultimately Achimi decided he could not keep his precious discovery to himself. Why? I'm not so sure. Perhaps he thought he'd simply burst otherwise. If it were me I know I'd have to tell someone, and, I suppose, who better than my three closest friends? So when the four partners next met, Achimi tried to explain to them, as best he could, what had happened in the cave.

"As you can imagine, at first the others thought he was joking. He'd neither proof nor witness nor evidence of that miracle. And when he tried to demonstrate what had occurred by trying to make the gem brighten once again, it failed to respond. Achimi could not figure out why the stone would not work a second time, and he was greatly embarrassed. Honestly, his three partners thought he was pulling their legs. It was only much later that Achimi was able to figure out that the gem worked only when the creature asking for help had a real and significant need — that is, one that couldn't be met by either good old hard work or a bit of ingenuity. In other circumstances, the gems were meaningless, no better or worse and no more precious than any others you'd come across.

"I believe Achimi was eventually able to convince the others of this truth. However, perhaps because the four were so successful in their business and their lives generally so secure and happy, the partnership found few occasions when they had to call upon the gems. In all honesty, I'm not sure they ever did again. Stories about their use have been bandied about, but I can't vouch for any of them.

"Naturally Achimi was very careful to guard his find. He'd told the other three but swore them to secrecy. Whether anyone revealed the secret to any other creature I cannot say, at least with any accuracy. But I can tell you this: some years later, the three stones disappeared from their hiding place. No one would admit to taking them, and no one could prove whether one or more of the other three had done so. Even though Achimi had found little use for the gems, he had come to regard them with great jealousy. Like any creature who lacks offspring, he valued his possessions above all else. So he was greatly angered and, worse, embittered by the theft. He concluded that one of his partners must have betrayed him, but as he couldn't figure out which one it was, he blamed all three and dissolved the partnership. He could not forgive them and, I understand, he never spoke to any of them again.

"After the breakup, as I understand, Obtala, Kelnek and Merithu tried other ventures, both together and on their own, but none ever achieved the same level of success. Eventually they went their separate ways, and I believe they remained well-off and satisfied for the rest of their lives. The three stones were never found again.

"Achimi — possibly because he had already obtained all the wealth he would ever need, perhaps because of his being saved from certain death — took a different path. He became a wandering sage and slowly, over time, gave away all his wealth to those whom he met on his travels. To his dying day he could never explain the origin of those three gems and was never sure whether to blame or thank them for what occurred later. But I like to believe he died a happy badger, for by the end of his days he had lived a full, complete and generous life." With this summation, Piro abruptly ended his extraordinary tale and emptied the last of his drink.

Fridis was dumbfounded but far from speechless. "And no one ever saw the gems again?" the duck asked.

"No. Well, at least not to my knowledge."

"And there were just the three?"

"Really, who's to know? Maybe there are many such sets of gems floating around the world, waiting to be found by creatures in dire need of something or other. That's a question I simply cannot answer."

"Did Achimi suspect any one of his three partners more than the others?"

"As to that, I cannot say either way. No doubt they all had equal opportunity, although it's too long ago to really know for certain. For my part, I'm not aware of any reason why any of the three would've stolen the gems. I understand they all liked and respected each other well enough. They did need each other, after all, in fact, I'd say more than they needed the magic stones. But who's to say what lies deep in the heart of another animal? I've often thought poor Achimi regretted there were only three gems. If there had been four, I'm sure he would have shared them, given one to each of the partners. As it is (or, rather, was), one can't divide three into four, at least in the case of gemstones."

"What a wonderful story, Señor Piro, although I must say I don't know how anyone could take offense at it."

The badger took another slow look around the cave, eying the rest of the company as if to make sure none of the others were paying attention to his rendition. Fridis followed his gaze. As far as she could tell, the rest of the dinner guests were devoting themselves to their own pleasure or to their immediate neighbor and not to anything else.

"Other creatures have different versions of this tale," Piro declared. "And others have been known to dispute the mine's origins and ownership. Frankly, my lady, these days one never knows who might take offense."

"How did you come by this knowledge?"

"Knowledge or a fabulous tale? Or a bit of both, perhaps." Piro heaved a little sigh. "While Achimi gave away his wealth, he never gave away ownership of this mine or what is contained within it when he dissolved the partnership. He simply never went near it again. Of course, only he knew all its secret passageways and entrances. The other three knew a lot, but only Achimi knew every detail. Over the years some scavengers tried to discover what they could, but they barely touched its surface. When Achimi died, he willed the mine and its secrets to a distant nephew, who passed it on to his offspring, and so on.

"I am one of those descendants. That is why I know so much. The amazing legend has been told and retold and passed on from one generation to the next. As you can imagine, the story may have been embellished with each retelling. Hah! Possibly more than a little. Thus I'm reluctant to say it is entirely the truth."

"Though, of course, it could also be completely accurate," Fridis replied.

"I would love to think so. Imagine finding those gemstones again! Who knows. They could still be lying about here, hidden under our very feet. What one could do with them! Just think of the possibilities."

"Absolutely, Señor Piro," Fridis said. "Absolutely."

❧ 14 ❧

MORE UNWELCOME NEWS

The quartet of birds was scheduled to leave the Miskens the very next morning. From there they'd make a brief stopover at Mount Ari to collect some diamonds, after which they'd start the long trip back to Blakfel. For Fridis it had been an astonishing trip of discovery, and for Aeron-Urd a relaxing respite from his responsibilities; neither animal was eager to return to the gray skies of Vigmar. Still, duty called, and both intended to respond to its onerous demands.

The four were on the very point of takeoff when word came of an unexpected visitor flying in from the north. Anything out of the ordinary in the Miskens demanded a vigilant response; fresh patrols were sent aloft, extra sentries were posted on the mine's periphery, and everyone not required above returned to the confines of the cave. Although an attack was seen as unlikely, given the current war footing, nothing could be ruled out, so every precaution was taken and every creature placed on high alert.

After several tense moments, word came that it was but a single falcon carrying a message for the Air Marshal. When the exhausted bird arrived and was ushered into the cave, the four saw to their mutual relief that it was Corvus. Without exception, each fervently hoped the falcon was bringing happier news this time.

Aeron-Urd, Raicho and Corvus huddled together while Fridis looked on from a distance, pacing back and forth. The duck wished she could participate as she tried desperately to gain a sense of the message and what it might augur for her. The last time, Aeron-Urd's dejected demeanor had revealed the great sadness of the news he had to convey to her. Now, watching her friend, Fridis longed to see some indication of good tidings.

Although the duck could make out no signs of sorrow this time, neither could she detect any signs of happiness. Rather, Aeron-Urd's expression manifested only disgust and anger. He looked so furious that Fridis feared he might strike at Corvus. Even the implacable Raicho began to lose his temper, flapping his wings in irritation and dancing about madly. An intense quarrel ensued. As it went on and on, Fridis became more and more puzzled about what was being said. Several of the mine's guardians had also begun to observe the unusual spectacle, as curious and mystified as Fridis.

As it turned out, the duck was the primary subject of the trio's discussion. At long last Aeron-Urd came over to Fridis, leaving Raicho with the weary, dejected Corvus. The Air Marshal led the perplexed duck over to a private corner of the garrison, away from the others.

"The last time poor Corvus brought us news," the gyrfalcon began, "I was forced to relay to you information of the most painful kind. I never imagined that he — or any bird, for that matter — could top that moment. However, it appears I was mistaken. The Squadron Leader has brought me an announcement so odious that my entire being revolts at the prospect of revealing it to you."

For a rare moment, the shocked duck didn't know what to say. Fridis waited impatiently while Aeron-Urd tried to get a grip on his fury.

"My lady, forgive me," the great bird said at last. "The message is so unbelievable, so offensive, at first I couldn't bring myself to accept it. I'm still not sure where or how to begin. I had to ask Corvus to explain it several times before I was able to grasp the thrust and logic of it. Frankly, I still don't understand what's happened, and I'm not yet certain what my next steps will be."

"You begin to worry me, Air Marshal. Please, how bad can it be?"

"I imagined there could be nothing worse than the death of Lord Eirwen. Bah! When I think of what you've been subjected to since your arrival in Vigmar, I am sickened. Sickened!"

"Aeron-Urd, I beg you, stop beating around the bush. Tell me before I collapse right here and now, on this very spot! The suspense is killing me."

"My word, if it were only that! By all the stars above, the Empire is rotten to the core. I've always had my doubts, but there's no getting around it now!" Aeron-Urd uttered a harsh *kyha-kyha*, clacked his beak and stomped around in a circle.

Watching the gyrfalcon marching about, Fridis wondered what could possibly be worse than Eirwen's death. Finally the gyrfalcon stopped his circling. Now he simply stared at the duck, apparently still at a loss for appropriate words to explain the situation.

"My good friend," remonstrated Fridis, more softly now, "I have lived through fear of being devoured by the wolf pack. I have been attacked by one of your own hawks and almost died. I've been seized in the dark of night for no reason at all and thrown into a cell. And I've had to face the death of Eirwen, my companion and best friend. Don't you think that by this point in my life I can take just about anything fate has to throw at me?"

"Yes, yes, of course you're right. Forgive me. I know you're as tough as any of our soldiers, perhaps even more so. It's just that the injustice of what has occurred appalls me so."

The duck did not reply, in hopes that her friend might continue.

Seeing he had no choice but to carry on, Aeron-Urd finally blurted out the news: "Fridis, you've been banished from Vigmar."

"What?" Fridis cried in response. The duck was as stupefied by the news as Aeron-Urd had been. Of all the possible scenarios, she had not expected this one.

"Exactly my reaction. I don't understand it either. The rationale is not entirely clear, at least not to me. However, I can tell you this: the Emperor is gravely ill and the Empress rules alone in his stead. The decision is obviously her doing."

"What exactly is the order? What was the reason given?"

"Crimes against the state, the Empire. Unspecified offenses, all suitably vague. Hints, rumors of activities on your part that were damaging to morale and — what's worse — could lead to insurrection. Really, I don't know more than that, and I can make neither head nor tail of it. Of course, we're not receiving this information from the original source; it comes from the mouth of Corvus, told quickly and with little detail. He did not have the authority, time or opportunity to ask pointed questions, not that anyone would have welcomed them. As you can imagine, the Squadron Leader was most anxious to relay this information to me."

"I imagine he was particularly apprehensive at the thought of facing your wrath." Despite the circumstances, Fridis managed a small smile.

"You can be assured of that, Duchess."

"Now what, Aeron-Urd?"

"I've been ordered to return to Blakfel at once," the Air Marshal said. "Hah! Perhaps the authorities suspect I'll be corrupted by you."

"I don't understand. What about the period of mourning you spoke about? What about the honor due to Eirwen — and to me, by extension — for his great sacrifice?"

The gyrfalcon looked shamefaced. "I'm embarrassed by my peers back home. Nothing about this story makes sense. Although ... "

"Although?"

"You've known for a while, from your own painful experience, that Vigmar is not a safe place, especially for the unwary and naive. I remember telling Lord Eirwen exactly that. 'Do not trust anyone,' I told him. That goes for you too, Fridis, although I never imagined you would be treated so cruelly. You're clearly seen as a threat to the powers that be. However, while they want to be rid of you, they also cannot kill you. Banishment is seen as their best, safest option. Exile renders you powerless and alone. Well, almost alone, but certainly with few resources and no allies to command."

"They?"

"As I said, I can only surmise this is the Empress's doing. And Vigmar's high command and bureaucracy have chosen not to object or resist."

"I thought I'd smoothed over any concerns," Fridis began. "I knew from — "

"From?" Aeron-Urd asked, raising his eyebrows.

"It's not important. The point is, I was aware of Dona Morana's suspicions. And of her collusion with the First Secretary. That's all that really matters." Fridis sighed. "Still, I felt I had won them over. Even Gloton seemed to have come around; after all, it was the wolverine who made this trip possible." After a brief pause, the duck continued, "I see now they were simply biding their time."

"You surprise me, Duchess. How did you come to know this?"

Fridis contemplated telling Aeron-Urd about the castle's secret passageways and listening posts. However, the duck didn't want to reveal her connection with Haidar or anything about the mountain goat's comings and goings. "I wish I could tell you, but I cannot. Let's just say I have it on very good authority. One day I hope to be able to explain everything. In the meantime, what should we — that is, I do? Clearly I dare not return with you to Blakfel. Where can I go? Where can I possibly find a semblance of peace and security?"

For the first time since he'd stalked over, the gyrfalcon smiled. That simple gesture comforted the duck greatly. "I have the perfect place for you," the other bird declared.

And that is how Fridis could now be found by a saltwater lagoon on the southeastern shores of Arundati. The spot was as far from Blakfel as any creature could get, in a sheltered tropical outpost well off the beaten path, protected from unwelcome visitors by both distance and jungle.

THE DUTIFUL AERON-URD, MEANWHILE, HAD RETURNED TO VIGMAR'S capital. The gyrfalcon might distrust the Empress and others in power, but he was loyal to his troops, believed in maintaining the struggle against Aeronbed and would continue to honor his oath to the Empire. The Air Marshal also recognized that giving up his command in a huff would achieve little for either of them. Only by maintaining his position of authority could the determined gyrfalcon hope to find out the true state of affairs in Blakfel. Only then could he decide on his next course of action.

Aeron-Urd sent Corvus and Rorbeg ahead, telling them to wait for him at the Arundati–Vigmar border crossing. Then he made a point of guiding Fridis and Raicho through the next set of mountains, where he'd planned to escort Fridis in any event. However, the trio flew right past the diamond mine at Mount Ari without bothering to investigate it; the gyrfalcon wanted to keep the duck's final destination a secret from prying eyes. Their exact route was carefully chosen to mislead and confuse any future pursuit.

The trio had started off in the direction of Vigmar but turned in the opposite direction at the first possible opportunity, taking a stealthy low-level route through deeper river valleys until they found themselves on the other side of the Misken Mountains. From there they followed another complicated and tortuous flight path until they emerged in the southern reaches of Arundati. There the mountains sloped away behind them and the land once again opened up into endless verdant jungle, while the emerald-green trees and distant turquoise ocean below beckoned them on.

It was at that point that Aeron-Urd, knowing that the duck and her protector were safely en route to their haven, took his leave of the two other birds. The gyrfalcon's faithful lieutenant would lead Fridis to the southern shore and maintain constant protection for her thereafter. Raicho, Aeron-Urd explained to the duck, was more than capable of dealing with any surprises or troubles. And, as his commanding officer, the gyrfalcon could easily explain away his underling's lengthy absence from regular duties.

It was another sad parting for Fridis and Aeron-Urd. It seemed to the duck that no sooner did she gain a friend, they were then forced to separate. Ahead of her lay isolation, certainly pleasurable, tranquil and safe, but isolation nonetheless. She had said goodbye to Eirwen and he had not returned. Would the Air Marshal encounter a similar fate? The prospect ruffled her feathers and sent shivers up and down her spine. The little duck, as brave as she was, could not bear to think about such a prospect. Thankfully Raicho was staying with her. Thus she had at least one companion, and they'd bonded as best they could under the circumstances.

But after many weeks of the same empty blue skies, the same abundant waters and the same swaying palm trees day in and day out, even distant, gloomy, unpredictable Vigmar was beginning to seem exciting — if not tempting — in comparison to the endless pristine tropics.

Fridis found it ironic, even grimly amusing, to think that — apart from the beauty of her surroundings and the consistently sublime weather — she was almost back to where she'd started when her adventure began. Save for Raicho, she was alone and friendless. Even more troubling, as a duck full of boundless energy and impatience, how long could she lie around sunning herself and waiting for a comforting word or surprise visit from Aeron-Urd? It certainly wouldn't be indefinitely. The duck was sure of that.

Aeron-Urd's attachment to Fridis had grown steadily over time. The fiercely loyal gyrfalcon was convinced that his separation from the duck would be short-lived. How could it be otherwise, since the decision to banish Fridis was so clearly unjust, not to mention stupid and ill-conceived. Vigmar needed Fridis, and everyone knew that.

Once the gyrfalcon had learned everything about the decree, once he had refined his arguments and begun to campaign on her behalf, the Air Marshal felt certain he could win the day for Fridis. Others might quake in fear, but Aeron-Urd would neither kowtow to nor be defeated by treacherous villains. Surely even the Empress would come to understand that exile could serve no useful purpose. And once he'd made them see things clearly, then he'd begin to plan for the duck's triumphant return.

❧ III ❧

AERONBED

THE GRAND COUNCIL MEETS

In the distance the panther could hear the slow tolling of bells telling the hours. It was late. The mist, especially dense this night, had closed in, shrouding everything in a miserably cold gloom. The warm, sunny days of early spring had come to an abrupt halt, as quickly and with as much surprise as they had begun so very few weeks ago.

Already most of the inhabitants of Manaris had forgotten about the unprecedented glorious sunshine and were now complaining about the never-ending enveloping damp. Rithild didn't mind, however; the huge cat actually preferred things that way. He liked slinking around unseen in the dark; he thought it suited his persona. In his mind, the fog helped him preserve an aura of mystery and intrigue. He could come and go surreptitiously, keeping everyone off balance and allowing him to catch them unawares. His fellow cats hated anything to do with water, especially the mists that hung over everyone like a heavy sodden blanket, soaking their fur and never allowing it to dry out. But Rithild was in his element and could not have been happier.

As the Baron prowled through the narrow streets and alleyways of the port, taking a carefully roundabout route to his destination, he kept a sharp eye out for any stranger who might be following too closely.

Although the panther saw none, he would be the first to admit that the heavy gray mists sweeping in from the sea were as challenging to his searching eyes as they were to someone who might be trying to track his progress. Rithild sniffed the air, but it smelled of nothing but salt and decaying seaweed. The scent rankled, and he hurried to distance himself from the water's edge.

The panther expected to find few creatures about at that hour. It was nearing midnight, and most honest, law-abiding citizens were abed — or at least they should have been. The nighttime travelers Rithild did encounter, the Baron was satisfied to note, were heading in the opposite direction, toward the shadowed light in the town's central square, where they doubtless hoped to enjoy Manaris's scant offerings of drink and entertainment. The only other creatures about were members of the town watch, guarding against evildoers as best they could in the dreary circumstances.

He finally reached his destination, the unremarkable door of a rather mean abode. The house was one of many humble three-story shops and grubby dwellings built cheek by jowl along a narrow, crooked alley; the top story of each overhung the floors below, adding to the darkness of the laneway. The Baron hesitated, looked around one more time to ensure he was truly alone, then rapped three times on the wooden door as softly as he could. Despite his light touch, in the utter stillness the noise seemed to resonate along the alley, and Rithild couldn't help but steal another glance in all directions.

The well-oiled door was unlocked quickly and he was received without a word of greeting. With a curt nod of recognition, Rithild entered just as quickly and soundlessly. Then the door was closed behind him, as silently as it had opened.

The light inside the dwelling was little better than outside. Fortunately, Rithild was well used to it; this was not his first visit to the place. His host, a smaller panther, said nothing but merely turned and ascended a narrow flight of well-worn wooden stairs, which led to a hallway on the second floor. Rithild, well used to the routine, followed right behind. At the top of the stairs, his guide opened a deep cupboard; in it, hanging from hooks, were two long, hooded black cloaks. He took one cloak out and carefully, almost reverently, handed it to Rithild. The Baron accepted the cloak with equal formality and put it on, arranging the hood precisely over his head.

As soon as Rithild was ready, his host knocked on a heavy wooden door leading off the hallway and stepped aside. This time a heavy bolt on the other side of the door was slowly dragged open, its jarring screech breaking the perfect silence. Rithild grimaced at the noise and glared at his host as if to say, *Fix it!* His host meekly acknowledged the reprimand, bowing his head. Rithild, meanwhile, entered the room alone, fastening the door behind him.

The apartment had little to commend it. It was a room, plain and simple, suitable for its task of providing a meeting place away from prying ears and eyes, and no more. It was, in comparison with the stairs, quite brightly lit. Three candles had been placed in a row on a low, broad bureau standing against the far wall; another two rested on a large round table in the middle of the room. Beside the bureau was another door, but this one was well disguised as a tall bookcase — a second, private exit known only to the Council, to be used in an emergency. Although it had never yet been needed, they had to remain cautious. Rithild was well aware of what lay beyond the door, for he had carefully scouted it out in days gone by, just in case.

The round table was large enough to seat six of his counterparts in addition to Rithild. The rules of the Council demanded that an odd number of members be present at all such meetings, for no vote could end in a tie. Rithild noticed immediately that he was the sixth to arrive, and he recalled seeing one cloak remaining in the wardrobe. As the Baron pulled back the heavy chair and sat down, he looked at the empty chair and then, turning to the panther seated next to him, raised his eyebrows questioningly. Barely moving, the other shook his head silently as if to say, *Don't ask me. And if I knew, I couldn't give the answer anyway.*

No one spoke. Rithild and the others sat patiently, breathing calmly, eyes cast down, without sharing a word of greeting to one another. The formality was typical; however, the period of reflection did not mean that Rithild was in a state of calm meditation. Perhaps the others were (although he doubted it), but his mind was turning over furiously as he continued to work and rework what information, misinformation and words of wisdom he would share with the other members of the Grand Council of Panthers.

Finally another knock came. It was doubtless as soft as the other had been, yet the noise seemed so loud in comparison with the stillness that Rithild almost jumped out of his seat. As he had been the last to arrive, it was up to him to open the door. He rose, went over to it and glanced down at the annoying bolt, which he knew would again disturb his peace of mind. He grimaced and tried to open it as carefully as possible, but the noise was as piercing as before. As he opened the door wide, he again glared at the host, but the latter, his eyes only on the newcomer, ignored him.

Frustrated by this disregard, Rithild could only bow respectfully to the new arrival and return to his seat. The newcomer shut and bolted the door while Rithild winced again at the noise. Then the panther took his seat. Still no one spoke. This time, however, all eyes, peering out from under the hoods, were on the latest among them to arrive. This last cat — their leader, Archduke Anishger — sat with closed eyes as if in silent prayer, ignoring them all.

When Anishger finally opened his eyes, he looked slowly around the table, nodding solemnly at each participant in turn. After this ritual, the cat raised his front paws and began a sacred chant. The councilors, who knew the words by heart, chimed in, following in plainsong fashion. Rithild usually found the beautiful chant quite soothing; at other times and in other places, he would find himself humming the tune quite unconsciously. Today, however, his mind was preoccupied with the news he was about to deliver.

At last they finished the chant. The Archduke called the meeting of the Grand Council to order and, to Rithild's great annoyance, they turned immediately to mundane administrative issues. Only when those matters had been dispensed with did their leader finally turn to the impatient Baron. The old cat spoke slowly, with an air of authority and gravitas that befitted his age, seniority and accumulated wisdom. "You asked for this special in camera meeting, Rithild," he said. "You also requested that the meeting take place where the Council cannot be observed or disturbed. Thus we meet here, in the House of Thorns."

The Archduke stopped to suppress a sudden fit of coughing. No one said a word. "I can only assume, therefore, you have something momentous to share with us, something requiring the greatest degree of secrecy," Anishger continued. "You are doubtless aware that merely holding such a meeting in times like this has its, shall we say, risks. You'll also be aware that Albiorix has an impressive array of informants who keep him well briefed on matters both large and small. If word got out about this session, it would raise serious misgivings in the minds of our cousins. Baron Rithild, we cannot afford to generate suspicion. Not now." He looked sternly around the table, catching in turn the eyes of each of the other six, as he declared, "Accordingly, I trust you've all taken the utmost care when making your way here."

Every Council member nodded vigorously, none daring to respond otherwise.

The Council's supreme leader was a cat of few words and little praise. "Having dealt with our administrative matters, let us waste no further time. Lord Rithild, you have the floor."

"Thank you," the Baron replied. "I trust I shall not disappoint any of you."

"We shall see, Rithild. We shall see."

"You will recall," the Baron said, "that a short time ago I visited with our forces in Heimborn, partly in response to concerns raised by Albiorix himself."

"You spoke of this the other day," interrupted the Archduke. "Is that matter not yet under control?"

"Not in any way you would imagine," Rithild replied, speaking to them all. "Before too long the Grand Council will have some difficult decisions to make. A disaster, I fear, awaits on our very doorstep."

A sharp intake of breath and a couple of muttered curses from the councilors, as calm, wise and experienced as they were, betrayed their surprise and shock.

RITHILD'S MOVE

"You certainly know how to get our attention," said the Archduke. "Go on, Baron. Speak plainly, sir."

"When we met the other day at our official headquarters, I spoke about the bears' uprising in Heimborn," Rithild said. "What I did not want to put on the record was the reaction of our own forces."

"What do you mean?" asked Rashtad, a senior member of the Council. "Were they inadequately equipped to deal with the issue?"

"All of you know that my nephew, Parthanyx, is one of the senior commanders serving in that region. He has proven to be both ambitious and forceful, so much so that he has taken upon himself the mantle of leadership of our many forces stationed there."

"Nothing wrong with that," Zlatan, the newest councilor, observed. "Let the cream rise to the top, I've always said."

"Of course, of course. But my only point was to note the family connection, so you will recognize that I speak truly and without bias on the subject."

"How is that relevant?" the Archduke snapped. "You're speaking in riddles, Rithild. Get to the point."

"I fear the issue is not how our forces will handle the bears. Rather, it is what will happen afterward. I don't want anyone to mistake my meaning here. It's not just the bears that are in open revolt — it's Parthanyx and the other commanders as well."

Several angry voices spoke at once. "What? What are you saying, Rithild? How so? Explain yourself, Baron."

Anishger held up a paw for quiet, giving Rithild the opportunity to continue.

"When our commanders have dispensed with the bears, they plan to march on Aeronbed. It will be the end of the coalition — perhaps the end of all of us."

The first reactions to his words had been loud and querulous, but now dead silence reigned round the table. The other six members of the Grand Council, including the Archduke, looked at one another, trying to comprehend the significance of Rithild's words.

"I don't understand. Why on earth do they want to march on Aeronbed?" asked Rashtad. "What would be the point?"

"For some inexplicable reason, they now consider the leadership of — and in — Manaris a corrupt, spent force, unable to comprehend the true nature of leadership, unable to do what is necessary to govern, and unfit to rule this kingdom. They will march here to overthrow the regime of King Albiorix. And in the process, they will discard all who are allied with the lions — including this council and its backers."

"Absolute nonsense. Albiorix is one thing, but the Grand Council as well? Are we not all panthers?"

"I did not say the move makes sense, or even whether I agree with it. I am merely reporting the facts."

Anishger now added his voice. "You witnessed this planning yourself? How can you be certain things will come to pass as you suggest?"

That question was one Rithild had not been looking forward to. He did not feel he could fool his colleagues as easily as he could Temorwig. "No, I did not," he admitted. "But I have it on very good authority. You all know my assistant, Lieutenant Eisa."

"The son of Kalishin of Dariah?" asked Zlatan.

"Yes, that's the one. I sent him to scout out the situation in the Heimborn borderlands; I also asked him to meet with Parthanyx. You all know the quality of Eisa's work and the accuracy of his reporting:

what he says can be relied on. It was he who relayed to me in great detail what he found out. I had my suspicions already, but Eisa confirmed my worst fears. It is for this reason that I mentioned Parthanyx by name when I began. I would not lightly condemn my own flesh and blood."

Although some nods of acknowledgment could be seen around the table, Anishger's face remained impenetrable. Rithild stayed silent as the others took in his words. Finally Zlatan made the leap. "You know what this means, of course. It means — "

"It means civil war," interjected the Archduke. "That is, if we do nothing to stop it."

"We are not in a position to do much about it," noted Zlatan. "The forces around Heimborn represent the bulk of our forces. They are battle-ready and tested. Moreover, if what Rithild says is accurate, they seem to have a cause they consider worth fighting for. We could not stand up to such an onslaught. What panther forces do we have in reserve here? Few indeed. What's more, what cause would inspire those few troops? The majority might also prefer a new regime under our commanders in the field."

"Let's keep our wits about us," the Archduke said. "Around this table we have many years of training, wiles and experience. It's far too early to skulk away in defeat." To Rithild he said, "You've had the longest to consider our options, Baron, and I'm sure you've not been wasting your time. What do you propose we do?"

"Hold on a bit," interjected Rashtad before Rithild could open his mouth. "Are we not talking treason here? This matter doesn't just concern us. It also concerns the lions, and the King. Long-standing allies and supporters, no less! We're not dealing with a trifling matter here. There'll be no pardons or forgiveness at the end of the day, should events unfold as the Baron has indicated. Mass executions will result, including more than one head around this table, I imagine. I, for one, want to know how Temorwig responded to this news."

"Well, Rithild?" asked the Archduke. The council members turned as one toward Rithild, every sense attuned to his next words.

"I did not tell him, my lords," Rithild replied softly.

"You did not tell him what?"

"I did not tell Temorwig anything about the rebellion threatened by the commanders. I only told him about the bears."

"You astound me, Lord Rithild," Anishger noted wryly, as the rest of the Council tried to grasp the implications. "It's a dangerous game you've chosen to play. Still, if I'd been in your position, I suspect I'd have played it exactly the same way."

"Coming from you, my lord," Rithild responded, smiling for the first time, "I'll take that as a rare compliment."

"You see, of course, what our good friend Rithild is doing," declared the Archduke. "He's playing for time so we can plan a course of action. Once Albiorix has been advised, there can be no turning back. Sides must be chosen. We have a few days yet — perhaps even longer — to determine what we must do."

One of the councilors, who up to now had been listening carefully, spoke up. "You yourself noted how well informed the King is," Dughyl said. "How long do you think we can keep this news from him? Perhaps he already knows and is watching for our next moves, to see how loyal we really are."

"I'm first to admit that my nephew is, ah, quite unpredictable," Rithild replied. "He seems to have no concern at all for secrecy in this matter. However, I suspect the King's spies are focusing on the bears, not on his allies. Even if he has heard something, he may interpret the comments of our soldiers as the normal grumbling of troops in the field. They always tend to berate the leaders back home, sometimes even more than they do the enemy. Should things come down to it, we can of course make that same pitch to the lions."

"I was not talking about our forces in the field," Dughyl objected. "I'm talking about us, tonight. Here and now."

More silence and concerned glances met this observation. How confident were they about each other's loyalty to the Grand Council?

"Let's not cast doubt on each other or our own affairs," the Archduke said. "We know and trust one another, and each of us has presumably taken every precaution while making our way here. Thus we have nothing to worry about ... well, not as yet. Let's turn to the matter before us."

"Am I correct in assuming Parthanyx and his fellow commanders are making no distinction between the lions and ourselves?" Zlatan asked. "Are we therefore all being placed in the same stewpot?"

"Sadly, that is so. It's beyond reason, of course. But there it is, and there's no getting around the fact. Nevertheless, we've still got a field to play on. However constricted it is, there we must play our very best game.

"Parthanyx may think he can accomplish this rebellion all on his own, but before too long I wager he'll come begging. As the Archduke has so wisely noted, around this table sits an accumulation of wisdom and skill far beyond what Parthanyx has encountered in his brief lifetime. He may command loyal troops and he may even be able to foment a revolution, but leading a country is a very different matter. That, my lords, is a matter of politics, not war.

"I think we could turn this awkward situation to our advantage and come out on top. Perhaps this event will prove to be serendipitous, a well-timed means to an end: the end of the era of lions and the beginning of a new one — the reign of the panthers."

After pausing briefly to let these words sink in, Rithild continued, speaking now with greater feeling. "Cousins, don't you think we've played second fiddle to the lions long enough?"

The others looked at him with enhanced interest and appreciation.

"Let's face facts. We've never really received due recognition," the Baron said. "We do what the lions ask and get little enough in return. They think we're living off the fat of the land in Heimborn. They've never appreciated what we do for them, how demanding it is to keep those wretched bears in check while the lions are free to enjoy their comforts and concentrate on other matters.

"In all honesty, I've thought a great deal about what Parthanyx has been putting about, his complaints and condemnations. Perhaps in his soldierly way he speaks some simple truths. Perhaps the lions have indeed led us into a soft and corrupt life. Perhaps our eyes have been opened just in time to do something about it. We could well be swept away along with the lions — that is, if we choose to do nothing. But, my friends, we also have a chance to swim on top of the wave and not be submerged by it. Who knows, possibly Parthanyx will merely be the means to our end, not his. Let the good soldier believe he is using us, but let us make sure it's really the other way around."

"Hear! Hear!" a couple of council members cried.

However, not all were so easily convinced. Rashtad, ever the voice of caution, interrupted the Baron's oratory. "Hold on. You're making quite a leap here. To avoid revealing what we know to the lions is one thing, and possibly we might be forgiven that omission. But — if I truly grasp your intent — you're now suggesting we become a party to what Parthanyx is planning. I won't even talk about the practical difficulty of trying to ride herd over a pack of infuriated, out-of-control cats. But now you're talking about active treason. Even discussing the idea, as we are this evening, can have consequences. I shudder to think what would happen if word got out."

"That's exactly why we're discussing this matter, my lords, in this house, in utmost secrecy, in the dead of night," responded Anishger. "No notes, no records. No word of what's being said must ever pass beyond these walls."

"Just so long as everyone realizes, Archduke, that when we leave this room tonight, we will have crossed a divide, one way or another," Rashtad answered. "In this case there will be no turning back."

"As I've said before, we can still play for time. Much will have to happen before we must reveal our intentions. Parthanyx and his fellow commanders have to deal with the bears first."

Once the Council had signaled its accord with this careful stance, Anishger turned back to the Baron. "Tell us, Rithild, how much do you know and how do you see things developing?"

Rithild revealed those things that he wanted to: Eisa's story, the Lieutenant's continuing role as an informant for the Council, and how the Council might yet play the game just getting underway. The Baron did not, however, disclose the three stark options he had presented to Eisa when he'd left that poor cat behind to fend for himself, nor some of his other ideas. To Rithild's way of thinking, the contest had already begun, and he was the only one engaged in the fighting. By the time the others had caught on, it would be too late for any of them.

Too many years of being a political animal had blackened the Baron's heart and soul; he might be old, but he was not so old that he lacked ambition. Unlike the others, he recognized that Parthanyx, for all his faults, had presented the panthers with a great opportunity, one that the brave and the ruthless could use to their advantage. And the bravest and most determined of all could ride to the very pinnacle of power.

By the time he left the Council meeting, Rithild had his colleagues where he wanted them. Even better, he was free to continue his maneuvering and conniving. The Baron already knew what he was going to do, but he was not ready to share that information with his panther brethren. For the present he controlled the communications and the next steps, as much as anyone could in such a free-flowing and unpredictable situation.

There was a great deal yet to be played out, and doubtless Rithild wouldn't be able to foresee and control everything. However, the panther could set some things in motion, things that should bring him the position of power he had long sought.

IV

HEIMBORN

17

EISA MAKES HIS WAY IN THE WORLD

E isa returned to the northern borderlands of Heimborn after his rendezvous with Rithild, his mood somewhere between dismay and despair. The Lieutenant had no idea what to do on his return to the panthers' encampment, except, of course, to stay as far away from Parthanyx as he could possibly manage.

Parthanyx frightened him deeply. Not that Eisa was by any means a coward. It was more that his physical bravery had never been tested in the relative comfort and security of Aeronbed's capital, and it had no opportunity of being confirmed on the front lines of Heimborn, where all good panthers were keeping a tight leash on the bears. In other words, the extent of his courage had yet to be determined.

To Eisa's way of thinking, the panther commander was a volatile creature, and right now he was out of control, perceiving enemies in all directions. It was a dangerous combination, and there was no telling what would happen when that panther was next annoyed. So, Eisa thought, it was far better that he be out of range when that blowup occurred.

As he made his way through the deeply forested hinterland, Eisa tried to focus on what he had been asked to do. *Keep your eyes and ears open and report back on everything important* seemed to be the gist of the Baron's commands. It didn't appear to be all that difficult or painful a task. For one thing, every soldier in the panther army — commanders, junior officers and other ranks — didn't hesitate to rant at length about everything from minor complaints to grand schemes, and to anyone who cared to listen. For another, given the loose control of their field units, Eisa thought he would have plenty of opportunities to sneak away whenever he wanted. However, he also knew he'd have to hone his acting (a skill that didn't come naturally to him) and maintain constant vigilance. The second, he judged, would be easier to achieve, for Eisa considered himself a cautious individual.

The trails the panther was following would take him up to the mountain gate that opened onto Heimborn's heights. There was no real gate, only a narrow gap that acted as a natural barrier to entry and exit. Since an enemy force could not enter en masse, it protected Heimborn from assaults. Not far from there, down the slopes and under the shadow of the mountains, the main force of panthers was garrisoned.

From that point on, the Lieutenant's precise destination was less certain. With whom did Eisa feel most secure? His oldest friend there, Samirxun, offered one possibility, but the cat was posted next in line to Parthanyx. Such proximity, Eisa reckoned, was much too close for comfort. Who, then, was stationed farthest from Parthanyx? Heimdell occupied that post, but the Commander was most like Parthanyx in character — too bellicose and too erratic for comfort. What about Hildric? Since the cat was given to gabbing away at length, he'd be a constant source of inside information, but that character trait also risked exposing Eisa's activities to others.

Eisa decided he needed to be surrounded by like-minded and more discreet counterparts, ones who minded their own business and spoke only when necessary. Perhaps Segomo? Although Eisa did not know her well, the officer was well regarded by her troops and seemed to possess a serious, moderate temperament. Best of all, her company was located far enough away from Parthanyx's own outfit. So Eisa had found his immediate destination — perhaps not as far away as dismay or despair, but certainly someplace in between.

As he veered off in the direction of Segomo's encampment, Eisa thought through what he would say to his sister panther when he arrived. What would make Segomo believe he'd experienced a change of heart and mind? Eisa had met the officer only once and talked to her only briefly. Naturally Segomo shared Parthanyx's extreme view of the bears and his disdain for the establishment back in Manaris. However, unlike Parthanyx, she was neither offensive nor crazed; one could at least have a rational conversation with her. Nevertheless, Eisa knew it would be wise not to test his cousin's limits; he would have to take on the guise of a true believer, with everything that entailed.

Dusk was approaching by the time Eisa approached Segomo's camp. It seemed like an eternity since he'd visited the encampments to investigate the state of affairs on Heimborn's frontiers, but it had been mere days since he'd completed that assignment. Thus his face and smell were known to the sentries and he was welcomed, if not warmly, at least with only a modicum of suspicion. To Eisa's surprise, despite the war footing, things were still quite relaxed.

Eisa immediately sought out Segomo but found only her second-in-command, Geifu. The latter explained that all the field commanders were assembled in one of the other encampments, and his commander would not be returning until the next day. Deciding he didn't want to tell his story more than once, out of fear of contradicting himself, Eisa offered no explanation for his reappearance. Fortunately Geifu seemed to accept his sudden turning up as normal and didn't pester him for a reason. Eisa was made welcome, invited to share in the company's dinner and allocated a place to rest his head.

Exhausted by the long march and the anguish of the preceding days, Eisa fell into a deep, troubled sleep, full of tormenting dreams. When he woke the next morning, the sun had been up for several hours and the camp was abuzz with activity. The company was on the move, intent on striking into Heimborn, and the entire camp was being dismantled.

Although he tried to find Segomo, once again Eisa could unearth only Geifu. The cat informed him that the Commander would be preoccupied with the impending move and too busy to deal with any other matters. However, Eisa was welcome to travel with the company until his position and duties were sorted out. The entire field army was marching into Heimborn, its plan being to occupy various sectors in order to re-establish the panthers' authority and bring about an abrupt end to the uprising.

Morale was high and the easygoing mood of the preceding day unchanged. Although the route into Heimborn required a circuitous and lengthy march uphill, the panthers remained confident of easy entry. Quick restoration of the status quo was expected. Nevertheless, no units would be staying behind at their current locations; every soldier was to be sent forward to maximize the impact. It would be a short, sharp and brutal confrontation to ensure that the bears' rebellion was short-lived.

Eisa wished he knew more about what was being planned. Unfortunately Geifu knew only the sketchiest details; he expected to hear more during the course of the day. As a result, the cat had limited information to provide and no advice to offer, and Eisa had to be content with what little the officer could share. The details amounted to the following: the panthers were to march into four key strategic points and occupy them, making a show of strength in the process, and — depending on what they found — do some damage to the bears, physically or otherwise. In other words, they would show the rebels who the real bosses were and quell the bears back into submission.

Once they got going, as they marched along together, Eisa tried to engage Geifu in conversation. However, his initial efforts proved to be relatively futile; the latter was often distracted by the demands of the advance and by constant interruptions from comrades seeking his help or counsel. Although Eisa was struck by Geifu's patience and good sense, he remained frustrated by the difficulty of engaging the cat in any sustained dialogue.

To Eisa the plan seemed straightforward enough and would incur minimal risk. In fact — considering Parthanyx's bellicose nature — a neutral observer might deem the approach restrained, even verging on diplomatic. Of course, Eisa reckoned, the scheme might not be of Parthanyx's choosing. It might be a compromise solution, perhaps pushed on him by another, less aggressive commander, possibly as an initial step only.

Geifu could provide no information on what had led to the choice of strategy, whose idea it was or why it had been chosen, nor did he demonstrate much curiosity about the matter. Like any good obedient soldier, he saw his primary job as accomplishing what was required of him that day. He would simply follow through on his orders to the best of his ability.

Eisa and Geifu found themselves striding along together near the front of the long line of troops now advancing toward Heimborn's border. Segomo was closer to the back of the line, so Eisa had not yet found an opportunity to meet with her. Thus his story (such as it was) remained untested.

As the panthers wended their way ever upward, the companies were forced to march through a series of narrow valleys and canyons. These darkly wooded gaps through the mountains made up the no-animals-land leading to the entrance to Heimborn proper. In normal times the panthers guarded the exit (or entrance, depending on one's viewpoint), keeping the bears locked in as virtual prisoners in their own land. Typically the cats stayed on their side of the border, entering the bears' territory only to conduct security patrols or search out offenders, whether they were guilty of real or merely suspected crimes against Aeronbed.

On the other side of the pass, at the actual entrance into Heimborn, stood a border sentry and a gate; this modest entry point was run by the bears, but only with the tacit permission of the panthers. Naturally Heimborn's control was more nominal than real, for the gate's function was primarily ceremonial. It was just window dressing, allowing for a pretense of independence on the part of the bears.

Although no one was fooled, the gate had an aura of legality that suited everyone involved. Rarely did any bear depart Heimborn, for they could not leave of their own free will. Permission for delegations of high-ranking bears to visit the capital of Aeronbed was granted on ceremonial occasions, again to keep up the pretense of independence and equality. In such cases the bears were escorted to and fro by the panthers, to ensure that no unsettling contact with local cats occurred and to guarantee that the bears did not "get up to no good." This long-established system was closely monitored and most efficiently run.

However, that had been before the uprising, and now the world was off its axis, so to speak.

While Eisa knew little about modern warfare, he knew enough to be unsettled by his new environment. To his way of thinking, the panthers were marching along as if off to a picnic. No forward patrols had been assigned; no one was watching the thick walls of forest alongside, and no escort birds were patrolling overhead. To Eisa the ravines presented perfect places for a trap; if attacked, the line of panthers, strung out and defenseless, had no easy escape route.

The forest was decidedly quiet. All the Lieutenant could hear was the footfalls of hundreds of cats marching along more or less in unison, and as for discordant scents, the panthers' odor easily covered up those of any other creatures lurking about. His discomfort grew apace.

After a while, Eisa, no longer able to hold back from expressing his anxieties to Geifu, suggested that the company needed to take greater precautions. Geifu, however, could only laugh at the Lieutenant's nervousness. In all the years he had served on the frontier of Heimborn and traveled along this and other routes in the area, Geifu declared — with no small degree of pleasure and derision — nothing untoward had ever happened.

"You must understand, Eisa, the bears don't think like us," the panther explained. "You see the perils and so do I. They'd be obvious to any half-witted soldier. Of course they could attack us here, where we're most vulnerable. But the idea never occurs to them. You see, the bears' appetite for resistance was wrung out of them an age and a half ago. These animals aren't warriors; they're not like us. You'll see soon enough. They're cowed and beaten down; they'll run as soon as we show up in force. Even before they started, the bears knew they'd lose." He spat derisively into the underbrush as he walked along. Eisa did not reply.

"Frankly, that's what's most surprising about this daft revolt," Geifu continued. "It makes no sense. Who's behind it? And what can they possibly hope to achieve? That's what I don't understand."

Eisa, far from convinced, glanced around nervously. He imagined a bear hiding behind each tree, keeping track of the panthers' every move. "But, given what you say about not understanding the bears' recent actions, shouldn't we be more on our guard?"

"Like I said, Lieutenant, I've marched back and forth on this trail so many times I've lost count," Geifu replied. "Not once has anything — and I repeat, *anything* — ever happened."

"But didn't you just say circumstances have changed," Eisa persisted. "Aren't the bears behaving differently now? Well, at least acting unusually?"

Geifu laughed. "Some things may change, but much more stays the same."

Eisa sighed. "Well, for all our sakes, I hope you're right."

"Rest assured, Lieutenant. If Commander Segomo saw a need for greater precautions, she would have ordered them already. She has not, and I trust her judgment in all things."

Eisa decided he'd beaten the subject to death. It was time to change tack. "How long have you been with this company, Geifu?"

The cat grunted and then laughed once more. "A very long time. In fact, I'd wager a lot longer than you've been walking the earth, my young friend. Hah! If I'd been properly rewarded for those young cubs I've trained and seen promoted, I'd be a rich panther by now. I came out to Heimborn when the very first of our garrison was stationed here, when I was still wet behind the ears. The army's been my life, it has."

"So what do *you* think of the bears?"

Geifu looked quizzically at Eisa. "That's an odd question."

"I'm just curious. You know, I've only been here a short time and I've never met a bear. I have no idea what they're like or how they behave. By now you must have met many."

"I try not to think about the bears. It gets in the way of my work."

"I don't understand. What do you mean?"

Geifu grunted again, but this time he did not laugh. "Nothing, really ... Look, it's just something to say. I don't like to talk about politics; it's none of my business. I care only about my brothers and sisters, my duty and my daily rations. You understand? But, since you're asking questions, you tell me something. Why are you here?

You finally decided to join up and have some fun? Didn't want to miss the action?"

Geifu's unexpected question provided Eisa an opportunity to practice his explanation. Why *had* he shown up unannounced? He threw off his earlier reserve and, on the spur of the moment, decided to adopt a bold stance. "Has no one told you?" he asked the other cat.

"Me? Hah! Why would anyone tell *me* anything?" Geifu spat out.

"I'm not sure how much I can reveal," Eisa said. "It's the reason I was looking for Segomo, so I could brief the Commander about my new assignment. But, given the situation, perhaps I'd better tell you now, just in case something happens before I get to her. After all, you're her second-in-command, and you should be made aware of such things."

At the mention of his exalted position, the cat straightened up, immediately taking on an aura of greater seniority. Without breaking stride, Eisa looked around slowly and carefully, first left and right at the darkening woods, then behind him to see how far they were ahead of the other cats, and then once again at the surrounding forest. Geifu's eyes followed his every move, his curiosity increasing with every step.

Finally, apparently fully satisfied with the security of his position, Eisa said, "I think I can trust you. Can you keep a secret?"

"What do you take me for?" the other said gruffly. "Of course I can."

"No offense meant; I just have to make sure. These are unusual — even dangerous — times. One can't be too careful, you know. I'm trusting you with my life, putting you in the know because of your key position. The point is, I'm going to need the help of an honorable and trustworthy soldier like you. You do wish to help me, don't you?"

Pleased by the compliments, the cat saluted, his curiosity at a peak.

Eisa drew his head more closely to that of his companion. "I'll be completely frank with you," he whispered. "I'm on a secret mission. Naturally I can't reveal who sent me out here, but I can tell you what I must do and why. Before I do so, you must swear to me that no word of this exchange shall pass your lips. Otherwise we're both dead cats. You hear me?"

Geifu nodded eagerly.

"You're certain?" persisted Eisa. "You understand?"

"Of course, of course," Geifu said impatiently.

"All right then. Here's the situation."

Eisa had had only the sketchiest of ideas about what he was going to say until he actually played it out. His whole narrative was completely spontaneous, although (like all good lies) it was based on a modicum of truth. "Your commanders have important friends in Manaris, but they cannot reveal themselves or their support — at least, not just yet. They've concluded that they need a secure means to get information back to them and a private way to communicate with the commanders. However, this communication channel must be totally secret. You understand what I'm saying?"

The other cat turned to look at him; his only response was to blink. Seeing Geifu's confusion, Eisa changed tack. "I volunteered to act in this capacity because your cause is dear to my heart. I've long had to pretend otherwise, to confuse my — *our* opponents. But here, among friends, I can be true to myself. I don't have to tell you about the personal injury that was done to me and how I've suffered as a result. That story will be well known to you as one of the more important and long-standing officers around here."

"Of course, of course, Eisa," Geifu replied, now mystified as well as confused.

"So I took it upon myself to appear as a regular soldier in the field, no different from you or anyone else of your rank. I had to blend in, you see. Spies are everywhere." Eisa glanced around, as if searching out those same spies.

"Naturally, Lieutenant, I understand completely," the other panther said, not really understanding at all.

"So this is where you come in, where you can help me. Do you think that would be possible?"

"Of course, Eisa, name it. You can count on me."

"Not long after we enter Heimborn and set up camp, I'll need to sneak away. Just for a bit, mind you. I'll have to do so several times, and at odd moments. I won't tell you what I'll be doing or where I'm going, but a smart officer like you will have no trouble figuring it out. I may need you to cover for me, or just look the other way when I leave. Do you think you could do that?"

"That's it?" Geifu answered slowly. "Just look the other way?"

"That's it. Or, if asked, shrug your shoulders and say you don't know where I am. Got it?"

Geifu nodded.

"Remember, whatever happens, I'll not forget your contribution. For that matter, neither will my superiors. The Grand Council values loyalty above all else. I'm sure I can see 'Field Commander' in your future, Geifu."

"I'm just trying to do my duty, to serve the army as best I can. I ask for nothing in return." However, as Geifu made this claim, his chest swelled with added pride. The panther was already looking forward to his next, long-awaited step up the promotional ladder.

"When I finally speak to Segomo about my role out here, I will brief her on our understanding. But, no matter what, you must never let on that we've spoken or repeat a word of our conversation to her. If you do, our arrangement will be broken. Naturally the Commander will deny everything, as she should. As, of course, will I. That's the way we agents do our job — complete secrecy. It's the only way we can work. Everyone here must act as if everything is normal and as if I don't even exist. You understand me?"

"Of course, Lieutenant. I'm at your service. If there's anything I can do to further the cause, I'm —"

"Excellent," Eisa interjected, cutting the other off. "Then we shall speak no more of this matter. Unless, of course, I need something from you or if anyone asks about my activities. No matter how innocuous the question may sound to you or how senior in rank the panther may be, you must say nothing and then report back to me as soon as possible, for they might just as easily be working for the enemy.

"I know, I know, it's hard to believe a panther could be untrue. But believe me, I could tell you a few stories. You can't imagine the lies a sly adversary will throw about. We — you and I — must be on our guard at all times. If asked, you must say as little as possible, only that I'm Lieutenant Eisa, come out to join the march on Heimborn because I believe so strongly in the cause. That'll be easy enough for you to say, because it's the truth. Agreed?"

Geifu nodded again. Eisa pulled him out of the line and embraced him, whispering in his ear, "We're now blood brothers, Geifu. Our futures are entwined. On to victory, eh?"

As the other panther's eyes filled with tears of emotion, Eisa almost felt sorry about how he had misled his new partner. Much later he would remember this moment, and, in particular, his hope that nothing bad would happen to Geifu as a result of his deception.

18

THE BEARS OF HEIMBORN

Little did Eisa or Geifu realize that the Lieutenant's instincts were far more attuned to the reality of the situation than either cat would have dared to guess. Perhaps Geifu's complacency even saved the panthers, for, as the pair and their fellow soldiers were marching toward the gates of Heimborn with so little concern, they were indeed being watched, and watched quite closely.

In fact, the bears of Heimborn had been scattered throughout the mountain ravines and dark coniferous forests, keeping track of the progress of each company as it moved ever nearer their realm. The cautious bears, however, were poised to attack only if discovered; they were not convinced of their capacity to take on the might of the panthers, and certainly not in a full-fledged battle. For the present they were content with assessing the strength and resources of the invaders.

Several weeks had passed since Goran-Art's death and Parthanyx's retreat from Heimborn. In those weeks much had happened. In the beginning, the bears had mourned the death of one of their brave clan chiefs, but very quickly they had thrown off their grief and moved to embrace Eirwen as Goran-Art's successor in the struggle against Aeronbed, and then as first among equals in the world of Heimborn. He was the only creature who had dared to strike back at the bears' overlords, especially the hated Parthanyx. Eirwen's evident courage was deemed to be more than sufficient reason for him to take on the mantle of Heimborn's military chief.

As such things go, Eirwen's fame spread quickly from bear to bear and clan to clan, until few remained in Heimborn who were unaware of what had occurred in Ethanead. Many of the stories, embellished and exaggerated for effect, bore little relationship to the reality. Those renditions served to ensure that Eirwen's reputation grew apace; the clamor to see him swelled weekly and the bears' reliance on him for answers increased exponentially, along with the majority's faith and prayers. Inevitably the expectations grew at a much greater rate than Eirwen's ability to deliver on them. The polar bear made no promises — at least none he couldn't keep on his own — but the combined hopes of the multitude and the commitments made in his name by others created an illusion of better days ahead, all to be easily achieved and with little sacrifice on anyone's part.

Unfortunately (and possibly predictably), not all the bears of Heimborn reacted with equal enthusiasm. For some, the news of Eirwen's arrival and attack on Parthanyx had the opposite impact. After so many years of submission, more than a few bears had grown accustomed to — even comfortable with — the status quo. Although they would never admit to liking the metaphorical collar that had been placed around their necks, in unguarded moments they might confess to preferring it to some unknown and, possibly, more precarious situation.

It must be recognized that, even in an unequal relationship between states or animals, some members of the subservient class still get to call the tune for the remainder, while those even lower down on the chain must be content with dancing to that tune. For the lucky few individuals at the top of that smaller heap, an upsetting of their measly apple cart would still be upsetting. And — to give those individuals their due — they may genuinely have feared the results of opposing the panthers' tyrannical rule. Any attempt at revolution could quite possibly lead to a far worse situation: not victory at all, but rather more punishment and greater suffering all around. So, although one might imagine Eirwen being heartily welcomed by every bear, the reality was much different. It was not long before the forces of conservatism in Heimborn tried to oppose the popular resistance movement that was springing up around them. And since they could not contain it on their own, they turned, ironically, to their very oppressors, the panthers, to help them put it down.

To Eirwen's great surprise, he soon found himself fighting on two fronts: a military campaign against the encroaching panthers and a political one against the bears' own fearful establishment. And the polar bear was rapidly tiring of the struggle. As he came to understand the daunting extent of the task he faced, he began to reminisce rather wistfully about his days in Vigmar, where all one required was the immediate decisions of a mercurial emperor to set things in motion. To be vaulted into a high position, as had occurred in Blakfel, with the support of the throne behind him — what a luxury that had been!

Eirwen began to think he'd been badly misled by Goran-Art and Somerled. They had made it seem as if the whole of Heimborn would rise up behind him en masse, after which the panthers would simply flee. At least, that was how the polar bear remembered their argument. But now Goran-Art was dead and Somerled was off spreading the word throughout Heimborn. Even Raven — Hunspek, as Eirwen had taken to calling him — was in the habit of disappearing for days on end. And without Fridis by his side, who could the polar bear confide in or pose difficult questions to? Surrounded though he was by his many relatives, he had never felt so lonely.

It hadn't taken many days after Goran-Art's death for the bear to grasp why the situation in Heimborn was so abysmal. The clans were demoralized and had become defeatist in spirit. Unfortunately Goran-Art had been the exception rather than the rule. Although many believed in Eirwen and the prophecy that seemed to foretell his arrival, beyond that belief they had no idea what to do. Generally speaking, the bears were passive and accepting, untrained in the arts of both war and politics. Initiative, assertiveness and enthusiasm had long been bred out of them.

In Vigmar, by way of contrast, things had been exactly the opposite: the Empire possessed trained armies and a tightly controlled officer corps. Eirwen began to understand how easy it had been for him in

Vigmar. To his dismay, he started believing that his success to date had had nothing to do with his own skills and powers. How could anyone in Vigmar have failed? To the bear it seemed simply impossible to fall short when all the authority of the Empire, its military might and skilled soldiers were behind one.

Eirwen's old self-doubts seeped back as he struggled to cope with the reality of the situation in Heimborn. On particularly difficult days the polar bear could be found stalking back and forth, muttering something to the effect that the bears deserved their awful fate. Some nights Eirwen considered sneaking off back to the wolves, who respected him as part of a highly trained team of professionals. More than once the notion came to him that — if only he knew where the wolves might be — he'd go off in search of them in the blink of an eye. But then, thinking everything through, Eirwen would feel guilty and ashamed of that short-sighted response. In his heart the polar bear knew he had to persevere, taking things one modest step at a time.

Eventually Eirwen determined that the best way forward was to put aside the world of political infighting. He concluded that success — any success — against the panthers would sway the political elites of Heimborn as much as any words he could muster to convince them to take on the cause of revolution. Fortunately Eirwen had learned a few things from Fridis, other things from the wolves, and a whole lot from his brief time as a general in Vigmar. He had learned that a good story could work wonders, that bravado could compensate for many other weaknesses, that solid information about your opponents' plans and movements was worth several of your own armies, that good training went together with good strategy, and, finally, that a small army can create havoc and confusion among the ranks of a much more powerful opponent. All those tactics he could employ when the right moment came.

Eirwen also began to think into the future, weighing the value of having a skilled and loyal fighting force of like-minded brethren at his command. In this dangerous world, such an army would serve him well in many ways over the years to come. After all, no one could forecast how the campaign would play out and what would be its final result.

Eirwen tried to put himself in the mindset of the panthers. Having seen some up close — Parthanyx and his vicious gang of thugs — he already had a few ideas. These cats were arrogant, proud, tough and cruel. They knew their way around and they were confident. They had good reason to be, for the bears had been a compliant bunch and, with a few exceptions, easy to dominate. Eirwen reflected that the panthers must have been quite surprised, or at least confused, by his counterattack, but that isolated incident would probably have amounted to little in their overall assessment of his kinfolk. While his attack on Parthanyx was well known — and often exaggerated — in the bear world, Eirwen suspected that any reports of the assault would have been suppressed among the panthers as too embarrassing or too dangerous to talk about. Still, the polar bear was certain that revenge would be on the mind of at least one cat.

How could the panthers' strengths be turned into weaknesses? Too much confidence can lead to being ill prepared; too much arrogance can lead to underestimating the opposition; too much toughness and cruelty can lead to alienating potential allies. This combination could present the bears with an opportunity: a combination of stealth and surprise, at least in the short term, might serve them well. Nonetheless, that advantage would wane as time went on. Once the bears had achieved some success, the panthers would see where they needed to build up their forces and reinforce their efforts. They would hit back where they could and doubtless would come down hard on the bear population with new repressive measures. While such repression would probably serve to drive more bears into supporting the revolt, the measures might be so dreadful that no one could endure them. That was the polar bear's greatest fear.

Eirwen was well aware of the risks. His only other option was to walk away without even trying, but he could not leave the bears to such a fate. He'd begun this revolt, whether intentionally or not, and he'd have to see it through. In the short term he needed a small group of determined fighters much like the wolf pack — a force that could hit and run, disappearing like a wraith into the darkness after each assault. They would need to harass their enemies and destroy their morale. If a few of the panthers began looking over their shoulders in the dead of night and wondering whether they should be occupying Heimborn, he would have accomplished something. It would not be enough, but it would be a start. Eirwen wondered whether time was on his side or on that of the cats.

Fortunately there was no shortage of volunteers, especially among the bears of Ethanead. They were enthusiastic, although undisciplined and unaware of the risks. Eirwen saw it as his job to fashion fighters out of these raw recruits and then to train others who could fan out across Heimborn to create and lead additional units. At the same time he would try to ensure that those not involved in the fighting would be kept out of harm's way.

The polar bear was surprised at how quickly things came together. In no time at all several companies were formed and readied to go into action. While Eirwen fretted that he might be underestimating what training was needed and, even more so, about what more he could hope to offer them, the bears soon mastered many elements of tactics and strategy. Luckily the panthers had made no move over the intervening period, affording precious time for the bears to practice and prepare themselves. And so, by the time the panthers did begin their assault on Heimborn, the bears were on the way to becoming a true fighting force.

Eirwen had no idea how large the panthers' army was and what they planned to do on their arrival. That was why he had stationed the well-hidden watchers along the routes into the bears' realm — watchers who could count, take note of what they observed and bring back reliable reports on what they had seen, but who would not provoke the enemy or give them any sense that an opposition force existed. Let the panthers think all was quiet and safe, just as always.

And what the bears saw was exactly what Eisa had observed: a degree of nonchalance and lack of preparation brought on by years of easily imposed rule. In other words, it was an attitude that created potential vulnerability. The question for Eirwen was, when and how best could he take advantage of it?

19

EISA FINDS HIS PLACE

B y the time the panthers had reached the now-deserted gates of Heimborn, crossed over to the other side and set up camp, Eisa was forced to acknowledge that Geifu had been right in his assessment of their opponents. Nothing at all had occurred, and the panthers' progress into the bears' homeland had remained unchecked.

Once sentries had been posted and the evening meal served, a large group of panthers, of both senior and junior ranks, assembled around an open fire in the very center of the encampment. The confident cats stretched out, relaxing and sharing war stories. Eisa, already accepted as one of Segomo's company, had been invited into the circle.

"Clearly Geifu's instincts are a lot better than mine," Eisa admitted openly to the assembly. "I could've sworn that eyes were upon us the whole time we were moving through the passes."

"An easy mistake to make, at least to those with less experience," one of the other soldiers replied. He spoke gruffly but good-naturedly. "The first time I was out here, I was completely spooked by these forests. Oh, you can see right enough, but the long shadows cast by the mountains make it impossible to tell friend from foe at twenty paces. The whole blasted place is as black and creepy as a rat snake. Hah! Not so different from the bears themselves."

"Everything about this country is creepy," another cat offered. "We just got here and already I can't wait to get out again."

"Nor can I," a third ventured. "I hope this exercise will be a short one."

"What? Didn't they tell you this will be an occupation?" Geifu said. "For the entire duration of the war?"

"For the duration?" his horrified colleague exclaimed. He began to swear profusely.

"Just joking, Draco," said Geifu, laughing. "Relax. It's just another show of force to remind the bears who's in charge."

"I thought they already knew that," Draco remarked sourly.

"Well, if they don't by now, they sure will after we're finished with them," interjected yet another soldier. "I hear Parthanyx really has it in for the bears this time."

"And where did you hear that, Labros?" Segomo asked calmly. The company's commander had arrived on the scene quietly, stepping out from the shadows. As Segomo spoke, she took her place among the circle.

"Sorry, ma'am, I guess I spoke out of turn," the surprised Labros sputtered. "But my brother, you know, he's one of Parthanyx's own company. He told me, on the q.t., like."

"Really?" Segomo said. "And what else did your well-informed brother tell you?"

"Well, ma'am, he told me about the fight Parthanyx had with that big bear."

"And your brother was there to witness the event?"

"Well, no, not really, ma'am. He was back at base. But he heard about it from one of his mates who saw the whole thing. He was right there in the thick of things when it happened."

"Beware of second- and third-paw tales, Labros. And I suggest that you don't tell them out of school. What we need to know, we will be told, and what you are told, you will hear only from me. Got it?"

"Yes, ma'am."

Segomo turned to face Eisa. "Lieutenant Eisa, I was told you'd joined up. Welcome to this merry band of cutthroats. No doubt we'll have plenty of work for you. Won't we, cousins."

Words of assent from round the circle greeted this remark.

"Has Geifu been looking after you?" Segomo continued.

"Indeed he has, Commander. I'm most obliged to him."

"Excellent. You and I will speak again later."

Eisa nodded as Draco asked, "Captain Segomo, ma'am, can you provide us with any details about our plans for the next few days?"

Segomo checked around the circle for her key subordinates. "Since we're all here, let me fill you in right now. I was going to tell you tomorrow morning, but now will do just as well."

The panthers stirred, sat up and leaned in; no one wanted to be missing crucial instructions.

"We will be occupying the entire northeast quadrant of Heimborn," Segomo continued. "The companies will fan out in teams, covering every compass point south of the mountain passes. Labros was right about one thing: we're searching for one particular bear, a newcomer who seems to have annoyed Parthanyx greatly. We're also looking for any friends the villain might have picked up along the way. When we find them, we will kill them. All of them. No prisoners. We want to put a stop to this uprising here and now, by cutting off its head."

"Do we know if the rebel bears are nearby?" Geifu asked.

"We can't be certain exactly where the agitators are hiding. But we're assuming they can't have gone far. That's why every commander has the same orders: no part of this region will go unsearched."

"What if we find civilians, ma'am?" Geifu pursued. "What do we do with them?"

"There are no civilians now. Every bear is suspect. No mercy will be shown."

There were a few whistles and sharp intakes of breath; Eisa even caught some muttered displeasure at the surprising news. These panthers were hardened soldiers but they were not murderers. Several looked at one another, discomfort written on their faces.

Segomo could read their thoughts. "Listen up, you lot. I know, over the many years we've been here, there's been some fraternization with the bears. It would have been impossible for that not to happen. Even I'll admit that — when you get to know the good ones — some of them aren't half bad. Naturally I'm aware that several of you have developed some profitable business arrangements with the better kind. No harm done, and I let that pass.

"Well, let me tell you, here and now, that's all come to an end. Parthanyx and some of the other commanders are fit to be tied with what happened. Clearly we've been too soft on the bears and they've been getting above themselves. The point is, we're starting to lose control. We need to show the scoundrels some backbone, to stop their taking advantage of our easy-going nature."

Eisa heard several more unhappy rejoinders to this announcement. Obviously not every panther viewed the bears as loathsome creatures.

"I don't have to explain to you," Segomo went on, "how the bears would treat us if the tables were turned. Down deep, they can't be trusted. They're a sinful, immoral breed, capable of only the foulest of deeds. Given half a chance, they'd slit our throats without a moment's thought. They'll never rise to our level but always fall prey to their basest instincts, make no mistake about it. So remember, don't turn your back on any of 'em. Especially now."

Some half-hearted grumbling continued.

"I trust I've made myself clear," Segomo said. "The sneak attack on Parthanyx's company must not go unpunished. If I see any signs of weakness — from any of you — you'll suffer the same fate as the bears. Got it?"

The panthers around the circle lapsed into silence. Looking around, Segomo repeated her question, more emphatically this time. "Have you got that?"

"Yes, ma'am," the cats replied in unison, some more heartily than others.

"Now I suggest you all turn in. Tomorrow will be a long day," Segomo commanded as she got up to leave. "Eisa, you follow me."

Eisa jumped up and followed after the company commander, who proceeded briskly down a trail leading away from the camp. Segomo padded ahead without further comment until the two panthers were well away from the others, near the perimeter of the encampment.

When they were truly alone, Segomo abruptly turned to confront Eisa. Bringing her face close to his, she hissed, "So tell me, cousin, why are you really here?"

Before he could answer, Segomo continued. "Don't forget, I'm not that simpleton Geifu. I won't accept sly words and clever stories. Give me the real goods or your stay here will be short-lived indeed."

"Er, what did Geifu tell you?" asked Eisa uncomfortably, stalling for time.

"He's told me nothing. He said you told him little of importance but that you'd tell me everything directly. So here I am. Speak!"

Better make it a good story, Eisa decided, *and better make it close to the truth.* "Do you remember when I was here last, on behalf of Baron Rithild? When I came to scout out things regarding the bears' revolt? You'll recall that the lions had asked him to check on the situation."

Segomo's eyes narrowed, but she nodded slightly.

"You know I met with Parthanyx and some of the others," Eisa continued. "Frankly, I heard a great deal more than I expected."

This time Segomo grinned broadly. "Parthanyx told me something of your encounter. Hah! It must have been quite a shock."

Although Eisa tried to return the smile in a collegial fashion, he suspected his expression was more as a grimace. Making an effort to respond diplomatically, he said, "He's certainly not what I would call predictable."

"Bloody crazy, if you ask me," said Segomo, laughing. "But we're all a little crazy out here. You will be too after a few years of watching this border. That is, if Parthanyx doesn't kill you first."

Eisa was encouraged by Segomo's easygoing response. It appeared that he had chosen the best point of return after all. The young panther began to relax.

"I understand what you're saying, really I do," Eisa went on. "I must confess that Parthanyx knocked the wind right out of me — literally. But as I went around talking to the others, I realized that he's far from alone in his views. Some of the other commanders feel more strongly and some less — Actually, that's not true. Some feel less and some about the same, but none hold more extreme views than he does."

"That's true enough; Parthanyx leads us in all ways. But rest assured, we're in agreement when it comes to the bears. And Manaris." Segomo's tone had become serious again, her good humor completely vanished. "They're both corrupt and evil — two rotten peas in the same pod, if you will. We see no difference between them."

When Eisa chose not to respond, Segomo continued her tirade. "We'll deal with both in turn. First we'll bring Heimborn under control and then we'll take care of Albiorix and his family. It's time for a new order, Eisa. It's high time the panthers ruled in Aeronbed. And not just any panthers. Don't think I'm talking about Rithild and the rest of the council layabouts. Those creaking politicians and lazy bureaucrats enjoying their fancy dinners and cozy beds? Bah! We've had more than enough of that lot — just cronies sucking up to the lions. It's the warriors like Parthanyx who'll take charge, and it's the Black Legion that'll finally establish a new moral compass, a new code of honor."

"The Black Legion?"

"That's the name Parthanyx has chosen for us. We're no longer part of Aeronbed's regular army. We are our own company of loyalists, reporting to no other creature. A new dawn awaits us, Eisa, you will see. An end to —"

"Yes, yes, I understand, Segomo," interjected Eisa, trying to stem the flow of words so terribly familiar to his ears. "You don't need to tell me. In all sincerity, I've come to recognize and accept your point of view. After meeting with you all out here, I had a great deal of time to think about everything I'd heard. Honestly, at first I thought only of fleeing back to Manaris. I'm a loyal soldier, Segomo, and Rithild is my immediate boss. I take my oath of allegiance seriously. What I was hearing here was very difficult to accept."

"We're loyal to each other here, and to the Legion, not to anyone else," growled the Commander, not liking being reminded of oaths of allegiance.

"No disrespect intended, Segomo. I'm only trying to explain how your situation differs from mine, and to explain my train of thought."

"All right, go on."

"The more I mulled it over and the more I weighed up my time back in Manaris, the more I began to see the logic of Parthanyx's message. It was a sorry life I'd been leading. So, by the time I actually reported back to Rithild, the blinkers covering my eyes all these past years had fallen away. I could see clearly for the first time in my life. I saw what you all saw — a vain, decayed old creature, as treacherous and fraudulent as you declared him to be. In fact, I'd say the Baron is a fitting representative for the regime, as decadent as the kingdom itself. I was so repulsed and horrified I could barely stand looking at him." Eisa grimaced dramatically to convey his disgust.

"I did not let on how I felt, however," he continued. "I played along as usual and Rithild took me for my regular dutiful self. Naturally, the Baron had no reason to think otherwise. Ironically, he ordered me to return here to continue working on his behalf. Unbeknownst to him, I was thrilled to do so, for I had already realized my true place is here. The Legion will be my home now, not Manaris. It was as if my secret prayers had been answered."

"And so you returned here?"

"Well, yes, although it took some time and thought to find an appropriate place. I didn't think Parthanyx would welcome me back, at least not right away. So I chose to join a company some way away — that is, until I'm truly accepted."

"Hah! After what he told us, I'd be the first to agree. It would've taken a very brave — or crazy — cat to go back there."

"I may be a fool, Segomo, but I'm certainly not crazy."

The Commander laughed and then asked, "So, what did you expect to do after returning here?"

"I admit I wasn't completely sure. Since I didn't know whether I would be accepted at all, I hadn't turned my mind to how I might be of greatest use. I'm here to serve, that's all I know."

"Service in the name of the Legion? That's all any officer can ask of a soldier."

"I'll own up, Segomo. I believed that you, of all the commanders, might be the most willing to take me in."

"You take me for a soft touch?" Segomo frowned.

"No, no. Er, it's just that, at the very least, one can have a civil conversation with you. Some of the others ... Well, you know ..."

"Say no more, Eisa. For both our sakes."

The two panthers were silent for a time, unsure about where the conversation might go next. Eisa decided he'd said enough. His story made sense, and Segomo either believed him or did not. Anything he might add now would more than likely look like desperation. He'd leave well enough alone now and not add any embellishments. *Keep things simple* would be his new mantra. He watched Segomo closely as his cousin weighed up the story versus her own suspicions.

Finally the Commander pronounced her assessment. "All right, Eisa, your story has enough currency. However, you should know that more than a few among us see your abrupt return as unwelcome or suspect, or maybe even both. I, for one, am prepared to give you the benefit of the doubt — for now. Don't make a fool of me, and don't cross me. Otherwise you'll be sorry we ever met. You clear on that?"

"Yes, Segomo. I appreciate — "

"Forget the thanks. You'd better go now. Get some rest. We've an early start and a long day ahead of us."

Eisa did as he was commanded. Saying no more, he turned and left with a curt but grateful salute.

But as he walked away, Segomo called out, "Wait! One question before you go. What was your arrangement with Rithild?"

"Arrangement?"

"Yes. Aren't you supposed to be keeping in touch with him in some fashion?"

"I'd forgotten about that. It's true, we planned to meet on a regular basis."

"You'd better continue with those meetings so you don't arouse any suspicion. When's the next one scheduled?"

Eisa told her.

"Your role as a channel to Rithild may prove useful to us," Segomo said. "Parthanyx may value the chance to spread misinformation back in Manaris. I'll have you escorted back through the pass when you need to leave. We'll speak more on this later."

Eisa could not believe his good fortune. The situation had turned out far better than he'd ever hoped or imagined. He could now play all the angles unimpeded. The panther returned to the campsite, feeling light-hearted and confident for the first time in many days.

20

A CHANGE OF PLANS

The king swept, unannounced, into Olwen's private chamber, strode over to the window and threw open the shutters. The harsh sunlight fell directly upon the surprised lioness, who was barely awake after her long night of labors.

"I've decided you won't return to the northern front," Albiorix said abruptly.

Olwen was immediately alert, and made no effort to conceal her disappointment. That opportunity to take command in the field — a rare honor for any lion — was dear to her heart. "What! How can you do this to me?" she protested. Her whiskers twitched angrily as she rose from the bed to confront her father. "I only returned to Manaris because of my meeting with the raven. I never intended to stay here indefinitely. And I doubt I can add anything more to understanding the bird's prophecy. I beg you, Majesty, let me return to the north! Too much time has already passed. My comrades —"

Albiorix held up his huge front paws to stop the rapid onslaught of words. "Hold on, daughter; don't get so worked up! I didn't mean you should stay here in the castle waiting on my needs and working on the meaning of the raven's message. Enough energy has been spent on that wretched puzzle."

The lioness, confused, looked up at her father with renewed hope. "If not here, then where? The south, with my half-brother? The east, with my cousins?"

"Neither, daughter. I want you to go to Heimborn."

"What?" the furious lioness growled. "How can you even suggest such a plan?"

"Now, don't get upset, Olwen."

The Princess, however, was just getting started. "That hopeless backwater? I'll have to hang about with those wretched panthers or the boring bears — or worse, both at the same time. Honestly, I don't know which is the greater punishment. How could you condemn me to such a fate? What have I done to offend you so?"

"Olwen — " Albiorix began

"I'm sorry, Father, you may be Aeronbed's king, but I simply won't go — no matter what you say. I want to be where the action is. I want to be with my own kind. Heimborn is even worse than staying in Manaris. Nothing ever happens there." Olwen began to stomp around her chambers in a majestic huff, as only a teenager can do.

"Daughter, you forget your place. Remember who you're talking to," Albiorix said. "I may be your father, but I am also your lord."

"I beg your pardon, Father. My heart was set on returning north. To be with my own kind, my comrades. Is that so much to ask of you? Anything else is, is — Well, it's such a comedown!"

"Olwen, you wish to serve me and Aeronbed, do you not?"

"Of course," the Princess responded, her heart sinking. The lioness knew her cards of youthful ambition and kinship could not compete with his cards: loyalty, duty, patriotism.

"Let me explain, daughter, and you will see why I have taken this decision."

As the old lion outlined his rationale, Olwen found she could not bear to look at her father. The Princess paced restlessly back and forth or stopped to stare out the high, wide windows. By this point the sun had disappeared behind a dense fog that seemed to have come out of nowhere. Thick clouds, which had already overwhelmed the town below, were now swirling around the castle's battlements. High above, the sun kept up its valiant but losing battle to pierce the misted skies.

Its thin rays barely warmed the lioness now, let alone the cool, damp ground below. Olwen's mind began to wander.

"Are you even listening to me?" the King snarled, bringing her back to the here-and-now.

"I'm sorry, Father. I was distracted by the, the — Oh, never mind," she replied heavily, not bothering to complete her thought.

"It's crucial you understand how this next step plays out," Albiorix went on. "Everything about the prophecy points to it. Whatever the details might be — whether we've misconstrued certain elements or not — some aspects are as clear as a tiger's eye. First, you are directly involved. Second, your fortune and our future are wrapped up with those of the panthers and the bears. In other words, your destiny and the fate of Aeronbed are intertwined, whether you like it or not."

"How can you be so sure?" Olwen protested. "In spite of all our deliberations, so much is still in doubt. I, for one, am more bewildered than ever."

"Naturally I understand your confusion. On many details we could only guess at the meaning. Equally, however, there was much we could decipher and several conclusions we could safely draw. The more I reflected last night on the raven's message, the more certain I became."

"But what am I to do in Heimborn? I've never been near the place before and I've spent little time in the company of panthers. On formal occasions, yes, but you kept me apart from them as a cub. And as for the bears, what do I know of them? Nothing at all."

"How would you reply if I said I've no idea what you should do in Heimborn?"

"I'd tell you it was a fool's errand, and I was the fool."

"Ha!" the king laughed. "Well said, Olwen. You are your mother's daughter."

Albiorix came over and embraced his daughter. "However, I'm not making such an admission, not by a long shot. No matter how things turn out in Heimborn, I can guarantee it will not be boring. The situation there has become most uncertain. You've heard me speak of this matter with Temorwig. Not only are the bears said to be in open revolt, something else is brewing — something far more serious.

"Temorwig has reported to me that our good friend Rithild has placed his lieutenant, Eisa, with the local forces. The Lieutenant will be his ears and eyes, and the Baron's seeking to find a safe way to stay in contact with him. I want you to play that role. Thus you will serve both the Grand Council and me, for I too need to know how and when to intervene."

The lioness frowned, and Albiorix read her mind. "I know, acting as an observer and go-between seems like the most simple and mindless of tasks, especially so since the lands between the capital and Heimborn are now at peace. But don't be fooled by appearances. Look to the greater picture. You know Aeronbed is being attacked on many fronts by Vigmar. Although we are not losing the war, we are not winning it either. The enemy seems to grow steadily in strength.

"Of course we can hold off Vigmar and, in time, we will persevere. But Aeronbed cannot survive if it also faces internal strife. If something evil is growing inside our land, we must nip it in the bud, before it spreads and kills us. It's that serious. Our future is at stake, and your presence in Heimborn is key to our survival.

"I wish I could explain more. All I can say today is that the prophecy you were so fortunate to witness has been a touchstone. If civil war lies in our future, so be it. But whatever happens, you hold the answers. I don't know exactly how or when. Perhaps you'll be able to find another way of looking at things. Perhaps you'll find the answers everyone else overlooks. Who knows?

"Do not be deceived by the peace that reigns around Heimborn. Danger lurks everywhere and the situation can change as easily as night follows day. Let me assure you, whatever you may feel about command and the thrill of combat, nothing will compare to the challenge I'm now asking you to accept. You will be the only lion there, with no support, no shoulder to lean upon. You will have nothing to carry you through but your wits, strength and character."

Olwen shivered and her eyes widened as the king's grave tone made itself felt. The lioness had never before heard Albiorix speak in such a manner.

"I thought you'd lost confidence in me," she said. "I'm ashamed of my earlier reaction. Now I feel quite the opposite. The responsibility you place on my shoulders is immense. Perhaps I am not yet worthy of such a mission."

"Never think so. Although you may believe yourself ill-equipped, I have great confidence in you. I have watched you mature and grow in wisdom. You can and will succeed. Beyond my own observations, the prophecy also tells me so."

"Father, how can you say that? From what possible evidence can you make such a judgment?"

"Olwen, do you doubt yourself? You, the daughter of Aeronbed's greatest king and greatest queen?"

"Of course I do. No sane creature would dare otherwise."

"Then let those doubts keep you watchful. I don't need boldness from you, at least not yet. I want instinct, scrutiny, careful assessment. I want to know what's going on; I want to know whom I can trust and whom I must fear. You will not need to act on your own just yet. We remain here for you back in Manaris. Can you do that for me, Olwen?"

The lioness smiled for the first time that day. "Of course, Father. I may be your beloved daughter, but I am also your most humble servant." Olwen bowed her head in happy deference. She'd remember this moment forever after.

21

EISA AND RITHILD

"What? Surely you can't be serious," the young panther fumed. "Princess Olwen? You must be joking."

"I know, I know, Eisa, that was my first reaction. Naturally, I could hardly say so. How could I object?" the Baron responded dryly. "We are talking about Albiorix's daughter, after all."

"But — "

"But as I thought some more about it," Rithild continued, ignoring his lieutenant's protests, "I tried to figure out what the old fox was up to."

"And what did you conclude, my lord?"

"Well, for one, if the king ever trusted us, he certainly doesn't anymore. Albiorix wants his own source of information, someone he can rely upon utterly."

"Still, it's an odd choice, to say the very least. The lioness is young and inexperienced."

"Not so inexperienced as you might think. The Princess spent the past year on the northern front and was about to take command of her own company. That's a great deal more than you can say. So don't be too arrogant when you meet her."

Eisa ignored the Baron's words. "Didn't you try to convince His

Majesty otherwise? It's clearly an error of judgment, even by my limited knowledge of such matters."

"Perhaps to you, Eisa, but once the King's mind is made up, he's not easily turned, not at all. You have to know when to pick your battles, and it was evident to me I could never win this one. In such cases you must accept defeat with grace, move on and live to fight another day. In any event, coming out here on a regular basis is no longer an option for me. I've a lot on my plate, Eisa, and my legs are not what they used to be."

"There was no other panther able to take this on?"

"No one. And, as I say, Albiorix's mind was already made up."

Eisa snarled as a wave of disgust welled up in his stomach. He continued to fume. "A lioness! A lion might have been acceptable, but a lioness? Words fail me."

"I'm disappointed in you," Rithild scolded. "Use your imagination, Eisa. Do you take me for a fool? If Olwen is as green as you think, she can be easily manipulated. If she proves far more able than you expect, she might prove to be a great ally. A personal link to the King himself — who knows how that connection might help us! It's up to you to determine her worth and make the most of it."

Eisa, shamed by this hearty rebuke, hung his head. "I should know better than to question your cunning, my lord. I forgot my place, and I beg your pardon."

"You're young and have much to learn, Eisa. Consider me your father and your teacher. However, enough of young Mistress Olwen for the present. I want to know what you've found out."

Eisa told him of his encounters with Geifu and Segomo and the sudden move into Heimborn. "They've adopted a new moniker for themselves: the Black Legion. It's not very original, but it does have a menacing ring to it. I don't know whether the entire panther force is involved or whether it's just the most fanatical leaders. Whatever the case, it seems they've no intention of reporting to Manaris ever again. Of course, I've only Segomo's word for it. You'll understand that I didn't want to appear too nosy. Asking too many questions could lead to suspicion, so I have to take the information as it comes."

"Yes, yes, of course. However, you must persevere. You're also going to have to take more chances. Things are moving much faster than I thought possible."

"I will, my lord; it goes without saying. I'd only just arrived when the commanders decided for some reason to march on Heimborn. None of my acquaintances asked, and no one ever explained, why that moment was chosen. They all simply marched off dutifully, leaving no one behind."

"No one at all?"

"Not a single cat. I thought it curious myself, although I'm hardly an expert on military tactics."

"Like no turning back ... " mused Rithild, more to himself than to his junior.

"Yes, precisely."

"What else?" the Baron asked sharply, coming out of his reverie.

"The real mystery became apparent when we got into Heimborn. Not a bear could be found! We searched for four days and nights without any letup. We could find no tracks or signs of their escape route."

"And nothing to indicate what happened to them?"

"Naturally there were signs of previous encampments, settlements, industry — that sort of thing. But every den we visited was completely deserted, and all the other commanders told a similar tale: there was no indication of where the bears were hiding out. I'd say either they were forewarned or they'd already created a means of escape and places to hide. We employed our best trackers, but to no avail. It was like the passing of winter — once gone, it's as if the season never existed. And so it was with the bears; we could find neither head nor tail of them anywhere."

"An impressive disappearing act. So the exercise was deemed a failure?"

"Well, that depends."

"Depends on what?"

"What your viewpoint is."

"Please enlighten me, Eisa."

"Well, on the one paw, the bears seem to be more observant and better prepared than we thought. Also, since we found none of them, we didn't have the opportunity to do any damage or at least instill fear among them. Their successful withdrawal may even embolden them further. However, the Black Legion now occupies a significant part of the bears' territory and the hunt for them continues. We're not letting up, not by any means. I can only assume that the bears are on the run and will have to run even farther. It's only a matter of time, of course. One day they will be found, and then ... " The Lieutenant paused as if for effect, made a gesture indicating a swift death and then carried on. "Moreover," he added, "it's significant that the bears did not see fit to attack us."

"So?"

"So I conclude that they have neither the means nor the strength to do so. They are not yet strong enough to defeat our forces, let alone inflict injury, with any chance of safe escape. Therefore, if it were up to me, I'd say we need to strike soon, before the rebels have time to generate more support and grow more powerful."

"You cannot strike what you cannot find. And, to my mind, another possibility looms even larger."

"What is that?"

"That they've merely *chosen* not to attack and are simply waiting for the right opportunity. A moment when the Legion's guard is down or its forces are spread too thinly or badly positioned and defenseless."

"It's certainly a possibility. Our forces may be tough and well-trained, but their approach is too cavalier for my liking. I believe the commanders have become overconfident after so many years of supremacy. They're too used to being overlords of a defeated race, one that was compliant rather than putting up any resistance. That's not the case anymore, but no one grasps that fact."

"Have you made your views known to anyone else?"

"Only indirectly, to one of the junior officers. But my observations had no impact on him."

"Have you met up with Parthanyx yet?"

"No. I'm still trying to avoid him, much as one stays clear of a rabid dog."

Rithild ignored the slight on his nephew.

"In any event, we've been too busy hunting for bears since I arrived on the scene," Eisa explained. "Segomo's marching orders took us some distance away from Parthanyx's company."

"There will come a time, Lieutenant. You'll have to steel yourself."

"I know, but it can wait."

"Very well, let things stand for the moment. We — you have a far more important task when you return."

"Oh?"

"Yes, I want you to give Segomo — or Parthanyx directly, if you run into him first — a message from me. The message has three parts. First, he and his fellow commanders have friends in high places in Manaris. Second, these friends have long identified with the troops' grievances against the lions. Third, certain members of the Grand Council are prepared to support a move on Aeronbed at the appropriate moment. However, for such a move to be successful, it must be coordinated with the Council, through me. Naturally this information must be kept utterly secret until the moment is right. Very few must know what is planned."

Eisa was struck by how close his story had followed what Rithild was now proposing, but he decided not to share that information with the Baron. "Do you think they'll believe such a tale?" he asked.

"Why not?"

"Even to me it sounds incredible that Council would adopt such a treasonous position. I don't see the Legion's commanders, suspicious as they already are, buying it."

"Yet it is true."

"It is?"

"Why do you not believe it?"

"Don't forget, my lord, I know the Council members."

"Perhaps you don't know them as well as you think."

Eisa looked at the Baron closely. Understanding was beginning to dawn on the young panther. "Perhaps I really do have more to learn," he admitted dryly.

"As I said earlier, you are young yet, and I am your teacher."

"My lord," Eisa replied, unsmiling, as he bowed his head.

"Is there anything else we need to discuss?"

"Two things. First, if Princess Olwen is to be an intermediary, we shall need a code to communicate our true intent to each other. Second, we'll need a new meeting spot. This place is too removed from the new front lines; it takes too long for me to get here. I'm afraid poor Princess Olwen will have to meet me on the very frontier of Heimborn."

"That first problem had already occurred to me. Fortunately I've had time to think about it and prepare something for you." Rithild passed him a rudimentary-looking code. "As for the second issue," he continued, "does the meeting place have to be at the very gates of Heimborn?"

"If not there, at least very close to them. Don't forget, the Legion's marching farther and farther into Heimborn, and I can get leave for only a few days. Even this visit has stretched things past my comfort level."

"It will increase the danger for her, and I can't say how the King will feel about that."

"You said she's experienced. It can't be any more dangerous than up north."

"True enough." Rithild sighed. "Do you have a place in mind?"

"Yes, a perfect spot, one I scouted out when I was coming here. I'll show it to you before we part, so there'll be no confusion. It's another day's march from here. Still, it'll be the last trek you have to make."

☙❦❧

WHEN THE TWO CATS FINALLY PARTED COMPANY, BOTH HAD NOTICED A change in the tone of their relationship. When they'd last met, Eisa had clearly been the subordinate. Now he had achieved (at least in the elder cat's opinion) a surprising level of confidence and forthrightness. They were not yet equals — far from it — but the change was now quite apparent. As Rithild watched Eisa leave, he wondered how much longer he would be able to control his young acolyte. Even more worrisome, Rithild began to wonder whether Eisa was likely to be influenced by the revolutionary ideas to which he was being exposed. If so, how long would it take before the Lieutenant cast off his past allegiance and began to identify with his new comrades? What would happen then?

For his part, the Baron was completely apolitical. He couldn't care less about ideas, whether they were espoused by the establishment or by aspiring revolutionaries. He simply enjoyed power for its own sake. It didn't matter what the views around the table were as long as he could sit at that table — and perhaps get far more than his fair share of the pudding.

As he began the long journey back to Manaris, Rithild turned his mind to Princess Olwen. Her presence at the gates of Heimborn would add a whole new dimension to his relationship with Eisa. His next priority was to prepare the lioness for what was to come.

22

A SETBACK FOR THE BLACK LEGION

More than three days had passed since Eisa had left Segomo's camp, almost a whole day more than expected. It had taken many hours to find a new rendezvous point, one closer to Heimborn, and the extra time weighed heavily on the panther's mind. Although Segomo had granted him leave to be absent, Eisa imagined the delay would have stretched the Commander's patience past the breaking point.

It was mid-afternoon and the sun was beginning to descend behind the surrounding mountaintops. Eisa was passing through the heavily wooded uplands leading to the gates into the bears' homeland when he heard a distant rumble. The ground around him began to shake violently, and he was forced to stop.

At first the panther took the event for an earth tremor, but it ended as abruptly as it had begun, and there were no aftershocks. Eisa sat down, considering the mystery and wondering if it needed exploring. But, hearing nothing more, he decided to carry on, more carefully now, more aware of his surroundings, attuned to the slightest unusual noise.

It wasn't long before he was forced to reconsider that decision. A new sound intruded upon his senses, less clearcut and more subdued, but growing steadily. Overcome by anxiety, he stopped again to listen, eyes wide, one ear close to the ground.

Someone was on the move. Many — no, an army was on the move, and it was heading in his direction. But from where? And which army?

The first question was easier to answer. The troops were clearly coming from within Heimborn. The answer to the second, however, was much more difficult to determine. The Legion had been stationed in Heimborn for the duration of its search for the rebellious bears. Considering the panthers' recent lack of success, in the three days Eisa had been away, it was hardly likely they had finished their deadly assignment, at least to his way of thinking.

Unless, of course, the bears had been foolish enough to take on Parthanyx in a full-fledged battle and had already been decimated, and what he was now listening to was a boisterous army returning in triumph. If so, Eisa felt a pang of sorrow that he had missed all the excitement. But even as the Lieutenant considered the possibility, he doubted it could be true. More likely it was the bears themselves, on the run from the Legion, pushed out of their enclave and racing for their lives.

But wasn't the direction wrong? Wouldn't the rebel forces be fleeing further into Heimborn rather than out of it? That would be true, but not if this path was their only way of escape. Whatever the case, Eisa decided it would be wise to leave the trail and hide in the deep shadows of the woods until he could discover whether the noise signaled friend or foe.

The panther had to move quickly, for the noise was growing ever louder. Whoever these creatures were, they'd be appearing within minutes. He found a good location not far off, a bend in the trail where he could hide and observe in both directions without being seen. In nervous anticipation the Lieutenant crouched behind a stand of thick bushes, keeping a sharp eye on the path.

He did not have long to wait. Before too long Eisa was relieved to see the panther forces appear, marching in double-quick time. To his alarm, though, the cats looked beaten down, nothing like a conquering army. Sparing no glances for the surrounding forest, they remained intently focused on getting to their next destination. Or perhaps, Eisa thought, on getting far away from Heimborn as fast as they possibly could.

To say Eisa was puzzled would be an understatement. This route march had not been in any plans he knew of, and the troops appeared to comprise the entire panther army, not just one or two companies. Keeping low to the ground, he searched their ranks for familiar faces. Eventually the panther saw one or two from Segomo's unit, and at last he spied a very haggard-looking Labros. With little hesitation, Eisa jumped out of his hiding place and sprinted over to the column of soldiers.

Several panthers immediately confronted him. A couple of stalwart fellows almost attacked him, forcing Eisa to back off. The line broke into pieces, creating a mighty commotion. Fortunately Labros noticed the fracas, recognized his comrade and pulled the others off him. As quickly as the brouhaha had started, it ended, and the march resumed its rapid, beleaguered pace.

Eisa, still mystified, joined the line and fell into step with Labros. "What the blazes is going on, cousin? Why's everyone retreating? I mean, why are we heading back into Aeronbed?"

The other panther looked exhausted. "You don't know? Yes, of course, you weren't there ... So where were you, anyway? By all the night's dark forces, what a fiasco!" He glanced behind him briefly, as if trying to recall what had occurred.

"Segomo knows where I was. She arranged —"

"Hah! Poor old Segomo," Labros interjected. After pausing for the briefest of moments, he added wistfully, "The Commander was a lot better than many other officers I've served under."

Stopping cold, Eisa pulled Labros out of the line. A couple of cats bumped into them and were forced to make a detour, greatly annoyed and muttering dark curses. The rest kept marching along without a glance.

"What are you saying?" Eisa demanded.

"You don't know anything, do you," the other replied.

"If I did I wouldn't be asking you."

"Look, we've got to keep going," Labros said urgently. He tried to rejoin the line, but Eisa held on to him tightly, his sharp claws gripping the other's shoulder.

"What's happening?" Eisa growled, tightening his grip. "Tell me!"

Before Labros could reply, another, rougher voice interceded. "What are you two yapping about? Get back into — Oh, it's you, Labros. And who's this?" It was clearly a senior officer, one Eisa did not recognize.

Labros said nothing but glanced toward his comrade. "Lieutenant Eisa, sir."

"Who the blazes are you?"

"It's a long story, sir. Segomo knows all about it. If I could just find her, I — "

He stopped and changed tack. "I have to report to the Commander, now that I'm back. I've an important message for her."

"Back? Where've you been, Lieutenant?"

"I'm sorry, sir, I can only tell Segomo."

"Well, Lieutenant, that could take a while, since the Captain's no longer with us."

"I don't understand, sir. No longer with us? Where's she gone?"

The officer stared at Eisa as if he were dealing with a dolt, while Labros looked on blankly. "Segomo's dead, Lieutenant."

Eisa still couldn't comprehend. He shuddered visibly. "Dead?"

"Deader than yesterday's dinner, if you'll pardon the expression."

"How did it happen?"

"You've no idea what's been going on, do you," the perplexed officer said. "How long have you been absent, Lieutenant?"

"Three days, sir. Well, three days and a bit."

"Three days! How the blazes did you get permission for such a lengthy leave in the middle of a campaign?"

"As I said, it's a long story. Segomo knew everything. And Geifu too; he can explain my situation as well."

"Ah, well, poor Geifu has gone the way of Segomo. Only Labros and a couple of others are left out of the entire company. Lucky to get out by the skin of their teeth, they were."

Eisa couldn't believe his ears. He could barely stand up; he could not speak. The panther was still holding on to Labros, but by now it was for support.

"Look, Lieutenant, we'll deal with you later. Fall back in line with Labros and we'll sort out things back at base camp. We've no time to hang about here."

Eisa did as he was told. Dazed by the shock, he marched alongside the others, trying to come to terms with the situation. Clearly the Legion had suffered a major setback. How could such a disaster have happened? Weren't the panthers the best-trained and toughest fighting force of all creatures? Were not the bears a mere rabble, hardly worth fighting, even for amusement's sake? He couldn't make sense of it.

It suddenly struck Eisa that, if he had not gone to meet Rithild, he too would be "deader than yesterday's dinner." It occurred to him to ask Labros — likely the only eyewitness — what had happened. "I don't get it. How could the bears have inflicted such a defeat? It's just not possible."

At first Labros was reluctant to relive an experience that had caused him great shame and distress. Although it took the panther a while to start speaking, when he finally did open his mouth, the tale came pouring out.

"Sometimes I think it would have been kinder of the gods of war to let me die alongside the others." Labros looked skyward and cursed his fate. "We were completely fooled, like bloody amateurs. I was fortunate — if you can call it that — because two of our blokes were lame, limping pretty badly. I was at the back of the line with both of 'em, pushing and prodding them to keep up.

"The entire company was scouting along a narrow trail up in the mountains, above what used to be the bears' main camp. So we were quite spread out. On our right was a sheer rock face with a high ridge above it, and on our left a nasty drop down to a river. All of a sudden, like, the front of the line spotted four or five smallish bears ahead of them. The bears see us and take off like scared rabbits. So we take off too, closing ranks as we speed up.

"You realize we hadn't even spotted a miserable ferret, let alone a bear. So everyone's pretty worked up about finally catching sight of the blasted creatures. There's no holding us back: we give chase like hot coals are tied to our tails. Except my two, of course; they can't move too fast. Between you and me, I figured that by the time anyone at the end of the line got there, there'd be nothing left to do. Or see, for that matter.

"So I figure, *What's the rush?* We get along as we should, but not nearly as fast as the others. The path begins to widen and the whole company begins to bunch up. The front squad's gaining quickly on the bears, followed right behind by all the rest. Everyone's blood is up — we can taste 'em now. But all of a sudden, like, the bears disappear round a bend in the trail and then — whoa, it's like the whole bloody mountainside was moving.

"In actual fact, it was. Because I'm so far back I can see what the others can't. I can see the rocks come tumbling down from above. I stop dead in my tracks and let out a howl so loud I bet you could hear it back in Manaris. But it's no use — it's already too late. I could see way far ahead, to the front. I spot Segomo looking up to see what the commotion is. She's taller than the rest, and I could see from her expression she knew she'd had it.

"Down over the ridge above comes half the blasted mountainside. I swear it's true, Lieutenant. Huge rocks come tumbling down over the entire company. Those who aren't flattened right there on the spot are swept over the side, down into the river below, before half of them knew what hit them.

"I watched our whole company fall, legs flailing, screaming, roaring and crying, trying to grab onto something, anything. But there was nothing they could do, nothing anyone could do. Draco, Geifu, Segomo — everyone. It was a massacre, and the bears didn't have to come within a hundred yards of us. It was brilliant — bloody brilliant. It's only 'cause of my two hobbling mates that I'm still alive. Hah! I guess the bears couldn't be bothered to wait for us to catch up with the others before unloading — "

Labros stopped briefly, as if reliving the moment in his mind. He shook his head. "It was unbelievable. We just stood there, watching in horror. I could see some bears on top of the ridge above, so I know exactly what happened. It was no accident, no natural cause, I tell you. I know they did it.

"Next thing I know, some of those brutes are pointing in our direction. Believe you me, the three of us didn't wait around for a second look. We're off like there's no tomorrow, because if they catch us, we know what's coming. You can well imagine any sore legs were forgotten pretty darn quick. We never moved so fast. Did they follow after us? I've no idea. We ran all the way back to camp. Never looked back, not once. Only to find out when we got there that it weren't just us.

"There were two other such attacks. No one fared as bad as our company, but it was a rout across the board. And the bears got away scot-free. A bloody massacre! Can you imagine the humiliation? What a shambles. That's why I say it would've been better to go over the side with the rest of them. I expect Parthanyx is bloody furious about what's happened. Heads will roll, except he'll find no heads left." Labros laughed bitterly at that little witticism and said no more.

Eisa shuddered at the very thought of what had occurred. So much for the invincibility of the Black Legion! What would Parthanyx do now? Regroup and go back in, he expected, but this time more carefully and deliberately. After all, it was only a couple of battles lost, not the whole war. Doubtless this foray was only the beginning; the next phase would likely be much nastier.

Eisa was dismayed by the reversal and saddened at the loss of so many of his new comrades. Like all the other members of the Legion, he would need to give the bears' strategic capabilities much greater respect. However, he took comfort in thinking that the setback might serve to slow down or even forestall Parthanyx's larger ambitions regarding Aeronbed itself.

With mixed emotions he marched along with the others until they reached their original encampment near Heimborn's gates. The cats were in a state of utter exhaustion. Eisa and the few other remnants of Segomo's company were folded into Hildric's unit. All were stood down to lick their wounds and rest up while the commanders met to determine their next steps.

23

EISA IS CALLED TO ACCOUNT

Early the next day, Eisa was called before a board of inquiry to investigate his questionable absence from the field of battle. The board, made up of senior commanders, was headed by Heimdell, and Hildric and Samirxun were its two other members. A few additional panthers were present to witness the event, which was held in a makeshift court set up some distance from the Legion's encampment. Eisa assumed the process would just be a formality, providing him with an opportunity to explain himself again and to advise the trio about what Lord Rithild had told him: that they now had support in Manaris for whatever they were about to do.

Eisa sat alone in front of the panel as Heimdell solemnly called the inquiry to order. "Lieutenant Eisa, you are accused of dereliction of duty and treason," she declared without any preamble. "How do you plead?"

Eisa could not believe what he was hearing. Were these cats out of their minds? "Commander, there must be some mistake. I can explain everything — "

"This is not the time to make speeches, Lieutenant," Heimdell continued severely. "It's your opportunity to make a plea. You have two choices: guilty or not guilty."

"But Commander — "

"Guilty or not guilty, Lieutenant. That's all I need to know."

Eisa was inclined to protest further or simply refuse to make a plea, but in the end he concluded that neither option would get him anywhere. Doubtless he would have an opportunity to give his version of the events during the hearing. He took a deep breath. "Not guilty, then."

"The court will take note," Heimdell declared matter-of-factly. "The prisoner pleads not guilty."

Court? Prisoner? thought Eisa. *What's going on here?* He began to rise to all fours and challenge the declaration. "Commander Heimdell, I need to know — " the Lieutenant began, but two guards appeared out of nowhere and forcibly restrained him.

"The prisoner is asked to remain calm and respect the authority of the court during the trial. Any and all evidence will be presented or revealed in due course and at the appropriate moment."

Eisa glanced toward Samirxun, but his old comrade returned the look without expression. When Eisa opened his mouth to make a direct appeal, the other shook his head and looked down at the ground. It was clear that a personal plea would be of no use.

Heimdell went on to inform Eisa that he was being tried under the authority of the local command of the Black Legion and charged with having betrayed his fellow soldiers, Segomo's company in particular. He was accused of secretly advising the rebel forces about the Legion's plans and specific movements in pursuit of the bears. Further, at an opportune moment he had surreptitiously left the field of battle and provided himself with a false alibi, only to return when the awful deed — the sneak attack on the company — had been executed.

Eisa's story — that Segomo had known of and given leave for his meeting with Rithild — was deemed by Heimdell to be "highly convenient" and "most improbable." Since the only witnesses who could vouch for him, Segomo and Geifu, were now dead, his tale could not be verified. Further, Eisa could not prove he had met with Lord Rithild, and the court was not prepared to wait until the Baron was contacted to prove his claim. The administration of justice in the Black Legion, it appeared, valued speed over getting to the truth.

Ultimately Eisa could bring no one else to speak in his defense. Labros was the only remaining member of the company who knew him, and their relationship had been minimal, to say the least. Labros could only attest to the Lieutenant's unexpected arrival some days prior to the move into Heimborn, his disappearance a couple of days before the bears' attack, and the curious nature of his return after the defeat — hiding in the bushes beside the trail. The cat could not say whether Eisa had been privy to Segomo's specific plans before he'd left, nor could he explain why he'd been absent. Finally, knowing so little of Eisa, he could not vouch for his character in any fashion.

Eisa's "excuse," as it was called — that his absence to meet with Rithild had been approved by his commander — was also seen to be suspect. He tried to give the same explanation for his reappearance in the territory that he'd first used with Segomo, but that story seemed pretty thin to every listener. Even to Eisa it sounded implausible. Either way, it appeared that the panther was a spy for someone. Thus the Lieutenant had no one to speak for him, no real opportunity to plead his case, no means to refute the accusations and no freedom to ask for time to investigate matters further.

On the other side of the fence, the evidence against him was pretty circumstantial and (at least to Eisa) equally meager. No one could prove he hadn't been away without a reasonable explanation, no motive for his "betrayal" was provided, and it appeared that he had missed the virtual destruction of his entire company by one of those lucky breaks in life. No more witnesses were called; they were all dead, in any event. Only Labros and his two comrades remained, and they could add no clues or evidence to flesh out the record.

However, as the painful day went on, it became clear to Eisa that the board's mind had been made up long before the trial began. The Legion, it appeared, required a scapegoat, someone on whom the humiliation could be blamed, thus permitting the stain of defeat to be erased. Eisa was simply the most convenient and most expendable victim. No one would mourn his loss, at least in that part of the world. Were the accusation and trial Parthanyx's doing? Eisa would never know, and it didn't really matter anyway.

In the end, the court's decision was unanimous. Eisa was found guilty of treason and was sentenced to death. The execution would be carried out the following day. His attempt to communicate Rithild's message — that Parthanyx and his followers had well-placed friends and supporters back at Manaris — was listened to with undisguised boredom, if not disbelief. Eisa was granted no opportunity to appeal the decision, and, with little ceremony, several tough guards abruptly led the panther away.

Eisa, too stunned by the suddenness of this turn of events to protest further, was imprisoned overnight in a roughly improvised jail. Left alone to await his fate, the distressed panther lay on the bare dirt floor of his cell, thinking about how things might have been, had he made other choices in his brief life.

☙❧

AT THE PRECISE MOMENT WHEN THE LIEUTENANT WAS BEING ESCORTED TO his makeshift prison, Olwen was hastening toward the meeting place Eisa had chosen for them. The lioness had met with Rithild the day before, some way along the principal route joining the capital of Aeronbed with the gates of Heimborn. The Baron had taken pains to describe the trail she must follow and as much as he was prepared to reveal about the situation in Heimborn, regarding both the bears and the Black Legion. Those revelations were far from the whole truth as Rithild knew it; they were, in fact, just enough to suit his purposes and no more. Of course, much more had happened since Rithild's last reunion with Eisa, so the Baron's bank of information was now far from full. In other words, over the days to come, Olwen would have a lot more to discover about many variables — discoveries that would change her life forever.

The Princess was unfamiliar with the territory, but she moved quickly and confidently, and by nightfall she was approaching the spot Eisa had marked out for their meeting. The lioness had arrived earlier than needed: the scheduled meeting was still a few days away. However, Olwen wanted plenty of time to explore the immediate terrain and neighboring lands. She took pride in not depending on any other creature for her survival and success. Other routes, safe exits and hiding places could well be necessary, some of which the lioness might reveal to Eisa and some she might just keep to herself. The future was ever uncertain, and her military training had taught the cat to be prepared for as many eventualities as possible. Having witnessed the importance of advance planning on the northern front, the Princess had taken a vow never to be caught unawares.

As a lioness, Olwen had a natural suspicion of panthers. They were, of course, related, but that relationship didn't make the bond any closer. She'd had little to do with these cats in her life so far, naturally preferring the company of her fellow lions. In addition, she'd taken an immediate dislike to Lord Rithild. The Princess had found his efforts to be ingratiating rather suspicious, and in her assessment afterward she concluded that the panther had hardly been forthcoming with his debriefing and accompanying advice. Assuming that any lieutenant of the Baron's must be of a similar nature, she was not looking forward to her first encounter with Eisa.

Despite her reservations, Olwen had not pressed the Baron on any outstanding points. Far better, she felt, to start afresh; far better to make her own assessment of the reality in Heimborn; far better to start with a clean slate than work through another's lies and deceptions. Although her father had provided a little information on the situation before she met Rithild, his guidance had been limited and vague. King Albiorix was either keeping his own counsel or his knowledge of what was going on had become severely limited. In sum, the lioness carried little with her but her own skills and quick mind. Nevertheless, her father's pronouncements about the prophecy and her role in the future of Aeronbed weighed heavily in the back of her mind.

After her arrival, Olwen worked to improve the hiding place Eisa had discovered. On the following days she scouted about until she felt at ease in this neck of the woods. It did not take long for the Princess to discover that she found the mountain reaches delightful, the fragrance of the early morning and the chill evening air much to her liking. She even began to venture into Heimborn itself, exploring for ways in and out of that territory that might not previously have been discovered.

24

NO WAY OUT

Over the course of his night in captivity, Eisa began to shake off the torpor that had felled his normal energetic spirit. When first incarcerated, he had given up hope, accepting his dire predicament. The Lieutenant viewed death as not just a release from his misery but perhaps also a noble and fitting end, leading to a place where he could join his recently killed brethren. Eventually, however, a deep anger took hold of the cat — anger at Parthanyx, anger at the injustice of his situation, anger at the slanderous charges brought against him (not forgetting the ensuing punishment).

Eisa's only question was who deserved the most blame. Rithild, for pushing him into this precarious situation and then abandoning him? Parthanyx, for starting the insane campaign? The bears, for murdering his comrades? Or was it the three judges who had chosen to end his life with so little concern? Whomever his fury was directed against, it did serve one goal: it motivated him, riling him up to do something about his quandary.

Although Eisa had given himself up for lost, now he began to wonder whether that fate was really so certain. He was not yet a carcass; while he breathed, he still had hope. Was there some way of escape just waiting to be discovered? The Lieutenant had not tested how secure the prison was, and in his initial daze he'd also failed to pay attention to how well guarded he was. Now that his eyes were accustomed to the dark interior, Eisa took a closer look at the structure in which he was being held.

It was a plain one-room wooden hut with only one way in and out. It was not finely crafted, but sturdy beams at each corner supported the entire structure. His eyes and nose told him there'd been no recent occupants; evidently the Legion had had few captives to worry about. If so, the panther figured, the guards would probably be inexperienced at keeping watch.

The walls looked sturdy enough. Eisa tried pressing against them; they flexed but did not break. He sized up the space: rectangular, with the locked door in the middle of one end. A small sliding panel high up on the door permitted someone to look in on the prisoner. The hut had a pitched roof, surprisingly high for such a small, mean structure. He could make out supporting rafters that indicated the quality of the building. If necessary, he could easily jump up to investigate.

Did the prison walls have any weak points? Repeating his earlier efforts, Eisa tried each panel in turn, pushing with all his might. None gave way sufficiently to give him any hope of breaking through. He found a small window high up in the wall opposite the door, but it was too small to wedge his body through. The panther drew himself up on two legs as tall as he could to look out. He could see stars in the night sky, the shadowy black tips of the trees on the surrounding mountain slopes, but, alas, nothing that could help his escape.

The earthen floor was unfinished. Could he dig deep enough to squeeze under one of the walls? But the compacted dirt was as hard and dense as a piece of granite. Eisa scratched at the most likely spot. Yes, he could make progress, but a single night would not offer enough time to dig a tunnel big enough for a well-muscled panther. Was a compromise approach possible? Could he pull away the base of the wall, half digging away the earth, half ripping at the wall with his teeth and claws, until he'd made a large enough opening? And, more important, could he do so without making any noise? How quiet did he need to be?

Eisa listened carefully, hardly daring to breathe. He could hear the sounds of the night: chattering crickets, frogs, a few evening thrushes, some buzzing insects. He could even make out the distant murmur of running water. That last observation surprised him, for he'd failed to notice any river or stream as he was being led away. Of course, his mind had been distracted by other matters.

As for his fellow panthers, their whereabouts remained a mystery. Were they patrolling some way off or were they simply asleep? He could hear no snoring, heavy breathing or other such noises that sleeping animals make. It was as if he'd been left completely alone. Perhaps the guards were making regular rounds, coming and going at intervals; if so, the patrols were spaced far enough apart that he hadn't yet remarked upon one. Or possibly, if the jail was so rarely used, his captors saw little need to guard it closely.

Eisa began to pace back and forth, judging the distance. Again he stopped to listen. No new sounds met his ears. Suddenly the panther broke into a fast run and took a flying leap against the far wall. Inside the hut, the resulting *crunch* was deafening. But, as before, the wall gave only a little; it certainly did not break. Eisa held perfectly still to see if his action had roused anyone. Several moments passed but he heard no outcry raised and no one came to check. A good sign, Eisa concluded; his effort had failed, but definitely no sentries were posted nearby.

So, which option to choose? Continue to batter against the wall or attempt to carve out a hole big enough for a breakout? Or was there yet a third option, one he had not yet worked out?

Eisa decided it would be faster to batter at the wall, so he took another run and leap at it. Again it bent, giving a little, but did not break. He squeezed himself against the opposite wall to maximize the running distance and took another charge. This time, as he leapt, Eisa thought he heard voices outside. He stopped himself in midair, veering to one side and landing with a thud in an embarrassing tangle just in front of the wall. He stayed huddled against the wall, holding his breath.

The voices were getting closer but stayed on the far side of the hut. It was two panthers, but he did not recognize either one. Eisa pricked up his ears and listened closely.

"Remind me, cousin, who are we waiting for?" The cat's voice was rough and low.

"Words fail me, Estrog. Surely you remember." The other panther had adopted a slightly superior attitude, his tone smooth and silky.

Silence ensued.

"It's Todog, you idiot," the second cat continued. "We're waiting for Todog."

"Take it easy, Vlad," responded the first. "They only put together this watch tonight. I've never met the sergeant before. I don't even know what the cat looks like."

"Well, I have. He looks a bit like that ugly sod Heimdell. Could even be her younger brother."

"And why are we waiting for him?"

"You're hopeless, you are. Todog's supposed to give us our orders."

"Like what?"

"How should I know? If I knew, we wouldn't need to wait for him, would we."

"Guess you're right at that."

The other panther sighed deeply. A pause followed, during which all Eisa could hear was the cats panting lightly.

"What do you think about this — " the first cat began.

"Quiet, you fool! These are secret matters. Even the forest has ears."

"Come on, Vlad, there's no one here but him, and he'll be dead by morning."

"It's not our place to express any opinions."

"Still ... "

A further silence followed, broken only by the sounds of wind gusting through the treetops. After a while Eisa could hear footsteps padding along from the other side of the jail. They crossed over to where the other two cats were standing.

"Who's there?" Estrog challenged.

"Todog," replied a gruff voice.

"Evening, Sergeant," the other two said in unison.

"I could hear you two idiots halfway up the valley. Have you never heard of keeping quiet?"

"Sorry, Sergeant, we — " Estrog began.

"Never mind, I don't want to hear your feeble excuses."

Vlad, however, responded more courageously, even attempting a bit of sarcasm as he tried to move the subject to safer ground. "Excuse me, Todog, we've been waiting for you so long we're growing stumps for legs. Where've you been all this time?"

Todog, however, was not to be drawn out. "Never you mind. If I'm late, you can assume there's a good reason for it. So let's get down to business. All quiet inside?"

"Not a peep out of the Lieutenant. Quieter than a sleeping cub."

"Good. Let's keep it that way."

Silence ensued again, broken only by increasingly strong gusts of wind that tossed the uppermost tree branches against their neighbors.

"Here's what you need to know," Todog continued. "We're moving out at first light tomorrow."

"Of course," Estrog said. "Back into Heimborn."

"No, you fool. Let me finish, why don't you. We're going the other way."

"The other way?"

"Toward Manaris."

"I don't understand."

"Between you and me, Corporal, it doesn't really matter whether you do or not. Just make sure that, once the Lieutenant's execution is done with, you start marching in the right direction. Otherwise you two will find yourselves all alone — surrounded by a few thousand bears! Ha ha ha!"

"Come on, Sergeant, what's going on?" Vlad said. "That makes no sense."

Todog heaved a long sigh. "Look, isn't it obvious? How you two misfits were chosen for this assignment, I'll never know. Commander Parthanyx, in his great wisdom, has concluded that our friend here is but one example of a whole host of miserable stooges and traitors."

"But he's one of us," Estrog dared to argue.

"Don't make me laugh. He might have been once, but not anymore. The Grand Council sent the Lieutenant here to sabotage the Legion. The traitor was betraying us to the bears. The *bears*, of all animals! Can you believe it? Can a panther sink so low? Parthanyx figures there may be — hah! probably are — plenty more where he came from back in Manaris. So we'd better put a halt to it right here and now. Otherwise we'll never know who we can trust. We can't afford to be stabbed in the back again. Right, comrades?"

Todog didn't bother waiting for the other two to concur. He kept right on talking. "So it's the root itself we're going after now, not the measly branches. It's time to move on Manaris. About bloody time, if you ask me. The sooner we get it done and take control, the better."

"Amen to that," Vlad responded.

"Now, don't forget, bringing about this death sentence was not an easy matter. And putting it into effect will not go down well with every cat. Our friend here is not unknown in the ranks, and not unloved. He's also well connected back at Manaris. So it's better for you — better for all concerned — that no one knows who carries out the actual deed. Got it? You should take the Lieutenant out before first light, when no one can see or hear you. And afterwards, keep your mouths shut about your part in it. This is not something to boast about."

"Yes, Sergeant," the two cats said.

"Fortunately our Lieutenant Eisa seems to have already given up the fight. All the easier for us. You know where to take him and you know what to do. No one must ever find the body."

After that last, chilling piece of guidance, Eisa heard only indistinct mutterings. The trio moved out of earshot and then dispersed. The Lieutenant was left with much to ponder, and little time to determine what he must do next.

25

OUT OF THE FRYING PAN

Eisa lay awake, contemplating what he'd heard. Everything had changed: the terrorizing of Heimborn had been put on hold and the march on Aeronbed's capital was about to begin. And here he was, a captive unable to provide any warning to his chief, Baron Rithild.

Instinctively the cat's thoughts had turned to his superiors back in Manaris, for it was with the existing regime that his first loyalty truly lay. Ironically, since he cared less about his own predicament, Eisa had to force himself to focus on his own immediate needs and rethink his plans of escape. The panther now knew how much — or rather how little — time he had. His execution was imminent. It would come even before the first shafts of dawn had a chance to light upon him; he'd never get to enjoy the sublime warmth of one more precious sunrise.

The big cat shook his head, trying to clear out the cobwebs and discordant thoughts. What hour was it? Eisa had no idea, having completely lost track of time. He needed to hurry if he wanted to make good his escape. That was all that mattered.

Although Eisa had no idea where he would be taken and how the deed would be done, he'd learned something about the two sentries who'd been ordered to carry out the execution. In sum, they weren't the most careful, diligent or brightest of soldiers the panther had come

across. Perhaps they were just competent enough to obey the order —
and well placed to end up as scapegoats. Could he convince the pair
they were mere pawns to be dispensed with later, and thus outwit
them?

Could he bribe them? But what could he offer except vague open-
ended promises of reward? If he had the gift of sufficient time, Eisa felt
that his ability to spin a yarn would be enough to do the trick. But the
panther doubted he'd see or hear the guards again until the moment
they came for him. It would be too brief an opportunity, he judged, to
talk his way out of a death sentence.

Nevertheless, if the guards remained out of earshot, he'd be free to
carry on with his rather noisier escape efforts. Better, Eisa concluded,
not to leave matters to the last moment. He went back to his half-
scratching, half-digging at the spot where the earthen floor met the
wooden wall. Every now and then he would stop and listen to
determine if anyone had noticed. Fortunately, no other creature stirred,
and he was able to pursue his labors unchecked. Unfortunately, his
valiant attempts produced little by way of results; the ground was as
hard and rocky as he had first taken it to be, and the walls stouter than
he had hoped. After much work and time spent, Eisa knew he would
never get through to the outside world by dawn. No, not by dawn —
before dawn, he reminded himself.

Frustrated, a furious Eisa again threw himself at the wall. Once
more the panel gave a little but did not break. The only tangible results
were a sore shoulder, a loud squeak from above and a voice from
far off.

"Did you hear that?" Estrog asked, yawning as if coming out of a
deep sleep.

His companion yawned too. "What? No. Didn't hear a blessed
thing. Hmpf, must have dozed off."

"You're useless. Sometimes I wonder — "

"Give it a rest. It's been a tough few days. You know it has."

"Aye, you're right about that. Sorry for being so hard on you. Still,
perhaps one of us should investigate."

"Well, go on if you want to. I'll just wait here." Vlad yawned
again.

"You're such a lazy sod," Estrog groused. "I do all the heavy lifting around here."

Silence ensued while neither of the panthers spoke. Eventually the sound of snoring revealed that one of them had gone back to sleep.

Finally Estrog declared, more to himself than his partner, "By all the stars above, words fail me. Okay, I'll go take a look. Lazy, good for nothing ... "

Eisa held his breath as he heard the soft padding of feet coming his way. The steps went all around the prison cell, finally stopping at the place where he'd been digging. Although Eisa heard Estrog nosing around, some desultory scratching and grunts, ultimately the panther didn't linger long. The cat seemed curious but clearly too tired or unconcerned to worry much about his discovery.

Finally Estrog retraced his steps back to their starting point. "Don't see anything out of the ordinary," he called out. "We don't have much longer to wait in any event."

Vlad, evidently barely awake, just grunted in reply.

Time was indeed running out. Digging was clearly not going to work. Eisa lay down and tried to think logically. A wave of exhaustion washed over him. The Lieutenant had been awake a long time now. The efforts of constant reflection and trying to escape were taking a toll; his energy was beginning to fade. No, the panther told himself, no time to rest; he must keep at it.

Eisa remembered the squeak he'd heard above him. In the darkness he could see nothing except the indistinct outline of the exposed beams supporting the roof structure. With a single easy bound, the panther leapt up unto one of them. It was wide enough to hold him — just. He jumped from beam to beam until he reached the far wall, just above the doorway. As Eisa looked down, it occurred to him that, squeezed right up against the wall as he was, if subject to nothing more than a quick glance he might remain hidden from view.

An idea came to him. He searched among the rafters until he found one that could be worked loose. Grabbing one in his mighty jaws, he pulled and pried until it gave way. The long piece of wood was not too heavy, but when it gave way, the panther could not keep his balance. With a heavy thud, both he and the joist fell to the ground. Although

Eisa's breath was knocked out of him, he tarried only a second before jumping back to his feet. He dragged the beam over to near the door and, with an immense effort, leapt up with it onto the closest rafter.

By carefully placing the pieces of timber side by side, the panther greatly increased his cover. Once that feat was accomplished, Eisa went back to the spot where he had tried to dig the hole and worked to make it appear that he had succeeded in getting through to freedom. Scratching, biting, gnawing and pulling, he made as big a mess as possible. Although to his eyes the result looked pretty lame, it might just convince two dimwitted guards operating in the dark and under a time pressure.

Now all Eisa needed was plenty of luck, combined with gullibility from his captors. While the panther waited, he tried to superimpose his mind onto theirs. What would they be thinking? How might they react when they found him gone? The minutes that had ticked by too quickly only moments ago were now moving far too slowly for the panther's liking. "Come on, let's get it over with," Eisa said half a loud. Adrenalin was the only thing keeping him awake, pushing him on now.

At last he heard his two executioners approaching. Neither panther said a word. Doubtless the significance of the deed was beginning to weigh upon them as much as the reality weighed upon Eisa. Perhaps the two cats were even more tense and nervous than he was.

It was likely the pair had never before been ordered to carry out an act like this — the killing of one of their own. It couldn't have been a welcome assignment. Had they simply been ordered to do the deed or had they been promised a generous reward for volunteering? Perhaps they were, after all, simply villainous cutthroats, happy to carry out the sentence. As these thoughts flooded his mind, Eisa tried to concentrate on what he had to do and the moves he had to make. It would all depend on how the pair reacted.

Finally the two guards were at the door and beginning the process of unlocking it.

"Pretty quiet in there, Vlad," Estrog said. "Do you suppose he's still asleep?"

"By the stars above, what a stupid question! How should I know, eh? Maybe the Lieutenant's killed himself and spared us the bother."

"Now don't start on me. I was just asking."

"Well, if our friend's catnapping, we'll wake him up soon enough."

Eisa heard another bolt being shoved open.

"I'll wait out here," Vlad continued. "You go in and fetch the poor sod."

"Me? Why not you?"

"You're not scared of him, are you? You tied him up before we locked him inside. What can he do to you?"

"What? I thought you tied him up."

"Are you telling me you left the prisoner untied? By all the stars, I should whack you one right on your thick head!"

"Hold on, Vlad. I'm no more to blame than you are."

"All right, all right, let's calm down. He couldn't get out anyway, no matter what. Still, one of us had better stay outside — just in case. Better I stay. Call me if you need any help. Go on."

Holding his breath, Eisa heard complaints, curses and finally acquiescence from Estrog in response to this one-sided proposal. The final locks were unlocked and the bolts unbolted. At first Estrog pulled open the slat in the door to peer inside. Not seeing anything, the panther began to pry open the door ever so slowly, peering in through the increasing crack as he did so. Eisa pressed himself with all his might into the wall, leaving no space even for a stray hair.

"Can't see anything," Estrog muttered, pulling his head out and looking back toward Vlad.

"Well, perhaps he's at the back end. Or around the corner. Go inside, then."

"I will, I will. Quit harping about it." He tiptoed inside, glancing about in every direction. "He's not here!" the astonished panther cried.

"This is no time for jokes, Estrog," Vlad said, still safely outside.

"I'm not joking. Look for yourself."

"What the blazes? No way I'm going inside! And there's no way the Lieutenant's escaped. Didn't you just check the cell not so long ago?"

"Of course I did. If you don't believe me, take a look for yourself."

Now Vlad's head appeared in the doorway. " What the — ? I don't bloody believe this."

"Look at the wall opposite," Estrog said. "Someone's been having a go at it. What do you think?"

Eisa was hoping the two panthers would set off in search of him, leaving him free to slink out unnoticed, or enter further into the cell to investigate. In the latter case, he'd jump down behind them and escape out the door before they'd grasped what was going on. Given half a chance, he'd even lock them in. If one did happen to glance up and spot him, he'd attack, hoping to dispatch that cat before the other could enter the fray. Then he'd turn his attention to the second guard. At that point at least the fight would be more equal.

However, only Estrog went over to examine Eisa's efforts. Vlad continued to wait safely by the door. Still, neither panther bothered to look up.

"I don't know," Estrog said finally, coming back to Vlad. "Maybe the Lieutenant got out that way, but I don't think so. He'd have to squeeze himself down to the size of a bloody ferret to get through. The whole thing beats me."

"Well, no good waiting around here trying to figure it out. We'd best start looking for the villain. At least he can't have gone far. By all the stars, there's going to be hell to pay when the Sergeant finds out."

The pair moved outside. "Yeah, but I sure don't want to be the one to tell Todog. What do you think? Should we sound the alarm?"

"Not just yet. We need time to get a bead on his escape route. It must start from the other end of the hut."

"This whole thing doesn't make sense. Something's not right."

"Whatever, let's split up. You head west and I'll go south. If we find nothing, meet you back here in ten. Call out if you catch his scent."

"Right."

Then the two cats were off on their hunt and Eisa heard nothing more. After a few minutes he leapt down as quietly as he could. The panther knew he had to move fast; his jailors would be back soon enough.

Ever so carefully, Eisa nosed his way past the open door. Then he was outside and just beginning to experience the welcome taste of freedom and the sensation of the cool night air, when he felt two strong sets of claws on his shoulders.

"Do you take us for fools, Lieutenant?" Vlad cried out in triumph.

"Yeah, who'd ever fall for such a simple trick?" echoed Estrog, chortling.

Eisa slumped down, crestfallen, and Estrog and Vlad relaxed their grip just a little. That was enough for Eisa's purposes — he jumped up quickly, grabbed the two surprised guards and threw them against each other. Their heads crashed hard together and the cats fell down, stunned. Eisa didn't hesitate this time. He was off like a thunderbolt toward the closest line of trees.

It took the guards a few moments to regain their senses, but then they took off in hot pursuit. All three cats were moving fast. Eisa, however, was running for his life, while the other two had to figure out how best to give chase and whether to call for reinforcements. Their resulting hesitation lost them precious moments.

However, it was not long before the Legion's hue and cry began in earnest.

❧ 26 ❧

FINDING SANCTUARY

E isa didn't know the region as well as his pursuers, who had been stationed in that stretch of Aeronbed for years. On top of that, his pursuers could bring in reinforcements to pick up his trail and they could fan out in many directions, cutting the panther off from potential escape routes.

It had occurred to the Lieutenant to head for the meeting place he'd arranged with Rithild, if only because he knew that area a little better than other parts, and that it held at least one satisfactory hiding spot. If all went really well, he could hole up there until the pursuit was given up and things had cooled down.

However, at the moment, all was not going really well. His old comrades — now his enemies — were on the hunt, following his scent, and despite his best efforts to shake the pursuit, they were closing in. Eisa could now hear his pursuers as they gained ground on him; he dared not stop to rest for a single minute.

The panther tried every trick he could think of. He backtracked up icy streams until his feet froze, climbed trees until he was dizzy from the height, ventured out onto rocky precipices and jumped over wide chasms. His pursuers, however, were not fooled and did not let up; they carried on after him as if they had no choice. Eisa had guessed the

Legion would not take his escape lying down, but he marveled at their stubborn determination to finish what they'd started. Nevertheless, after so many hours, Eisa was still alive. He'd seen another sunrise after all, and then another day and a second sunrise after that.

Soon enough the panther would be getting close to the meeting place. Eisa took extra precautions to mislead the pursuit. Then at last he found the spot and, taking special care to disguise his entry point, dove headfirst into the longed-for sanctuary. He burrowed down as best he could and then turned around to set up a vantage point from which he could catch sight of any pursuers.

Eisa panted heavily, exhausted and footsore. The panther had not eaten or slept in three days, and he had drunk only a little water to sustain himself during his getaway. From around his neck he removed the blood-red gemstone his father had given him as a talisman, so many years ago, and hid it deeply in a recess of the burrow. He'd leave it there for safekeeping should he have to run off again. However, beyond that single act, the panther was not prepared to break his vigilance.

Statue-like, he focused his attention entirely on the world outside, watching for intruders and listening for any unusual sounds. Although Eisa felt safer than he had for two whole days, something still seemed amiss. His instincts told him to be wary, but exhaustion had numbed his senses.

It was now mid-afternoon. The weather had turned warm during his flight to freedom, but his underground hiding place remained refreshingly cool. The sun was beginning to descend behind the not-so-distant mountains. Eisa could hear the hunt continuing, his pursuers calling out to each other, but so far his former comrades were merely circling around him, not getting any nearer.

His entire body ached and he desperately wanted to shut his eyes, but whatever was troubling his thoughts also served to keep him alert. Finally that same nagging doubt told Eisa to turn his head and look behind him. The hairs rose on his back — had he really seen a pair of golden eyes staring back at him?

He could not be certain. Perhaps he was so exhausted that he was imagining things. But yes, there was a definite scent — unfamiliar yet familiar. Eisa snarled; he could not help himself. Suddenly he heard his name being called very quietly, almost like a gentle purr.

"Eisa, is that you?"

It came from behind him. Despite the need to keep a low profile, he immediately jumped up and turned to face the rear of the burrow. But it did not help; whoever was present remained hidden. An unseen enemy or a friend?

"Sit down. You'll give us away." The disembodied voice was calm and quiet, but it also had an air of authority.

The panther did as he was told. "Who is this?" Eisa hissed. "And where are you?"

"It's Olwen," the voice replied. "Lord Rithild told you I'd meet you here, did he not?"

Eisa was relieved but still perplexed. "Yes, he did. But why can't I see you?"

"Crawl straight forward four steps, very slowly and carefully. Then stop in your tracks."

He followed her command to the letter.

"Now look a bit to the right. Do you see a small hole in the rock face? Head toward it. You'll think it's impossibly small, but you can squeeze through. I could, so I know you can. When you get through, you'll find a short passageway leading to a proper lair. Follow it. You'll find me soon enough. I'm waiting for you inside."

The hole was minuscule. He doubted that any creature could have found it without guidance, let alone gained entry through it. But the lioness was right; he was able to contort his body through the opening, just barely. As instructed, he crawled down the narrow passage and found Olwen in a rough den that was well stocked with provisions.

"Are you hungry?" the lioness asked simply.

He was hungrier than he'd ever known. Olwen offered him what appeared to be a substantial feast, and he wasted no time. The lioness waited patiently while he ripped, gulped, chewed and swallowed. Every now and then she would turn her head to look through the tiny peephole from which she could see the entire meeting place.

"You picked an excellent spot," she said at one point. "It just needed some fine-tuning. I was wise to show up early enough to finish it off." Olwen went on to explain about her premature arrival and subsequent scouting around. The lioness had clearly not wasted the opportunity. "Something told me things were not going as planned. And then I sensed it might be even worse than I'd guessed. So I lay in wait, figuring this was the most logical place you'd come to, since we did have a rendezvous planned." Olwen smiled enigmatically.

Eisa, despite his misgivings, could not help but be both impressed and grateful. The panther started to speak, but she silenced him. "I believe they've picked up your scent again — I can hear a great deal of commotion not far away. Doubtless you can sense it too. We should hunker down. I imagine you need to sleep. I've had an easy few days here, so I'll stand guard. You rest now. We'll speak later."

Eisa didn't need to be asked twice; he was utterly bushed. Now, with his stomach full for the first time in several days, fatigue quickly overtook him. He was grateful for the help and felt secure enough to let his guard down; within minutes, the panther was fast asleep.

❧

WHEN EISA AWOKE MANY HOURS LATER, THE LIONESS SILENCED HIM WITH the slightest of signals. Very quietly she hissed, "They're all around us now. I'll assume these panthers are no longer your friends. They know you've been here, but they can't figure out what happened to you, and they can't find us inside here. I've taken extra precautions to make sure no one can get in."

The panther started to speak but she silenced him with a paw on the shoulder. "Better not to talk now," she whispered. "There's quite a party of them outside."

For several more hours they said nothing. While Eisa slept off and on, his pursuers hunted around vainly outside their secret lair, went away, came back perplexed, went away again and then returned one more time. Finally they gave up completely and went on to search elsewhere, in greener pastures.

Finally the two cats felt secure enough to talk freely. By this time Eisa had recovered from his ordeal and begun to learn about his new companion. Olwen was indeed very young, but only in years. Eisa understood right away that the lioness was self-assured, self-reliant and no fool. She was also far more experienced than most lions of her years; certainly she'd had far more exposure to combat than he'd ever had. Although Olwen was not one of his kind, Eisa found himself being irresistibly drawn to her. Of course, the Lieutenant already owed his life to the lioness, but respect and attraction quickly followed.

For Olwen, however, things were not so clear-cut. While the lioness still had no idea what was going on in Heimborn and elsewhere, she'd already noted that events had marched along much faster than anyone would have thought possible, and certainly not in a way she or her father could have predicted. Naturally Olwen had expected to meet up with Eisa, but not in such circumstances. But here he was, and on the run not from the bears but from his fellow panthers. Olwen felt greatly confused and not quite sure what to make of her new companion.

Eisa explained in detail what had occurred over the past several days. Olwen was horrified by the slaughter of the panther companies and appropriately sympathetic when she heard how Eisa had been blamed for it. Unlike Rithild, his lieutenant was honest and forthright. The panther held nothing back — what would be the point? It was far too late for dissembling now; Eisa needed a friend badly, and the lioness was the only potential ally around.

When Olwen heard about the Legion's decision to march on Manaris, she was furious. Eisa's news threatened the end of Aeronbed, at least as she knew it. Her thoughts quickly turned to the threat to her father and Temorwig. The Princess wasn't sure whom she was more enraged with, Eisa or the rest of the traitorous panthers. Her second thoughts, however, went to the prophecy. But she wasn't prepared to share that story with the panther just yet.

"Why didn't you tell me earlier?" Olwen's tail lashed furiously. "We have to warn Manaris! We have to get word to the King. Right away!"

"I tried to explain but you told me not to speak. And then you told me to get some rest. What was I to do?"

"You should have told me anyway!"

"With that hunting party ranging about outside?" Eisa retorted. "You would have gone out to face that nest of vipers? You against the whole lot of them? They're not playing games, you know. You may be a lion, Olwen, but they'd have cut you to pieces. Both of us would be dead by now. We've survived only by keeping quiet — exactly as you suggested."

"But ... " she began. Her voice trailed off as Olwen realized that Eisa was correct. Even if she had known his dreadful news right away, they'd been prisoners of their own making. "How many days' head start have your cousins had?" the lioness asked.

"My guess is two to three. Maybe four, depending on when they started, how long I've been on the run and how long I've slept. Except for my pursuers, I assume the bulk of the Legion started off toward Manaris immediately."

Olwen could have roared with frustration. If Eisa's guess was right (it sounded logical enough), the panthers would already be in the capital and taking charge. With all Aeronbed's lion forces in the north, Manaris would be largely undefended, open to an easy conquest. Unless, of course, her father was as well informed as he claimed to be. Even so, how many troops would Albiorix be able to call upon on such short notice?

And now there the two of them sat, isolated in a no-longer friendly world: Eisa facing a death sentence and she the daughter of a soon-to-be (or already) overthrown monarch. Both outcasts, they would be on the run from the new overlords of Aeronbed. The very thought of it was almost too much to bear.

Yet Olwen had great faith in her father. Could Albiorix possibly have triumphed against the odds? The King would not give way easily, she knew that; he was strong and courageous. She still had hope and faith to guide her, but how could she find out what had happened? What to do next was the most immediate question facing her. Could she find a safe way back to the capital to find out? Or should she make for safer terrain, where no one could find her? And if she chose the latter option, where would she find such a place now?

And what of Eisa? Olwen's eyes turned to the dispirited-looking panther. Eisa was not of her kind, and she knew very little about him except that he was Rithild's lieutenant. Could he help her? Would he help her? What were his plans for the days to come? Olwen was full of doubts and fears, and Eisa was all she had to offer support. They had been thrown together by the fates, and that fact alone meant something to her. But could she really trust the panther? Where did his loyalties truly lie, to Aeronbed or to his own kind? Was her future now to be bound up with his? Would they end up facing the world united, or separately and at odds?

❦ V ❦
BLAKFEL

27

AN EMISSARY FOR VIGMAR

Old Man Winter was lingering on in Blakfel. The brief glimpse of spring some weeks earlier had created hope in its inhabitants, but ultimately it had proved to be only a frustrating peekaboo glimpse. The howling winds, driving sleet and ice-covered streets returned with a vengeance to torment the creatures huddled within the walls of the capital.

Everyone declared they'd never seen anything like it. With Fridis banished, there were no amusing spectacles or uplifting performances to lighten the mood or break the monotony, but no one complained publicly. Who would dare take the risk? It would only draw attention to the complainant, and anyway, it wouldn't help — or so everyone said. Behind closed doors, however, many did ask one another what had happened. Why had the duck been so precipitously exiled? Few satisfying answers were to be found, in or out of doors.

The only good thing to be said in defense of the foul weather was that it had delayed the spring campaign against Aeronbed. Potential grieving mothers, fathers and spouses were thus grateful for the small mercy.

The Emperor lingered as well, his condition neither improving nor deteriorating. This generated both praise and condemnation for the doctor — praise by some for keeping him alive and condemnation by others for failing to heal him. Many, hoping against hope that recovery was still a possibility, welcomed the donkey's amazing ability to survive. Others viewed the situation only as a source of stagnation and instability. They felt that Don Grimezel's death, however distressing the prospect might be, might potentially clear the air, allowing for some movement among the dynastic factions. At least life would be moving forward rather than going in circles, or so they claimed.

The war planning went on. What else could the generals do? It was their job, after all. All were committed to winning the long-standing struggle against Aeronbed. Further conquests or holding on to recent gains were the only plausible goals that anyone put forward.

The astute Empress realized she still had work to do to consolidate her tenuous position. Loyal favorites or those who were most pliable had to be moved into higher positions. Critics and enemies had to be replaced and dispatched as far away as possible, either to the regions or the front lines. However, Dona Morana saw no point in winning the political battle only to lose the military one. Since good generals were important, she was limited in some of her potential moves. The imperial donkey had to put up with leaving in place some future rivals and promoting others who would never deign to be true allies but were too popular and competent to be ignored.

The Empress had been delighted by her successful banishment of Fridis. At long last she had found a way to remove her chief rival, a bird whom she would never deign to call princess, let alone duchess. Although the naive might see only an innocent and harmless duck, the Empress knew better. She could see through the wily bird's elaborate pretense.

The throne of Vigmar was too great a prize for the ambitious to resist. The Empress had witnessed the duck's rise in popularity and constant attempts to connect with her subjects. To the donkey's way of thinking, no one with an inkling of political guile could doubt that Fridis would make a move against her sooner or later. The threat had to be nipped in the bud, and Dona Morana had the stomach for such calculating moves. Far better to remove the Countess from the scene while she still had the power to do so. For once, Gloton had deserved the rare praise she heaped upon him: the wolverine had found a way to get Fridis to leave Blakfel willingly, even happily, opening the door for the Empress's unopposed masterstroke.

Fridis's departure did generate a few questions, but no opposition, violent or otherwise, had resulted. Only a few members of the capital's medical team — they had come to rely on the duck's healing powers — dared say anything. Naturally none had the nerve to make a single direct comment to Dona Morana. Even if they had, she would have cared little about such whining. With Fridis's aid, their life had been getting too comfortable and they'd been getting lazy. From now on they would have to buckle down and earn their keep.

Lucky Gloton was rewarded with a baronetcy, a lavish estate in the country and resources of his own. The red fox Vulpé, the wolverine's loyal agent, was promoted and given the title Grand Inquisitor. He was now responsible for Vigmar's security, reporting directly to the Empress. Gloton hadn't welcomed the appointment, having sought the position for himself, but he knew better than to object. The Empress, of course, was wise enough to avoid concentrating too much authority with any one functionary. Such power, she knew, could easily go to a creature's head. And a head, once swelled by prestige and a sense of entitlement, might one day need to be removed. Dona Morana could not afford to lose the wolverine — at least, not yet.

To an impartial outsider, the fact that the Emperor's uncertain state of health failed to bother the Empress might seem curious at best and repellent at worst. However, from her standpoint, Dona Morana was now able to do whatever she liked in both their names, and no opponent or underling could question her decisions. Don Grimezel's illness was a small price to pay. Besides the Empress, only the owl Seanan was permitted to see him. Given the Emperor's pitiful state, only she could claim to communicate with him, interpreting his indecipherable mutterings and vague sighs in any way she wished. It was, Dona Morana considered, almost too good to be true.

If Grimezel were to die, however, everything would change. Dona Morana was, like any stalwart monarch, determined to be ready for every eventuality. She had one more brilliant move to make, one that would secure the throne from all potential usurpers and win the war against Aeronbed in one fell swoop. It was not without its risks, but only a ruler with true imagination could even conceive the idea, let alone bring about its successful execution. But who among her many pawns and knights could be trusted to successfully carry out her bold gambit? And who was also expendable, should things go wrong?

After much thought, the Empress called for Vulpé. The fox arrived in the throne room and stood before her, crouching down and keeping as far away as he could while still making his low growl heard, thereby appearing both fearful and unctuous at the same time. The Empress began to have misgivings. Was Vulpé really the crafty, wily creature she needed? Was he capable of completing the task she had in mind?

Gloton had at least proven his worth time and time again. But the wolverine had (for both good and bad reasons) become too important to Dona Morana; she could not afford his extended absence from the capital. Contemplating her dilemma, the Empress realized she needed to groom some additional sycophants and hirelings. That job, however, could wait.

"Come closer," Dona Morana called out to the fox. "I don't want to have to yell."

Vulpé did as she bid, practically crawling his way toward her. The Empress rolled her eyes toward the heavens, her unease increasing. *What a vile creature he is*, she thought, and then wondered, *What made Gloton pick this strange fellow?*

When the fox managed to reach an appropriate spot, the imperious donkey sighed audibly and muttered something under her breath. Then, stamping a hoof, she ordered loudly, "All right, Vulpé, enough! That's far enough."

He stopped and bowed low again, which was difficult because the fox was already nearly as close to the floor as an animal could get.

"Vulpé!" the Empress brayed suddenly.

The fox yelped and leapt into the air. Catching his breath, he stammered, "Your Highness, I'm sorry, you caught me by surprise."

"Tell me again," Dona Morana asked. "What is it you did for our friend Baron Gloton?" The donkey almost snickered at the wolverine's new title; the idea of the First Secretary as a baron was truly laughable. However, she managed to restrain the impulse.

"It's better you don't know the details, Highness," Vulpé replied carefully. The fox was clearly a quick study. He had learned that useful response from the wolverine.

"All right, never mind. I don't really want to know." Idly waving one foreleg in the air, Dona Morana paused to consider her next salvo.

The fox, meanwhile, looked searchingly into her face. "How can I be of service to you, Highness?" he blurted out.

"That's a question I hope to hear from every creature who crosses my path or enters my humble abode." She smiled broadly, showing her teeth, at this fanciful remark.

"I am here to serve," the fox continued, bowing again, not quite so deeply as before. Feeling more confident in the donkey's presence, Vulpé had begun to relax.

"Don't push it. I get the point," the Empress countered, quickly destroying his newly upbeat mood.

Deciding silence would be the most appropriate virtue to display at that point in the conversation, the fox nodded meekly.

Dona Morana thought she'd better launch into the point of the meeting. "You've been well rewarded by us, have you not."

That remark set Vulpé's whiskers aquiver. Clearly the Empress was about to ask for something particularly difficult or say something particularly demeaning — or both at the same time. "It is true, Majesty, you have favored me greatly," the fox observed prudently. "Equally, I trust I have met your expectations."

"So far, Vulpé, so far."

As he did not reply, she carried on. "But now I'm going to task you with the most important commission ever given to any of the Empire's humble servants. Nothing in the annals of time will ever come close to touching it. Are you up to the challenge, Vulpé?"

The fox swallowed hard, thinking quickly. Would it be dangerous, painful, unachievable? Possibly all three together? Was it time for him to stand up straight, appear both resolute and agreeable, and accept the commission? Or should he point a paw at the next creature in line? As he'd learned from Gloton, it was always a guessing game with the Empress. At least, Vulpé thought with relief, she wasn't insulting him

— at least, not yet. His mouth dry, as he croaked out an unintelligible response.

"What did you say?" the donkey asked, holding a graceful hoof by one cocked ear. "Perhaps I'm getting a trifle deaf in my later years."

"Highness," the fox managed to utter, his valor now overcoming his caution, "I hope I shall rise to meet whatever expectations you have and accomplish whatever test is placed before me."

"Well, well, Vulpé, a fine response indeed. If all our subjects had answered thus, this blasted war would have been over and done with years ago, when I was but a mere foal."

The delighted fox raised himself to his full height and bowed low again.

"Have you ever been to Aeronbed?"

The question was totally unexpected. Vulpé cringed visibly. "*The* Aeronbed, Your Majesty?"

"Is there more than one such country?" Dona Morana responded caustically. "Does your sense of geography fail you?"

"Of course not, Highness. Only one Aeronbed exists, as far as I know. I regret to say I have never visited that unhappy realm," Vulpé said. "But, Majesty, are we not at war with Aeronbed? How could I possibly have gone there?" He hoped this reply might save him from what he supposed would inevitably come next. It was a vain hope.

"We have not always been engaged in pitched battles. The war was suspended from time to time, and some creatures did go back and forth between empire and kingdom, notwithstanding the precarious situation," Dona Morana replied.

"No one I know of, I'm sorry to say."

"Well, that's a great pity, because, Vulpé, you're going to Manaris. On my behalf, that is — as my personal emissary. So you'd better find someone to take you there, or at very least show you a route that's safe enough to allow you to return in one piece."

She was not asking; the Empress had already chosen him. His fate was sealed. The fox hoped the commission would not turn out to be an omen of doom. "Can you tell me more, Highness?" he asked politely. "What exactly do you wish me to do, and with whom am I to parley?"

What Vulpé really wanted to say was: *But, Dona Morana, what you're demanding means certain death! These two nations are at each other's throats; creatures are slaughtering each other on every field of battle; neither side is seeking, let alone willing, to talk now. The whole idea is crazy!* He was wise enough to know that such a reply would be not only fruitless but met with scornful derision, so the fox resolved to put on a brave front. At the same time, however, he continued to hope against hope that possibly, just possibly, when she answered his questions and revealed the relevant details, the scheme would fall to pieces — as surely it must. Then he would never have to actually execute it.

"Vulpé, you surprise and please me," Dona Morana was saying. "This is the kind of positive and practical response I seek from my councilors but receive so very rarely. I shall have to mention your impressive demeanor to our friend Gloton."

"Your Highness is too kind." He rose up and bowed again, rather pleased with himself. It was a rare day one received a compliment from the Empress, let alone two of them.

"Listen well to what I have in mind. And as you listen, Vulpé, remember that the line between enemy and friend is not always clearly drawn. More to the point, they do not always remain static."

As Dona Morana went on to explain her scheme, Vulpé nodded carefully, still not quite sure what she had meant by that last observation. The more the fox listened, the more horrified he became. At the same time, he could see the brilliance of the donkey's mind at work. What the Empress intended to pull off was incredibly audacious, but it was so unexpected it might actually work. Perhaps, the fox considered, that was what distinguished rulers from the ruled: the ability to think up the most outrageous ideas and will them into reality.

The problem was that it would now be up to him to make the scheme come to pass. Vulpé had never done anything close to what Dona Morana envisaged. His life had amounted to small, grubby deeds done quietly and efficiently in dark alleyways. This plan was on another scale, far beyond his ken. At first he could not conceive of accomplishing it, but the more Vulpé listened to the Empress, the more logical his choosing seemed to be. Dona Morana had asked *him* to do this, and she would not have done so unless she had faith in him.

The fox was fleet of foot and quick of mind. Possibly, just possibly, he could pull it off. His confidence began to grow and his anxieties to recede. He started thinking about the hurdles over which he'd have to leap. But then Vulpé remembered he'd never even been close to Aeronbed. Who could show him the way?

The fox interrupted her speech flow. "Your Highness, I still have one major obstacle: getting to and from my destination safely. Let me say again, I've never visited Aeronbed, and I know no one who can be of service to that end."

The Empress paused to think. In truth, she had no ideas. Outside of those in Vigmar's military who had seen action in Aeronbed, the donkey knew of no one, and they certainly could not be involved in her scheme. Indeed, they could not even be told of her plans. "As to that small matter, I cannot help you," Dona Morana said dismissively. "You must find someone on your own. You are our security chief, are you not? You must have flunkies, cutthroats, spies under your sway who can help. Ask around — but I warn you, do so with the greatest care. This matter is of the utmost secrecy. In particular, do not speak to our military cousins. They must not know, not even suspect anything. If any — I repeat, *any* word gets out, it will be your head on a plate."

Vulpé was a quick learner. He already knew there was no point in raising more questions or objections. The fox had thrown in his lot with the Empress, so he had better get on with following his new marching orders as best he could. "When all is in readiness, Your Highness," he said, bowing, "I will report back to you."

"Excellent. As I said before, I wish all my minions were more like you," the Empress replied agreeably, much to the fox's satisfaction.

This third, sort-of compliment, one that reflected Dona Morana's unvarnished thoughts, was an exceedingly rare event. The donkey was beginning to think that Gloton, who was always — in comparison with the obliging Vulpé — so quick to raise objections or concerns, was less than forthcoming in his dealings with her. Nevertheless, the Empress knew fine words did not a cupboard make, and she could not discount the wolverine's record of success. Time would tell: the proof of Vulpé's pudding would be in its eating.might

28

VULPÉ SEEKS HELP

Shortly after he had met with the Empress, the incredible challenge facing Vulpé began to sink in, slowly at first, and then with a rush that left the wily fox gasping for air. Whatever first blush of optimism — possibly even enthusiasm — he possessed had already worn thin, until there was nothing left of either emotion. Once again Vulpé was overcome with doubt and uncertainty. How and where to start? To whom could he turn for advice and help?

Fearing Gloton's ability to glom onto any opportunity and then steal the eventual credit, Vulpé was initially reluctant to call upon the wolverine. But not only did the First Secretary know everyone, he was better placed than any other creature in the Empress's employ to call in a favor or two. So, after some hesitation, the anxious fox bowed to the inevitable.

The fox's appearance in his private chambers took the wolverine by surprise. "What's the matter, Vulpé?" he said. "You look like you've seen a ghost."

"The Empress," croaked the fox. Enough said.

A fleeting expression crossed Gloton's face, as if he'd eaten a very sour pickle. But Vigmar's First Secretary carried on happily enough, apparently in a fabulous mood. "Say no more, my friend. I'm eternally thankful you've come to share the unwelcome duty of interviews with the Empress. My, er, visits have been reduced immeasurably, and as a result, my life has become much calmer, even relaxed. You know what I always say: 'Be careful what you wish for.' Now you are your own creature, no longer beholden to me, what say you, Vulpé?"

"I can only admit your words of advice were perfectly correct. The joy of meeting with the Empress is a mitigated pleasure."

"*Pleasure. Joy.* Now those are two words I wouldn't have used in the same sentence as 'meeting with the Empress.' Ha ha! Nevertheless, good for you for looking on the bright side of things." Gloton laughed heartily while the fox scowled.

"So, what can I do for you today? Some state security problem needing my intervention? Some miserable wretch who requires the promise of a reward? Or, even better, some foe needing to be taken down a peg or two?"

"None of those, I'm afraid," the glum fox replied.

"Well, then, speak up. What is it?"

"The Empress has set me a task unlike any previous assignment. Frankly, I've no idea where to start."

Gloton's interest was quickly piqued. The Empire's most senior bureaucrat liked to know everything that was going on, in every nook and cranny. Information was the key to staying alive and accumulating power, and because of Vulpé's recent appointment, the wolverine had been cut off from many palace secrets and interactions to which he'd previously enjoyed unique access. He needed to stay on top of things to keep one step ahead of his rivals. Now Gloton saw an opportunity to gain a couple of steps and obligate the fox to him in the process. "Tell me everything, my good fellow. Only then can I really help."

Although Vulpé's need was so great that he had been forced to confide in Gloton, the fox was no simpleton. Far from his days as a mere hireling of the First Secretary, he had risen to the heights of power through the good offices of the Empress. He had learned a thing or two on the way up that slippery pole, and he was not about to start sliding down by giving away all his leverage. So the fox told the wolverine just enough to whet the latter's appetite and indicate the nature of his immediate problem, and no more.

Gloton, meanwhile, having played the game for much longer, understood Vulpé's modus operandi for what it was. Although the fox's lack of candor frustrated the wolverine, his admiration for Vulpé only grew. Indeed, he even gave himself credit for the latter's growth in wisdom and wiles. The Baron was prepared to bide his time and join in the sport. No doubt Vulpé would be back again when no other recourse was available.

"You need a guide into Aeronbed, do you? Not an enviable task. No, not at all."

Vulpé merely nodded, his expression one of abject misery.

Gloton's expression implied deep contemplation and deliberation, although he had known the answer all along. Of course, he had to make his choice appear as difficult as possible, in order to increase the fox's resulting obligation. At last he said, "I may have someone for you. But you'll need to leave the matter completely to me. Broaching a subject like this requires a deft and delicate touch. I need not tell you your task is dangerous, even foolhardy; you know that already. The creature I have in mind may take some convincing. However, it so happens you've come to the right individual, for I'm the only one in a position to undertake such a commission — I may have to use some inducements that are at my sole disposal. And even then he will need leave to forgo his duties within the palace. Her Majesty will also have to agree."

"Can you tell me who it is?"

"I will not reveal the individual's name. Not yet, anyway. He might feel the need to refuse and, given his position, I cannot force him."

"If I can help in that regard, just say the word."

"There's nothing you can do, Vulpé. Leave it to me."

"Thank you, Gloton."

"Don't thank me yet. This is going to be a hard nut to crack."

"I have complete confidence in you, First Secretary. And I'll be utterly in your debt."

Yes, you will, thought the wolverine. *And you can be sure I'll never forget your obligation — that is, should you manage to return in one piece.*

Promising to deal with the problem that very day, Gloton escorted the fox out of the castle. Vulpé was left to wonder whom Gloton had in mind, and ruminating upon what else would be required to complete Dona Morana's seemingly impossible quest.

❧

THE CRUEL, RAIN-SOAKED WINDS OF LATE WINTER WERE WHIPPING AROUND the bleak courtyard outside the palace kitchen, creating small but vicious whirlwinds of grit and sleet. The weather made it a painful exercise break for Haidar and Alsvid, forcing the two friends to walk around with their eyes half-closed. Eventually the mountain goat and the pony gave up on their afternoon constitutional to seek shelter inside. There the warm atmosphere generated by the large open fires and simmering pots of hearty food provided a welcome relief.

"Why did we even bother to go outside?" Alsvid said, shaking off the rain. "That's what I'm asking myself."

"We're gluttons for punishment, I suppose," the goat responded, shedding copious amounts of water onto the stone floor.

"Force of habit, rather. But, speaking of punishment, don't forget that Gloton wants to see you later today."

Haidar groaned loudly. "What can that odious creature want from me? I keep trying to come up with a reasonable excuse not to show up. Unfortunately we're not that busy these days, and he knows it."

"Still —"

"There's no *still* about it. The wolverine's the last creature I want to lay eyes on, and I certainly wouldn't bet on hearing good news. You remember the last time he and I met. I cringe just thinking about it."

"You don't know for sure. Perhaps it's nothing more than a palace dinner being planned. Perhaps the unexpected arrival of some foreign dignitary."

"Of course that's always possible. But the First Secretary doesn't need a one-on-one meeting to inform the kitchen of state occasions." The mountain goat groaned again. "Ahh! I suppose I'll just have to grit my teeth and make the best of it. He can't be avoided or denied in the end. He'd just ask the Empress to order me to go."

"You might learn something of value, something that'll serve the cause."

"I love your optimism, Alsvid. I certainly do."

⚸

"H<small>AIDAR, MY GOOD FELLOW</small>," <small>EXCLAIMED</small> G<small>LOTON, JUMPING UP FROM HIS</small> comfortable seat to welcome the mountain goat.

The Baron's finely appointed chambers were illuminated by several candles at this late hour of the day. Haidar, who had not entered the private domain since Guntram's departure, now so many months ago, glanced round to see what changes the wolverine might have made. *My good fellow,* the goat thought. *That's rich. He must want something awfully badly. The Baron will see soon enough that I've got nothing for him.* However, he only nodded solemnly by way of reply.

Gloton carried on in a similar vein. "I do appreciate your making the time to see me. Sit down, sit down. I know we haven't spoken recently, but let me tell you, I've heard much praise of your fine work this past winter."

Although the goat was suspicious, like any creature he welcomed a compliment. "Thank you," he said carefully. "It's always satisfying to hear that my efforts are well-regarded." Haidar took a seat in a plump armchair the wolverine had generously pushed into place near the fire. Sitting down in the presence of the First Secretary was unusual, to say the least, and the goat's antennae immediately rose.

Remaining standing, Gloton paused as if not quite sure how to proceed. He began to amble awkwardly about the room as Haidar followed his movements with his eyes. Finally the wolverine stopped directly in front of the goat.

"What I have to say to you is most important," Gloton declared. "Indeed, it's of crucial importance to Vigmar's future. You may well be surprised at some of the things I have to reveal today. Just remember this: appearances can be deceiving, and all things have their backstage aspects. Do you understand me?"

Haidar understood the distinction probably better than any other creature in Blakfel. Still, surprised by Gloton's words and tone, all he said in reply was, "I do."

"Excellent. Then let us begin." After pausing briefly, the wolverine said, "First, I want to tell you that the news concerning Countess — I mean, Grand Duchess Fridis has caused me no end of concern. Not only was her, er, involuntary withdrawal from Vigmar most uncalled for, it was also most unfortunate. It pains me to admit that I was unable to convince Her Imperial Highness that her decision was, let us say, intemperate."

Haidar tried to make sense of the First Secretary's carefully chosen words.

Gloton, meanwhile, after a short pause, blurted out, "I'm aware that Fridis was a particular friend of yours, so I wanted you to know where I stand on this matter."

How did he know that? thought Haidar. *Of course. Fridis and I never tried to keep our meetings secret, and I imagine Gloton has spies everywhere.* Suspecting the wolverine was trying to worm out of him some compromising admission, the mountain goat responded as vaguely as possible. "I had the pleasure of meeting the Duchess a few times. Fridis was most obliging, and she particularly liked my cooking. Naturally that was the principal basis of our relationship."

"I remain hopeful that the Empress may change her mind one day," Gloton carried on, showing no interest in Haidar's response, "and Fridis will be able to take up her rightful place in Blakfel once more."

"Indeed." With that, the goat clamped his mouth shut.

Seeing that Haidar was not about to let down his guard, Gloton realized there was little to be gained in continuing in that vein. He decided to jump right into the matter of the day. "All that is by the by, however. Let me turn to the reason for our meeting. I know I can rely on you for complete discretion. What I'm going to speak about is something that must remain between the two of us. No one else must ever hear a word of it. Can I rely on you, Haidar?"

The goat's nod was almost imperceptible. Although Gloton was tempted to ask again, just to make sure Haidar had heard him, he decided to carry on. "The truth is, I need your help. For a great cause. And not just me — the Empire needs your help!"

This last declaration took Haidar completely by surprise. Not being sure how to respond, he simply nodded again.

"Some of us in Blakfel — I cannot name the others, but if I did you'd recognize many of those involved — have been concerned about the current state of affairs."

"Current state of affairs," repeated the goat.

"The relationship between Vigmar and Aeronbed, the direction in which the Empire is heading — or, to be more precise, not heading. My good fellow, I know you are a loyal and faithful servant of Her Majesty. I am not suggesting anything improper by telling you this." The wolverine paused dramatically and then added, "The point is, the conflict with Aeronbed has dragged on far too long, and some of us have come to believe that an alternative solution to the war must be found. There, I've said it. There's no getting around the fact."

Gloton stopped to see if the mountain goat had taken in the import of this amazing assertion. Haidar, for his part, was feeling unnerved by the First Secretary's unexpected revelation. What the wolverine was suggesting was a reflection of his own deeply held views and, more than anything, he wanted to agree wholeheartedly with it. However, being deeply suspicious of Gloton and convinced the wolverine was trying to trap him into saying something treasonous, he couldn't bring himself to respond nearly as enthusiastically as he would have wished.

Had Gloton stationed a third party — a witness hidden from view — to listen in on their conversation? The goat peered into the corners of the room; it was a good-sized apartment, and he, more than most creatures in Blakfel, knew that plenty of eavesdropping opportunities existed in the castle. Perhaps he'd misjudged Gloton. Had the wolverine been playing a game all along, using his rank and his loathsome appearance to deceive even the Emperor and Empress? Was the wolverine actually on the same side as Haidar?

In the end, the mountain goat decided the safest course of action was to ask another question. "Why are you telling me this?"

"I understand your hesitation, really I do," Gloton answered in a light-hearted fashion. In truth, he could not help but admire the goat's forbearance. "Under the circumstances it's most understandable. You barely know me, and it's always wise to be careful. But have no fear. Come, look around."

The wolverine escorted the goat around the room, into every nook and cranny, even opening the door to the hallway outside to assure his guest that he was not under surveillance.

When Haidar was satisfied and had sat down again, Gloton moved his own chair closer, so the two could speak in absolute confidence. "To answer your question, I'm telling you this because, as I said earlier, I need your help. There may be others in Blakfel with your knowledge, but if there are, I know them not. I understand that you are the only current resident of the capital who has traveled to Aeronbed and returned. Now, don't be alarmed — it's not a treasonous matter and this is not an accusation. On the contrary, in this instance it's turned out to be a valuable, maybe even crucial asset. The reality is, because of the long-standing war with Aeronbed, few — outside of our military forces, of course — have ever traveled across the border and returned safely. More than that, I don't know of anyone who has had actual contact with the big cats."

Haidar jumped out of his chair, almost taking off the wolverine's head in the process, and stumbled over to the nearest wall. He was too shocked to speak. How had Gloton come by this knowledge? If Haidar had been unnerved before, now he was certain he'd be arrested any minute. Better, he decided, to say nothing at all and get out while he could. That is, if he was still able to leave.

"Don't worry, don't worry," the wolverine declared, waving his paws about in what he took to be a soothing fashion. "I keep telling you, you've nothing to fear from me. You and I, we're on the same side. If my words ring true with you, it's a welcome confirmation for me. Because then, Haidar, you're in a position to help us — to help Vigmar — bring this long and costly struggle to an end."

The anxious goat looked at the wolverine for a few moments. Neither spoke. Then Haidar sat down again. If Gloton was telling the truth, he could not afford to pass up the opportunity.

Nevertheless, the goat did not want to lose his head through carelessness. "Let's say — only for the sake of conjecture, mind you — that I travelled to Aeronbed and met someone, long ago and in a period of relative peace. What then?" he asked cautiously.

"Then I would say you are the very creature for us."

"And why is that?"

"Because you know how to get into and out of Aeronbed safely and without being noticed. But more than that, you know someone on the other side of the mountains with whom Vigmar can start a dialogue."

Although no mission could have come closer to Haidar's deepest wishes, Gloton was the last creature (apart from Dona Morana) the mountain goat would have expected to express such thoughts. The stunned chef was both perplexed and thrilled. He squirmed in his seat, literally not knowing which way to turn. Was Gloton presenting him with an opportunity too good to let slip, or was it a trap?

Once again the wary mountain goat tried to tread the thinnest of lines. "Tell me more," he requested.

Although to Haidar his response seemed perfectly neutral, at that point Gloton knew he had him. The rest would involve only further massaging, stroking and encouraging. The cat was in the bag, so to speak. The wolverine went on to explain what he could, putting a positive spin on the enterprise. But he did not minimize the dangers, for he knew that the mountain goat, who was brave and committed enough for several animals, would be thrilled by a daring undertaking.

Gloton did not know the whole story about Haidar's father, but he knew plenty. And he knew that the son was proud enough to want to set things right and restore the family's good name. Haidar was also a true believer, an ideologue rather than a practical creature, one who could be manipulated into sacrificing himself for a just cause. He'd be the perfect naive dupe and companion for the cynical Vulpé.

29

AN UNWELCOME WELCOME

"Welcome back, Air Marshal," Aravat exclaimed cheerfully as he spotted the new arrival. "We've missed you around the table, have we not, colleagues?" A chorus of assenting voices sprang up from every corner of the packed room.

Aeron-Urd, however, not in a particularly jovial mood that night, paid them little heed. The great gyrfalcon had already been infuriated, if not horrified, by Dona Morana's decision to forbid Fridis from returning to Vigmar (he couldn't bring himself to say *exiled*). Now, back in Blakfel from the outer reaches of Arundati after several hard days' flying against strong headwinds, he was bone tired and feeling ill-tempered. Learning that the meeting of generals was already in progress, the bird had not stopped to eat or drink upon arriving at the castle. Rather, the Air Marshal had made his way directly to the war room.

Aeron-Urd, his sour expression saying more than words could convey, headed directly toward Aravat. He tried to pull aside the elephant as discreetly as he could, but it was not an easy task, given the circumstances and their size difference. After a couple of failed attempts, the gyrfalcon was finally forced to yank up Aravat's ear with a wing and declare, "General, we need to speak. Now, and in private."

The elephant was put out by the bird's lack of deference. "Can't you see we're in the middle of planning the spring offensive?" His tone was severe, and loud enough for some of those nearby to overhear. "We've been at it for several days now, Air Marshal. And though we haven't benefited from your contributions, somehow we've managed. But now we must get on with things. Your arrival is most timely, in fact; your input is required at this very juncture."

The gyrfalcon scowled. His fierce gaze surveyed the assembly, as if ready to attack at the slightest insult.

Aravat, meanwhile, having received no satisfactory response, carried on, more forcefully now. "Right now, as it happens. Any other matter between us will have to wait."

But Aeron-Urd would not be denied. "General, this is urgent. I need to talk about — "

"Air Marshal," Aravat interrupted sharply, waving his trunk aloft, "the only subject I'm prepared to discuss right now is the forthcoming campaign. That is our only urgent issue. If Vigmar's troop movements in the months to come are the subject of your inquiry, that's all well and good. Everyone around this table will be eager to hear your words of wisdom. Anything else, however, will have to wait."

The elephant glowered even more fiercely than the gyrfalcon, which was quite a feat. "Frankly, Air Marshal, we've been most indulgent about your little holiday for these past few weeks. I've been trying to remain good-humored about the whole thing — so far. The fact is, you're late to the war table, which is inexcusable, given the circumstances. I'm prepared to overlook it for the present, but not for much longer."

The room was deathly quiet. Acrimony between old comrades had become rare since the departure of the apes. Some at the table were looking at the floor or their hoofs, paws or talons, their discomfort evident, while others turned to watch the two generals with increasing curiosity or disquiet.

Aeron-Urd, almost speechless with fury now, would not let the matter drop. "I will not be spoken to in this manner. Who do you take me for?"

"I take you for a creature that has verged on neglect of duty, Aeron-

Urd. I won't hazard a guess as to what excuse you might have, but your ill-judged behavior stops here. Am I understood?"

The gyrfalcon, close to boiling over with rage, was on the verge of stalking off, but some inner voice told him to calm down. He clamped his beak down hard, turned away from Aravat and walked over to the table. He rested against it, staring off into the distance but seeing nothing. Clearly the situation in Blakfel had changed during his brief absence, and not for the better.

Things were indeed different. The cast of characters around the war table of the previous summer had changed markedly. Of course a few were the same, such as those from the Army of the North who were able to attend during the winter stand-down: Nashorn, Grishon and Dorkal. The wolf pack, however, stuck in the wilds of Aeronbed, was not represented. The eagle Rad-Alya, an old friend, had disappeared without a trace, and the whereabouts of Emer-Sigr and Harclan, commanders of the Army of the South, were still unknown. The traitor Don Baaldulce had vanished. And most important of all, with the loss of Lord Eirwen, Aravat had assumed overall command. Among the new representatives, the gyrfalcon knew only An-Mot, the golden eagle who had replaced Rad-Alya. Later he was to be introduced to Vulpé, Vigmar's new head of security. Where had that strange little red fox come from? The turnover was both extraordinary and dismaying.

While Aeron-Urd was pondering these major changes, Aravat had brought the meeting back to order. The elephant was in the process of summing up the state of affairs and the generals' progress over the past two days. Although the recap was really for Aeron-Urd's behalf, the gyrfalcon was barely listening. Still steaming inwardly, he was thinking about Fridis.

The discussion began anew. Aeron-Urd heard other voices chime in, but he paid them little heed. In front of him lay a huge map of the continent, and on it the positions of the various armies were laid out, at least as far as they could be ascertained this far away from the front lines. Instinctively the gyrfalcon began to refocus his energies, studying the map in earnest.

Suddenly Aeron-Urd noticed the room had gone quiet. Everyone was now staring pointedly at him. Evidently they were expecting him to say something, but what had they been talking about? He glanced around. "My apologies, generals. It was a long and arduous flight. I have not rested or supped in two days, but came here directly I landed. I am not my usual self."

This apology seemed to mollify the others; the bird saw a few appreciative nods. They had all been through the wars, and they knew what it was like to be hurt or dog-tired.

Still, Aeron-Urd felt he should add something substantive to the discussion. "You have evidently turned to me for some of my usual brilliant and incisive comments," the gyrfalcon said with a small smile. "I may be exhausted, but I will make an observation, one that I trust will prove timely.

"You will recall the now justifiably famous incident when one of my squadrons caught up with the two messengers from Adarix's wolf pack. Even though my officers had been instructed to keep a talons-off approach while they were scouting about, their decisive actions turned out to be instrumental in repelling the enemy's attack, both land and air forces. Those two messengers would never have made it back alive without that timely intervention.

"I don't mean to toot my own horn or boast about their bravery; those involved have already earned sufficient accolades. What I want to emphasize is that a small force operating with surprise and speed completely overwhelmed a much larger army. The immediate result is well known: we learned the location and strength of the wolf pack and can now plan our next moves accordingly. Without that information, we would have been operating in a complete vacuum. As well, in the longer term, the enemy may well have suffered a major blow to its morale and confidence."

"Your point, Air Marshal?" someone asked.

"The point is that, even though that encounter was unforeseen, we were able to inflict a decisive blow upon the enemy forces. Just think what we could accomplish if we planned more combined air and land operations. While we have lost touch with Rad-Alya's forces, my hawk and falcon squadrons are intact, highly trained and ready to go."

Aeron-Urd looked over to An-Mot for support. Seeing no reaction, the gyrfalcon carried on. "Further, we have established forward posts throughout a large part of central Aeronbed. They can coordinate their efforts with Lord Adarix in the months to come. In fact, I can envisage a brand-new way of conducting war in the future — more efficient, more effective, more deadly."

When Aeron-Urd had finished speaking, an uncomfortable silence filled the room. Finally Aravat spoke. "Well said, Air Marshal, as usual. Unfortunately, that was not what we were discussing."

"What?" the surprised gyrfalcon exclaimed. He glanced around the room. Most of the others avoided meeting his eyes.

"We were actually speaking about holding our present positions in the north while sending Adarix south to find Emer-Sigr. Only when that mission has been completed successfully should we return to the offensive. That is my considered opinion."

No one uttered a word. Aeron-Urd suddenly felt overwhelmed by fatigue. The tune was beginning to sound all too familiar: stand pat; maintain defensive positions; take no risks. He tried to imagine what Lords Eirwen and Adarix would have proposed.

"I don't believe — " he began to say, then stopped. There seemed little point in making an objection. No point at all, in fact. Aeron-Urd was too tired to take up the argument that night, and maybe ever after.

The others were staring at him like vultures watching a dying buffalo.

"Well, my friends," the great gyrfalcon said with a wan smile, "I guess the future will just have to wait a little while longer."

30

AN INTERVIEW WITH THE
EMPRESS

T he next day, after a brief sleep that only partly restored his sense of well-being, Aeron-Urd went looking for the Empress. He found Vigmar's chief bureaucrat instead, patrolling the corridors of power.

"So it's Baron Gloton now," the gyrfalcon began as he approached the wolverine. "Hah! The last time I saw you, First Secretary, you were but a mere lord! You are to be congratulated, sir, for your speedy climb to the top rungs of the Empire's slippery ladder."

The wolverine would not take offense. "Thank you, Air Marshal," he said, bowing. "I am ever grateful to the Empress for her generosity. That she saw fit to reward me for my humble services goes beyond words. Indeed, what more can I say?"

"I guess not very much at that, First Secretary."

"How can I be of service to you, Aeron-Urd?"

"I won't beat about the bush — I need to speak to Her Majesty. Unless the Emperor has, by the grace of all that's good in this world, recovered sufficiently to speak with one of his old commanders."

"I regret to say that Don Grimezel still remains in the same pitiful state as when you left Blakfel. He sees no one but the Empress. And his doctor, of course." The wolverine shrugged. "It's a mysterious business ... his decline, that is."

"Indeed, and a great tragedy for Vigmar. Still, we must make the best of it. Soldier on, what have you," the falcon said awkwardly.

Gloton nodded soberly.

"That being the case," Aeron-Urd continued, "I would like you to arrange an audience. I need to speak with Dona Morana before we are consumed once again by our war efforts."

"I will need to review Her Majesty's crowded schedule. In the current circumstances with the Emperor's illness, Dona Morana is busier than ever. Can you tell me, my lord, what the purpose is?"

"I would prefer to keep the subject matter confidential. Let's just say it's a private matter, one that requires her — only her — particular attention."

"I'm afraid I must tell you no such matter exists. What concerns Her Highness concerns me as well. If I don't know the reason, the meeting does not occur. It's as simple as that."

What a pompous, interfering Johnny-come-lately! Who does he think he is? Despite his feelings, the gyrfalcon held his anger in check. "Surely matters of great delicacy exist," he said as patiently as possible. "Ones that require such a high degree of discretion that they must be kept from even your privileged ears."

Gloton smiled brightly. "There might have been at one time, but not anymore. The Empress has come to rely upon me totally, in every respect. I advise, I vet, I dispense favors, I protect, I promote ... and so on. You know how it is. In essence, Dona Morana and I are one and the same being."

Although Aeron-Urd tried to imagine such a creature, it turned out to be beyond his creative powers. Feeling increasingly impatient, the gyrfalcon wondered whether the wolverine was bluffing, overstating his authority. The bird decided he would accommodate Gloton, at least to some extent. "As you wish. Advise Her Highness that I want to talk about Grand Duchess Fridis."

"Oh, dear, oh dear. Not Her Majesty's favorite subject, I'm afraid. Unless of course ... Well, you know ... " the wolverine stopped.

Aeron-Urd stared at the wolverine with utter contempt. "I'm afraid I do *not* know," he replied.

"There are always, er, matters the Empress would like to know more about. Certain kinds of information she appreciates receiving, if you grasp my meaning."

"Really? Well, then, explain to Her Highness that I have some valuable advice and *information* about the Duchess. For her ears only."

"In that case, Air Marshal, I'd say you're in luck." Unrolling a parchment he was carrying with him, the wolverine peered closely at it. "Yes, I'm certain we can move some things aside and fit you in. Leave it with me. You'll get word later today, one way or the other."

After pausing for a brief moment, the wolverine went on. "If you'll allow me to provide you a bit of guidance, I'm only a humble public servant but I've benefited from spending many hours observing Her Majesty. I can tell you, whatever you're after in your meeting, if you want any hope of success, focus far more on the information and less on the advice. The Empress does not take kindly to unsolicited opinions — not at all."

Aeron-Urd stood straight and proud before the Empress. Dona Morana, decked out in fine clothing and exquisite jewelry, looked particularly regal on her raised throne. The gyrfalcon could not help noticing that Her Majesty now occupied the larger of the two thrones while the other one sat sadly empty on its slightly lower dais. He approached and bowed low.

She waved him in closer with one elegant hoof. "Thank you for coming to see me so soon after your return to Blakfel. I trust your recent journey was profitable, and not too exhausting, I hope." She smiled beatifically.

"On the contrary, Highness, it is I who should be offering thanks — that you found time in your schedule to grant me an audience."

"I always have time to meet with my general staff. They who serve and sacrifice for Vigmar rank above all else. Do they not, Baron?"

Gloton, who was standing a little off to one side, said nothing but smiled carefully and bowed low.

"You may leave us, First Secretary. I wish to speak with the Air Marshal in private."

"As you wish, Majesty," Gloton replied without expression.

As soon as the wolverine had departed, Aeron-Urd approached the throne. He spoke quietly and firmly. "I imagine the First Secretary has explained why I wanted to meet with you."

"Indeed he has. I must tell you I was delighted to hear the news. I welcome such loyalty and candor. Those are rare commodities around here."

"Perhaps you're spending too much time with the wrong crowd," Aeron-Urd replied.

"Hmm, perhaps I am at that. We shall see. In any event, do go on with your story. I'm all ears, Air Marshal."

"I have not come here to plead a case for Duchess Fridis — "

"I hope not," the regal donkey interrupted him. "You wouldn't get very far, Aeron-Urd, I can tell you that right away."

"But, Your Highness, as I came to know Fridis — "

"It was you who rescued the duck from Baaldulce's prison, was it not?" Dona Morana interjected. Her eyes narrowed as she took the opportunity to peer more closely at the gyrfalcon.

"I had that honor, Your Majesty."

"So the duck's bewitched you too."

Aeron-Urd was taken aback. "Highness?"

"Have you or have you not come here to tell me where the Countess is hiding?"

Aeron-Urd, thrown off track by Dona Morana's sudden charge, was not about to be bowled over that easily. "Did you not exile Fridis from Vigmar?"

Normally Dona Morana would never put up with any questioning of her authority. However, she decided this was an opportune moment to promote an appropriate rationale. "Of course I did — in my poor husband's name. It was one of Don Grimezel's last instructions to me before he lapsed into unconsciousness. Naturally I would never have enacted such a delicate matter on my own." The donkey sighed deeply, as if the illness of her husband caused her heart to ache.

"The Emperor can speak, Your Highness?"

"Only to me, only a few words at a time. Don Grimezel remains in guarded condition. However, the subject of his health is by the by. You and I are talking of Lady Fridis, not the Emperor."

"Indeed we are, Your Majesty. I came to ask you — no, to appeal to your devotion and love for Vigmar — to rescind your order of exile. I believe the loss to the Empire has been too great. Fridis was the closest friend and companion of Vigmar's great champion, after all."

"Ex-champion, I'm afraid. The white bear didn't even last a whole year. More's the pity — he showed such promise." The donkey sighed once more.

"I implore you, Dona Morana, think carefully before you spurn my request. I must confess, I simply cannot comprehend why the Duchess was sent away. It makes no sense to me, not at all."

"That is your failing, Aeron-Urd, not a virtue. True understanding is not given to every creature. That is why only one Empress at a time can rule."

"But Fridis's powers of healing and her selfless ministering ... Can you not — "

"You are beginning to bore me, Aeron-Urd. I do not have to explain to you, or to anyone else, for that matter, why and how our decisions are made. You are here for only one reason: to answer my questions. And what I want to know is, where is the Countess?"

Aeron-Urd realized he had nothing to gain by pursuing the matter. "I escorted Lady Fridis to the Misken Mountains. She obtained gems, as had been arranged by Lord, er, Baron Gloton. As we were about to fly back, word came of the decision forbidding her return. As a good and loyal soldier, I left her there and came back directly."

"But where is the duck now?"

"I do not know. I flew with Lady Fridis only to the other side of the mountains, where she could carry on safely to her next destination. From there I returned directly to Blakfel."

"That's it? You did not stop en route?"

"I did, to meet with one of our squadrons on the Vigmar-Arundati border."

"Why?"

"To review their state of war-readiness and revise their orders."

"And you didn't see Fridis again?"

"No. As I've already stated."

"Then tell me one last thing. Where do you think the Countess is now?"

"I have absolutely no idea. I left her sitting on a mountain ledge. As far as I know, Fridis could still be sitting there in that very same spot, or she could have flown off in any direction."

"Where would you have gone if you had been her?" persisted Dona Morana.

"I am not a duck, Your Highness. Therefore I cannot think like a duck. It would be useless, even misleading, for me to speculate."

The donkey leaned back on the throne, contemplating the gyrfalcon for several moments, hoping that the silence might push him into some fateful admission. But it did not. Aeron-Urd remained at attention, unbending, expressionless, giving nothing away.

Finally the Empress dismissed him with a languorous wave of one hoof. "All right, Aeron-Urd, you may go back to your war."

The gyrfalcon, however, did not budge. "One last word before I go, Majesty," he said. "You and Don Grimezel know that I have long been a fearless and loyal servant of Vigmar. I state this in case there is any misunderstanding on your part about the thoughts I've just expressed. I wish to assure you that, when I speak on behalf of the Duchess, I do so with Vigmar's best interests at heart. Nothing else."

For a several more moments the donkey merely looked at him, unblinking, with only the slightest touch of scorn on her lips. But as the gyrfalcon began to take his leave, the donkey stopped him. "Well said, Aeron-Urd — simple and to the point. I will forgive you your impetuous actions and disrespect. In return, let me give you a word of advice. Recognize that you are not privy to everything that goes on around here. Heavy is the head that wears the crown, and heavy is the duty of one who bears so much on behalf of our great empire. Be assured, our decisions are not taken lightly."

Aeron-Urd nodded soberly. He had heard and understood.

"You may go."

Once the Air Marshal had left the throne room, Gloton reappeared as quietly and quickly as he had departed.

"You heard everything?" the Empress asked the wolverine.

"I did."

"Tell me, what kind of soldier is Aeron-Urd?"

"Capable, strong, fearless — just as he describes himself — and a skilled leader of our air defense forces. Also loyal ... well, at least up to now."

"Aeron-Urd knows more than he is saying. Can the bird be bribed? Could he replace Aravat?"

"As to the latter question, yes, he could, easily. However, regarding the former, since he seems to be singularly devoted to Lady Fridis, I'd say we have nothing to offer him."

"Pity. The gyrfalcon is a danger to us. Watch him closely, Gloton. We may yet need to dig some tunnels under our stalwart air marshal."

31

WAR PLANS

Although Aeron-Urd was known as an excellent commander of his own troops, he was also considered to be intemperate, even hot-headed, when dealing with his peers. His behavior since coming back to Blakfel had exhibited new depths of poor judgment — at least, that was how the other generals viewed it. Very quickly the bird had lost former allies and made new enemies where he could ill afford it, and all through his concern for and loyalty to his friend Fridis.

The bird was smart enough to realize he was doing his cause and his own fortunes little good with his self-destructive actions, but he'd begun to care little about such matters. Perhaps Aeron-Urd's position had ceased to hold great importance for him, or possibly his life had become just too complicated and unfathomable. Whatever the case, the gyrfalcon remained ill at ease and unsure as to who to ask for help or guidance.

If the falcon had been normally inclined to seek support, he might have recruited some of his winged colleagues to band together against the regime, for he was by no means alone in his views. However, Aeron-Urd was by nature a solitary creature who did his own thing in his own time, trusting in his own merits and not given to falling back on others for support. Rad-Alya might have been of help, but she and her legions of eagles remained missing in action. As a result, the forces that might have united against Dona Morana remained divided and impotent.

Aeron-Urd was the first to appreciate that on his own he was no match for the Empress. There was nothing he could gain by making further entreaties on behalf of Fridis. Naturally the Air Marshal had not believed the donkey's words. However, since he lacked the power to question Dona Morana's credibility, he was forced to accept her lies. And his oath of loyalty to the regime was not easy to overcome. Thus Aeron-Urd was forced to give up his quest to restore the Grand Duchess to her former status in Blakfel. For the time being he would let the matter lie, hoping that the Emperor would recuperate sooner rather than later. In the meantime, the bird had a war to win, one he could neglect no longer.

The Air Marshal had already ordered Lorcan and Corvus, along with their squadrons, to catch up with Emrin-Can and Amlich (already en route) and to meet up with the rest of the wolf pack and work together with them over the months to come. Now the high command wanted them to move south, not north. Aeron-Urd wondered how those new orders would be received by the wolf pack. Not happily, he thought.

In the meantime, since current operations were being well managed by his field commanders, the gyrfalcon would embark on a new endeavor. He would create and train an entirely new team of hawks, fresh squadrons that would be based nearby. When the spring fighting season began, he told the other generals, the inevitable fatalities would occur and reinforcements would be required. His peers were quick to praise his acumen, but they did not grasp the whole truth — that Aeron-Urd had recognized his reduced status in Vigmar. He could see the day when he'd need additional loyal forces to command. The only question was, against whom would they ultimately be fighting?

EMRIN AND AMLICH, ACCOMPANIED BY THE TWO SQUADRONS COMMANDED by Lorcan and Corvus, had a much easier time returning to the wolf pack's mountaintop retreat. Thanks to the withdrawal of Aeronbed's troops to their winter quarters and the vigilance of the accompanying birds, the wolfhound and the wolf were able to avoid significant encounters with the enemy. Freed from the need to hide and use roundabout routes, they made much better time. The hawks, with their ability to scan great distances and cover more terrain, even found another route back to the wolves' sanctuary. This allowed the pair to avoid the pack of big cats waiting on the other side of the mountaintop — an encounter the two companions were not looking forward to. As a result, Emrin and Amlich were able to sneak back into the wolves' winter lair almost as efficiently as they had left it so many months ago.

By the time they arrived back, winter was on the wane, even in these higher elevations. The army of wolves welcomed their return, as well as the added support from the hawks and falcons, with great enthusiasm. Celebrations were arranged to mark the incredible success of their venture, and the wolves and birds made much of the stories of action and heroics. Despite his initial misgivings about returning, even Emrin was thrilled to be back and at the center of these tales of courage and daring.

Time had passed. The wolves may not have forgotten Eirwen, but they were now looking forward, not backward. In the need to turn their minds to the spring campaign, thoughts of past wrongdoings were now put aside. Adarix had expected the mission to succeed, despite the challenging odds; after all, he had selected Emrin in the first place. That was how the wolf operated — he did not bank on failure. Nevertheless, while he had expected Amlich to return, Adarix had not been certain he'd ever see the wolfhound again. Now, despite his own misgivings about the dog, the return of both animals was both a relief and a pleasant surprise. After carefully observing the pair's interactions, Adarix realized that the duo worked well together, even bonding on the adventure. He sensed that Emrin and Amlich would have much more to contribute to the campaign in the days to come.

The presence of the air squadrons was an added bonus, giving the wolf leader an opportunity to rethink his next moves. This surprising turn of events excited Adarix. He understood immediately the potential impact of a combined air and land operation: it would allow the pack to shed its guerrilla role and pursue a more intense offensive. Adarix was grateful for Aeron-Urd's generous offer, believing that the added complement could not only turn the tide in Vigmar's favor but also permit the wolves to meet the goals Eirwen had set for the pack when the campaign started.

However, fresh orders came within days, via another squadron of hawks; they were now commanded to move south to try to find Emer-Sigr's forces. Adarix was greatly displeased. Considerable discussion ensued among the pack's senior officers about whether the orders could be "reinterpreted," disputed or even ignored. At the end of the day, though, the call of duty and their innate obedience to the orders of the high command overcame natural ambition. The wolf leader argued that, if the tables were turned and he were in Aravat's position, he too would expect to be obeyed by his troops in the field, without question or delay. Nevertheless, Adarix took pains to propose an alternative, a plan that enabled the wolves to turn once again toward the north. This proposal Adarix sent back with the returning squadron, although with little hope of its being adopted.

Reluctantly the wolves embarked on the long trek southward, traveling along the path the wolfhound had discovered when he'd left in midwinter. Eventually they'd turn southwest instead of traveling east as Emrin and Amlich had done. However, Adarix planned to march as slowly as possible, just in case the high command saw fit to change its mind. It wouldn't be the first time, and the wolf didn't want to find himself too far from the fray when plans changed once again.

VI

HEIMBORN

32

DISAGREEMENTS

A s the disappointed wolves were starting their slow trek toward the south, Eirwen was savoring the results of the bears' attack on the Black Legion. With a little ingenuity and a lot of groundwork, they'd achieved the impossible — a successful first strike against the panthers, inflicting maximum harm while suffering no losses of their own. They had simply taken advantage of their size, strength and better knowledge of the locale to lure the panthers into the perfect trap.

Eirwen's authority had reached heights he'd never dared imagine, and the bears' confidence had risen in tandem. The only puzzle facing them now was how to make the most of their success.

At first the bears had expected immediate and particularly cruel reprisals from the Legion. Over the ensuing days the clans had been careful to seek shelter, hiding away from the enemy. However, nothing occurred; there were no signs of hunters, no destruction, no taking of revenge. Then word filtered back to them that not only had the panther forces vanished from Heimborn, they'd also retreated from their camps along the borderlands. Exploratory sorties revealed that no troops of any kind had been left behind to guard the passes.

This turn of events was as controversial as it was mysterious. Some of the clan chiefs claimed that the bears' unexpected success had so demoralized the panthers that they had simply given up and retreated for good. Others suggested that their departure was merely a ploy, that they now knew not to underestimate the bears and were planning their own version of a nasty surprise. Still others maintained that the troop movements might have nothing to do with either possibility; perhaps King Albiorix had needed the panthers to reposition themselves on battlefields in the north or the south, where their presence would be essential to shoring up the battered divisions of lions. Of course no one came up with the real reason; it would have been beyond anyone's imagination.

However, the debate caused the bears to hesitate. Rushing into a possible defeat would sacrifice that wonderful feeling of success they'd so quickly gained. Eirwen's doubts about the readiness of the bears to take on the panthers in a head-to-head battle remained. Of course it was essential to make the most of the initial victory. Boosting morale and cementing cohesion of the clans was all to the good, but moving forward required preparation. While fortune favored the brave, Eirwen knew it also punished the foolhardy. It was a thin line, and too easily crossed.

Still, despite Eirwen's desire to avoid unnecessary risk, he was the first to push for a discussion on next steps, now that the bears were in a position to take the initiative. As it turned out, decisions were not up to him alone. The bear clans as a whole had to agree on this potentially decisive move, and Eirwen was forced to bring together their leaders to reach a consensus. Assembling the chiefs in one place was no easy matter, given how dispersed the clans were throughout Heimborn, and it took time to gather even a majority of them. While he was waiting, Eirwen asked his scouts to find out what they could about where the panther forces were.

News of the Ethanead rebellion had spread throughout Heimborn. After the panthers had departed, messages were dispatched to every clan, asking their leaders to assemble as quickly as possible. Five of the chiefs lived close enough to make the arduous journey with reasonable speed. They were enough, it was felt, to make decisions on behalf of the entire bear population; some were deputized to represent those that lived too far away. Hunspek had been delegated to consult with the remainder, but he had not yet returned when the meeting began.

With the retreat of the panthers, the Ethanead clan had immediately reoccupied their home territory. The clan chiefs, along with Eirwen and Somerled, met in one of Ethanead's larger caves. Somerled, the wisest of the elders, had been asked to lead the discussion and mediate where necessary. The old black bear tried to present a balanced appraisal of the situation, taking not one side or the other. As usual, Eirwen chose not to speak his mind until later in the day. As things turned out, opinions among the clan chiefs were as divided as night is from day.

Haefan, of the clan Adelgrid, representing the bears who lived in central Heimborn, sought to preserve the current status quo. He was satisfied with the results of the recent revolt but did not want to press on any further. "We are like the hornet," the brown bear declared. "We have stung the mighty beast on his nose and scared him off. From now on he will be wary and keep away from our nest. However, if we torment him further, his ire will be raised. He will feel the need to strike back, to return in force and perhaps even destroy our home for good. We have gained much, cousins. Let's not throw it away by being too hasty. Perhaps over time, but as for now — "

Vidar of the Sethadi clan cut in. Sethadi occupied a wide swath of territory along Heimborn's northern borders. Having no barrier between it and Aeronbed, other than the mountain heights, those bears were literally on the front lines of the relationship with the panthers. "Clever words, cousin, but don't fool yourself," she declared, glaring at Haefan and waving a paw dismissively. "Accepting the status quo and carrying on as we have will be our death sentence.

"I needn't remind you how much the Sethadi clan has suffered. More than the rest of you put together — with the exception, of course, of our brothers and sisters in Ethanead. We grieve for Goran-Art, who dared to stand up to Parthanyx, and we owe many thanks to Lord Eirwen for his stalwart actions in responding to that outrage. He has struck a blow they'll never forget.

"Somerled has told us about the prophecy. Is it true? I don't know; I'd never claim to be an expert in such things. But what I do know is this: results speak for themselves. For the first time in living memory we can hold our heads high and stand up on two feet before our overlords. No, let me go even further — we have risen to new heights and now stand *over* our hated tormentors."

Several approving nods and growls could be heard.

Vidar carried on. "Let's not fool ourselves. They'll be back. Maybe not tomorrow, but one day. And, I'll wager, sooner than anyone around this table would like — I'd stake my life on it. So we'd better prepare for the difficult days ahead."

Bakman of the Alciburg clan was next to speak. A rough-looking black bear with intelligent, penetrating eyes, he rose slowly to all fours. "I would suggest, Haefan, that we are far more like bees than hornets — bees with a precious hive full of honey, too valuable to be left alone for very long. Mark my words, we haven't seen the last of Parthanyx and his thugs. Vidar speaks most wisely, but each of us can judge matters only according to our own experience.

"The day-to-day life of the Sethadi clan has been a sorry one, and humiliations and cruelty are commonplace. Everyone here knows this. The Alciburg clan has been more fortunate, lying as it does nearer Heimborn's southern boundary. Our lands are well protected and, it appears, of less interest to the panthers, so Parthanyx and his ilk rarely trouble us. But I too grate at Aeronbed's brutality and oppression. It is wrong, and we are right to oppose it. Now we have an opportunity to do something about this evil — for the first time in our lives — and we must seize it."

"Hear, hear!" some voices exclaimed.

"Anat," Somerled said, "you are both sister and heir to Goran-Art. Although you are the youngest and newest of the clan chiefs, you have suffered the most personal loss of us all. What say you?"

All heads turned to watch this bear whom few knew or had even heard speak of before. Anat, her shaggy coat almost blond in color, spoke slowly and carefully. "I bow before your combined experience and wisdom, cousins. This new responsibility weighs heavily on my shoulders, for Goran-Art shared little of his duties and knowledge with me before his death. He was hasty to a fault; this we all accept. Nevertheless, my brother was correct in his views.

"He saw in Lord Eirwen the champion we all sought. As Vidar has said, the results speak for themselves. Only a warlord experienced in the ways of campaigns could have pulled off such a brilliant coup. I'd say Eirwen's victory is less like an insect's sting than a bite through the tough hide of our tormentors. It may be small but it still goes deep, creating a nasty wound. We must savor it even more for the surprising manner in which it was orchestrated.

"I say we've only just begun. We must carry on, for my brother's sake as well as for our common good. The Ethanead clan will defer to the wise direction of Lord Eirwen and will follow him wherever he wishes to take us."

Eirwen would have blushed if a polar bear could. He was pleased to see several nods of approval for Anat's contribution.

"We can all agree that Eirwen's arrival has changed things for Heimborn," Somerled said. "Our relationship with the Kingdom of Aeronbed will never be the same from this point on, no matter what happens."

"How shall we follow up this triumph?" interjected Aedelborn, the oldest of the clan chiefs. "That is the issue before this council. Do we hunker down and secure our border defenses at the most strategic places or strike out from here? I suggest that we've been living with defeat and submission for so long we've lost any idea of our real power. Goran-Art and Eirwen have shown us the way. They stood up to the panthers. If we carry on standing up for what we believe and harness our power, not only can we secure Heimborn for good, we also have an opportunity to expand our range.

"I ask you, cousins, if our hearts and minds are set to the challenge, what can hold us back? Is not the whole of Aeronbed rightly ours for the taking? Would it not be fair and just, after all these years of suffering, that the Kingdom of Aeronbed should be ours? Now that we have our noble Eirwen to lead us, what force can stand in our way?"

Aedelborn and the others turned to look at Eirwen, as if expecting the polar bear to say something profound. But he kept his counsel.

Somerled spoke up. "You've said nothing as yet, Gullhinder," the elder said, turning to a good-looking younger bear. His elegance and confident manner reminded Eirwen of Don Baaldulce. Of a russet hue and with a striking golden mark on his back, he sat in a rather relaxed fashion a little apart from the others. "Where does Sethana stand on these matters?"

For a long moment Gullhinder said nothing. Then he sat back on his haunches, raised his head as if to study the den's rocky ceiling, and shut his eyes. His eyes still closed, he started speaking. "Comrades, cousins, I must confess that this brave talk worries me. I understand you all, yes I do. But have you considered where such violence would lead?

"You suggest that the panthers will treat us with more respect. Hah! I think none of us can imagine the manner in which that *respect* will be shown. You may think we've struck the Black Legion hard, but — despite what Anat has said — it still amounts to nothing more than a mosquito bite, not even a flesh wound. Aeronbed's resources are vast and the panther forces are professional, experienced and unforgiving.

"This, cousins, is not the end of things. It's just the beginning. War, and all the suffering that accompanies it, will follow. None of us will be spared. And for what? Goran-Art was a hothead and a troublemaker. None of you can deny that; let's not forget that the clan chiefs censured him more than once.

"We've lived in peace for so many years. Of course it hasn't been perfect, but whose life is? Can any of you here promise a better future for Heimborn when all is said and done? I doubt it. However, let's assume for the sake of argument that we're the easy victors in a war with the cats and — by some miracle — we even conquer Aeronbed. Where would that leave us?"

Gullhinder finally opened his eyes wide and then slammed his front paws down on the table. "I'll tell you where, cousins. *We* would become the panthers — evil overlords obliged to crush and brutalize the rest of Aeronbed's inhabitants to maintain peace and order for the benefit of the new regime. And do you think for one minute the lions would roll over and play dead or run away to Vigmar? Not bloody likely! They'd fight tooth and nail to keep their lands. And that constant struggle could well be the *best* possible result. At worst we'd be the losers, living for ever after in fear and deprivation. So let's not be too eager to give up what we already have."

These words provoked fury among some of the clan chiefs, and

Anat had to be physically restrained from going after her cousin. The others looked on, either perplexed or with increasing anxiety.

"Outrageous!" Aedelborn howled, jumping up.

"You take us to be formed of the same clay as those panthers?" Vidar growled. "You insult every bear with such claims."

"Beware the corrupting force of power," Gullhinder countered. "Be careful what you wish for, Vidar, because you might just get it."

"Perhaps for you, cousin," Vidar shot back. "But not for the rest of us. Never!"

"And what would *you* propose, Gullhinder?" Bakman called out at the same time.

Gullhinder didn't bother to reply. He merely slumped down in his place and shrugged.

Eirwen was beginning to see what ailed the clan chiefs. Not only were they quarrelsome, their views were all over the place. Forging a consensus — especially one that would give him a mandate to move forward — would be tricky at best, perhaps even impossible to achieve. Eirwen asked for a break in the meeting while he went out to see if Hunspek had returned and whether there was any further news of the panthers' position.

There was still no sign of the raven, and the only information on the panthers was the lack of any news. To all intents and purposes the enemy had completely disappeared. The Legion had either traveled a very long way from Heimborn or they were extremely well hidden, lying in wait until the bears' next move. Since neither approach was typical for them, nothing could be assumed.

During the break, Eirwen asked Somerled how the bears had previously managed to work together on difficult issues. The old bear sighed deeply. "Either we all agree or we do not act. And as you can see for yourself, we agree about little, even on such a crucial matter as this one. So we make do with small decisions and modest steps. These differences have made it easy for the panthers to rule over us."

"No one sees this problem but you?"

"No, we all see it. That's what's most infuriating. No one wants to give up power to anyone else, so we continue in this pathetic fashion. As you have seen, even the interpretation of the prophecy divides us.

Doubtless if you'd arrived in the territory of another clan, those bears would have embraced you just as enthusiastically, leaving everyone else suspicious of their motives. The problem is that there is as much resentment and rivalry as there is mutual regard among the clans."

The polar bear was horrified. "You — *we* can't carry on like this, Somerled."

"Of course, I agree. The question is how to get them to understand and to make it happen."

Eirwen paced back and forth outside, racking his brain as he tried to think of an answer. The task proved particularly challenging. Was there some lesson from his past that might serve him now? At last the polar bear remembered one old legend that he felt might be of use.

Somerled called the bears together, and Eirwen began to speak.

33

EIRWEN'S STORY

"Let me tell you a story about my old friend Fox," Eirwen said. "Mind you, this is not the plain red fox you know from around these parts. Rather, it's his distant cousin who lives up in the Far North, where I hail from. This fox's coat is silvery white, somewhat like mine — well, at least it is in the wintertime. And he lives a rather solitary life, as I did, once upon a time."

The polar bear sighed as he recalled those calmer times. He began to stride around the cave, gesturing to accentuate the key points of his tale.

"Actually, the story is about an ancestor of his," continued Eirwen, "one who lived a long time ago, before animals of different species cooperated with one another as they do in these times. It was quite the opposite then: only the hardiest and most determined survived. Every animal lived for itself and life was harsh and brutal. In the Far North that was especially true, for summers there are short and winters long and difficult. Food is scarce for the land-based animals, and not easy to find or catch even at the best of times. One's stomach sits empty for much of the time.

"In the days I speak of, this white fox often went without dinner, for the creature wasn't the masterful hunter he is today. In fact, many would have called him bone lazy — though of course not to his face, for he was pretty touchy and didn't take criticism at all well. But, if the stories are accurate, to label this fox as brother to the sloth would have been spot on, for the creature hardly bothered to put himself out. Searching far and wide as he does today to find his prey would have been unthinkable back then.

"The fox particularly loved the taste of lemmings — little fellows pretty much like your mice, but without tails — but he wasn't very good at catching them. Lemmings are small and have no teeth or claws to defend themselves with, but they can turn in a flash and scurry off in every direction. Hunting lemmings can drive you crazy — I can tell you that from personal experience!

"Anyway, as I heard the tale, one fine summer's day when the fox was groaning about the effort it took to find a good meal, one of his kin let him in on a secret — or so he said. According to his cousin, once a year, at a certain spot on the rocky shores of the northern sea, all the lemmings that live in the area run into the water by the hundreds and drown. It's as if the lemmings have no care to live, no care for anything else, as if their minds have become fevered, without rational thought.

"If the fox so desired, he was told, all he would have to do to catch a huge number — enough for an entire winter's worth of food — was wait at the edge of the sea and pounce on the lemmings as they dashed by, heedless of their fate. They would even, it was said, run right into his mouth. It was just that easy. Even better, the date of the lemmings' annual race to the sea was fast approaching and that very shoreline was not so far from his den.

"The fox was delighted with this news, seeing the opportunity as the answer to his prayers. No great hunting skills needed, hardly any work involved, a big payoff — how could it fail? So he took the advice to heart. Really, given his idle nature, it would have been surprising if he'd done otherwise.

"The fox had been told that the lemmings would start running down the ridge in the morning. The night before, he got himself into what seemed to be the very best position from which to attack and, hugging close to the ground, he began to wait. The conditions seemed auspicious:

the water was serene, the winds blew gently from the land to the sea, the gentle slope provided a comfortable spot to rest, and the ridge was not far from the water, so he would be hidden from the lemmings until the very last moment. Everything, the fox decided, was perfect.

"Dawn broke over the eastern horizon and the beach was flooded with light. However, there was no sign of the lemmings. 'No problem,' the fox declared; he was not in a rush. Morning had only just begun, so he would keep waiting. Soon the sun began to rise in the sky, higher and higher, and still he waited. When the fox could no longer pretend it was early morning, he rose stiffly, stretched and looked all about. He could see nothing out of the ordinary, certainly no sign of lemmings rushing to their death.

"So the fox crept up to the top of the ridge and peeked over the edge to see what was happening. I'm sure you can guess, cousins — nothing, absolutely nothing, was going on. Dismayed, he jumped to the top of the ridge, rose up to his full height and peered way off into the distance. Still nothing. Not one single creature was on the move, nor could the fox catch the scent of any prey. He was puzzled and more than a little irritated. Still, patience was one of his strengths; he was prepared to continue waiting. He went back to his perfect spot and lay down again.

"The day passed slowly. At one point the fox fell asleep under the warm sun, only to wake with a start, hoping he hadn't missed his prey. He cursed himself for his inattention, but there was no sign that anything had passed by. Although the fox was thankful for that small mercy, he was becoming a tad curious. Perhaps he'd been misinformed about the location, or maybe he'd confused the day.

"By this time the fox was pretty hungry but he wasn't starving. So he decided to remain there another night and see what the new day would bring. As you can probably guess, the next day produced the same result: no sign of lemmings. By the next night, the fox's stomach was growling something fierce. Still, while he was rather annoyed with the creature who had told him the tale, it was awfully convenient to remain convinced of its truth. At least he wouldn't have to run about and waste a lot of energy for nothing. Indeed, lying in wait for dinner to arrive was about as easy as it could get. So the fox decided to give his endeavor just one more day.

"One day eventually turned into four, and by that point his very survival was in question. The fox was at his wits' end, but all he could think about was who to blame for his predicament. He was furious with the cousin who'd confided in him, because clearly the story was false. Nevertheless, the fox was astute enough to direct his anger where it really belonged. Had *he* not been the foolish one for believing the tall tale so easily? His laziness and greed had simply overcome his judgment and good sense.

"Utterly exhausted, the fox struggled to his feet. By now, however, he could only totter unsteadily for a few steps before his strength failed and he collapsed."

Eirwen stopped and looked around. He had certainly captured the bears' interest. All eyes were fixed on him and not a sound could be heard apart from the combined chorus of their breathing. Someone muttered, "Go on. What happened next?"

Smiling inwardly, Eirwen continued his tale. "As I was saying, it looked like a sorry end for the fox. However, as luck would have it — and there has to be some luck involved, or this story would be pretty short and meaningless — a large snowy owl happened by the very spot where the fox lay near death. She was on her way to her nest, back from a fabulously successful hunt. Holding lemmings in both sets of claws and with two more in her beak, she'd already gorged herself on the little creatures. Curious about the apparently sleeping fox down by the ocean's edge, the owl decided to take a closer look. She circled a few times, just to be on the safe side, and finally descended to settle down right in front of the fox's nose.

"Although foxes and owls were not quite mortal enemies in those days, they were certainly not friends either. Let's just say they had a mutual respect and kept their distance, rarely speaking to one another — which is one of the reasons why this story is amazing. The owl knew that the fox presented no danger. Indeed, she could see that he was dreadfully weak, almost on the point of death. She dropped the lemmings from her beak and asked him what was going on.

"The fox did not respond, so the owl poked his forehead with her right foot and then, just in case, hopped back out of range. 'What's the matter with you?' she demanded. The fox could not move. He could barely even open his eyes, but with a huge effort he managed to gaze up at the magnificent fat bird. He was much too weak to talk, too weak even to notice that two dead lemmings lay right in front of him. The effort hurt so much that he closed his eyes again.

"The owl, her curiosity kindled, was not to be denied, however. Feeling more secure, she poked him again, a little harder this time. This roused the fox, who, although irritated at being prodded, managed to croak out the story in as few words as possible.

"'Who told you that extraordinary tale?' she quizzed when he'd finished. The fox closed his eyes once more. At first the owl thought he'd fallen asleep, but then, sighing mournfully, he opened them again and uttered a faint reply: 'I don't remember.'

"'Sorry to be the bearer of bad news,' the owl replied, 'but that's nothing but an old worm's tale. I've heard it several times, and from several sources. Naturally I never believed a word of it. Of course I should know, for I fly far and wide over these parts and I see much more than you ever could. And I've never seen such a thing.'

"'Oh' was all the fox could think of to say. Tears began to roll down his furry cheeks as he realized how foolish he had been and how miserable, famished and faint he was now, all at the same time.

"Fortunately for the fox, this owl was a kind-hearted creature. His pathetic tears moved her deeply. She'd eaten more than her fill of lemmings and had already collected more than enough to store in her nest for the weeks to come. So the owl ripped a small piece from one of her freshly caught lemmings and placed it in the fox's mouth. The fox was moved to even more tears, for he'd never experienced such gracious and generous behavior before. Eating slowly, he felt his vigor beginning to return, and thanked her profusely.

"'I have a suggestion,' the owl said after the fox had swallowed several more pieces. 'And if you take what I have to say to heart, you'll never run into this predicament again.'

"'What do you mean?' the fox asked. He had never before been given advice by a bird.

"'What I mean is, you'll never again find yourself starving to death all alone by the northern sea.' The fox still didn't understand, so again he asked the owl to explain.

"'The point is, you can't catch a lemming simply by being a fox.' The fox hadn't the faintest idea what she meant. 'The only way you can catch a lemming,' the owl continued, 'is to think and act like a lemming.'

"The fox was so weak that his mind still wasn't working terribly well. All he could think of to say was 'What?'

"When hunting, the owl explained, it is essential to mimic the actions and movements of your prey. Then you can predict its behavior and remain one step ahead all the time. At first the fox was dubious. How could he think any differently? After all, a fox is a fox, just as a bear is a bear. He racked his brain, but though his stomach was filling up and his head was clearing fast, true understanding still eluded him.

"The owl was aware of the fox's reputation for laziness, for it was well-known throughout the animal world. But she also knew that her old rival wasn't stupid. She waited patiently while the fox closed his eyes and tried to work it out. After a while she wondered whether he'd fallen asleep. After a longer while, she gave up waiting.

"'If you use your brain as much as your speed and agility, you will be more successful,' the owl explained at last. 'Once you know where the lemmings live and how they get about, you won't have to expend so much energy and time racing about after them. As a result, you will have your fill of lemmings instead of dining on berries and grubs.' She shuddered at the thought of such a wretched diet.

"The owl wasn't stupid. She understood that the more successful the fox was at catching lemmings, the less attention he'd pay to her chicks. She gave him another lemming as a parting gift and the fox thanked her profusely, not grasping her real motivation. As a final gesture of goodwill, the owl told him where to find the best supply of lemmings in the neighborhood.

"It wasn't long before the fox went to check it out and reflect on her advice. She had been telling the truth, and this time, instead of running helter-skelter after the lemmings, he took the time to watch his prey carefully. The fox observed how they behaved, how they jumped about in their curious fashion. Then he practiced mimicking their behavior until he was able to move exactly as they did.

"And that's the way the fox of the Far North learned to be an accomplished hunter of lemmings. He persevered by learning when and how they will jump, and by always being one step ahead of those tasty morsels with his jaws at the ready. As for the owl and her offspring, they prospered as well — at least when there were plenty of lemmings to go round."

34

A CONSENSUS OF SORTS

Having finished his parable, an expectant Eirwen looked around at his audience. He had been expecting approval and acclaim, but all he saw was puzzled looks. His cousins had evidently enjoyed the story, but it appeared that none had managed to understand its underlying meaning — just like the white fox.

Sighing loudly, Eirwen returned to sit across from Somerled. The old bear had caught his story's point, which was doubtless why he was considered a particularly wise creature. "What Eirwen has been talking about, cousins — what he is providing us with — is an allegory. It is an explanation of our current predicament intended to reveal what we must do to escape from it."

Eirwen quickly indicated his agreement and opened his front paws wide in a plea for responses. Somerled fell silent also, hoping that one or more of the others would catch on. An awkward silence ensued while the baffled bears looked at one another or down at their huge paws.

After a while, Bakman spoke up, not without some hesitation. "I take it we are like this poor fox, caught up in some fanciful notion — perhaps even one of our own making — that keeps us weak and powerless. And because we are so caught up in that fantasy, we are unable to make any progress. Is that it?"

"Precisely," Somerled responded kindly. "Yet there is still more to it."

Vidar interjected, more forcefully than her cousin. "I see it now! The tale tells us exactly how we must move forward. We must use our minds. We must watch our enemy, know how he will act and react, mimic his behavior, prepare ourselves and be ready to strike when the moment comes."

"With our jaws at the ready," Eirwen added with a sense of relief.

Small, round eyes glistened around the table as everyone began to comprehend. Finally Eirwen witnessed a spark of enthusiasm as an eager discussion broke out among three of the clan chiefs. But one well-told story was not enough to ensure that reaching a consensus could be so easily achieved. Gullhinder remained immovable.

"Forgive me, cousin. I enjoyed the tale, really I did, and I'll be sure to regale the rest of the clan with it when I get back home. It changes nothing, however. You are counselling war, Eirwen, asking us to discard years of careful practices and measured behavior. To what end? I would like to know."

"Careful practices and measured behavior!" Anat scoffed before Eirwen could respond. She rose to her full height. "What has *measured behavior* ever brought us? Nothing but misery and humiliation. I say, 'Enough!' If there's to be war, so be it. We've been crawling around on bended knee for too long. I would rather die a free bear than live like a shackled prisoner."

"I agree!" Vidar jumped to her feet to stand by Anat. "There can only be one choice — war!"

"Anat and Vidar are right," echoed Bakman, also rising. "There's been enough talk, cousins. More than enough. It's time to act. If we're united, victory will be ours for the taking."

Aedelborn struggled to his feet and looked around the room at the other chiefs. "I speak not just for myself but for several of Heimborn's smaller clans as well. I know they will abide by my counsel. I too say the time has come to throw off our chains. We must take back what is rightly ours. I will put my trust in Lord Eirwen."

The others turned to stare at Gullhinder and Haefan. Both had remained seated without saying a word. "Well, cousins?" Vidar asked pointedly.

Gullhinder remained defiant-looking, while Haefan shifted about in obvious discomfort. The latter stared down at the table, avoiding the glares of those who were standing.

Gullhinder began to speak. "My position remains unchanged. The Sethana clan will not —"

But Eirwen too had risen and began to speak over him. "I thank you for your vote of confidence, cousins," the polar bear stated flatly. "But it is not enough."

The bears stared at him. A perplexed Somerled looked up from where he sat, his face full of questions.

"We are already at war with the panthers, whether we like it or not," Eirwen continued. "Yes, my fable of the white fox was one way of describing how we must work together in the days to come. But it's only a partial answer to determining our fate. This method of decision-making — " He swept a paw around to include all those present. "This method may work in times of peace, but not in war. We will need to make hard, quick decisions — even painful ones — in the days to come. There will be no time to meet again like this. In war there can be only one decision-maker, only one leader.

"If you agree today with this course of action, then it must include investing me with supreme command of all the bear clans. And with total authority to make those decisions until this struggle is over. When that time comes — and I promise it will — I will step down and you can resume your old ways, if that is what you desire. This path is the only way forward. There can be no other and I will accept no other. If you want me to lead, cousins, those are my terms."

A shocked silence ensued as the full meaning of Eirwen's words sunk in.

Finally Bakman spoke up. "You speak truly, Eirwen. There can be no going back. I'm with you." Eirwen's other supporters were quick to voice their assent.

Then Haefan got up. "The members of the Adelgrid clan are wary and slow to accept change. I know they will not be comfortable with such an aggressive stance. However, it's clear that no viable alternative is open to Heimborn. So, cousins, I declare to you this day that I will personally support this strategy. Once I'm back home, I will make every effort to convince my family to support the new, er, direction. That's all I can promise."

"Well said, Haefan," declared Somerled. "And enough said."

All eyes now turned to Gullhinder, who alone had remained seated. "Well, well," the russet bear said. "Even Cousin Haefan sees fit to join this mad rush to slaughter. It appears I am alone in my opposition to this dangerous scheme. If I cannot make you grasp the folly of what you're about to embark on, at least I can make my disagreement known.

"At first I took our new friend to be nothing more than a reckless adventurer, but now I see him for what he is — a ruthless tyrant! First he attempts to trick us into making war and then he seeks to rule us all. And we walk happily into his trap, like witless sheep into the waiting pen. Do you really think Eirwen will walk away from power so willingly at the end of this great struggle? Hah! If you believe that, cousins, you're all bigger fools than I thought. No matter what happens — win or lose — we'll find ourselves under his thrall."

"Enough!" Vidar growled. "You insult us all, Gullhinder, *and* you humiliate yourself. You know from Somerled how unwillingly Eirwen came to this task."

"Can't you see through his guise of reluctance?" Gullhinder said. "It's just a sham, an act so clever you've all been hoodwinked."

"If you had some other strategy to propose, we might listen to it," Anat countered. "But all you can do is throw around abuse like an angry wolverine."

"That's where you're wrong." Gullhinder smirked. "I propose that we negotiate with the Legion. I grant you we've managed to hurt the panthers. Aye, we've certainly got their full attention, and for that advantage I give full credit to our noble Lord Eirwen. Now, for the first time in a long while, we can speak from a position of strength. We can demand better terms and we can insist that our sacred territory remain untouched. This time they'll listen. They know now we can strike back at will."

Eirwen noticed that Haefan was looking around at the others with increasing uncertainty. He was hunched over and seemed ready to sit down again.

But Anat spoke up quickly. "I chose to ignore your insult to my brother, who gave his life in the cause of Heimborn's freedom. But in the name of Goran-Art, I declare there can be no more negotiation, no more deals, no more bended knees. If I must stand all alone against the cats, I will do so. I will not parley with those who have so cruelly abused us — never again! If you think you can do business with those murderers, Gullhinder, then it's you who are the fool, not us."

"Hear, hear," cried some of the other bears. Haefan straightened up again.

Gullhinder saw he could not convince the others. "So be it. I wish you well, cousins, with your splendid war — and your new *king*," the black bear spat. "But let me be perfectly clear. In making this choice, you forsake the path of peace and compromise. The Sethana clan will not support you in this futile endeavor, and no self-appointed despot will ever rule over it. The era of this council has come to a pitiful end. In the long, dark days ahead, I trust you will remember my words." He rose at last and swept out of the cave without another word.

It was a painful moment, and the chiefs were very conscious of the momentous turn of events. For better or for worse, life would never be the same for Heimborn.

❧ VII ❧

ARUNDATI TO VIGMAR

35

FRIDIS SEEKS A LIFE OF PURPOSE

The days on Arundati's southern shores had been too easy and trouble-free for Fridis. It was as simple as that. If the duck had come across but one grating grain of sand to disturb her rest or some other such thing that caused discomfort, she might have stayed in her tropical paradise, happily attending to such irritants. But as it was, Fridis was bored to tears.

Of course she had regrets. Her friend Eirwen was dead and Fridis missed him terribly. Once more she was alone, and once more she was a prisoner of sorts. Still, her punishment amounted to nothing more than exile; no one could seriously call it captivity, and to be honest, the surroundings were more than hospitable. As a result, the duck's mind turned often to the polar bear and to the end of their great adventure, rather than her own plight. Fridis speculated about how things would have turned out if Eirwen had not gone off to fight, or if she had insisted on going as well, or if both had opted for a safer path in life. There were too many what-ifs in her life — she was plagued by the wretched words.

Although Raicho had proven to be an excellent companion, the falcon was not Aeron-Urd. And he was definitely not Eirwen. Raicho never engaged in entertaining banter or conversations about grand ideas. He didn't even mention her fine plumage, which she felt was becoming even more beautiful — if such a thing were possible — in the sultry tropical environment.

Fridis suspected the peregrine falcon was as unhappy as she was to be stuck in this distant hinterland. He was so far from the war's heroic encounters and had nothing to do but keep watch over her and practice his flying skills. They'd seen no interlopers since arriving, not a single creature that threatened danger or even evoked interest. When the diligent Raicho was not carrying out one of his interminable patrols, the two birds would chat and exchange the odd story. But the falcon was a bird of few words and always careful in what he said. The duck learned more about the history and geography of Vigmar, but nothing of consequence to her own life. Moreover, those few moments of conversation were never long enough or frequent enough to satisfy Fridis's curiosity.

The duck had grown used to the presence of other creatures during her time in Vigmar, with all the surprises, mysteries and complications that arose from interacting with them. Fridis no longer sought out solitude as she had done in the northern forests; her own company was not enough to satisfy her need for companionship and adventure. And so, ironically, exile to this land of impeccable beaches, dramatic sunsets and fragrant breezes was indeed a punishment. Perfection, at least in terms of climate and topography, was simply not sufficient to occupy her energetic mind.

After so many weeks of enforced rest, Fridis realized she needed to get back to doing something, anything but just eating, paddling about and contemplating the vexations of her life in Blakfel. Of course the duck was too small to participate directly in the war and — by decree of the Empress — she could no longer attend to the sick and wounded. But couldn't she resume her sleuthing career?

Fridis was fascinated by Señor Piro's story about the discovery and disappearance of the magic gemstones. She could not help but be curious about how the gems had made their way from the Misken Mountains to where she'd found them, in the icy passageway that connected her former world to Vigmar. Now that was a real mystery! Could she possibly solve it? Why not?

Her mind turned to the possibilities facing her. Besides satisfying her curiosity about the gemstones, could she also contribute to the war effort? No. Even as the idea popped into her head, Fridis knew she would do nothing to support the meaningless war with Aeronbed — meaningless, that is, ever since Eirwen's death. All she was prepared to do was support and help those who had come to mean something to her: Aeron-Urd, Haidar, perhaps even the hapless Emperor.

So, after much hesitation, one fine day — a day not unlike all the others that had preceded it — Fridis broached the subject with Raicho. Unsure whether the falcon would need convincing, the duck asked him straight out whether he would help guide her back northward. She did not, however, mention her idea of finding out more about the gems.

Raicho listened carefully to her request but gave no sign of leaning either way, instead asking leave to fly about for a few minutes while he considered his answer. Fridis watched him nervously as he flew his distinctive slow, graceful, swooping figure-eight pattern way above. Finally, flying slowly in big circles, he descended and landed right beside her.

The peregrine falcon did not hem or haw. "I have been commanded by Aeron-Urd to protect you with my life, to serve you, to submit to your every request and to keep you here, unmolested by any possible attack, until we hear from him again. As a result, Grand Duchess, my orders represent an essential contradiction: I am bound to reply both yes and no to your request. I doubt the Air Marshal ever imagined you'd ask to leave here without hearing further from him. So, my lady, you see my dilemma."

"I do. If you agree to my request to leave, you'll end up obeying one part of your charge. However, at the same time you'll be breaking the other part. And vice versa."

"Exactly."

"What would you like to do, Raicho?"

"What I want is immaterial."

"Please call me Fridis. After all this time together, 'Grand Duchess' — even 'Duchess' — seems ridiculously formal."

"Yes, Duchess — sorry — Fridis."

"Thank you. Now, even though you don't consider your wishes relevant, tell me anyway. What would you want to be doing if I wasn't here? And don't worry, I won't hold your words against you."

"Since you ask, I'd rather be with my fellow officers in the thick of things. My first loyalty lies with the squadron. It's like my family; to be here without them is like trying to fly with only one good wing. And, with all due respect to the Air Marshal — I understand the rationale for his choice, for this spot is agreeable beyond belief and safe beyond words — it can also lull any thinking creature to sleep.

"After a good while here, I suspect, nothing but being at one with nature would matter to anyone. And that's where the real danger lies: in becoming accustomed to and enamored by the softness of life here. When that happens, you'll be satisfied with doing nothing more every day than watching the palm fronds being tossed about in the wind and worshipping the gorgeous sunrises and sunsets. And when that point arrives, you won't even notice life passing you by."

Raicho had never spoken at such length in response to her questions. The duck was both surprised and impressed by the thought he'd put into the answer. "That's quite profound," she replied. "At least, I think it is. It certainly mirrors my own feelings. We can't stay in this paradise for too much longer or we'll become ensnared by its web of beauty."

"However, saying so does not absolve me of my responsibilities to protect you and to keep you here. I cannot get around Aeron-Urd's orders, however contradictory they may be."

An idea occurred to Fridis. "In that case, let us simply say — to Aeron-Urd or to anyone else who might ask — that we are not leaving or even going very far. We are simply taking a short trip up the coast for a change of scenery. A little bit of excitement, if you will. Of course we shall return, just not right away. The Air Marshal has not forbidden excursions, has he?"

Raicho, suspecting that the duck was merely playing with words, looked a little dubious. "No, he has not, and I can certainly see how such a stance would provide a way around my dilemma. However, what if Aeron-Urd returns in our absence?"

"Do you really think that's possible?"

Raicho thought for a minute, even raising his penetrating gaze to the northern sky as if expecting the gyrfalcon to make a sudden appearance. "In all honesty, I do not," the bird said at last. "Unless, of course, we're away for a very long while. Given the time of year, the Air Marshal will not get leave to return, not this far south, and not for some time to come. The season for war approaches; every creature who can serve will be called upon." Then the falcon laughed. "Although the very idea of combat seems impossible to conjure up in this beautiful place."

"Excellent. It's settled, then. But just in case, we should leave some kind of a message for our friend, something only he will comprehend. Can you do that, Raicho?"

"Of course."

"By the end of this, er, little holiday, I hope you too will get your wish."

The skeptical Raicho was anxious about Fridis's scheme. Going somewhere else would certainly generate the ire of his boss, and the chance that she would be discovered and end up in harm's way would increase greatly with any move. But the falcon was just as bored as the duck, and the likelihood of encountering anyone else on a short trip up the coast was minuscule. As long as they stayed to the south of the two mountain ranges, they should be safe enough.

After weighing it all up, the falcon finally responded, "Thank you, Duchess."

"Fridis," she reminded the falcon.

"Sorry. Fridis."

36

A SHORT JAUNT UP THE COAST

Although on most days the duck would have been satisfied with a short trip up the coast, on this day the jaunt represented only the first stage of her intended journey. Fridis's real destination was Blakfel. There she could retrieve her two hidden gems — but she had no intention of traveling directly to the capital.

Along the way, the duck wanted to stop once more in the Misken Mountains. There she would speak at length with Señor Piro, trying to pull out of him whatever more he was prepared to share about the history of the gems. As Fridis would now be searching in earnest, she would need any information that might help her figure out how and why the gemstones had moved about the Empire.

Naturally Fridis kept her true plans from Raicho. While the falcon had been persuaded to help her travel a little way up the coast, she knew her companion could not agree to the radical departure from Aeron-Urd's orders she was envisaging. When the two birds came in sight of the mountains, Fridis would ask Raicho to arrange a visit. One step at a time: that was how she'd play it. After the mines, she would head further north along the eastern coastline until she could find a safe way to enter Blakfel. The duck hoped her escort would stay with her; however, if at some point Raicho would not or could not agree to that, Fridis was determined to go off on her own.

As soon as Raicho had fashioned his coded message for Aeron-Urd, the two birds set off toward the east, following the coastline. The pair flew with great caution, staying low to avoid being spotted. Raicho insisted on taking frequent breaks to scout out each new region they approached. Fortunately the winds were at their backs and they made good progress. The scenery below and the weather above remained constant. To their left were endless emerald forests of towering trees thick with climbing vines, ferns and mosses; on their right were aquamarine lagoons and pristine white sand beaches. All around them at every stage were the ever-present moist, perfumed air and the heavenly blue sky.

After a few days of careful flying along the southern coast, they turned toward the north, and both birds enjoyed the change of scenery. Eventually the Misken Mountains appeared on the distant horizon, like an inviting beacon. Fridis wasted no time in broaching the subject of revisiting the mines, as if the idea had just occurred to her.

Initially the falcon wouldn't even hear of her suggestion. He was reluctant to make the request to the mine authorities, let alone actually undertake a trip to the site. The mountains were a secure zone, after all. Unlike the first time, when they'd visited with the Air Marshal, now the two birds had no permission to enter the area. Raicho was aware that Aeron-Urd's rank and connections had been responsible for their swift approval on that earlier occasion. The peregrine, however, was merely a junior officer, a nobody in the pecking order. And Fridis's protector had even more serious concerns. Contact with anyone else risked revealing the whereabouts of the Grand Duchess, something the Air Marshal had wanted to avoid and had strenuously warned against.

The falcon did his best to argue the point with Fridis. The duck, however, was unrelenting in her efforts to convince her companion. In the end Raicho agreed — against his better judgment — to approach the first point of access to the mines. He committed to seeking approval there to proceed. The duck's noble rank would doubtless count for something, and since Fridis had visited the mines in recent memory, hopefully its guardians would be more inclined to accept her rationale for returning. If those in authority turned down her request — which Raicho guessed would be the case — then he and Fridis would immediately return to their place of refuge as surreptitiously as they'd departed. Such was the falcon's final word on the matter, and Fridis agreed to abide by it.

However, as is often the case when making a request, their simple appeal, posed honestly and without pretense, produced a surprising yes. Those on the mine's first line of defense hesitated only briefly before passing it on. The positive response from those higher up came quickly, fast enough to unnerve Raicho much more than an outright rejection would have done.

The falcon did not hesitate to warn the duck about his misgivings. "Don't forget what happened to you in Blakfel," he declared when they were alone. "Things are quiet here, but you still have determined enemies in the capital."

The duck shrugged off his concerns, annoying the falcon. "Look, Fridis, we've not been hiding out for your amusement but for your protection," he insisted. "The Air Marshal made those arrangements under the assumption that Dona Morana's persecution of you would not end at mere exile. Although we've had a delightful 'holiday,' it doesn't mean all is well. It only means they failed to find us."

Still Fridis would not be dissuaded.

Raicho persisted. "Don't think for a minute they've forgotten about you. It would surprise me if envoys of the Empress haven't already been to the mines, since Misken is the last place you were known to have gone. Perhaps after that they continued to search further afield; perhaps they're searching still. Possibly they left spies behind at the mine, just in case you were fool enough to return.

"We've covered our tracks since we left here last time, as well as any bird could. If we leave right now, I'm certain we can remain out of harm's way. To fly on to the mine site, however, means taking a great risk, perhaps courting disaster. And don't forget, your safety is my responsibility. I'll be the one answering to Aeron-Urd, not you."

Fridis, meanwhile, was becoming more and more impatient with Raicho's concern. She chose to ignore it, for the duck was determined to proceed. Dismissing his fears as exaggerated, she took the welcome from the mine authorities at face value. Whatever trouble or danger might await her, Fridis was supremely confident she could deal with it. The memories of her awful imprisonment had faded completely, and her mind could go in only one direction — forward.

The two birds, both a little put out with each other by this point, flew in grim silence through the checkpoints, stopping at each to reconfirm their identity and purpose. The pair finally arrived at Misken, where the head official of the mine, who remembered the Grand Duchess from her recent visit, greeted them warmly.

Once more Fridis was asked about the reason for this second visit, and whether she sought to acquire additional jewels. Despite Raicho's misgivings, it appeared that no one back in Blakfel had thought to advise the authorities of the change in the duck's status. Just like the previous time, she was treated as an important and distinguished visitor. Whatever lingering apprehensions Fridis might have had, they dissolved immediately. Raicho, for his part, remained distrustful and on his guard.

The duck explained that she was returning home from a long holiday in the south and, realizing that her route took her close to Misken, she'd decided on the spur of the moment to take one last look at the magnificent site before moving on. Although she had no need for more gems, she was keen to continue her fascinating conversation with Señor Piro, if the badger was available.

Her reply and simple request were met with easy acquiescence. After offering the two birds the inevitable tokens of hospitality, the mine director sent for Piro, who turned up promptly and offered to escort Fridis through the maze of tunnels to where the jewels were kept. Raicho stayed above, having no interest in the mine or the gems, while Fridis and Piro wended their way down into the dramatic cave rooms far beneath the surface.

Piro led the way, with Fridis following immediately behind. The two had not gone far when she tentatively introduced the reason for her visit to Misken. "If anyone were to find the missing gems you told me about," the duck asked as innocently as she could manage, "who would the rightful owner be?"

If Fridis had wanted to get the badger's attention, this unexpected question certainly worked. Piro stopped in his tracks and spun around to face the duck. Fridis almost tripped over him, he'd moved so fast.

"The Misken gemstones? What a strange question. Why do you ask?" He sounded suspicious. All she could see of the badger were his intimidating black eyes, squinting in the gloom.

Fridis had no intention of revealing her new plan, at least not yet. At this point in the conversation she was reluctant to explain to Piro even the supposed reason for her inquiry. Struggling to find the right words, the duck was, for a rare moment, speechless. At last she blurted out, "Your story of Achimi and the AKOM partnership intrigued me greatly. During my travels since then, I found I couldn't let it go. I'd lie awake at night, mulling over the possible paths the gems might have taken, and then I'd come up with so many ideas and theories. Frankly, the question of ownership is merely the first of many I have."

Piro did not deign to answer, merely shrugging impassively and turning to continue the trek through the dark tunnels. Fridis wondered whether he recalled having told her about AKOM. She hoped the badger was just being careful, feeling a need to respond with the same caution she was employing as she posed her questions. Piro did not speak as he scuttled from one passageway to another, veering this way and that along the well-memorized path. They proceeded in silence until Fridis almost despaired of a reply.

However, the badger had clearly been thinking about her question. Out of the blue, and without slowing his progress or even glancing back, he said, "If I'm being quite fair, I have to admit there's more than one way to reply to such a question. Some would argue, 'Finders, keepers' — whoever possesses the jewels and can manage to hang on to them deserves to own them. Others would insist — because of the gems' great powers — that they belong to no single creature but to all animals, and therefore should be owned in common. Bah! I ask you, what creature could be trusted to use them wisely for the good of all?"

Although tempted to add an opinion, Fridis decided it was better to hold her tongue and let the badger hold forth.

"Still others," Piro said without missing a beat, "would declare that whoever created the stones remains the rightful owner, no matter what their destiny. As for me, I'd point out it was Achimi who discovered the stones, after who knows how many centuries of their being abandoned. And then he held them for a good long while before they were stolen. Therefore, Duchess, I'd say the descendants of the original makers and owners have no claim to the stones — not anymore. None at all!"

Piro interrupted his harangue as he worked his way up a steeper slope and made an awkward turn into another passageway. It seemed to Fridis that the route they were taking was different from before, but it had been many months and she couldn't really be sure.

"In any event," the badger continued, "who's to say who the original creators or owners were? That knowledge has long been lost to the world, and any creature today would be hard pressed to put forward — let alone prove — such a claim. So, in sum, I'd argue that Achimi's successors were — are — the rightful owners of the Misken gems."

"In other words," Fridis said boldly, "*you* are the rightful owner."

37

THE RIGHTFUL OWNER

Once more the badger stopped in his tracks and twisted around to face her. Even in the gloom Fridis could not help but notice the cunning grin, the gleam in his eyes and a new intensity in his voice.

"Aye, Duchess, that's exactly what I'm saying. The story of the gems may have sparked your curiosity, but I've been thinking about them my whole life. I would give anything — *anything* — to retrieve them. The badgers are their true and rightful owners. *I* am their rightful owner. No one else!" Piro's voice had risen and his words echoed down the long tunnel. The grin was gone, replaced by a look of anger, as if the badger had fought this battle of words many times before.

Fridis was undaunted by the other's passion. "But Achimi lost the gems," she began. "Doesn't —"

"Not lost — they were stolen. When one is robbed, one doesn't give up a claim to ownership."

Fridis realized that pursuing this line of questioning would get her nowhere. "Was there anything you left out of your story about the discovery of the gemstones?" she asked. "And their subsequent loss?"

"*Theft*," the badger reminded her.

"Sorry, theft."

"Why do you ask?" Piro replied.

Fridis sighed. "I'm sorry for taking such a roundabout path to get to my point. As I said, your story has burned within me since we met, but it's more than a matter of simple curiosity. I've decided to make it my mission to discover the trail those stones took after they went missing. And so I need to know every detail of what happened. You know, I'm actually quite the detective. If I can find the route the gemstones took once they were taken from Achimi, I believe I can trace them all the way to where they might be hiding today."

Even in the dim light, Fridis could see that the badger was unconvinced. "Don't be fooled by my small stature, Piro, and do not underestimate me. When I set my mind to do something, I will not be deterred, by anything or anyone. And I already have some ideas, ideas worth exploring. I just need a trail to follow."

Piro's eyes had narrowed to mere slits and he stared at her doubtfully. "What ideas?" he asked, a little more sharply.

"They're more like hunches, really. I'd rather not go into detail until I've had a chance to pursue them. But I can say this: if I do find the gems, I pledge to you I'll bring them back here."

Did the duck really mean it? Could he confide in her? The badger didn't trust any creature completely; he even doubted the loyalty of his own family. But Fridis's gumption and her forthright, determined manner had struck a chord with him. He'd opened up to her before with the story of Achimi and the gems, and that act alone had been a rare enough gesture. Perhaps the little duck could indeed help him achieve his long-held ambition of restoring the gems to the badger family. No one had ever made such an offer before. Piro began to feel that he'd little to lose and much to gain from telling Fridis what he knew and had been holding so tightly to his chest.

"Such a pledge should not be given lightly."

"I do not give it lightly."

The badger paused as he thought it over. "Then I take you at your word, Lady Fridis," he said at last. "And I will hold you to it." Piro pondered for a few moments, looked up and down the tunnel, just to make sure they were alone, and then said, "Follow me."

He scuttled off, following a heretofore hidden offshoot of the tunnel system. Fridis followed as fast as her legs could carry her. After the inevitable circuitous twists and turns, the tunnel opened up into a cave, where a modicum of light filtered in from some unknown source. There the badger settled down and indicated that she should do likewise.

"As I explained to you before," Piro began, "I was told that the four partners had never used the gems again but that stories — only stories, mind you — were being bandied about some years later that in fact they had done so. Here's what I was told.

"In those early years the whole of Vigmar, including these southern lands, was at peace, and creatures lived in harmony and comfort. Well, more or less — you know how it is — but signs of what was to come were there for those with keener eyes. Like the little acorns that grow into great oak trees, they were lying about waiting for the right combination of soil, sun and water. Achimi and his partners were creatures of business. Their talents meshed; they knew how to manage the mine and keep up with demand. So they prospered mightily and became very wealthy. However, they were not so astute at reading the winds of change. Although signs of decay were scattered everywhere, they ignored them.

"Success breeds envy; it's as inevitable as night follows day. Oh, it begins innocently enough: a few spiteful thoughts, some dishonest desires. Aye, my lady, none of us is immune to the sin of envy. There's nothing wicked about wishing and brooding, but if unchecked, such thinking can turn upon itself, brewing and stewing until it becomes a veritable soup of evil intent. When the wrong sort of creature starts weighing up the pros and cons, that can lead to the next step — the foul deed itself."

The badger's intensity began to worry Fridis. Was it too late, she wondered, to back out? Yes, it was. Piro was already in full flight.

"The four were very choosy about whom they hired. They were also secretive about the location and extent of their holdings. Rivals and thieves tried everything — bribery, spies, raids on shipments, you name it — but none were successful at seizing AKOM's riches. However, commoners are one thing and powerful rulers another. It was when Vigmar's king decided he deserved a share of the spoils that things changed — changed for the worse, that is. The king was unrelenting in his pressure on the four partners, and he had the power, the forces to command and the will that mere competitors and criminals did not."

Piro had spoken with great vehemence, but now he calmed down a little. "Those are the things I know to be accurate," the badger continued. "The remainder, I'm afraid to say, is conjecture or legend. I was never able to verify the truth of it; I can only say the tale makes sense. At the point when the four partners decided to give way to the king, when they believed they could resist the pressure from Vigmar no longer, seemingly out of thin air, an army showed up to save the partnership. No one, to my knowledge, had ever before heard of these rivals of Vigmar. They were called the Knights of Arundati, and they became the founders of this kingdom. They repelled Vigmar's king and army, thus saving AKOM."

For a few seconds Piro exulted in the ancient victory, but soon his bitterness returned. "Although the four partners were saved, their rescue came with a price. AKOM was left to conduct its affairs as before and to prosper as never before, but the new rulers took their pound of flesh. The Knights taxed the resulting wealth heavily, so in the end, it was a victory in name only.

"I've never been told, one way or the other, whether the gems brought about this rescue — and the unintended consequence — but I can see no other possibility. And which of the partners implored the stones for help, I can only guess. Of course, in the end it was all for nothing. Only a few years later, Vigmar invaded, conquered Arundati and took control of the mines. But by then the three gems had long since disappeared.

"One more thing. I said Achimi had no idea which of his three partners to suspect, but that's not completely true. I believe he thought all three were involved. To my way of thinking, that would explain his reaction — his decision to cut off relations with all of them. It's the only explanation that makes sense to me."

The badger paused briefly before continuing. "I'm not sure how this information really helps your search, but right now there *is* one way I can assist you."

"Go on," said Fridis.

"Soon after you and the Air Marshal left Misken, a deputation from Vigmar visited the mine. They were looking for you and they asked for our help. A hefty payment was promised for any information and a bigger one for your capture. If you were ever seen in the area again, we were to report the news to Blakfel — immediately. So not only have you been seen, you've walked right into our fortress, like an innocent fly into the spider's web, as it were. I'm sure the directors of the mine are already calculating their reward as we speak."

"What!" quacked Fridis, horrified, despite Raicho's warnings.

Piro nodded grimly.

The duck looked frantically about, as if expecting long claws to reach out of the darkness and grab her. "Why are you telling me this?" she asked.

"What would more riches mean to me? Nothing. Your promise to find the gemstones, however — that is something I truly hold dear. It's as simple as that. The hope that I might possess the original Misken jewels is worth far more to me than any monetary reward. Your capture wouldn't serve one bit of good — hah! not to me, anyway. Whatever is amiss in your relationship with the Emperor or Empress is not my concern. These are matters beyond my ken or my care." The badger shrugged, made a face and held his front paws open as if to dramatize his lack of concern for the imperial family.

"I have a feeling that you know far more than you're willing to tell me," Piro added. "So be it. I don't need to know all your secrets. But I do want the gems back, and something tells me you're capable of anything you set out to achieve."

Fridis was about to respond when the badger said, "Don't forget, I will hold you to your pledge."

From Piro's menacing tone the duck concluded that he was capable of anything. She quickly changed the subject. "But you just told me I'm about to be arrested," she protested. "What good will any promise do now if I'm about to be taken back to prison?"

"Hah! Prison? You'd be so lucky. I'd say your fate will be far worse."

Fridis was doubly shocked, and dismay overwhelmed her. How

could she have been so naive? How could she have so blithely ignored Raicho's advice to play it safe?

To her great surprise, Piro's face broke out in a wide grin and he began to chortle heartily.

"It's hardly a laughing matter — " the duck began.

"Oh, that's all by the by," the badger interjected, still laughing. "Remember what I told you? The directors may run this place, but I alone know all the pathways in and out of the mines, including the most secret routes of all. I can lead you out by a hidden tunnel to the south. Trust me, no one will see you leave. From there you can make your escape."

"But what about you? And what about Raicho?"

"Hah! I'm safe. The mine owners need me too much, and I can be awfully vague in my answers when I want to be. I'll just tell them you asked to go back up top and I pointed the way out ... or something like that."

Piro shrugged again. "As for your friend, I'm sorry to say I can do nothing for him. Since his name was not on any list, either he's already been clapped in prison as your accomplice or he's regarded as an innocent party and is still a free bird. Whichever, his fate is already sealed. Still, if I can manage it safely, I'll get word to him about your escape."

After thinking for a moment, Fridis said, "Tell Raicho I'll return to the signal marker, the one he created before we left the south."

"The signal marker ... yes, got it. Meanwhile, time's running short. It won't be long before the others start wondering what's keeping us. You'd best be off before they send a search party."

The secret exit turned out to be nothing more than a small hole in the rock face. However, it was well disguised and well away from Misken's observant guardians. Fridis never bothered to ask why it existed. The opening was more than adequate for a smallish bird desirous of making an escape, which was all she cared about. Piro pointed out a safe route to follow and, with the briefest of salutes, she left.

The badger's gruff last words, however — and his menacing scowl

— stayed with the duck for many days to come. "Remember your promise, Fridis, for I'll never forget it. Not until the day I die."

38

ON TO VIGMAR

Fridis was winging her way north in the dead of night, flying low over the eastern seaboard of Arundati as she followed the ins and outs of the ever-changing coastline. Not so far below her the duck could hear the waves rhythmically washing up onto empty beaches and rugged rocks.

After several days' flight, she was finally nearing the border with Vigmar. Fridis had trusted that her unusual flight path from Misken would help her avoid running into anyone of consequence, someone who might pose a threat to her life and to her latest scheme. So far, fortune had favored the duck: only the stars had shown up to accompany her nighttime flights. The region had turned out to be an uninhabited, even desolate stretch of the Empire.

Fridis had not told Piro the truth. She had no intention of returning to the hiding place she'd shared with Raicho. Only a fool would have advertised her route and destination, and the duck was no fool. Even before leaving the mine, the reality of her situation had become crystal clear: the peregrine falcon would never be able to meet up with her, back at the little lagoon or elsewhere.

Either Raicho was already a prisoner and thus going nowhere, or, if by some miracle the authorities considered him innocent, they would be insisting he lead them to the meeting spot. As a dutiful servant of Vigmar, he could hardly plead innocence and refuse such an order at the same time. Neither option suited Fridis. No doubt Raicho would stall or mislead them as much as possible, but at some point his own neck would be at stake.

It was only a question of time. Sooner or later they would find her — that is, if she chose to prolong her stay on the southern shore. Fridis could not take that risk; far better, she decided, to leave everyone in the dark and get a good head start. The duck had not revealed her real intentions to Raicho, so he could tell them nothing more. They'd never imagine that she'd be returning, of her own volition, directly to the place where she'd be at greatest risk: Vigmar's capital, Blakfel.

The duck felt some pangs of remorse about poor Raicho. The falcon had been right all along about the danger of returning to the mines, and she'd been dead wrong. Fridis hoped that nothing bad would happen to her loyal companion. He had simply been following orders; he'd been stuck with her, playing nursemaid, when he would much rather have been in the thick of battle. Perhaps because of her rash decision, Raicho would finally get his wish, that is, if he wasn't already locked up as her accomplice. Fridis shuddered at the very thought; having recently suffered that fate, she wouldn't wish it on her worst enemy. But what could she do about it? She was powerless to help him. Anyway, she had her new mission to accomplish.

Even worse, Fridis now viewed the trip to the mines as having been an utter waste of time. She'd gained so little from her conversation with Piro. What, after all, had he revealed to her? Nothing you could put a wingtip on, just a bit more of the unsavory history of Vigmar. It amounted to nothing more than a suspicion that the three partners had acted together in the theft. Not a smidgen of proof existed one way or the other. What's more, she'd gathered no clues to guide her toward her next destination. Fridis wished she'd had more time to cross-examine the badger, or at least had prepared more questions in advance.

So, where should she go to investigate the disappearance of the gemstones? Thankfully, she had plenty of time on her long flight north to think and plan her next move. As she flew on, enveloped in darkness, Fridis felt truly alone for the first time in a long, long while — in fact, since her meeting with Raven and Eirwen in the northern forests. She had coped well enough on her own then; now, in this strange land, she would have to do so again.

It wasn't long before the obvious question occurred to Fridis. Why had she decided to embark on this new — and likely foolhardy — quest? She had been out of harm's way and well guarded by Raicho. Life had been a trifle boring, but at least it was calm and comfortable. Why couldn't she have left well enough alone? Now here she was without help, flying off into the unknown, where doubtless yet more danger lay in wait. She already knew where the gems were; two were hidden in the castle and the other — yes, the other lay with Eirwen. Poor Eirwen! She could not dwell on his memory; it was too distressing.

And where could that third gemstone be now? Surely the wolves would have noticed it. But in the message relayed to her about the polar bear's death, not one word was said about the gem or, for that matter, whether Eirwen had used it before he died. Of course, that kind of information would not have been shared freely with just anyone.

Perhaps the gem still rested with Eirwen, in death as in life. If so, would it ever be found again? The duck wished she knew more about the circumstances of her friend's sacrifice. Then she wondered whether Adarix and Alberic had taken possession of the stone before Eirwen died and were keeping it safe for her. She would have to ask the wolves when next they met. Unless, of course, they were now jealously holding on to the gem, using it for their own ends, with no intention of ever giving it back. What then?

The possibilities were endless, and Fridis's thoughts began to veer off on many tangents. She tried to refocus her mind. What was the question? Yes, why was she going on this foolish mission if she already knew where the gemstones were? What was the point? She already had a partial answer to the only pressing question, which was where the missing jewels were now. But as quickly as she admitted this to herself, she was ready with her response: that was not the real mystery. Not at all. The real mystery was how the gemstones had traveled from mines deep within the Misken Mountains to the ice cave that separated one world from another. She wanted an answer. And to find that answer, she had to follow the trail.

But the trail, Fridis had to acknowledge, was pretty cold. No, it was more like ice, frozen as solid as a northern lake in deep midwinter. It had happened so long ago that any search was a matter for a historian rather than a detective. Finding the answer would have to go beyond her normal line of approach. There were only three suspects, no living witnesses, little evidence, no clear motivation and the most minimal of clues to go on. All she had were circuitous suspicions repeated to her these many years later by a creature whose point of view was, without a doubt, heavily biased. In sum, the duck had very little to go on and no clear starting point.

But that wasn't completely accurate. There was a starting point: the disappearance of the stones and the breakup of the AKOM partnership. Most important of all, Fridis had to keep reminding herself that she had found the gems and knew where two of them were hidden. No other creature could make such a claim. The intrepid duck felt in her heart that there was a reason why she had discovered the three and had then come across Señor Piro. There had to be. She just didn't know what it was yet.

Fridis tried to put herself into the minds of Achimi's three partners, Obtala, Kelnek and Merithu, the snow leopard, the falcon and the brown bear. She knew little about them, only the facts that they'd reunited after the original partnership broke up and they were skilled at running a mining operation. How had they all got together in the first place? Where did they go afterward? What kind of creatures were they — honest, well-meaning, unscrupulous, greedy, mischievous, devious, envious? Piro had said nothing about them at all; the badger cared only about his own family history. One could hardly blame him.

But did Piro speak the truth? The badger had acknowledged that more than one version of the story existed. Also, ownership of the mine had generated no end of envy and greed. Piro had told his story warily, as if merely repeating the old tale could get him in trouble. Fridis conceded that, by the time she reached the end of her quest, the result might be four separate versions of the truth. Then she'd be no further ahead at all.

Fridis shrugged off that possibility. Whatever the outcome, much of the fun was in the chase. Just thinking about the hunt got her mind and heart racing. It was at the very least something to do, a whole lot better than lazing around in the sun on some distant southern shore.

Fridis decided that her first point of attack would be to discover where the three other partners had gone after they split up. But where could she find such information? She had no idea where those animals had lived. But no, that wasn't completely accurate. The big cats, she'd been told, were in Aeronbed, and while the duck had never heard anyone speak of leopards, she assumed that they too must live there. Unfortunately there was still a war on, and the cats were the enemies of Vigmar. So that approach could be — had to be — put aside for the present.

Where did the bears live? She had no idea. The only bear Fridis knew was Eirwen, and of course he had come from another world. She'd never thought to ask about others. Who could tell her? Since no possibility leapt to mind, the duck was left with the falcons. There were certainly plenty of falcons in Vigmar. Aeron-Urd, for example, was one. Wouldn't it be amazing if he was related in some way to Kelnek! And if he wasn't, her friend might know something about that bird or someone else who could help her.

Thinking of Aeron-Urd warmed her heart and gave her renewed vigor. Fridis planned to sneak back into Blakfel through the secret cave-and-tunnel system she knew so well. That memory caused her to think of Haidar, who was a mine of information about the history of the kingdoms. He too would be an excellent and unbiased resource for her quest. Fridis's original determination to head for Blakfel was thus reconfirmed. The capital simply had to be her destination. Spurred on by this greater purpose, the duck flew a little faster.

However, Blakfel also held unpleasant memories: the attack by the hawks when they first arrived and the Empress's later threats. She would have to take care with her route and her flying pattern. So Fridis continued up the coast, staying away from the central part of the Empire. She hid in coastal marshes by day and flew by night, the sound of crashing waves below her a constant guide.

In spite of her lack of experience with migrating, the duck knew instinctively which way to go, where to make subtle turns and which junction points were of real consequence. She avoided the direct route to Blakfel, which was more likely to be patrolled, planning to head inland toward the capital only when she was near the northernmost point of Vigmar. Fridis felt certain that no one would be searching for her in these eastern regions. What's more, if her adversaries suspected she might be bold enough to return to the capital, they'd never expect her to arrive from that direction.

The duck's trek was long and circuitous. She flew over an ever-changing landscape: lowlands thick with grass, wide river valleys and vast deltas opening into the ocean; barren cliffs, their sharp rocky points extending like claws into the foaming sea; dense, impenetrable, unending forests; the decaying ruins of fortified castles, now devoid of all life; and rolling sand dunes that fell away into surging tides. Fridis encountered calm, starlit evenings of great tranquility and tumultuous storms in which she had to employ all her strength to avoid being blown far inland and way off course.

No matter the obstacles, Fridis flew on and on. Now and then she saw other birds or heard their calls, but always from afar. Sometimes she overtook them at night while they were resting on the ground; at other times she could hear them passing overhead as she crouched hidden in her daytime shelter. Occasionally she would spy groups of animals moving about below her, but she did not recognize them; if they saw her in turn, they did not react. Once or twice she got a scare — just a sensation or perhaps a shadow flitting across her line of sight during an early evening takeoff or a late morning descent — that caused her to dive for a safe haven, searching for whatever cover she could find on short notice.

Fridis was invigorated and strengthened by her journey northward. Whatever the final outcome, she'd already concluded that her new quest was offering a great deal more than her prolonged holiday in the sun.

En route, she passed over the verdant but empty grassy plain where she and Eirwen had first arrived in the land of Vigmar. The sight of it felt comfortable and welcoming. *Strange,* the duck thought, *how quickly that happens. The familiar — what little there is of it and whatever it amounts to — becomes so quickly agreeable.* She was tempted to retrace their earlier route toward the capital, despite its dangers, because she'd come to know it so well. But Fridis resisted the impulse and carried on northward, until she reached the hills and mountains far beyond Blakfel.

Only when Fridis was well past the mountains did she veer off to the west, her intention being to double back toward the capital. The closer Fridis got to her destination, the more apprehensive she became and the greater her precautions. On occasion she walked instead of flying, hugging the ground where she felt too exposed, although that slowed down her progress even further.

At last Fridis came within sight of the capital, its familiar high walls, towers and fortifications looming before her. By contrast with the empty lands she'd passed through, Blakfel seemed awe-inspiring, which of course it was meant to be.

It was early morning when the duck arrived near the city wall. She would hide out in the underbrush until nightfall, when she would sneak into the castle through the tunnel system. It had been a long haul, but now she would be rewarded for her efforts.

39

LOOKING FOR HAIDAR

F ridis easily found her way to the cave entrance and entered the tunnel beyond without incident. At intervals throughout the day and evening, the duck had heard the calls of patrolling hawks flying overhead. But she had remained low to the ground and had been extremely careful with her movements, timing her approach to avoid being discovered. She found no signs of recent activity in the tunnel, and its familiarity was comforting.

But the entrance, Fridis knew, was only the first and simplest step. She was more than practiced at getting inside the castle, but where should she exit at the other end? As the duck could no longer move about freely in Blakfel, this visit would have to be kept secret. Her most obvious choices were Haidar's room or the kitchen cellar.

The cellar was more accessible and led directly to the kitchen, where Haidar would most likely be found directing affairs as usual. But given the usual frenetic activity there, many others would also be present, and who among them were friends and who were enemies? Apart from her very few close confidants, no creature could now be above suspicion. Fridis concluded that Haidar's personal quarters would present the safer choice. It might take longer to connect with the mountain goat, given how rarely he seemed to take a break, but her top priority now had to be personal security.

Remembering all the pitfalls along the route, Fridis took plenty of time to make her way to the secret entrance to Haidar's room. The later the hour, the better, she figured, and the greater the chance she'd catch the goat in his room. It was by now well into the night and the castle was as still as a sleeping dormouse; evidently Blakfel's inhabitants — save the ever-present watchful guards — were safely tucked into their beds. Fridis hoped that even the conscientious Haidar would be taking his rest.

Fridis had painful memories of the way out of the goat's quarters: past the edge of a carpet hanging above a chest of drawers. She hoped that nothing had been moved in the interim to block her way back inside. It was quite a tricky maneuver to hover in midair while she poked her head past the heavy material and squeezed into the room, but she made it through nonetheless.

The mountain goat's chamber was as dark and quiet as the secret passage. Fridis felt she'd made an immense racket as she entered, but no one stirred. If Haidar was there, he was certainly a heavy sleeper. She had expected to find some sign of life, but the duck was sorely disappointed. She perched on top of the bureau and listened. No one was there.

Frustration overwhelmed her. Fridis had come such a long distance and was so eager to see her friend again. More than that, the duck felt a pent-up need to talk to him. She had had plenty of time during her long flight to accumulate a list of questions. Now she needed to speak to the goat right away and get some answers.

It had been a strenuous journey and a long day. In spite of her disappointment, the goat's absence presented a welcome opportunity for Fridis to catch up on her sleep. Feeling truly secure for the first time in weeks, she immediately dozed off. Still, just to be on the safe side, she settled down where she'd entered the room, curled up on top of the tall chest of drawers, out of sight of any unsuspecting visitor.

THE DAY WAS WELL ALONG WHEN THE DUCK WOKE UP AGAIN. A DIM LIGHT entered the room through a tiny, almost opaque window she'd not noticed before, and Fridis could see no sign of Haidar. Had the goat returned and then left again without even noticing her? That seemed unlikely.

The room was neat and tidy and the goat's bed looked untouched. In fact, now that she checked more closely, she could see a thin layer of dust over everything. It appeared as if no one had been in the room for weeks. Was Haidar now employed elsewhere? Had he moved? But the picture of his father with his lion friend was still on the wall; he wouldn't have left that valuable keepsake behind.

Was Haidar on an extended trip, a holiday perhaps? But why and where would he be traveling, and how could he get leave from his duties? If anything, it seemed more likely that the goat was now so busy he was forced to sleep in a corner of the kitchen. The frustrated duck couldn't wait indefinitely in the bedroom; she had to press on.

Hearing voices in the corridor, she opted for the longer, safer route to the kitchen, back through the tunnel and the cellar. Fridis was well rested and ready for action, so it didn't take her long to get to the cellar storeroom. By now she was adept at opening its secret entrance. The place was unchanged, its maze of barrels, boxes and foodstuffs lying or hanging haphazardly everywhere, so it was easy to creep through the space unseen. The duck could hear the usual hum of activity in the kitchen above: shouted instructions, hoofs rushing to and fro, and crashing pots and pans. Fridis assumed that lunch preparations were in full force.

As she made her way toward the stairs, wafting down from above came the wonderful aromas of cooking: spicy stews, fresh breads, sweet puddings and delicacies of all sorts. Fridis realized she was famished, and that reality drove out every other thought.

The duck worked her way along, carefully flitting from one crate or barrel to another. At one point some creature descended from the kitchen and rummaged close to her, peeking and poking in a huge barrel until he found what he was searching for, hefted it aloft and carted it back upstairs. Fridis remained completely still, not even breathing, behind some massive sacks of cornmeal. She had not been seen, but equally the duck had had no opportunity to determine who the other was. Even if she had, could Fridis ever hope to distinguish between friend and foe?

No one else had come down by the time she reached the stone staircase. Fridis had reached a point of decision. There were no more hiding places; she would be going out into the open. She halted a minute, pressed low against the rough wall, just in case Haidar might show up to save her, or perhaps in case some animal she'd prefer to avoid suddenly appeared up top and forced her back into the cellar's recesses. But no one did. It was up to her now. Fridis took a deep breath and hurried up the circular stairs, wings flapping. She almost flew, she moved so quickly, and soon enough she was at the kitchen doorway.

Gazing inside, the duck experienced once again the full effect of the kitchen's intense activity: the shouts; the furious pace; the rattle of pots and pans; the bubbling stewpots; the smell of meat roasting on a spit in the big fireplace; the piles of cut-up carrots, potatoes and greens; the intense heat and glare of the roaring fires; steam escaping from under half-closed lids on the simmering soups; the wonderful fragrances of exotic herbs and spices. It almost took her breath away. She remained huddled in the shadow of the doorframe, peering in and hoping not to be noticed while she took it all in. Fortunately, the eyes of the kitchen staff were focused on their tasks, not on her.

But among all the animals present, Fridis could neither see nor hear Haidar. The mountain goat was not at his regular command post; in fact, no one was. *Strange*, she thought. *What about* —? And then she found herself looking straight into Alsvid's eyes.

The pony looked about as surprised as Fridis was. For a second or two they both stood stock still, their gazes locked in mutual shock. Then Alsvid had the presence of mind to sidle toward the door, block Fridis from view and gently push her back down the stairs into the cellar. Once they were there, the pony shut the door behind them.

Alsvid's questions came thick and fast. "Princess, what are you doing here? How did — ? *Why* did you come back? Don't you know there's a price on your head?"

"A price on my head?" was Fridis's surprised reply.

"A reward is being offered just for reporting sight of you. Finding you, catching you, or bringing back your head commands even more. My lady, it's not safe here!"

Fridis was unfazed. "Is it safe anywhere?" she said coolly.

"Perhaps not, but there can't be a more dangerous spot for you than right here in the middle of the castle, with the Empress herself sleeping right above our heads."

"On the contrary," said the duck, flapping her wings. "All eyes will be focused everywhere *but* here. In fact, this precise spot may be the least dangerous place in the entire Empire. No one would think I'd be mad enough to return to Blakfel, let alone to the palace kitchen. But listen, Alsvid, I need to speak to Haidar. Do you know where he is?"

"He's not here, Princess," the pony replied, stone-faced.

"Oh no," Fridis lamented. "Not that old game!"

Alsvid almost broke out laughing at the memory of that encounter. "It's too long a story to tell now. Can you find a place to hide until my break?"

"Haidar's quarters? If you think that's safe."

"That'll be perfect. But be careful how you make your way. I'll meet you there at midday. And don't worry, Princess," Alsvid added with a big smile, "I won't forget to bring a tray of your favorite pastries."

Fridis thanked the pony profusely and scurried away, back through the tunnels to Haidar's room.

40

ALSVID'S ANSWERS

"So tell me, where is Haidar?" Fridis asked Alsvid between beakfuls of delicious quiche. "And please don't say he's not here."

"Ha ha! This time it's the truth. It's quite a mystery, actually, and I confess I don't quite understand what happened. Haidar left some weeks ago. He told me he had been entrusted with a secret mission, something very dear to his heart. Those were his exact words, in fact. He couldn't — or wouldn't — go into detail. Nevertheless, he did say that if he met with success, his actions would 'change the course of our history' and 'right many a wrong that has been done.' I must say, Princess, I hadn't seen Haidar so enthusiastic in ages."

"That's quite a declaration, especially coming from Haidar," Fridis observed. "Do you have any idea where he went?"

"He didn't say, but I have a feeling he was heading for Aeronbed."

"Aeronbed? But Vigmar's at war with Aeronbed! Crossing the border would be dangerous enough for anyone from here, but for one creature all alone? That's madness!"

"Of course, of course. But doesn't it make sense? You know the story of his family as well as I do. His greatest regret is what happened to his father, and he would do anything to redress that terrible injustice."

"Surely, but how could Haidar hope to do such a thing? And of all times, why now?"

"I'm the first to agree with you. But since Haidar told me nothing about his plans, I'm really just guessing." Alsvid let out a weary sigh. "I'm sure he's doing what he thinks best."

"He's so obsessed by the wrong done to his family. That could easily have colored his judgment."

"I wish I could say otherwise. But, as I said, he didn't provide me with enough details to know one way or the other. However, I can correct you on one point: Haidar did not go alone."

"What? He didn't?"

"Someone else was involved. I've no idea who exactly, but I believe it was someone in the employ of Dona Morana."

"The Empress?" Fridis quacked. "Is it really possible? How do you know?"

"First, because Haidar learned about his commission from First Secretary Gloton. And second, one day he inadvertently said 'we' instead of 'I' when talking about his trip, and then immediately tried to cover up his error. I pretended not to notice and didn't press him on it, but he never did that again."

"Haidar trusted Gloton? After everything we know about the wolverine?"

"No, Princess, he did not. Well, at least not completely. Just enough, I suppose, to sell him on whatever was being proposed."

"Was it Gloton who went with him?"

"No, I've seen the wolverine around the castle since Haidar left — the Baron is pretty hard to miss, after all. It was definitely someone else."

"Then who?" Fridis mused, as much to herself as to Alsvid. "Who else is absent from court?"

"I rarely frequent such elevated circles, Princess, and only as part of my work. So I couldn't say."

"Is there anyone we could ask?"

Alsvid thought for a moment. "A mission of such importance

would have to be kept quiet," the pony said after several seconds. "Only a few would have been in the know. Still, it can't be a complete secret. I suggest you ask your friend Aeron-Urd. As a member of the high command, the falcon would have been involved in the planning, or at very least kept apprised of such an important initiative. He should have some idea of Haidar's purpose."

"I was planning to meet with the Air Marshal, but as things stand now I'm going to need your help. You've made it plain I can no longer come and go freely."

"Always happy to help, Princess."

"In fact, I have two favors to ask of you." Fridis told Alsvid about the two leather pouches still tucked away in Eirwen's bedroom. Then she described her trip to the Misken Mountains and asked the pony if he knew anything about the badgers, the mine and the history of the jewels.

"With regard to your first request, I'm sure I can make up a story that will allow me to visit that part of the castle. I'll certainly try my best. As for the second, unfortunately it's Haidar who's the master of history around here. He revels in it, as you know, particularly where it involves his own family. Many's the time we talked late into the night as we sat around the kitchen hearth — or rather, he spoke and I listened as he told me tales of the past."

"Did he ever speak of the mine?"

"Hah! I have to confess that I didn't always listen as well as I should have. He did go on and on, and the fire's heat often put me to sleep, so I probably missed as much as I learned. However, I do seem to recall Haidar talking about an AKOM partnership and their falling out."

"AKOM? Yes, the name came from their initials: Achimi, Kelnek, Obtala and Merithu. What else do you remember?"

"The AKOM discovery was so vast that it was responsible — almost solely responsible — for all the wealth of Arundati. The kings of Vigmar were jealous, and they tried to get their paws — or rather, their hooves — on it several times. They finally succeeded, as you learned. In fact, according to Haidar, it was the theft of the gemstones that led to Vigmar's success and the demise of the Arundati regime. Those gems, he declared, held the key to their power. Hah! Haidar used to say that whoever controls the gems could rule the entire world.

"Of course, that's the kind of thing Haidar tends to say. He often comes up with such dramatic claims. The bitterness he holds against the Emperor and Empress is equal to that of an entire herd of mountain goats. Not that I necessarily disagree or wish to speak ill of my friend. He knows well enough my views on the subject."

"But there were no members of the donkey family among the four partners. How did the rulers of Vigmar manage to gain control of the gems?"

"How can you ask such a question after what happened to you?"

Fridis sighed. She recalled what Eirwen had been told about appearances being deceiving and the need to trust no one. "So one of the partners could have been in the pay of Vigmar. Or bribed or even intimidated ... "

"Or possibly a combination of all three."

"Hmm. If you had to guess, which of the three partners would you pick as the thief?"

"Difficult to say, Princess, but if I were forced to choose, I'd say Kelnek."

"The falcon? Why?"

"Because the leopards have been allies of Aeronbed for as long as anyone can remember, and the bears are allied with no one at all. The falcons, on the other hoof, have traditionally been identified with this regime." Alsvid sighed again. "It's a pretty thin argument, I admit, but better than nothing."

"Is there anything else you can recall from your conversations with Haidar?"

"Nothing that comes to mind. But if I do remember anything, Princess, I'll surely tell you."

Alsvid went off to arrange a meeting with Aeron-Urd and to retrieve the two pouches. Meanwhile, Fridis ate her fill, reflecting on everything she had learned so far. The gems, the duck knew already, could work great magic: one healed the sick and injured and another provided a brilliant light to guide the way. But perhaps she and Eirwen had barely glimpsed the stones' capacity. Perhaps they held many different kinds of power, and far stronger and more wide-ranging than she could ever imagine. Even their reputation alone would give them a degree of power — as long as everyone shared in that belief.

Fridis thought back to how Piro had reacted to her story. The badger had risked a great deal by helping her to escape, just in the meager hope that he might yet get them back. How had the kings of Vigmar managed to lose control of them? Would they not have protected the stones with their very lives? Their loss didn't make sense. Yet they'd already been stolen once. Why not a second time, or several times? And then, of course, after so many years had passed, someone had decided to hide them in the ice cave. Why? And how? And when? She wondered who had been the last creature to hold the gemstones before she found them.

The duck also wondered (rather more apprehensively) whether anyone else might be on the hunt for them. Was it really possible that every other creature in Vigmar had completely forgotten about the gems and that she alone was taking up the quest? Although it seemed unlikely, no one she'd met in Vigmar had even mentioned their existence, let alone their powers.

More and more questions assailed her. Although Alsvid had added somewhat to her store of knowledge, what she knew still provided very little to go on. But Fridis was determined to pursue her new goal. She would not stop until she'd found some answers.

First, however, she had to turn her mind to meeting with Aeron-Urd. While Fridis was looking forward to seeing the gyrfalcon again, her anticipation was muted. The Air Marshal was both fond and greatly protective of her, and through her trials they had developed a deep mutual attachment. Since the death of Eirwen, Fridis had considered Aeron-Urd the only true friend she had left in Vigmar. But how would he react to her risk-laden decision to return to the capital, a place full of significant dangers for her? And what would he say about her impetuous and ill-conceived trip to the Misken Mountains, which had landed his lieutenant Raicho in grave peril? Fridis intended to beg his forgiveness, for she was truly sorry for her actions and hoped that Raicho had avoided coming to harm. She also trusted that Aeron-Urd would understand her reasoning.

As promised, Alsvid returned with the two gemstones and the arrangements for meeting her old friend. The pony had made up a story about delivering a special dinner order to that part of the palace. However, as it turned out, he had met only a few creatures that might have questioned his presence, and none of them bothered to do so. Alsvid had entered Eirwen's now empty room unseen and without difficulty, found the pouches under the floorboards just as Fridis had left them, and hid them on his covered tray to bring them back to her.

Now that it was all over, he was rather pleased with himself. "If I may ask, Princess, what's in these pouches that's so important?"

Fridis had not told Alsvid about the gemstones, and the pony had not thought to ask until that very moment. "They contain keepsakes of great personal value to me," she replied. "Lord Eirwen and I found them on our travels, and I'm deeply grateful to you for bringing them to me."

Apparently satisfied with that vague reply, Alsvid asked nothing further.

"One more thing," said Fridis. "How did the Air Marshal respond when you told him about my return?"

"He was greatly disturbed. Not so much about your showing up, but in general. I know Aeron-Urd only by reputation, Princess. Today I met him for the first time, but even though I cannot compare him to how he looked in the past, to me the bird did not look at all well. Sunken eyes, low in spirit — I'd say the Air Marshal is carrying a heavy weight upon his shoulders."

"Did he at least seem pleased that I'm here?"

"He conveyed little emotion one way or the other. He was all business, so there was no small talk. As you can imagine, to any outside observer it would seem most unusual for me, a humble member of the kitchen staff, even to speak with so exalted a figure. A lengthy interview would have been highly suspect. So we had to discuss the meeting arrangements quietly and carefully, as if we were talking about some matter of food provision."

"Again, I'm most grateful, Alsvid. You have been a true and loyal friend."

"Haidar would have asked nothing less of me. And to be honest, I rather enjoyed the departure from routine. It's been my pleasure to serve you." The pony bowed low.

Fridis was genuinely moved by Alsvid's insight, support and kindness. The duck remembered how she'd once thought the pony a fool. Now she could not help but remark upon how Alsvid carried himself — simultaneously professional and modest. It was far more than the duck had expected, or felt she deserved.

It had been arranged that Fridis would meet Aeron-Urd in the kitchen cellar the next evening. Haidar's room was too confined and the duck didn't want to chance incriminating the mountain goat in her dealings with anyone else. The cellar would also permit a quick escape should something go wrong.

41

IN THE CELLAR

From her well-chosen vantage point, the duck could see everyone who entered the cellar, while she remained hidden. She watched Aeron-Urd stepping and hopping carefully among the scattered crates and barrels, his talons clacking on the hard-packed floor. The pony remained just out of sight by the cellar's entry, keeping an eye out for interlopers.

Alsvid's observations about the gyrfalcon's state were borne out by the bird's appearance and his weary posture. Even in the cellar's dim light, Fridis could see that Aeron-Urd had lost quite a few feathers and there was a melancholy air about him. Had she been the source of what was troubling him? Although Fridis was delighted to see her friend — indeed, her rescuer — concern now outweighed pleasure in her mind. More than anything she wanted to run up to Aeron-Urd and give him a big hug, but she held back.

Neither spoke until they were face to face, perching uncomfortably on two large oak barrels across from each other. Aeron-Urd frowned, sighed loudly and peered down his imperious beak. Then he asked, half sadly, half frostily, "Why did you come back, Fridis?"

The duck saw no sign of joy on the falcon's part at seeing her, nothing that matched her own feelings. Certainly there were no words of affection after so long a time apart. Was she mistaken, or was his tone almost harsh? Instinctively Fridis felt insulted. Had she taken all those risks and suffered through the long and arduous flight only to find she was nothing better than a miserable outcast? There, in contrast, stood the Air Marshal with his exalted rank, secure position and creature comforts. Aeron-Urd didn't have to skulk about, hiding in dark rooms, meeting in secret in cellars, or worry about whether his head would still be on its shoulders the next day.

"Is that it, Air Marshal? No 'It's good to see you again, Fridis'? No 'I hope your long journey didn't exhaust you'? No — "

Aeron-Urd held up one of his long, powerful wings to stop the flood of complaints. Fridis saw a pained look on his face; she had wounded him, as she had meant to. But the duck took no pleasure in her little victory, for at the same time she had inflicted an injury upon herself. She fell silent.

The gyrfalcon slowly brought his wing down and asked again, this time more softly and thoughtfully, "Why did you come back, Fridis?"

This time the duck tried to respond in kind. "I, I came — " she started to say. But she could not go on. Her rationale — that she was determined to find out what had happened to the gems — now seemed so insubstantial, so trifling, especially when she considered how others' lives had been jeopardized as a result. Fridis saw her grand plan unraveling, being revealed as nothing but a vain conceit, without justification.

Huge tears welled up in her eyes, quickly streamed down her face and plopped magnificently onto the floor. *Like water off a duck's back*, she thought, at the same time both stricken and amused. Suddenly all the pent-up tension of the past days was released and she began to weep unreservedly. Fridis felt foolish. She had not meant to act like this; she was a strong, confident duck, more than able to stand on her own two webbed feet.

At first Aeron-Urd simply perched there without moving. Then he hopped over to embrace Fridis, hugging her wordlessly until the storm of sobs and tears ended.

They separated. "I'm sorry," she said, amazed at how much better she now felt.

"No, it is I who should apologize — for being so ungracious," the gyrfalcon responded kindly. "I *am* happy — very happy — to see you, Fridis. It's just that I've been so concerned. I was anxious when we said goodbye at Misken, but I'm even more so now. I hoped you'd remain out of harm's way during this turmoil. Now that you're back, I have to worry about your safety all over again."

"You don't have to fret," the duck retorted, instantly on the defensive. "I can more than take care of myself!"

"Really? Are you so certain? Truthfully, I don't think you'd survive very long here without your friends and allies."

"I made it this far, didn't I."

"I was meaning to ask you about that. How on earth did you penetrate our air defenses? No creature — least of all you — should have been able to fly in unnoticed. Heads will roll, let me tell you!"

Fridis was caught. She didn't want to reveal her secret way into the castle, but equally she didn't want to cause trouble for the sentries. "Er, well, I, I guess it was a combination of being very careful and, er, having great luck," she stammered. "I must have made it through just as the guard was changing."

"Where exactly did you get in, and what time was that?"

"I don't really recall," she said quickly. "I wasn't paying close attention."

Aeron-Urd's ferocious stare was fixed upon her as only a bird of prey can manage. Although unconvinced by her attempts to obscure the time and place of her arrival, the gyrfalcon decided there was little to be gained by pressing the duck. Clearly Fridis was not prepared to divulge the information, even to him. Perhaps it was a secret best not shared.

Given what her experiences in Vigmar, Fridis knew that Aeron-Urd's comment about the need for allies was accurate. Despite her bravado, she badly needed support. The duck was small and largely helpless in this terrible place, and — apart from her smarts and quick thinking — her only defense amounted to hiding out and lying low. Still, she hated to admit that to anyone else.

The Air Marshal's reproach reminded her of his dutiful lieutenant. "Tell me, is Raicho safe?"

The gyrfalcon paused before replying. Finally he spoke, a little less kindly this time. "He is, but no thanks to you."

This fresh assault wounded her deeply. Fridis stiffened, preparing a rejoinder, but then her entire body sagged once more. "I'm sorry," the duck started to say. "I did not mean — " Her words trailed off; they felt useless, meaningless now. Fridis realized she'd been so careless, in so many ways.

"Of course you didn't mean it to happen; no one ever does." Although Aeron-Urd's words were meant charitably, they provided little solace.

"What happened to — "

"His arrest and imprisonment were naturally reported to me. Fortunately, I still had enough seniority and sway to help in such matters. I was able to free Raicho, and now he's back where he wanted to be. Life is much simpler on the front lines, believe it or not. At least there it's clear who the enemy is." After a brief pause, the gyrfalcon added, "Unfortunately, that event and my response did not go unnoticed around here. To tell the truth, Fridis, my fortunes have changed greatly since I last saw you."

From his whole demeanor Fridis knew those words to be true. Even worse, the duck was aware she was largely the cause of his undoing. She wished to make amends but could think of nothing that would help. "I have wronged both you and Raicho," she said bravely. "I beg your forgiveness, Aeron-Urd."

"You could not have known the extent of the evildoing around here," the gyrfalcon replied, somewhat more gently. "I tried to make that clear to you when I took you to the southern shores, but obviously I failed miserably." He sighed deeply. "Since you've been gone, Blackfel has been plumbing new depths of villainy, which surprises even someone as jaded as I am."

His comments dismayed her, but the duck said nothing.

"Evidently, Fridis, we're never too old to benefit from life's painful lessons. Hah! I make a fine pupil, learning something new every day. Well, you're here, and we must deal with that," Aeron-Urd continued. "What is your intention now?"

That caught Fridis off guard. Beyond asking him for information, the duck wasn't exactly sure what she wanted to do or where she planned to go next. Further, having seen her friend brought so low, she now had great concerns about Aeron-Urd's health and state of mind. She wished she could nurse him as she had the other wounded souls of Vigmar. "Before I answer, I want to know how you are faring."

"All the better for seeing you again," the gyrfalcon replied, and permitted himself a smile. "But," he carried on, the smile quickly disappearing, "I admit that the past weeks have been exceedingly trying. I have no confidence in the cabal that's running things now. Hah! Perhaps they feel just the same about me. There's a merry thought." He paused to reflect upon that idea. "I despair about the future now. How things will turn out, I've no idea."

"You look dreadfully tired."

"I haven't been sleeping well, that's true." He decided not to tell her about his conversation with the Empress. Things were already miserable enough between them.

Fridis feared it was much more than lack of sleep. Although the duck wanted desperately to ask her many questions, she felt he would not be capable of dealing with them. The falcon appeared far too strung-out. "Take a few moments to rest now. There's much that I wish to discuss with you, but your health comes first. Would you like to find a quiet place where you can be alone?"

"Rest? That's ironic — it should be me looking out for your welfare. In all honesty, Fridis, I doubt it would help. You should ask your questions now. We may not get another chance."

The duck still hadn't revealed the real reason for her return. She knew that researching the fate of the three gemstones in a time of war would seem awfully trivial to an outside observer, but something told her the answers to those questions might ultimately prove of tremendous importance. She just didn't know why, how or when it would come to pass. "My questions may seem nonsensical or even pointless. But I will ask them notwithstanding — that is, if you're sure this is a good time."

"No time like the present. As I said, who knows when the next opportunity will come? One or the other of us may have to leave suddenly and without notice. You can well imagine that happening, can you not." The gyrfalcon winked, amused at the thought.

Fridis, however, shivered. She knew it to be only too true. "All right, if you're sure. My first question has to do with Haidar."

"Haidar? The head of the palace kitchen? Why? What's happened to him?"

She told him what she had heard from Alsvid. "I'm trying to figure out where he's gone and who's traveling with him. I know this is a difficult question; instead of asking what doesn't belong in a picture, I'm asking the opposite. What — or rather, who — isn't where they should be? In other words, have you noticed if any of Dona Morana's entourage has been absent these past few weeks?"

Aeron-Urd closed his eyes, putting together a mental picture of the corridors of power and the palace salons. He thought for a long while, so long in fact that Fridis thought he might have fallen asleep. After a while, he opened his eyes and said simply, "Vulpé."

"Vulpé?" Fridis said.

"I doubt you know him. You probably didn't come across the fox when you were last in Blakfel. He used to be one of Gloton's minions, one of those invisible characters, if you know what I mean — always around but never noticed by anyone else. Vulpé's risen in stature since you left, so much so he that he now fulfils Baaldulce's old role as head of Vigmar's internal security."

"Wow, that's quite a promotion!"

"Indeed. To my mind, his specialty was managing to stay out of sight and out of mind. That's a little more challenging now with his exalted post. Although perhaps he's found a way to achieve absolute invisibility." The falcon laughed.

"What can you tell me about him?"

"Not much. As I say, he's quite the cipher. But, like Gloton, I would not trust him with one feather from my head."

"Do you have any idea what they may be up to?"

Aeron-Urd shut his eyes and once more kept them closed for the longest while. Finally he opened them wide and said wistfully, "No. Sorry, no idea at all. But that's a mystery in itself. We are at war with Aeronbed, and unless Aravat is beginning to cut me out of key discussions, I should have known something about any scheme involving the fox. By all that's sacred, this is too much! Such cavalier independent adventuring could compromise authorized missions!"

Aeron-Urd jumped back to the barrel he'd previously occupied. "I could ask Aravat," he offered, "but if I'm not meant to know, he'll just stonewall me." Fridis was about to respond when the falcon added, "I'll ferret around and see what I can pick up. That is, if we're given the grace of enough time."

"Thank you. My second batch of questions may seem to you even more bizarre and irrelevant, but I'll ask nonetheless."

The Air Marshal nodded.

"Have you ever heard of a falcon named Kelnek?"

"What an extraordinary question. Are you asking for a history lesson now? Why on earth do you ask about him?"

"I said my questions might seem weird. It has to do with the reason I went back to the Misken Mountains. I'm interested in the origins of three gems found there and what's happened to them since. When I was there, I heard quite a story from that old badger Piro. It has quite intrigued me."

"You didn't get enough jewels when you visited Misken?" he said, chuckling. "So what did Piro tell you?"

Fridis gave him the gist of the story, adding what little more she'd learned from Alsvid.

The falcon snorted. "It's too bad you didn't ask Raicho about it; he actually knows a bit about those things. You know he's a peregrine falcon, right? I'm a gyrfalcon — different families, different stories. I think Kelnek was related in some fashion to Raicho, although I have to admit I wasn't paying much attention when he told me about it."

"Raicho is related to Kelnek? Extraordinary! The possibility never occurred to me."

"Why should it have?"

"True enough. And how was I to know? All you birds of prey look alike to me." Fridis laughed, but inside she was kicking herself for missing a wonderful opportunity. All those wasted weeks in the south!

"I don't hold much for family lore," Aeron-Urd continued. "I know something about it, of course. Who wouldn't? The stories get passed around often enough, but only as folktales to fill the idle hours — a source of amusement, don't you know. Of course a few still hold with the old legends, the ones who really care about them. The badgers? That doesn't surprise me; it's part of their history. As for me, I'm a professional soldier, and my focus is on the here and now — and the morrow, for that matter. No time to grind over old myths."

"You think it's just a story?" Fridis was disappointed by Aeron-Urd's skepticism.

"Naturally every story has a basis in fact. But you know how creatures love to embellish the simple truth with their own fancies. Yes, there was a mine owned and operated by those four fellows. Yes, there was a theft and the partnership was disbanded. After that, who knows? Listen, Fridis, fortunes and nations can't rise and fall on the strength of three little gems. Now, if you had proof that they existed and that they worked real magic ... Well, then I might sing a different song."

Fridis's first reaction was to ask herself whether Aeron-Urd was right. Did the gems really hold as much power as she and Piro thought? Perhaps it was more a matter of blind faith plus good luck. Perhaps everything had happened just as it would have anyway, and only when events happily coincided were they taken as related. And then, as her friend said, stories became garnished and exaggerated over time and then were accepted as gospel.

But quickly enough Fridis changed her tack. After all, hadn't she and Eirwen personally witnessed the power of the gemstones — and more than once? But should she reveal that to Aeron-Urd? What were the risks of explaining everything to her dearest friend? Fridis was torn between opening up to the gyrfalcon and keeping her secret truly secret. She recalled an old saying: *Three birds can keep a secret, but only if two of them are dead.* She also considered her knowledge of the stones' existence a great responsibility, and one that lay only with her. Aeron-Urd, despite his misgivings about Vigmar's rulers, might consider it his duty to tell someone else. And then what?

"If it were true, what then?" Fridis asked him.

"Well, then the creature who possessed those stones would hold awesome power, power that would have to be wielded most carefully. I'm not sure I'd like to be someone in that position."

"If Kelnek was the one who took the gems, what would he have done with them?"

Aeron-Urd bristled at the suggestion. "A falcon worthy of his name would do no such thing."

"But what if he was not so worthy?"

"I'd hope never to meet such a vile creature."

"Aeron-Urd, please don't take this so personally. I'm only trying to understand — "

"It would be just like those badgers to cast aspersions on everyone else. For all we know, there never was a theft and they hold the jewels still. They could have spread the tale so no one would ever think to search their own backyard."

Fridis had to acknowledge (at least to herself) that such a clever strategy was entirely possible. Although, given Piro's vehemence, she doubted it greatly. "But if the story is true and Kelnek ended up with them — I won't say he stole them, but perhaps he found them or was given them — where would he have gone?"

"Even if I could come up with an answer, it would be based on too many what-ifs. As a result, it would more than likely be worthless."

"Doesn't matter," she responded. Fridis was becoming rather annoyed with his repeated hesitations and delaying tactics.

Aeron-Urd finally understood that Fridis was not to be denied. "*If* it's true," the gyrfalcon sighed, "and *if* Kelnek was in the pay of Vigmar, he would obviously come here. If not, he would most likely return to his homeland. That is, if it's true, which I still can't believe or accept."

"Where is the homeland of the peregrine falcons?" Fridis asked.

"Approximately due west of here, in the borderlands between Vigmar and Aeronbed. But of course, that was in the past. Now the peregrines have dispersed everywhere and are intermixed with other birds of prey. You would be hard pressed to find the remaining enclave there."

"But it's not impossible?"

"No, not impossible," Aeron-Urd admitted wearily. "You're not thinking of going there now, are you?" he asked, suddenly realizing that it would more than likely be Fridis's next destination.

"No, have no fear of that. But I am going in search of Haidar. I think my friend the mountain goat has become embroiled in some terrible scheme of the Empress, and I fear it will not go well for him. Something tells me he needs my help."

"And would it be only coincidental that Haidar's route and the homeland of the peregrine falcons lie in more or less the same direction?"

"Amazing, isn't it?" Fridis responded with a laugh.

"Fridis, your persistence is matched only by your beauty," the gyrfalcon declared ruefully. Aeron-Urd had grasped that nothing he could do or say would persuade his friend to stay or return to the south. In any event, the capital was a dangerous place for her, and all eyes would be focused elsewhere than the borderlands. If Fridis took great care — though he was far from convinced of that likelihood — she might survive well enough in those mountainous regions.

Fridis, feeling that she'd learned everything she could in Blakfel, would not stay a second night. The Air Marshal offered the duck what help he could provide. He created safe passage to the west for her by ordering his air defenses to focus on other sectors during the following evening. Thus she could fly off without worry, covering much ground in very short order.

Fridis said her farewells to the Air Marshal, thanking him and urging him to take care. "Aeron-Urd, you didn't go into detail about what is troubling you. I understand that you don't want me to worry, so I won't press you further. But please remember that you will always be in my thoughts. I will pray for your welfare and success while I am gone. If ever you're in need, just think of me, and I will do my best to be of equal service to you. Promise me that."

Although the gyrfalcon was highly skeptical that Fridis could do anything to aid him, he thanked her for her good wishes and promised to do as she requested. They parted again as good friends, each deeply concerned about the other's welfare far more than for their own.

42

THE BORDERLANDS

Thanks to Aeron-Urd, Fridis escaped Blakfel Castle as easily and as secretly as she had entered it; none of those guarding the its environs were the wiser. Alsvid sent her off with invaluable provisions and wishes for safe travels. Feeling well rested, the duck flew with renewed purpose and confidence.

The initial hours passed without incident, and in the damp night air she made great progress. Eventually rain began to fall, first as a persistent drizzle and then harder. Undaunted by the turn in the weather, she followed a chain of placid lakes and meandering rivers. These led to the foothills of the long mountain range dividing Vigmar and Aeronbed. From what she could see, it appeared that few, if any, creatures lived in those parts.

As Fridis reached the mountains, the inclement weather eased off. In the tranquil light of early dawn she focused her gaze on the few trails she could see, on the off-chance that she might spot Haidar. Of course the duck thought it most unlikely that she would see the mountain goat, given the length of time since he had left the castle and having no idea of his route. By her reckoning he should be well into Aeronbed and already descending the slopes on the other side. Still, she figured little would be lost by keeping her eyes open.

The duck had two chains of mountains to fly over or through before reaching Aeronbed, the second of which was the higher and more treacherous. Between them lay an isolated alpine meadow, a kind of no-go area, little traveled because of the on-again, off-again war between the two countries. In the more distant mountains, according to Aeron-Urd, a colony of peregrine falcons had resided for many generations.

Once past the first set of mountains, Fridis knew she would have to take greater care with her flight path. Physically, she'd completely recovered from the earlier hawk attack in Blakfel. Emotionally, the experience would never leave her; she would always remain on her guard where raptors were concerned. To the duck's way of thinking, the wartime neutrality of this family of falcons meant that they might not be particularly aggressive toward strangers. But the birds' natural predatory instincts might still hold sway.

The duck hoped to spot the peregrine falcons well before they caught wind of her. Then she'd have a chance to use her introduction from Aeron-Urd instead of having to flee or fight to survive. The closer she got to the site of the colony, the more she scanned the skies above and less the ground below. Concern for her own safety now took precedence over any hope of spotting Haidar.

What strategy should she adopt on meeting the falcons? Would they be impressed by her titles? Could she offer them anything in return? Should she act high and mighty or humble when asking her questions? Aeron-Urd had been unable to give her any advice — not that she would have taken it anyway. Perhaps, because she was an outsider, they'd tell her nothing; perhaps they had nothing new to reveal in any event.

The second mountain range appeared on the horizon, its looming, shark's-teeth peaks still covered with a deep snowpack, despite the fact that spring had arrived long ago. Thick mists hid much of the lower slopes. The awesome heights made the Misken Mountains seem like pathetic hills, and Fridis was overwhelmed by their magnitude. The duck wasn't used to flying at altitudes where the air was so cold and thin.

Fridis had never been certain about the exact location of the falcons' colony. The mountains extended to the north and the south as far as the eye could see. While Aeron-Urd more or less knew the territory, he had never visited it and couldn't give her precise directions. All Fridis could see was a vast emptiness; all she could hear was the wind swirling around her. There were no clues, no traces of life anywhere. Nevertheless, although her misgivings were increasing, it was far too late to turn back.

Fatigue began to take its toll. Fridis needed a rest in order to think about what to do and where to search. Otherwise she'd be flying about aimlessly. She was a great detective, was she not? Better start acting like one. Surely she could figure out something about the location of the falcons' settlement.

She began to soar in circles, looking for a safe landing place on the closest mountain, one that would provide both a commanding view and some protection from the buffeting winds now enveloping her. After a short while she discovered just what she needed. It was not much for a web-footed bird used to flat wetlands, but the ledge was just wide enough. It would more than do.

However, as Fridis huddled against the rock face with the wind whistling past her sleek head, she found the outlook nerve-racking. The spot was, she declared to herself, hardly the place for a duck. Still, now that she had landed, she had to make the best of it and think like a falcon. What would the birds need for their habitation? It would have to be a place with an expansive view over the endless skies beyond and the deep lands below, a place sheltered from the elements where they could rear their young safely, easily concealed from what few predators they might have. In fact, it would be a great deal like the spot where she was now resting.

Fridis began to examine her surroundings. It wasn't long before she found evidence that some other creature had settled on that very ledge, recently even. However, while the duck recognized the residues of a meal or two, there was no sign of a nest or anything else of real consequence. Did the falcons just use the spot as one of several resting places, or was it something more?

She was awkwardly hopping and stumbling about when a sound from above attracted her attention. She raised her head to look straight up the cliffside. Given the occasional wind gusts, the experience was a bit dizzying, if not unnerving. Fridis's eyes were watering so much she had to keep blinking to clear her vision. Then, as she opened them one more time, Fridis spied two beady eyes and a hooked beak looking down at her from about fifty feet directly above, fixed on her every movement.

Startled, Fridis let out a harsh quack, flapped her wings and instinctively jumped into the air, veering away from the rock face. The eyes and beak followed her movements but did not otherwise react. The duck, meanwhile, was struggling in the stiff breeze while she tried to keep a close watch on whoever it was looking back at her. Although the eyes continued to stare, the creature did not communicate or even move anything but its downy head.

After a few anxious moments, Fridis concluded that the bird posed no threat. Chances were the creature was either incapacitated or merely curious. She flew up and hovered at its height, then circled around, investigating more closely, until her confidence returned. Finally feeling secure enough, Fridis approached — a trifle unsteadily — to land beside the bird, far enough from it that she could jump away if it struck at her.

Fridis quickly discovered that the creature was not alone. It was one of several similar birds, all sheltered in a huge makeshift nest that was cunningly hidden from view until one was right on top of it. The duck stood on a nearby rock ledge looking at them. They kept very still and quiet, watching her intently.

Best to be assertive, she thought. "Greetings, my friends. My name is Lady Fridis, Princess of Vigmar. Can you tell me who you are and where I am?"

Princess was stretching the truth, but she'd got used to the mistaken title and thought it might come in handy when meeting strangers.

"Princess," the largest of the birds answered brightly, "we are the offspring of the Lord and Lady of Sesteros, who rule this mountain region. We await their return, and in their name we bid all visitors welcome."

So that was it: they were mere nestlings. Definitely polite and well brought up, Fridis decided. However, since the young birds were as big as she was, the duck wondered with some anxiety how huge the parents must be.

"I thank you for your most gracious welcome, young ones. And when do you think the Lord and Lady will return?"

"It should be very soon," responded the same chick. "It's rather unusual for both to be away at the same time, but given our advanced age, they are confident we will be secure from all enemies."

"I'd imagine your enemies must be few and far between, especially so high up in the mountains."

"That is true, my lady, but one can never be too cautious."

"Are there more of you?"

"Oh yes," answered another. "We have lots of cousins; our family is quite large. There are many sheltered places in these mountains, and they're all well hidden. And there are caves where we can shelter from the worst winter storms."

They may be cautious, Fridis considered, *but they're certainly forthcoming with information. Lucky for them I'm not an enemy.*

"Listen, young ones, do you happen to know a falcon by the name of Raicho?"

"Raicho? Yes, my lady, he's our favorite cousin!" replied several of them in unison, delighted at hearing the name.

"A great warrior," one said proudly. "I'm named after him."

"Do you know him, my lady?" asked another.

"Indeed I do. Raicho and I are very well acquainted. We spent several weeks together in the south of Arundati this past winter. Do you know where that is? Your cousin was looking after me, as a matter of fact."

This news created a deal of excitement. It turned out that Raicho, en route to join his squadron in the borderlands, had recently traveled through the falcons' homeland to pay his respects to his many relatives. The bird was clearly a hero to his younger relations, who immediately asked for tales about his exploits.

Just as Fridis was beginning to regale them with her story, she heard far behind her a harsh, sharp *rehk-rehk-rehk*. All eyes turned to the eastern sky. The Lord and Lady in question were circling gracefully overhead, soaring on an upstream of air. With increasing anxiety Fridis watched the pair descend. The newcomers were large indeed, and they appeared — at least to Fridis — quite ferocious. Their huge talons were loaded with food.

Fridis began to prepare her words of greeting. However, as the parents glided in, even before she could open her beak to explain her arrival, the enthusiastic nestlings were telling them about their royal visitor and her connection to their illustrious cousin. The adults dealt first with their chicks' needs, as good parents must, all the while eyeing Fridis carefully and somewhat imperiously. Meanwhile she bowed low to them and tried to pay her respects in spite of the commotion.

When the screeching had abated and things had calmed down, Fridis was able to explain her unexpected appearance in the falcons' territory. The duck presented her introduction from Aeron-Urd and gave them a gift: one of the many jewels she had obtained from the Misken mine. The longer she spoke, the greater the two birds' obvious relief. Fridis's status quickly changed from intruder to guest, the falcon parents relaxed and harmony reigned.

Fridis went on to tell her hosts about Raicho's role in her rescue from false imprisonment, the trip south to Arundati and recent events in Vigmar. The duck was relieved to learn that the falcon had not spoken ill of her, despite what had occurred at Misken. Aeron-Urd was well known to them and held in high regard, although the same could not be said for the two warring factions.

"We have long held ourselves apart from those contemptible adversaries," said Lady Sesteros, gazing out over the valley beyond. "This demanding location may not be the most sought-after home on earth, but it suits us just fine. And it's ours to command, without interference from either party — or anyone else for that matter. It's rare that anyone bothers us here."

"And we certainly don't bother anyone else," her husband added.

"But your cousin Raicho and many of his brethren seem to have chosen otherwise," Fridis said. "Why is that?"

"It's true we're not all of one mind on this important matter," Lady Sesteros replied. "Unfortunately, not all the hawks and falcons are as well situated as we are. The valley you see below is undisturbed and virtually inaccessible. Perfect for us, but for few others. Other branches of the family could not avoid getting caught up in this endless fighting. Although we invited them to join us, only a few saw fit to accept our offer. Oaths of loyalty weigh heavily in the falcons' world." She shrugged as if to say *There's no accounting for the judgment of some birds.*

"I understand Raicho visited here only recently."

"Yes, but that information is not well known," Lord Sesteros said, eyeing his young ones severely. "Our cousin asked us not to tell anyone." Then he smiled indulgently. "But you know how excitable nestlings can be; they can't control their tongues at this age. And I'm sure there's no harm done, since you and Raicho are well acquainted. In point of fact, our cousin took quite a detour to get here, as his new squadron is stationed far to the south. It was a rare opportunity for him to pay a visit and bring us news of the outside world, and vice versa. Raicho is dear to us, and we had not seen him in a long while."

In a bitter tone the falcon added, "Who knows — we may not see him again. This wretched war!"

"Tell me, if you feel you can," said Fridis, "who is at fault for starting the war? Or, more to the point, who's to blame for continuing it?"

"Both sides!" the two falcons replied quickly, in unison.

"Some creatures never learn," continued Lady Sesteros. "Can you believe it, carrying on a war from one generation to the next? How crazy is that? How pointless! And have you heard the latest? In Aeronbed they're now turning on each other."

"No," Fridis answered. "What do you mean?"

"The panthers have attacked the lions and pushed them into the far north. A civil war has broken out, on top of the war with Vigmar. How long Albiorix can hold out while fighting on two fronts, I can't imagine. Of course, the old lion may have already given up by now. Our news is always a little dated."

The details didn't really make much difference to Fridis. The duck knew very little about who was who and what was what in Aeronbed. "How do you know so much about what's going on with your neighbors?" she asked. "I mean, since you keep apart from everyone else."

"We keep our distance, that's true enough. But we birds see much from on high and can cover a lot of territory in a day or two. A lot of information gets passed around at the watering holes and in the wetlands. And, of course, since it's migration season, relatives and old friends are stopping by to gossip and pass on the latest tidbits," Lady Sesteros said, smiling broadly. "You're a duck — you know how birds are."

"Have you heard much about what happened farther south?" asked Fridis. "Where the wolves invaded Aeronbed last year?" The duck hoped she might hear some news of Eirwen's exploits. She felt a pang of heartache throughout her very being; it had been a while now since she'd thought about the polar bear.

"Not so much from that region, I'm afraid," Lord Sesteros said. "An army of wolves, you say? Haven't heard anything about that. Different migration route, you know. Why do you ask?"

Fridis told the solicitous pair about Eirwen, recounting the story she'd heard of his tragic death. They were appropriately dismayed, adding that they would pay attention to any news from that region, should it come their way.

They feasted and gossiped for the whole day. It was a rare respite for Fridis; she felt truly at ease with these sensible, affable, matter-of-fact falcons. They were not at all like what she had expected, but then again, the whole land was a constant source of surprise. In her enjoyment of their company, Fridis almost forgot why she had come in the first place. By late afternoon, when they were still in the jolliest of moods, the duck decided she'd better get to the point or her moment would be lost, probably forever.

"Your hospitality has been most generous. Really, I'm overwhelmed by it. I haven't felt so happy in ages. Your welcome has been more than I ever expected, and your chicks are treasures — so polite and well brought up."

The two falcons beamed, like all parents when their children are complimented and their own role is recognized.

"I've been having so much fun," added Fridis, "that I forgot completely about the purpose of my trip here."

"So you didn't drop in just to exchange news of our cousin?" Lord Sesteros said, winking.

Fridis laughed.

"You see, Fridis," Lady Sesteros added, laughing as well, "at this rate we'll be inviting you to stay with us, even though you aren't a falcon. And then you won't ever be able to leave."

"Perhaps not such a far-fetched thought — or desire. Since the death of my dear friend I have been at loose ends, a bird without a proper roost, so to speak." Fridis paused briefly as she contemplated the suggestion of staying on. "But I still have a mission that I must complete before I'd ever contemplate accepting such an invitation. My Lord and Lady Sesteros, here is the reason I am here — " The duck went on to describe a good part of her experience at the mines and her search for where the mysterious Misken gemstones had gone after they disappeared.

The falcons looked at each other, their eyes wide.

"Now, that is old family lore," exclaimed Lord Sesteros.

"It's a shame you didn't ask Raicho about it," Lady Sesteros said. "He knows far more than we do."

Fridis sighed inwardly at receiving that advice for a second time. Would she ever get a chance to quiz Raicho? "But I gather you know something of the story," she persisted. "And of Kelnek."

"Naturally, but I'm afraid much of it cannot be verified," replied Lord Sesteros. "It occurred a long time ago, and many accusations were bandied about that no one was ever able to prove."

"Yes, so I've heard. Is there something you can add to what I already know?" Fridis looked at both of them in turn and hesitated. "But please, only tell me what you feel comfortable about saying. I don't wish to pry or bring unhappy memories back into your lives."

"Fear not, Princess. As I said, it was a very long time ago," replied Lord Sesteros. "I don't think anyone really cares about the gems anymore. Well, except you, perhaps. In fact, it's been a long while since we've even spoken of the affair."

Lady Sesteros took up the tale. "There appears to have been an orchestrated effort to blame Kelnek for what happened. As you can imagine, we peregrines are rather sensitive about that accusation. To steal the gemstones would not have been an honorable act — so unlike a falcon."

"Aeron-Urd said the same thing. But still, not impossible?"

"No, of course not impossible. Bad eggs turn up in almost every nest over the course of time. But Kelnek? I don't think so."

"Why not?"

"Because of everything else we know about him. Usually if one has an evil streak, it comes out in different ways. But no other charge was ever leveled against that bird. In fact, to our knowledge, Kelnek was always well-regarded by his peers. No one else had anything ill to say about him. Nothing at all."

"What was said?"

"Well, some maintained that Kelnek had the motive and the opportunity. And a means of easy escape — being a bird, that is, he could cover a lot of ground."

"What possible motive did Kelnek have that the other partners did not?"

"Exactly," Lord Sesteros said.

"Well, not exactly," Lady Sesteros countered. The other two looked at her.

"You're not going to bring up that old chestnut, are you, my dear?" Lord Sesteros said, his eyebrow feathers raised in question.

"It must be admitted, in all honesty, my love."

What could this be about? wondered Fridis. She didn't want to interrupt the flow of information by speaking.

"We've heard it said," Lady Sesteros continued, "that Kelnek believed the badger — What was his name? Achimi? Yes, that was it — that this Achimi was not prepared to use the gems to their full potential. What I mean is, the badger didn't see or couldn't understand the forces for good they could be put toward. So the gems just languished, hidden underground and neglected, because he kept them a secret. It was also suggested that only Kelnek — and again I must admit that no witnesses ever came forward to verify this — saw their true potential. Somehow or other, the King of Vigmar came to know about the stones. And the story goes on to say that the King ... Gosh, now I've forgotten his name too. What was it, my dear?"

"Berkulan," Lord Sesteros said.

"Yes, that was it. So Berkulan, or possibly some creature allied with him, convinced Kelnek that he could make far better use of the stones. Only a ruler of true nobility, he was told, would use them for the good of all the world's animals. And so Kelnek was urged to take the stones from Achimi and give them to Berkulan. The story is that he actually did so, but only after much convincing."

"But you do not believe it," said Fridis.

"We don't know what to believe, Princess," Lord Sesteros replied. "The point is, we have no evidence one way or the other. And no details of that story can be corroborated or denied. So we simply refuse to pass judgment."

"It would account for the sudden rise in power of the kings of Vigmar," added Lady Sesteros.

"But it does not confirm how they got hold of the gems," her husband responded. "Only that they did so."

"That is very true, my dear. It could have been any of them."

"This story was bandied about for many years," continued Lord Sesteros, "but no one ever saw fit to accuse Kelnek of the theft — at least not directly. So that says something."

"Whatever became of Kelnek? Were the gems ever seen again?"

"I know he came back here, at least for a time. Word had it that Kelnek was greatly saddened by the turn of events, but he never spoke much about those days to anyone around here. One day he just disappeared and never returned. As for the gemstones, I don't think anyone ever saw them again. Perhaps Raicho can add something to this tale. When next you meet him, you should ask him."

Fridis thanked the two birds profusely. Her time with the falcons had been much more pleasurable than she'd ever imagined. Indeed, the suggestion that she return after her mission was the best invitation she'd received since arriving in Vigmar. While the mountain heights were hardly suitable for a web-footed, water-loving duck, this colony of falcons had quickly become the closest thing to family she'd ever encountered.

With a full heart, Fridis told the Sesteros family that she looked forward with enthusiasm to their next encounter. Then, with real sadness, she bade them farewell.

VIII

AERONBED

❧ 43 ❧

A CHANGE IN REGIME

Albiorix's informants, whoever they were, had let the old lion down just when he needed them most. Perhaps those sources had never really existed, except by rumor and reputation. Or possibly the king's past success had been due more to a combination of his sharp instincts and excellent judgment. Whatever the case, in the animal kingdom — in any kingdom, any world — one is only as good as one's last battle.

King Albiorix had expected something, his nerves on edge and his whiskers on high alert. He had sent Olwen to Heimborn because he was highly suspicious of what he'd been hearing about turmoil in the hinterland and misinformation from the panthers' Grand Council. What he hadn't expected was the suddenness of the Black Legion's move, ironically brought on not by victory but by defeat.

The king was used to dealing with more predictable and less mercurial cats than Parthanyx. One can study and plan for the behavior of rational, well-balanced creatures, but the mad animal is impulsive and erratic in his moves. How — unless one is similarly crazed — can an individual prepare for such an enemy? Such an animal makes unexpected moves, takes huge risks and attacks out of the blue, even though it makes no sense and before it is properly ready. But surprise counts for much in war, and in this instance Albiorix was taken completely by surprise.

By the time the Legion's assault was determined to be not just some troop maneuver or a strategic repositioning, but rather a full-fledged onslaught and occupation, it was too late to do anything but beat a hasty retreat. Albiorix had few forces to call upon, loyal or otherwise, between the capital and the army of panthers. Thus, not only was the lion surprised, he was also at a severe disadvantage in terms of numbers.

One truism about conducting war is that, when an army meets an opponent of overwhelming size, it's generally best to take a step backwards and live to fight another day. With the bulk of the lion armies stationed elsewhere — mostly in the north, fighting Vigmar — Albiorix and Temorwig knew they had little chance of success against Parthanyx.

As a last resort, the two had turned to their few remaining panther allies in Manaris. But that faction, after some soul-searching (such as it was), gave the lions the cold shoulder. Rithild was not to be found and Anishger blathered on, offering to act as a mediator to try to find an "honorable and peaceful resolution to the crisis" — when of course there was none to be had. Albiorix had no time for such discussions, and he also saw through the Grand Council's scheming.

In the end, Albiorix was sensible enough to acknowledge that his reign had come to an end — at least temporarily — and astute enough to realize that pleas for mercy would receive short shrift. With great sadness the king left his capital, the city his family had largely envisioned and shaped. During his retreat, he was preoccupied by thoughts of Olwen's vision. If the old lion found comfort in that recollection, he revealed it to no one.

The remaining inhabitants of the capital tried to escape as well, following after Albiorix's retreating stalwarts. For the most part those creatures, being too young or too old for fighting, were not able to flee fast enough. They were dealt with brutally by the panthers, who took out their anger and lust for revenge on the lions instead of the bears.

Parthanyx was sending a clear message to the rest of the kingdom: the new ruler of Aeronbed would exhibit little patience and even less empathy for those who failed to submit to his regime.

The entire operation — the attack and overthrow of the old guard — was executed quickly and efficiently. Within only a few days the Legion had occupied the central part of Aeronbed and installed a new and much tougher administration. Albiorix and Temorwig, along with their remaining supporters, had fled to the north to join their army there, which was already fully engaged in bloody battle with Vigmar's forces. As a result, while the lions still held the far north and far south of Aeronbed, the center and its highly prized capital now lay within the tight grasp of the panthers.

The venerable Archduke Anishger met Parthanyx at the gates of the castle to welcome the kingdom's new commander-in-chief. He was wise enough to recognize youthful vigor, audacity and power when it stood squarely before him. More than that, he knew better than to take on a younger opponent in a struggle for dominance, especially when the latter was backed by a huge contingent of loyal comrades. For his part, Rithild reappeared once the dust had settled, as mysteriously and as quietly as he had previously vanished.

In this rare instance, Parthanyx was not to be outdone in acumen and political instincts. Most of his followers had expected the panther to place Albiorix's crown upon his own head. But the cat did not choose to glorify himself or strut about in a regal manner. Instead, to everyone's surprise, he asked Baron Rithild to act as Aeronbed's regent and interim ruler. Parthanyx would continue to head the army in his drive to eliminate Albiorix's loyalists and capture the rest of the kingdom.

Parthanyx knew he had to move quickly to take advantage of the disarray in the lions' camp. The panther commander had realized what others had failed to observe: that in point of fact the lions had yet to be defeated in battle. They had merely been pushed aside, leaving a vacuum that the Black Legion now occupied. Albiorix and his beleaguered supporters were on the run and forced to fight on two fronts, but the old lion was far from crushed; he still had many battle-hardened followers. It was time for Parthanyx to pounce again, before those tiresome creatures were able to lick their wounds and regroup.

The Legion's leader also understood that remaining in Aeronbed's hospitable capital would only serve to soften and corrupt his troops. His legionnaires had been hardened, in both body and mind, by their many years in the field. Insisting they remain so, Parthanyx wanted to move quickly to take up the battle once more, this time to achieve total victory.

The bears' surprising triumph had amounted to nothing but a step backward for Parthanyx, only strengthening his determination to succeed. Moreover, it had taught the panther a valuable lesson: that Heimborn was but a distracting sideshow. Controlling the whole of Aeronbed was the real goal, and occupying Manaris would be the jewel in his crown. So he had immediately changed course and taken his first major step forward. There would be time enough later to settle scores with the bears, something that he made clear to his commanders when they'd left the mountains of Heimborn far behind.

The Archduke, seeing the writing on the wall, took early retirement and wisely disappeared from the scene, never to be heard from again. No one was more surprised than Lord Rithild when he became the new ruler of Aeronbed. Even though the cat had always coveted the position, and even though his power was held at the behest (or sufferance) of his nephew Parthanyx, he was content — more than content — with his exalted new rank — at least for the present.

As wily and conniving as ever, the Baron always looked forward, never backward. The notion of what might yet be stood foursquare in his mind. Although his nephew was unpredictable, Parthanyx was still family, and he might even be controlled if Rithild played his cards adroitly. And, as reckless and ambitious as Parthanyx was in pursuing his conquests, anything could happen, including an untoward death on the battlefield. *Just as long as it doesn't happen too soon,* thought Rithild. *At least, not before the lions are well and truly disposed of and the new order is made secure.*

The rest of the Grand Council knew where the cards lay, and they picked them up with alacrity to serve the new regime. Those panthers had no great loyalty to the old Archduke and no love at all for the lions who'd dominated them for so long. A new springtime — a panther-led spring — had arrived at last, and they were more than happy to serve the regime and take whatever spoils fell from the table.

In the midst of his rejoicing, Archduke Rithild, as he was now titled, had remarked on one slightly disturbing, discordant note: the absence of his young acolyte, Eisa, among the hordes of panthers now occupying the city. He had expected the Lieutenant to show up sooner rather than later, to pay his respects and report on his observations. When that did not occur, his curiosity was accordingly aroused.

Rithild knew well enough not to ask Parthanyx directly, but he did scout around, casually asking some Legion commanders about Eisa's whereabouts. It was only then that he found out the awful truth about his former assistant's alleged crime, subsequent trial and intended punishment.

It was not clear what had happened to Eisa after his escape; no one wanted to talk about that embarrassment. It was assumed that the panther had somehow died of starvation or exhaustion in the wilds of the mountains bordering Heimborn. Rithild felt a little sorry about that, for he had lost an able and obedient assistant. But he did not spend too much time thinking about his loss; he had a country to run now. Assistants were awfully easy to come by when you ruled the roost.

THE WAR WITH VIGMAR CARRIED ON. IT WAS AS IF NOTHING HAD CHANGED in Aeronbed. It took some time for word to filter east about the change in regime, and even longer to figure out its implications for all the concerned parties.

Adarix and his wolf pack, now aided by the squadrons of Lorcan and Corvus, finally gave up stalling. Having received no word from the high command in Blakfel to change course, they were forced to follow the original directive: to proceed south to meet up with Emer-Sigr and her forces.

Vigmar's northern army, under the command of General Nashorn, continued to struggle onward through the mountainous border region.

Suffering from the absence of Fridis's interventions to restore the wounded to health, the rhinoceros was determined to proceed even more cautiously and deliberately. Fortunately for him, the lions, their attention now divided between the panthers to the south and the rhinos and dogs to the north, were forced into a defensive position on both fronts. Thus Nashorn was able to maintain his slow advance.

The apes, who had fled Vigmar so desperately to join the forces of Aeronbed, were now caught in a dilemma. They could not change sides again, fearing absolute humiliation — if not outright slaughter — at the hoofs of the Emperor and Empress if they dared to return in that direction. Nor could they see hanging on to the losing proposition of the lions. So, once again, the ape forces chose to melt away in the middle of the night. No one was quite sure how they managed the feat or where they had gone. One thing was clear, however: their new calling card seemed to be the art of slipping out of a noose.

Eirwen continued his efforts to mold the bears into a vigorous fighting force and to edge them out of their apparently secure shelter. Slowly and carefully he began to work his way beyond the borders of Heimborn and into Aeronbed proper. His first move took him into the areas recently vacated by the panthers. Fortunately, the Legion, its attention now focused on destroying the lions to the north, had not remained in any strength. As a result, the bears had free rein in those early days to establish a strong presence in the central region. The clans that preferred to stand on the sidelines, led principally by Gullhinder, did so, remaining in their Heimborn enclaves. They were waiting to see which way the wind would blow, much like the panthers of the Grand Council.

Parthanyx wasted no time carrying on with his bold assault against the lions. At first, well rested after the winter, the lions were able to hold the Legion at bay. But, faced with the unrelenting pressure of Vigmar's forces on his eastern flank, Albiorix was forced to give way. He retreated with his shattered army even farther, to a redoubt at the far northern tip of Aeronbed. There the lions held on as best they could in rough, dense terrain while the panthers consolidated their hold in the remainder of the north and then turned to deal with Vigmar's northern army.

The only hope remaining to Albiorix was to link up with what remained of the lions' forces in the south and with any other cats still loyal to his regime. However, by that point the besieged King was so isolated he could do little but stand his ground and hope for a miracle. Unfortunately for the old lion, miracles were in very short supply.

❧ 44 ❧
HAIDAR'S TREK

"I've been wondering, Haidar," the red fox asked with a surprising degree of admiration. "How did you come to know your way through these mountains? The safe passages between Vigmar and Aeronbed are few and far between, and none of them are easy — at least to my knowledge."

When the mountain goat failed to reply, Vulpé added, "You know, Gloton told me nothing about why he asked you to, er, participate in this mission. Nor, for that matter, why you agreed to do so."

This time Haidar chose to respond, but only to the first question. "It's simple enough. I keep my eyes, ears and nose open," the goat said dismissively. "And I work just as hard to remember what I've learned. It's nothing that you or any other creature couldn't manage. That is, if you bothered to try."

"I understand that," persisted Vulpé. "But how did you find this particular route?"

"I used to get out and about more — a lot more. In the old days, that is. And don't forget, I am a mountain goat, so great heights and narrow ridges are nothing to me."

"Of course, of course. But with all due respect, we're already well into Aeronbed. Nobody goes for a holiday stroll this far from Vigmar."

"You'd be surprised how far some do — or rather, did — roam about, before the war began."

"Since when has there not been a war?" groused the fox. "I'd be hard pressed to remember one day of real peace since I was a mere kit."

Haidar just grunted. Vulpé noted that the close-mouthed goat hadn't bothered to reply to his other questions.

The two animals were creeping through a dense forest of tall pine trees, over ground carpeted with long-dead needles and low, sparse underbrush, in the lands just west of the mountain range dividing Aeronbed from Vigmar. Trusting in the goat's guidance, the fox had little idea as to his exact location. They'd passed unmolested along treacherous trails and through difficult narrow chasms, little explored and even less traveled, seemingly remembered in this time of hostility only by the mountain goat.

The fox was hoping he'd be able to remember the roundabout and seemingly devious route Haidar had chosen, so that he would be able to find his way home again. Vulpé knew that pretty soon the pair would have to part ways, very likely never to see each other again, if what Gloton had told him was accurate. One of them would be going one way — toward the lions — while the other would be searching out the panthers. Unless, of course, Gloton's source had erred in his assessment of Aeronbed's evolving political situation. If so, the First Secretary's trust would represent a rare lapse of judgment.

But Haidar had given the fox no clues as to the logic of his chosen path, and Vulpé found the route, despite his careful questions and crafty brain, very difficult to figure out. The twists and turns, the switchbacks, the rugged trails, the fords across anonymous rivers, the impenetrable stands of pines and cedars — the fox kept trying to store in his mind the scents and visual aspects, retracing the course over and over again. Unfortunately, with each passing day he had more to remember, and the effort was proving challenging.

Vulpé knew he would have to pick his moment of departure perfectly, for once they'd split up, he would be well and truly on his own. Indeed, the fox reckoned he might have to place his faith in the panthers to provide him safe passage back.

"Haidar, let's stop a while. We need to speak further."

"What's there to talk about?" Haidar asked gruffly. He disliked the fox's questions and was tiring of the constant interruptions. "We must push on. Time does not stand still, you know." As if to accentuate the point, the goat leapt ahead.

Not to be outdone, Vulpé seized one of the mountain goat's legs in his jaws in an attempt to force him to a stop. Haidar tried to pull away, but the fox held on tightly, although not hard enough to draw blood. He was tempted to squeeze harder but didn't want to antagonize his guide. Finally Vulpé's persistence paid off, and the goat was forced to acquiesce.

"The time has come," said the fox, "to talk about the specific details of what we are to do."

"Can't it wait?" the mountain goat said with undisguised irritation. "We still have a way to go before nightfall."

"No, Haidar, it cannot," replied the fox forcefully. "We must deal with it this very minute."

The goat sighed deeply and turned toward his partner. "Well?" he said.

Although the fox had thought carefully about this moment, he'd come to understand that Haidar was both prickly and unpredictable, and not easily pushed around. Could he convince the mountain goat to go his way? Vulpé thought it highly unlikely, but he had to try.

"You know our mission is to seek a peace accord with Aeronbed, one that will bring about a just, lasting and honest end to this war."

The goat glowered at the fox, as if to say, *Do you think I'm stupid? Do you think I need reminding? What other reason could there be?*

"Don't get impatient. I'm just recapitulating the situation before I get to the point," Vulpé responded quickly. "And you're aware that grievances over the years have brought about a situation where both sides no longer trust, let alone speak to each other."

Haidar said, his voice dripping with sarcasm, "Am I supposed to nod or what?"

"Haidar, I'm just putting the context in perspective."

"Just get to the point."

"I'm trying. Bear with me a little." The fox realized that the goat was not going to make it easy for him. "So our friends have been searching for an intermediary, someone with whom we can enter into discussions. Someone who hasn't been a party to the years of past misunderstandings and built-up enmity. Someone who might have a fresh perspective on the matter. In sum, a creature who can break free of past prejudices. Are you following me?"

"Yes, of course." A little more calmly now. "What you say makes sense."

Well, that's a break, thought Vulpé. *Now for the tough part.*

"We concluded that we can't speak directly to the lions," the fox continued. "No offense meant, but we needed another creature, one that could relate to the leadership but was not one of them. Someone who could speak their language and whom both sides could trust." Vulpé paused to see if Haidar was still onside.

"Go on," the goat said carefully, wondering what creature could ever live up to such a buildup.

"So you'd agree that our go-between needs to be one of the big cats, but not a lion?" It was a jump, but a logical one.

The goat hesitated, reflecting on what that implied. "Possibly," he said after a while, not completely swayed by the fox's reasoning. "It depends on which individual you propose."

"Do you know everyone in Aeronbed?"

"I know a few, although some by reputation only."

"Then how can you judge who I might suggest?"

That was a good argument, but Haidar was not yet prepared to give way. "True enough. Equally, however, neither can you. You know even less about the cats than I do."

The fox didn't dare pretend otherwise. This line of attack was leading him nowhere. It was time for a big lie. "Don't forget, we're very well informed. I wouldn't have based a trip into Aeronbed on mere speculation, not at all. On the contrary, we've received word from our contacts that certain parties are prepared to deal with us."

"Indeed." The ever-skeptical Haidar had yet to be impressed.

"Yes," continued Vulpé, warming to the task. "We believe this is the breakthrough we've been looking for. The point is, Haidar, go-betweens have been conducting talks — in secret, mind you — for a while now. It was only recently we received confirmation that the time is now perfect to reach an accord."

"If that's so, why do you need me? If you've been conducting these *talks*, someone else must know a safe way through to Aeronbed."

The fox was taken aback by the quick retort. He had overstepped, underestimating the goat's intelligence and unrelenting distrust. Haidar was not to be as easily swayed or fooled as Gloton had let on. Vulpé had hoped to push him into going with him to approach the panthers instead of the lions, but now he realized that strategy would not work. Deciding that he'd better move to another tack, the fox paused for effect and looked about him before responding.

"I'm sorry," Vulpé said, hanging his head in mock shame. "You are absolutely correct, Haidar. If we indeed enjoyed such an excellent situation, we'd have been positioned to go it alone. The truth is, we are not — nowhere near. Forgive my foolish boasting. It was my feeble attempt to make us — to make me seem more successful in your eyes. The fact is, my good fellow, we've had no such luck. That's the reason why we need your help, pure and simple.

"We have made contact, but it's only that. Contact and connections that are limited, peripheral and with not much to show for them. We understood that you have family history with these cats and a feeling for them. Don't worry. I assure you, I don't know the details of that story. It's just that we believe you might succeed where we cannot." The fox hung his head even more deeply in apparent shame. His neck began to hurt from the effort.

Haidar had listened in noncommittal silence. He began to reflect on the fox's confession. While some creatures might have walked away from such a situation — an admission of lying, a story of failure and deceit — they had the opposite impact on the mountain goat. In fact, Haidar found those words of apology far more affecting than Vulpé's previous arrogance.

"I appreciate your honesty, even if it comes so late in the day," he said at last. "You have need of my unique knowledge and position. Of course, it makes perfect sense. Although it won't be easy, it's possible I can make the connection you need. I say 'possible' because the world has changed a great deal; the situation may be too far gone for any hope of peace to succeed. Still, we're a long way from abandoning hope. We will proceed as planned. Who knows, Vulpé, if we're lucky, we'll meet up with someone who can aid us in our quest."

Vulpé smiled inwardly. The cautious goat had been restrained in his reply, promising nothing and naming no potential intermediary. However, the fox knew then that he'd finally found the key to Haidar, one he resolved to use again whenever it proved necessary. The moment of decision could wait for another day.

🐾 45 🐾

ON THE MOVE

After surfacing from their hideout, Eisa and Olwen made their way by less traveled byways back to the outskirts of the capital of Aeronbed. While the panther remained hidden nearby, Olwen entered Manaris via a discreet, circuitous route the lioness had used in her younger, more rebellious days. Although her escapes from the capital's confines had been rare, the Princess had always thought it would come in handy later. However, the lioness had never imagined the current scenario: the overthrow of the lion regime by the rebellious panthers.

Once inside the city, Olwen was able to contact those few lions that the panthers had left alive as useful to their new overlords. Much to her dismay, those townsfolk confirmed Eisa's suspicions. The Black Legion had thrown out her father, King Albiorix, and instituted a new government. The usurpers, led by the recently promoted Rithild, had imposed harsh restrictions and an administration managed along strict military lines. General Parthanyx, as he now called himself, had not tarried in the capital but had hurried on toward the north of Aeronbed. There he was pursuing his campaign against the King's remaining supporters.

Olwen's only consolation was that her father was believed to be alive and nowhere near giving up his fight for the kingdom. That was the only good news; the rest was much less positive. Word in the laneways and markets was that the struggle was not going well. The King and his loyalists were being backed inexorably into the northwest corner of the kingdom.

In despair, Olwen left the capital to relay the news to Eisa. The two big cats were sheltering at a deserted farm, only a stone's throw from the castle walls, while they contemplated their next move.

Eisa, in his naivety and continuing faith in authority, had been sorely tempted to arrange a meeting with Rithild. The panther wanted to make his terrible predicament known to his former chief, to avow his innocence and pledge his continued loyalty to the Grand Council. Despite the false charges leveled by the Legion, he wanted desperately to restore his place in the ranks of his extended family, and he knew that only Rithild could vouch for him and prove he had remained true to the panthers' cause.

Restoring his position, however, was just one side of the equation. The other side was the situation facing Olwen. As the King's daughter, the lioness would be a target for every Legion soldier. She was a creature on the run, without any safe haven. Eisa, with his empathetic heart, felt increasingly entwined with the Princess's fate. And she had saved his life with her quick actions. He was indebted to the lioness, and that fact was of great importance to the panther.

When the moment came to face the crucial decision about whether or not to seek his own redemption, Eisa was greatly torn. If he actually managed to restore his position, he would be leaving Olwen to a terrible fate. In all good conscience, how could he do so? But if he chose to walk away from his family and remained with Olwen, what about his future? He'd be casting his lot with her and, by extension, the former lion regime, with which he felt little in common. Eisa was a panther born and bred; surely he belonged with his kin. However, the Lieutenant had rejected the vicious path chosen by Parthanyx. That malignant cat now ruled Aeronbed, and after what had happened to him at Heimborn, Eisa felt alienated, abandoned by his own kind. The choice seemed impossible.

The two cats had left the farm during the night and made their way through some nearby woods. They were now holed up in a small cave to the south of Manaris. The cave was more like a thin crack in the rock face, hardly big enough for two big cats, but it was well concealed and afforded them all the privacy they required. From there, if he so desired, Eisa could sneak back to the castle without being seen. Getting into the former king's chambers, now occupied by Rithild, would be another matter.

Despite his divided mind and misgivings, Eisa broached the subject of meeting with his former superior. "You know, this could well be my only opportunity — " the panther began.

The dismayed lioness was one jump ahead of him. She cried out, "You can't possibly be thinking of going to see Rithild! If so, you're ... " Her voice trailed off, leaving the thought unfinished. If Eisa had been her brother she would have called the panther a fool, but the two were not close enough friends to allow for insults.

Eisa realized that Olwen understood exactly what was on his mind. Yet the panther had been hoping, even expecting, some respect for his painful position. She knew his story of injustice, so why did the lioness not understand the need to state his case and right the wrongs done to him? Could she not see how heavily that awful accusation weighed upon him? "How can you object to my trying to set things right?" he protested. "If I can't make Rithild understand what really happened, I'll be a criminal forever, outside the law, on the run for the remainder of my days."

"I applaud your desire to *set things right*," Olwen said, with more than a hint of scorn. "Of course, one's sense of justice is always at its strongest when applied to one's own situation. Perhaps you've forgotten what happened here: the overthrow of the legitimate government and the imposition of a brutal regime bent on vengeance.

"But let's leave that trifle aside. I'm sorry to tell you, Eisa, that your problems count for nothing. Don't you see the world's been turned upside down? Do you honestly think you can march in, get a fair hearing and achieve *justice* in an afternoon? I would laugh if the idea didn't make me feel like weeping."

"But Rithild is the only one who can vouch for me," the panther protested. "And as Aeronbed's leader he has the authority to deliver me from that death sentence."

"Rithild's but a sham leader. You know that just as well as I do. Parthanyx commands in all matters. Can you not see that? Do you think Rithild would free you on his own? At best you would be clapped into prison to await orders from Parthanyx. At worst you would be quietly disposed of and your carcass left to rot in some distant field. Mark my words, Eisa, you'd simply disappear off the face of the earth."

"But Parthanyx would be forced to release me once the truth is made known."

"Really? Why?"

"Because that's the right and just thing to do."

"And in your experience, Eisa, that's how Parthanyx conducts his affairs?"

The panther opened his mouth but could think of nothing to say. He knew how Parthanyx conducted his affairs; he was harsh, merciless and already on the edge of madness. Eisa had seen for himself how his former brother officer commanded. "But Rithild is no fool! Surely my loyalty counts for something," he exclaimed. "Would he not think of some clever way around the situation?"

"Hah! The only thing that will be worked around is you. And on top of everything, your association with me would add yet another charge to the list of your crimes. You think that little detail won't come out? It'd be Rithild's second question. *So tell me, Eisa, did you ever meet up with the Princess?* And you're so innocent you'd blurt out the answer without even thinking."

The embarrassed panther was speechless as Olwen went on. "Listen, Eisa, you and I are different, in so many ways. But for the past couple of weeks we've had one thing in common: Parthanyx wants us both dead. He is our common enemy, and that fact binds us together. Perhaps that bond won't last forever, but it certainly does for the present.

"If you choose to seek out Rithild, I must flee. If my father dies, I become heir to the kingdom. I have authority and legitimacy and I'm an experienced commander in the field, so Parthanyx has more than one reason to have me killed. Right now I am alone and powerless; my only hope is to seek out allies and build up my strength. You must choose what you wish to be — my enemy or my friend."

It was a stark choice. Eisa had only one tool at his disposal: he could betray Olwen in return for his own restitution. Everything the panther wanted (or thought he wanted) could be his — or would if his mind worked like that of Rithild. But it did not; even he was aware of that. At the back of the panther's mind, Eisa was far from sure whether his mentor retained any residual loyalty toward him.

So Eisa already knew he had no choice but to leave Manaris with Olwen and throw in his lot with the lions. The Princess had saved him and now he must repay the debt. Still, it was a painful choice. He was leaving his own world for good; there could be no turning back. Although neither cat spoke of it, they were both aware of the significance of his choice. His sacrifice now matched her courage. They were united in a new cause.

"Let's get away from this place," Eisa declared. "I'm not sure where to go, though anywhere but here would be a vast improvement."

They left their narrow cave and crept down the mountainside.

"Let me tell you a story," Olwen said by way of reply, "as the two of us journey together into the unknown."

The lioness then told the panther all about her meeting with the raven, the prophecy and her efforts to unravel its meaning.

❦ 46 ❧

A NEW DIRECTION

The two big cats had been traveling along long-forgotten and densely overgrown hidden trails known only to Olwen. Dusk was approaching, and they were now far enough away from the castle to feel safe and relaxed enough to drop their guard.

The lioness's story of her meeting with the raven, what was then revealed to her, the subsequent conversations with King Albiorix, and their collective — and frustrating — attempts to decipher its meaning had taken considerable time to tell, especially as Olwen had gone into great detail. Eisa listened thoughtfully and without interruption.

By the time the lioness was nearing the end of her long tale, darkness was falling over central Aeronbed. The two companions pressed on notwithstanding, putting as much distance as possible between themselves and Manaris. Although they had encountered no other mammals along the way, the pair were now being serenaded by the typical sounds of early evening: the muted hums, chirps, croaks, buzzes and whatnot of the deep woods.

When Olwen came to the end of her monologue, Eisa turned his head toward her and asked his first question. "Where you were standing when you witnessed the raven's prophecy? What I mean is, what was your position in relation to the vision?"

The eyes of the surprised lioness opened wide with astonishment. "That was exactly the question my father posed!"

Eisa laughed. "Then your father asked the right question. His Majesty is clearly an excellent practitioner of the discipline."

"Divination has always been an interest of his. But how did you know to ask the same question? Surely you too aren't skilled in the wizards' domain."

"To answer that question, Olwen, requires a story of my own. That is, if you'll bear with me."

"Surely. Eisa, you begin to amaze me."

"It was common knowledge," said the young panther, "that the King held fast to the notion of wizardry and prophecy even in these modern times. Your father is a rare advocate of the practice — its champion, even — since, as you probably know, that whole field largely fell out of fashion with his generation. Indeed, some critics label the pursuit 'black magic,' decrying it as nothing more than evil superstition. For the most part it's given no credence at all, and placed on the same level as useless old folktales. Few creatures hold with it now."

"I know. His friend Temorwig is always at him about it. He's the greatest skeptic of them all."

"Well, Temorwig's view certainly prevails these days. It's rare to see an entire complement of wizards being kept on retainer, as your father did. Who knows, perhaps Mirati and his associates will be the last of their kind."

"You seem to know a great deal about my father."

"My own father told me a great deal about the King's interests. He was pleased that someone still held to the old ways."

"Your father? Why?"

"Because, you see, my father was a wizard."

"You're joking!"

"I knew that would surprise you. Kalishin — that was his name — of the famous house of Dariah. He was the last official chief wizard of the panthers. When he retired, the Grand Council decided to give up on the position. To them as well, the idea of prophecy had fallen out of fashion. They wanted to move with the times. Of course, you've seen for yourself how difficult it is to make sense of the clues, and then how impossible it is to verify the results. There were always creatures that doubted the use of prophecy, even when it was all the rage."

Olwen laughed. "You should talk to Temorwig about that."

"I'd say he and the Grand Council would get along just fine ... well, at least on that topic. As for us, whenever my father's work produced answers the Council didn't like — and that became the norm more and more — protests and concerns were raised. Over time, the objections became more frequent and were voiced more loudly. His contribution was seen as being — well, no longer essential to their deliberations. In fact, some of the Council members began to see my father as an annoyance, as frustrating their desires."

"You speak quite matter-of-factly about it."

"I do, don't I." The panther sighed. "It happened a long time ago. Seems like ancient history now."

"What did your father do about it?"

"Really, what could he do? He served at the Council's pleasure; if they didn't need him, they'd stop calling upon him. But my father came from a noble line and was well placed among the ranks of the panthers. And even if they didn't appreciate what he said, they liked and respected him. He maintained his position but was more and more shunted off to the sidelines. Eventually he got the message and retired to teach what he knew to whatever willing pupils were out there. As you can imagine, there weren't too many."

"What about you?"

"When I was quite young, I was willing — at least at first. But you know how it is with the young. At some point your parents become an embarrassment and you think they've nothing worthwhile to teach you. You hear what others — friends, relations, the cynical, the jealous — are saying and you take their words at face value. Whatever the case, it became clear to me that my father was becoming more of a curiosity than an honored elder. So I began to turn away from him and his ideas.

"About the same time, one of my uncles found a position for me with the Baron. As you can imagine, it was pretty exciting for a young cat to be at the center of things, meeting everyone, going all over the place, having the confidence of one of the most senior members of the Grand Council. I grabbed at it and relished every moment. I was so busy I had little time for those at home."

For a while Eisa stopped talking as they walked along, still side by side. All that could be heard was the sounds of the night and their soft tread on the grassy trail.

"And then what?" asked Olwen.

Eisa sighed. "I realized my father was no longer an embarrassment, but someone I truly loved and respected. But by that time it was too late."

The lioness looked directly at the panther. "Too late?"

"He died while I was out on some meaningless errand for Rithild. I never got to say goodbye or tell him how much I cared for him or thank him for what he'd given me. It's something I regret to this day." Eisa shook himself as if to change his mood. "I'm sorry, Olwen, I didn't mean to bother you with my regrets. We were talking about your prophecy, not me and my problems."

"Don't apologize, Eisa," the lioness responded. "I'm glad you told me."

"I guess no one's ever asked me about my life before. It just came pouring out."

Despite the increasing darkness, Olwen could see his eyes glisten and she sensed the pain Eisa must have been harboring for so long. Suddenly she experienced pangs of longing for her own father, now so far away and doubtless in great danger. The lioness hoped desperately that she'd live long enough to see him again. As a cub, she realized, you take for granted that your parents will live forever and that there'll always be another day to thank them and express your love and admiration. The lioness could take comfort in knowing that her relationship with her father had always been an excellent one.

They walked on in silence, each with their private thoughts. After a time, Eisa asked her again, "So, what *was* your position when you saw the vision?"

"I've often tried to remember. Don't forget, many days have gone by since I witnessed it. Also, it happened so fast. What if my memory is faulty? Wouldn't that mess up the whole message?"

"No, not at all, and you're still clear on many other details. We're just trying to figure out the time frame for the prophecy to take effect and what efforts are required to make it happen. Why don't we rest a while and work on it."

The two cats moved off the trail and into a sheltered grove.

"Take a moment and let the scene swim before your eyes," Eisa instructed. "Let your mind go. Think of nothing else."

For several minutes Olwen sat with her eyes closed. Neither spoke. Finally, without opening her eyes, she declared, "I'm looking up toward a mountain. Yes, I think so. Certainly not down. I can see a mountain pass — at least I take it to be one — and I'm standing at the base of the mountain."

Olwen opened her eyes. "Yes, I'm sure of it now. The mountainside was sloping down toward me. It was an easy slope, without trees — just one huge clearing or open meadow. And the creatures I could see were moving from my left to my right along the top of a ridge, not getting closer or moving away from me."

"In that case," Eisa responded, "according to my knowledge of prophecy, what is to occur will not happen quickly or without struggle. Also, you will not be directly involved. However, look what's already happened in the kingdom. You said yourself that the world has turned upside down. Your father has been forced to flee to the far north, the Legion controls the center of Aeronbed, and the bears of Heimborn have turned the tables on the panthers and struck out for the first time anyone can recall. I'd say we're witnessing tumultuous events. And they're not moving slowly at all. Rather, they are overtaking us at every turn."

"I see what you mean. Perhaps I was mistaken after all."

Eisa laughed. "That's one of the main challenges with visions and prophecies. The retelling relies on some creature's memory, which inevitably is far from perfect. You can't be faulted. It's a shame no one else was present to witness it."

"You don't believe me?"

"Not at all. It's just that two heads — that is, two memories — are always better than one."

"In that case I regret it as well. That would have simplified my life considerably." Olwen sighed loudly. "Can you explain anything about the stars in the pond?"

"Did your father ask how many animals you saw?"

"Yes, he did. How did you know that?"

"It's one of the first questions all wizards ask. And what did he conclude?"

"It was not perfectly clear to him. The truth is, I was uncertain. Did I see two or three creatures? I don't know if I can really say," the lioness replied with evident frustration. "Not with any accuracy. Not anymore."

"Always trust your feelings and intuition in such matters. If you thought you saw something, you certainly did."

"In that case it was three, one after the other."

"And your father told you the meaning of the numbers."

"Yes, he did." Olwen explained how the king had interpreted this detail to her.

"I agree with your father's analysis. You know, I went back to studying prophecy on my own in the off-hours, employing my father's tools and books. I learned a lot, though of course I would never claim to have attained his level of expertise. It's only been a part-time effort, and one meets few cats that have actually experienced a vision. So it's a rare day when I actually get to practice these skills." The panther laughed. "So thank you for the opportunity."

"That goes both ways — if you can help clarify the meaning."

"From what you've told me, the white bear — if it does exist — would be something to behold."

"Surely no such creature exists."

"Did you know there are white ravens?"

"A white raven? That's impossible."

"Indeed not. I've seen one myself. Those birds are rare, but they do exist. The impossible is only what we have yet to witness, discover or achieve."

"So you think, somewhere out there, there's a white bear walking around?"

"Of course. Haven't we already experienced several extraordinary events? No, it wouldn't surprise me at all."

"And the stars?"

"How many did you see?"

"Too many to count. The sky was filled with stars. And a full moon as well."

"For you I see an incredibly bright future. Your father was correct; the prophecy concerns you directly. Whatever ails or troubles you will disappear — perhaps not immediately, but in time. For you personally, all the signs are auspicious."

"Well, that's comforting." She laughed. No matter what misgivings she still had about the world of prophecy, this picture of the future pleased her no end.

"Was there anything else?"

"The tree — the abaster tree."

"Oh yes, I'd quite forgotten that detail."

"Temorwig thought it might be the tree of life or some such thing."

"Well, not quite. Do you know the tale of the abaster tree?"

"Afraid not."

"Then I shall tell you. When the world was first fashioned and lands were set aside for cats both big and small, powerful and weak — the lions, panthers, tigers, jaguars, and so on — our creator was very pleased with what had been shaped. There were big smooth rocks upon which to bask in the warm sun, deep grasses to hide in and high ridges for spotting prey. Everything seemed perfect.

"But it was not long before the creator realized some important things had been missed: shelter, shade, sustenance in lean times and so on. The trees were called upon so they could be placed where they would be of greatest benefit to the cats. The most aggressive and boldest trees approached immediately. The conifers, whose branches give deep shade all year long and whose needles provide a soft bed upon which to sleep, came first and the creator accorded them many places to grow.

"Next came the broadleaf trees with their long, thick, twisting branches, perfect for cats to perch on while keeping watch. Then came the many fruit and nut trees, a source of abundance and nutrition in times when the hunt goes badly. Understanding that those trees were crucial to our survival, the creator placed them in many spots around the land. Finally, many splendid flowering trees presented themselves. The creator, realizing that cats need beauty in their lives as well as sustenance, allowed them to grow wherever they took seed.

"When the creator's work was finished, everything seemed perfect. But then, at the very last minute, along came the abaster tree. It had been too shy to push forward with the others, and now it stood quietly before the creator, seeking its own place in the sun. 'But where shall I live?' it asked sadly. 'Sorry, abaster,' replied our creator, 'all the fertile lands have been taken. Indeed, I have even given the rocky and desert lands to those that can survive best there. There is no place left for you.'

"'But what should I do?' lamented the abaster. The creator took pity on the tree, thought long and hard and then declared in a loud voice so that all could hear: 'Abaster, you may have come late, but I hold you in my heart nonetheless. You will become a special tree, one that will always remain exceptional and distinctive. Only a few of you will be discovered, but in each one a little of me will be found, to remind every cat of the mysteries of life. And so every cat will understand that life holds within it something both sacred and transcendent.'

"And so the abaster found its place, hidden amid all the other trees of the world, to exist as a rare, special find. Supposedly, whenever we come across such a tree, it is meant to reveal something. In your case, Olwen, it served to bring you a foreshadowing of what was to come."

"But are we supposed to meekly accept what is foretold," the frustrated lioness demanded, "or is the prophecy's purpose to give us a warning, so that we can prepare ourselves to fight against something we fear or reject?"

"An excellent question, probably the most important question of all," Eisa replied. "What do you think the King's answer would be?"

"I think — since he believes so much in prophecy — that if he could be assured of its meaning he would accept it, whether for ill or for good. He would see it as knowledge to guide us forward, not to fight against."

"In that case I would say that your father is most wise. I too would adopt such an approach."

The two cats remained silent as they resumed their trek away from the coast and deeper into the central hinterlands of Aeronbed. It occurred to Olwen that her first impressions of Eisa had been badly mistaken. She had taken her distant cousin to be another hot-blooded, dull-witted panther, unfit for lion society. However, as she had come to know him through his careful responses and intelligent observations, the lioness realized that he was exactly the opposite.

The lioness hoped that one day Eisa and her father might meet. She felt they would indulge in wonderful, intense conversations about wizardry. Olwen began to see the panther's smooth black pelt not as an imperfection but as attractive, even exotic and handsome. It was a feeling she'd never experienced before.

Eisa, for his part, had already come to admire Olwen's self-confidence, her skills as a warrior, her common sense and wisdom. Now he had also found a confidante, someone who listened to his ideas and took him seriously. She was a rare and beautiful creature with whom he could share his innermost thoughts and feelings. He too had never felt like that before.

IX

BLAKFEL

❧ 47 ❧

AERON-URD IS REVITALIZED

To the inexperienced eye, the squadron of merlins was nothing more than the tiniest of dots in the distant sky set against the morning sun, now rising sharply in the eastern skies behind them. An unwary victim would not have noticed them until it was too late, far too late to react in time.

From an isolated peak a day's flight from Vigmar's capital, Aeron-Urd surveyed his new band of attack birds as they flew in tight formation in the valley below. The squadron had been formed and trained quickly by the Air Marshal himself, bringing in recruits from regions he knew particularly well — birds he thought would be utterly loyal, and to him alone.

From his vantage point Aeron-Urd could judge every maneuver. The gyrfalcon was mightily pleased with their progress. Figure eights, pairings, peeling off, dives, hovering, stealthy gliding — they had already mastered everything, and probably better and faster than he had done at their age. All that remained to establish was nerve under pressure and a killer instinct, but most falcons came by those naturally, and the ones that did not would learn them quickly enough. He would keep his prized new squadron sequestered away from Blakfel, so they would remain untainted by intrigue, pressure and temptation.

Aeron-Urd, reinvigorated by all this activity, was enjoying renewed confidence for the first time since his return from Arundati. The news from the northern front was promising; the forward air defense forces had been deployed effectively in Aeronbed's central border regions; no counterattacks had been experienced elsewhere; the gyrfalcon's opponents in Vigmar were either ignoring him or at least had stopped criticizing his every idea; and now he had molded these new units of predators into fighting form. Life, the Air Marshal thought, was on the upswing. His lethargy had dropped away, his fatigue vanished.

Aeron-Urd had even stopped musing daily about how Fridis might be faring. The falcon had heard nothing from the eider duck, although that was to be expected; since her banishment, there was no way to communicate with her. The Duchess was on her own, pursuing her foolish quest to follow the trail of the Misken gems. The very thought of such wasted effort gave him heartburn.

Still, the gyrfalcon missed the duck terribly. Not much time would go by before he would stop what he was doing, gaze into the western skies and wish that Fridis would suddenly appear on the horizon. And when she inevitably didn't show up, he would ask himself the inevitable questions. Where could Fridis be? Was she in harm's way? Would he ever see her again? Aeron-Urd promised himself that, should the war reach another stalemate or, by some miracle, a satisfying resolution, he would go off in search of the duck. But when that might be, he could only guess.

❧

"What orders has he given you?"

"None, Baron."

"The Air Marshal just keeps you practicing and practicing?"

"I assume he's getting us in shape for a transfer to the front lines in the weeks to come. Reinforcements are always needed, as you — "

The wolverine cut off the bird in mid-sentence. "Why are you stationed apart from the other squadrons? Why is he keeping you in isolation, off in the hinterlands?"

"We were told it's best to be kept separate during our training period. Helps to develop an esprit de corps, you know. That is, at least in the beginning."

"You've no idea at all where the Air Marshal might use you?"

"We are sworn to do his bidding. That is, of course, the way of all attacking birds. Aeron-Urd is renowned as a fearless leader. We respect his ability, and in turn his care for and belief in us is beyond compare. When the time comes, we merlins will do whatever he asks of us."

"Your loyalty to Aeron-Urd is most commendable, Captain. I trust that your loyalty to the Emperor and Empress is no less strong."

"Sir? I don't think I — "

Once again the wolverine interrupted the bird. "Don't make the mistake others have. Your ultimate oath is to the Empire, to their Imperial Majesties, not to one of Vigmar's many generals, no matter what his qualities and reputation may be."

"Of course, First Secretary, that goes without saying. Though, I might add, I could hardly imagine a difference between the two."

"One would always hope so."

The merlin had no rejoinder.

"You may go, Captain. I appreciate your taking the time to pay me a visit today. I trust you will keep our conversation in the strictest confidence."

"Naturally, Baron. It need not be said."

"SOMETHING IS AFOOT, GLOTON. I FEEL IT IN MY BONES," DONA MORANA declared. "We must act soon."

"We have little evidence upon which to act, Highness."

"Since when has that little detail ever stopped you?" snapped the elegant donkey.

"A wicked jest, your Highness," he replied, glancing round as if concerned about who might have overheard. "You, of all creatures, know I keep well within my bounds. I haven't managed to survive this long by playing fast and loose with the rule of law."

"I am the law now, Gloton."

"I'm afraid it's not that simple, Majesty."

"Bah! So what do you suggest?" She leaned back in her throne and languidly waved a hoof at him.

"Ever since the Air Marshal's return from Arundati, he's been behaving strangely. First it was the arguments with his colleagues. Then his bizarre plea about Fridis. Next, his mysterious wanderings and meetings with suspect individuals at late hours. Finally, his setting up an elite air corps answerable only to him."

"Exactly my point. Yet you maintain those actions are insufficient grounds to condemn him?"

"Let's not forget that the Air Marshal is one of Vigmar's most successful officers. He has many supporters, despite those colleagues he has recently alienated. You cannot simply remove someone of his caliber. Indeed, Aeron-Urd might well argue that he is merely tired, sick or suffering from battle fatigue. What could we do then?"

"You're beginning to sound like a bureaucrat. Where's my trusty ally of old?"

"Perhaps I've grown wiser and — "

"— more cautious," Dona Morana interrupted. Her long ears stood straight up. "Now that you've got something to lose."

"Empress, how could you?"

"It's not so difficult a speculation. In truth, Gloton, I'm beginning to regret sending Vulpé off to Aeronbed. The fox would not shirk his responsibilities. He would not hold back from fulfilling his duty to me."

"It's you I'm trying to protect, Majesty, not anyone else. We must be careful about dealing with someone of his position and standing."

"So you keep repeating, but you have failed to come up with a workable solution. Just one, that's all I ask."

"If your Imperial Highness would let me finish, I believe I have a strategy."

The donkey sighed impatiently. "Get on with it then."

"As I started to say, Your Majesty, as matters stand now, the evidence against Aeron-Urd remains thin. Beyond bad manners, we have no particular offense with which to charge him. But if we were to dig up an appropriate crime and a credible witness to the act, we could proceed."

"So? Tell me something I don't already know."

"What if we — if I were to come up with such a witness?"

"You have someone who will swear to treasonous activity?"

"Let's just say, Majesty, I have the power to influence this particular individual."

The annoyed donkey sighed again. "Then get on with it. You know there's not a moment to lose."

"In such undertakings we must act carefully. And be prepared for a strong reaction from his supporters."

"Then make his crime that much the worse. Make it stink to the highest towers of Blakfel. Make it so repugnant that no one will speak up for him."

"Yet the charge must be believable."

"Of course, of course, that goes without saying. Creativity and imagination — is that not what I pay you good money for? Not to mention the fancy titles and valuable properties."

"Results, Highness. You pay me for results, and you've been good enough to — "

"Once Aeron-Urd is charged, he must be tried and condemned," Dona Morana brayed, interrupting the wolverine once again. "The longer we wait, the more time for busybodies to show up, asking the usual awkward questions."

"I would suggest, Majesty, that as soon as we charge him, other officers must be rewarded with appropriate promotions. Thus they will understand that, where one may fall, others may yet rise and thus be beholden to us."

"To *me* don't you mean, Gloton?"

"Of course, Majesty, my mistake. I meant to you."

"Make it happen then. Ensure that Aravat is briefed and primed."

"It will be done as you command, Highness."

✤ 48 ✤

AERON-URD RUNS OUT OF ALLIES

I t was just before dawn. Such things always happened in the early morning, Aeron-Urd mused afterward.

The old gyrfalcon had been woken up abruptly, in as rude a manner as he could ever imagine. Only the slightest hint of daylight shone into his austere military quarters. Hearing an unexpected noise, he had come to, blinking his weary eyes, and saw before him a security officer and four burly dogs. The officer, a white donkey he did not know, was no one who'd be embarrassed or feel conflicted about the evil deed.

"Air Marshal Aeron-Urd, you are hereby charged with high treason," declared the donkey. Her tone was both imperious and stoic, as if she had performed the task a thousand times. "You will be so good as to accompany me."

"This is preposterous. Who charges me?"

"The state charges you, sir."

"The state?"

"The Empire, if you prefer that term."

The gyrfalcon snorted contemptuously.

"You are to be held in Blakfel pending your trial," the officer added, as if that made any difference.

"Tell me the nature of these charges."

"As I have no details, Air Marshal, I can provide no explanation. That is not my affair. My business is to execute my orders. You will be provided with this information in due course."

Aeron-Urd doubted that last statement. The gyrfalcon was neither naive nor innocent in such matters. What an irony, he thought. He had rescued Fridis from one hateful tower and now he was to be held, probably, in one quite similar. He had no illusions about his ultimate fate. Such charges were not brought forward lightly.

But he was a member of the established order, a general in the high command, with a sterling reputation and his own loyal forces to back him up. Would that be enough to save him? Could he get word to his squadrons? No doubt his opponents would be working hard to keep one step ahead of him. At that very moment they would be destroying his reputation, separating him from his followers, planting seeds of doubt, bringing forward a variety of trumped-up charges, ones not easily refuted by his allies. The powers in Blakfel were masters in the art of destroying someone's credibility. It was a shame, he considered wistfully; they were so inept at waging war and so successful at this vile game.

Were these the rewards of long service and loyalty to the Empire? That was a stupid question. The gyrfalcon knew the answer already; in point of fact, he'd known it long ago. Although he had been taken by surprise, he was not really shocked. In Vigmar such things happened all the time, just not to him. Of course he'd been expecting something, but the recent calm had lulled him into false hope.

But didn't Vigmar need him to win this war? Were they so foolish as to think otherwise? Some generals were expendable, but he was not — at least so Aeron-Urd had believed. The bird knew he'd made enemies; he was too easy to anger, too ready to criticize the failings of others and too quick to defend his own troops. But he also had his share of stalwart comrades, faithful friends and loyal followers. Could he warn them in time? Could he organize some resistance?

"I need to advise my —" the gyrfalcon began.

"That's been taken care of," interrupted the officer, betraying no emotion.

Physical resistance was useless, escape futile. The bird knew that truth as well. To try either would only serve his adversaries, providing proof of guilt and an excuse to kill him immediately. So the former hero of Vigmar acquiesced, accepting the fateful summons and coming without further protest.

As Aeron-Urd walked awkwardly between his captors, weighted down by chains, toward his new, less than agreeable chamber, he stewed over the many questions that came to him. Which of his rivals or enemies was to blame? What kind of hearing would he get, if any? Would he be granted the opportunity to defend himself? Would anyone be permitted to speak on his behalf? Could he call witnesses? Could he cross-examine his accusers? Finally, if all else failed, could he get word to his loyal squadrons in time to be rescued?

If only he'd kept faithful Raicho around. No, on second thought, that would be worse; his lieutenant would have been killed trying to help him. He was glad then that he'd allowed the falcon to depart for the front. He would be safer there.

Aeron-Urd's mind turned once more to Fridis. Of all his musings, this one saddened him the most. The gyrfalcon generally hoped for the best, but this time he suspected the worst. It came to him like a lightning bolt that he would never again see the duck. He tried to capture Fridis with his mind and communicate his affection to her. He prayed for her safety and good fortune in the difficult days ahead.

⛊

"GENERAL ARAVAT, I ASSUME YOU'VE HEARD THE NEWS — " BEGAN Garfreg, one of the junior members of the high command. The war room was abuzz. Senior officers were chatting in groups of two or three, dissecting the latest rumors, trying to figure out what had happened overnight.

"Of course I've heard the news, Colonel. I've already appointed the gyrfalcon's successor."

"*You* have appointed his successor?" exclaimed the gray falcon.

"Given the, er, unfortunate circumstances, the Empress has given me the authority to act in this instance. Several other organizational changes will be required as a result — you know, chains of command, that sort of thing. Those will be announced in due time. Naturally you'll be notified of any shift in your status."

"That wasn't my worry, General. The question I was about to ask had to do with the charges themselves."

"Your meaning, sir?"

"Isn't it obvious? If I may speak plainly, how can anyone believe such a pack of lies? The claims against the Air Marshal verge on the bizarre. Aeron-Urd was — still is, as a far as I know — a staunch and loyal soldier. Some may have their differences with the gyrfalcon, but Vigmar has no finer commanding officer."

The elephant pulled Garfreg off to one side, where they could speak more quietly and not be overheard. "I'm grateful for your honesty, sir. In return, let me give you some advice, words of wisdom you'll perhaps thank me for one day. If you continue in this vein, you'll find yourself voicing a distinctly minority opinion. The case against Aeron-Urd, as vile a tale of betrayal as ever I've heard, is well documented and sufficiently credible. Plenty of witnesses — plenty, I repeat — have come forward to bear witness to the Air Marshal's folly. And the consensus among his peers is that the damning testimony is entirely accurate."

The elephant flapped his ears in a menacing manner. "Do I have to remind you of Aeron-Urd's rash decision to send two squadrons into the field, a move that left Vigmar's defenses depleted? That was without consultation and implemented without authority from the high command. In my opinion, it was a sign of things to come."

Aravat heaved a deep sigh of regret and disappointment and added, "In sum, we've witnessed an unfortunate turn of events and a sad end for an illustrious career. Still, it's a fact, nonetheless."

"General Aravat, I beg to differ. One can't be condemned to death for an unfortunate turn of events."

Aravat looked down at the gray falcon. His eyes narrowed, his trunk tensed and his magnificent tusks rose high in the air. Shaking his massive head, the elephant decided to drive the point home. "It appears I've failed to make my meaning abundantly clear. If you do not already know it, the charges come from the office of the Empress. I shouldn't have to explain what that means. In brief, there is nothing more to be said."

Garfreg opened his beak as if to protest. Aravat beat him to it. "And I would suggest that you take great care with any future comments you choose to make about this business."

The courageous colonel tried one last time, but the elephant quickly shut him down. "I do not intend to argue the merits of the case with you, sir, here or anywhere else. You can rest assured that Aeron-Urd will have his day in court. And just in case you know of others with similar concerns, tell them that they too had better speak and act with great caution. One never knows, sir, who will be next."

A long silence ensued while Aravat stared fixedly at the falcon. Then the great elephant turned and stalked away as Garfreg stood glued in place. It was the last time they would ever speak about Aeron-Urd's fate.

⚜

"I TRUST ALL THE MEASURES ARE IN PLACE," DONA MORANA SAID.

"They are, Highness," the wolverine answered. "The witnesses are primed and the generals are onside. Aeron-Urd's private squadron has been dispatched to the front for training — save for one crucial witness. And, of course, the Air Marshal is safe and sound under lock and key. All that remains is due process. It's a matter of days, if not less."

"Good. I want no slip-ups. Make sure of it."

"Things will unfold exactly as you have commanded."

"One more thing, Gloton, before you go."

"Majesty?"

"Do you think Aeron-Urd knows where Duchess Fridis is?"

Vigmar's First Secretary thought for a moment. "Given everything we know and suspect, I think it highly likely."

"Do you think he'd share that information with you — for a fair price, that is?"

The wolverine thought again. "Not to save himself, not for the usual rewards. Only to save another. Frankly, Empress, in my view, the gyrfalcon has an overdeveloped sense of honor and duty. Also, he's no fool. The Air Marshal knows — and has accepted — the fate that awaits him."

"Perhaps in this instance some enhanced interrogation techniques might be in order."

"We can but try, Majesty," responded Gloton, without a trace of a smile.

"Then do so. But keep the wretch fit for his trial. We don't want any embarrassments, even at this late stage. Report back to me tonight." She waved him away with the flick of a hoof. "You may go."

As he turned away from the Empress, Gloton permitted himself a rare smirk of triumph. He had shown the donkey what he was capable of, despite her doubts.

The implacable donkey watched the wolverine bow, turn and depart. Gloton had, it appeared, managed things to perfection. A wave of smug satisfaction washed over the Empress. Although she doubted Aeron-Urd would succumb to further abuse, she took great pleasure in knowing that another potential threat was soon to depart this world. One by one she was rooting out the regime's enemies. With any luck the wolves would never return, leaving only those who owed her true and complete loyalty. Then, when Don Grimezel was dead, she'd be able to do as she really wished.

❧ X ❧

AERONBED

FRIDIS GOES WEST

Before they parted company, Lord and Lady Sesteros guided Fridis through the safest mountain passes west of the great mountain range — the less demanding secret routes known only to the local colony of peregrine falcons. Her hosts took care to instruct her on the signs to look for: a specific rock formation here, a crevice shaped like an X there, a singular waterfall, an outcropping of white marble amid the gray of the rock face, and so on. Those markers would lead her back to that part of the world, should she ever choose to accept the birds' invitation.

The duck had so enjoyed her stay with the Sesteros family that she had delayed her departure more than once. Even now she could not help but take her time as the three birds wended their way through the mountains and she thoughtfully absorbed every instruction.

When Fridis bade farewell one last time and watched the falcons depart for home, it was not with the heavy heart she'd been expecting. She had thought she'd feel quite bereft to be on her own again. On the contrary, the lightness and contentment she had enjoyed during her brief stay remained with her for some time, as if enchanted dust had been sprinkled over her — a magic aimed at sustaining her high spirits for as long as possible.

The craggy mountains soon disappeared, followed first by deep, shadowed valleys and then dense woodlands. Over the course of the descent into Aeronbed, Fridis's delight at encountering a new land competed in her mind with the two challenges she'd set for herself just days ago — uncovering the history of the magic gemstones and finding Haidar.

The duck had learned more than she had hoped from the Sesteros family, especially a motive for the theft of the gemstones that made sense. The pieces, she felt, were falling into place. Nevertheless, Fridis had to keep in mind that those stories amounted to little more than fables that — even as they were being told to her — no one admitted to putting much stock in. Still, it was a start and something to go on. Might Haidar and Raicho add to what she had learned? She was certain of it, and the duck knew she had to find them both. Where the trail would lead next was anyone's guess.

Even though Fridis had stayed longer than planned with the falcon family, the duck was convinced she must have gained ground on Haidar. She'd been flying freely in a direct line rather than having to walk, climb, scramble and stay under cover, as Haidar and Vulpé must surely be doing. But she was also sure that the secretive mountain goat had his own resources and shortcuts known only to him. Could Haidar's head start and knowledge have matched her advantage of speed?

But as she began to fly over Aeronbed's vast plains, the immensity of the task hit her. How could she hope to find any creature in this unfamiliar territory? Thinking like a falcon had helped locate the Sesteros home, but sheer blind luck had played a much larger part.

The falcons had taken great efforts to explain the lay of the land in this part of Aeronbed. Flying over this region regularly, they knew it quite well. Manaris, the capital of Aeronbed, lay on the coast, due west of the spot where Lord Sesteros had left her. All she had to do was fly in a straight line. Unless Fridis came across unexpected impediments or strong crosswinds, she simply needed to continue in the same direction. It was the route Fridis imagined Haidar had chosen. And if impediments did arise for her, they'd arise for Haidar even more.

From there on the duck would have to take extra care. She was in enemy territory, after all, and knew precious little about the state of affairs in Aeronbed. And with a civil war now in full swing, who could tell what was going on or who now controlled which lands. Fridis knew from Lorcan and Corvus's reports that the enemy used buzzards and vultures in their air force. Encountering one of those would not be a pleasant prospect, although she suspected they were not nearly as deadly as the raptors of Vigmar.

In that relatively optimistic frame of mind, Fridis flew on without incident until dusk, spotting no creatures of either air or land. Finally she made her descent to settle for the night on a small shallow lake. She'd not seen such a welcome spot in a long time. It was perfectly suited for ducks, and she was determined to make the most of it. There she took shelter amid the reeds and bulrushes that predominated at one end.

All was still except for a gentle southerly breeze rippling the water and the sounds of bullfrogs and cicadas. Fridis heard no end of noises, but nothing to disturb her peace of mind. Well hidden and therefore feeling quite secure, Fridis slept deeply and peacefully — that is, until she awoke with a start in the dead of night.

Something had disturbed her sleep, although everything seemed quiet. Even the creatures of the night had finally taken to their beds. Above her shone a myriad of stars, and a half-moon was slowly sinking toward the western horizon. As she floated gently on the water, contemplating her situation, the breeze began to pick up. It gathered in strength until the tops of the trees around the lake began to whip back and forth.

Definitely something was amiss. But what could it be? An unusual noise? No, not a noise. Was something moving? She could not be certain of anything over the tempestuous gusts. Fridis remained still for several minutes, hardly breathing, as she would if she had spotted a predator. Nothing stirred except the tall grasses and reeds, now being tossed pell-mell.

Slowly Fridis began to relax and breathe more deeply, but she remained fearful and ill at ease. And then she felt a shadow pass over her. Instinctively the duck dove under the surface, swimming quickly into a denser area of reeds. She rose for a quick breath and just as quickly descended even deeper — as deep as she dared — switching directions more than once and staying under as long as she could. Fridis ascended to the surface again only when she was desperate, when she thought her lungs might burst. She came up as quietly and smoothly as possible, looking around apprehensively, ready to dive again.

Whatever the shadow was, it had felt like the embodiment of dread and death. Fridis continued to cower in the reeds, trying to make herself as small as possible. She couldn't stop shivering. That shadow, that thing of nightmares, was still present, grasping her soul with a deadly grip.

Suddenly an image of Aeron-Urd flashed through her mind. At first she was puzzled. What did it mean? The juxtaposition was too odd, the feelings evoked too contrary to comprehend. Thoughts of her good friend were welcome and comforting, but the preceding sensation had been alarming, even blood-chilling. And then it struck her. Aeron-Urd was thinking of her; he needed her help.

Something must have happened to the gyrfalcon, something awful. Fridis wanted to cry out in horror, but the sound died in her throat. Was he dead? No, if he was still able to send his thoughts to her, to communicate in such a fashion, that terrible event had not yet happened. What could be wrong? What danger was there for Aeron-Urd at home in Vigmar? Alas, Fridis knew only too well. Having experienced the darker side of Blakfel's political world, she realized anything was possible in that wicked place.

Just before they parted, Fridis had told Aeron-Urd to think of her if he was in dire need of assistance. Then the duck would do what she could to help him. But hadn't that offer been just a fanciful idea, part of a friendly exchange of farewells, rather than meant to be taken seriously? Now, so far away in this strange land, what could Fridis possibly do for the gyrfalcon? Should she go back to Blakfel? The duck doubted she could return in time to help her friend. And even if she did manage such a feat, once there, then what? It wasn't as if she had any power in the place or could command legions of followers — not anymore, not by a long shot.

Fridis's mind raced. Resting on that little lake so far away, she felt completely powerless. Well, not quite powerless. The duck still had the two gemstones and they had worked miracles before — at least, so she'd reckoned. Could they help now? Would their powers work at a distance? She had no idea; she'd never tried such an experiment before. Was it possible?

Fridis knew she had to try, for the sake of her friend, even if it meant the risk of revealing her presence to potential enemies. Although the duck had no idea of the stones' capacity or range, if the tales she had been hearing were even half true, they held immense power, even more than she had originally guessed.

Detecting nothing dangerous nearby, Fridis felt her confidence return. She paddled over to the far shore, searching for a hiding place. Something was telling her to hurry. Aeron-Urd's life hung in the balance, and if she acted right away she might be able to tip the scales in his favor. Any threats lurking nearby would have to be ignored.

Fridis found a small thicket not far from the shore. Although it was far from perfect, it was better than being completely exposed. She hurriedly opened the two pouches. Which gemstone to choose? Was Aeron-Urd ill or was he in danger? The duck was in a quandary, sensing that she had only one chance to provide help. Perhaps it didn't really matter which one; perhaps they all did the same thing. She had never really thought it through, given everything else on her mind.

Then it occurred to Fridis that, because of the apparent gravity of the situation and the great distance involved, she might need to use both gemstones. Her need to act immediately was competing with her need to get the request right. If only she weren't forced to keep guessing! In her confusion, Fridis began to despair. Her fumbling attempts to unwrap the two stones caused her to drop one. It tumbled into the underbrush and became lodged between two roots. It took what seemed ages to retrieve it. Cursing her ineptitude, she took a deep breath and forced herself to slow down and pay more attention.

Taking greater care, she laid each stone on its respective pouch. Then she closed her eyes and began to picture her good friend who had done so much for her. As tears welled in her eyes, Fridis asked for his rescue and prayed for his safety as she tried to picture Aeron-Urd escaping whatever fate was in store for him. As had always occurred in the past at first, nothing happened. Fear washed over her — perhaps this time it would fail to work.

Just as despair began to take hold, the stones' appearance began to alter. Their evanescent inner light grew and grew until Fridis had to shield her eyes with her wings. Because both gems were at work, the intensity was like nothing she had ever experienced. It was as if she was looking directly into a pure white sun. As the jewels continued to glow, the duck, her eyes closed, recited her mantra on Aeron-Urd's behalf. After a few minutes, as mysteriously as always, the radiance began to fade, leaving only the darkness of night, which now seemed blacker than ever.

Fridis shuddered. She tried to flap her wings but, confined by the surrounding thicket, gave up. She replaced the stones in their pouches and made them secure. Instinct told her to get moving, to get as far away as possible. Danger lived in every nook and cranny. Who knew what creature the light might have attracted?

The duck crawled out of the thicket and then soared straight up. Suddenly overcome by exhaustion, she flew to the other side of the lake and found a new sanctuary. Once more hidden out of sight, satisfied she had done everything she could for her old friend, she fell into a deep sleep.

50

THE BEACON

"Did you see that?" Haidar asked, suddenly wide awake.

"I certainly did," Vulpé replied, rubbing his eyes. "What do you think it was?"

"No idea." The goat struggled to his feet, his gaze still fixed in the direction of the mysterious glow. "I've been surprised by many strange things in my lifetime, but I've never seen anything like that. What could make such an intense white light and then suddenly disappear?"

"Certainly not an explosion. There was no sound attached to it."

"Unless it happened too far away for us to hear anything."

"No, we'd have heard something. How far away, do you reckon? Do you think we should check it out?" The curious fox, quickly warming to the idea of investigating, began to pace about.

"Several miles, maybe more. But I'm not so sure about checking it out. We might end up like the proverbial moths drawn to a flame."

"We face risk every day we're in this wretched country. Look, Haidar, it's the first sign of life we've seen. It must mean something. We can't ignore it."

The mountain goat did not respond.

"You'd think we'd have come across someone by now," the fox

complained. "By my grandfather's whiskers, we've met no one. Where are the armies of Aeronbed, for pity's sake?"

The mountain goat had no answer to that question.

"Back home they must be wondering what's become of us," Vulpé continued. "*I'm* wondering what's become of us!"

"I told you before we left that our progress would be uncertain. This whole mission is fraught with uncertainty. We're trying to be careful, to stay under cover and keep out of sight. We can't just meander about mindlessly. What if we meet up with someone who kills first and asks questions later?"

"I know, I know, we must proceed cautiously, but how much longer will it take? For all we know the war is already over and we're just wasting our time out here."

"Or perhaps Vigmar's already been defeated and we're just risking our necks for nothing."

"What? Don't say that, Haidar, not even in jest."

"But you must admit — "

"I admit nothing. But I do vote that we investigate the source of that light."

Haidar sighed. One part of the mountain goat was reluctant to stray from his chosen route and schedule, but a larger part was deeply curious about what they'd just seen. The light had been most unusual. It didn't belong out there in the countryside, not at all — unless it was some kind of beacon, meant for him.

Although the goat could not come up with a logical explanation, he felt that the light was beckoning to him somehow. He had also been wondering why there were so few signs of life. Where were the inhabitants of Aeronbed? At very least Haidar had expected to come across a lion regiment or two by this point in their journey. He'd begun to worry, but he wasn't about to admit that to Vulpé.

Possibly the mysterious light was the key to the puzzle. He would have to meditate further on it. In the meantime, he was prepared to give in to the fox. "All right, Vulpé, have it your way. We can strike out at sunrise."

"Excellent, Haidar. Now you're talking."

⟨✦⟩

THE PANTHER NOTICED THE REFLECTION IN THE LIONESS'S EYES BEFORE HE saw the light itself. Eisa looked around instantly, just as his companion rose to all fours.

"What the — ?" Olwen cried. The two cats stared into the distance until the glow disappeared.

"Have you ever seen the like before?" Eisa asked.

"Never, never," she replied. "Whatever can it mean?"

"No idea. It was as bright as the sun at midday, but it came from over there." The panther pointed toward the spot. "Some kind of magic, I'd say, or ... " He shrugged. Was it another omen, another part of the puzzle the lioness had revealed?

She didn't pick up on his hesitation. "Certainly not lightning; there are no storms about anywhere. And it came without any sound at all."

"How far away, do you think?"

"Not so far. But then again, I have no idea what we're dealing with. Was it something small close by or something large a long distance off?"

"We need to investigate, don't you agree?"

"I do." She purred with anticipation. "What are mysteries for but to solve?"

Eisa couldn't agree more. Curiosity might kill the cat, but the fear of death never stopped one from trying. It was in their blood.

"No time like the present. Let's go."

The two cats were well rested and eager to solve this latest enigma. For some days they had been wandering about central Aeronbed, trying to figure out a safe route north to join the remnants of Albiorix's army. It was, both acknowledged, not much of a plan, and their progress had been frustratingly slow. However, they were also aware that few other options existed. Every direction led to danger or to an unknown of some kind. The situation in the north, however dire, was at least familiar to them both.

51

CALAMITOUS NEWS

I t was a calm evening, without any wind. Smoke from the dying embers drifted lazily into the sky. The wolf pack's leaders sat in a large circle around the firepit, feeling relaxed and comfortable, savoring the fruits of recent victories. Their trek to the south had been one of twists and turns. They had fought many battles against tough and determined opponents. Although they had relished the action, they had not come away unscathed.

As Adarix had expected, Lorcan and Corvus had proven to be of immeasurable help, if not decisive, on several occasions. Eventually, however, it appeared that Aeronbed's southern forces had figured out the raptors' movements and daily tactics, and they had begun to deploy more air patrols of their own to counter them. That effort had evened things out but did not stop the wolves' progress. Still, after many weeks, they were a long way from reaching the southernmost part of Aeronbed and had discovered not one sign of their own army under Baroness Emer-Sigr. The disappearance of the horse and the animals under her command remained a mystery.

It was now late spring, and signs of the oppressive summer heat to come were beginning to be felt by the wolves. On this particular night, a moment of peace reigned after several days of hostilities. The birds of prey were roosting off by themselves. The wolves were engaging in much good-natured banter amid the celebrations.

"I appreciate your words of praise, Adarix," Ammarich called out to his brother, in reply to some well-earned complement. "But in all frankness, have we not been chasing our tails as much as not?"

"Hold on, Ammarich," interjected Asteel with a broad grin. "You may be the oldest and wisest of our clan, but are you daring to question our dear lord and master?"

"Since you put it that way, brother, yes!" Although they all laughed at the reply, Ammarich persisted. "Really, you know I have no quarrel with Adarix's leadership. Have we not met with success after success? And not just on this campaign but also in years past. No one dares stand in our way. Rather, it is our friends in Blakfel who cause me grief. For weeks now we've been fighting our way to the south. I ask you, to what avail? It's as if we've been digging a deeper and deeper pit for ourselves. I tell you, one day we'll find we're dug in so deeply we can no longer climb out."

"I'm not sure I understand," Amrin said.

"Amrin, Adarix — all of you, you know I speak plainly."

"And most sensibly," added Asteel. Much nodding of heads resulted. The pack knew that Ammarich always spoke his mind — and the truth, at least as far as the wolf knew it.

"Go on, brother," said Amteil.

Ammarich needed no further invitation. "For weeks now we've been hunting down the cats in southern Aeronbed. And, as I said, meeting with our usual success. We have lost some good friends and noble cousins, but that is the price of war. Nevertheless, we are no further along in finding what seems to be a ghost army, and we just keep moving around in circles. We don't have the strength to break through the enemy lines and we don't have the ability to go around them. Yes, we prick and poke at them and make them bleed, but over time they have begun to target us and match our efforts. I tell you, brothers, we don't want to find ourselves on the run again like last year."

All was now quiet around the dying fire. Ammarich had said what many were thinking, but only he had the gumption and the authority to say it out loud. The wolves looked at each other, then at Ammarich and finally at Adarix. Their leader had been listening attentively without any indication of where his thinking lay.

"You speak for many of us, Ammarich," Alberic interjected. "But are we not obliged to follow the directions of the high command? We are loyal soldiers of Vigmar, after all. Are we really in a position to judge how the entire war effort is being conducted?"

"What do the generals in Blakfel know about what's going on out here? Have they actually listened to our reports? Have we heard a single word from them since we began this latest campaign?" Albelin complained. The young wolf jumped up and stalked about angrily.

"Is that not a traditional complaint of the soldier in the field?" persisted Alberic. "We think that those who command back home have no idea how to fight a war. Meanwhile, they think we're failing to obey their intelligent orders and successfully execute their brilliant strategies. Is this situation really so different?"

"I'm convinced of it," Ammarich said. "And in my opinion, we're wasting our time down here. The key to victory lies in the north; it always has. That's where Lord Eirwen directed us to go. That's where the final battle is supposed to occur."

So intently focused were they on their own discussion that the wolves had failed to notice an increasingly raucous disturbance among the birds of prey. Now becoming aware of the fuss, all heads turned to where the hawks and falcons were roosting. The wolves' conversation ceased.

"That's not like them," Ammarich commented, a little annoyed by the commotion. "Asteel, go tell those birds to pipe down. We're at war, for pity's sake."

"Hold on, Asteel," intervened Adarix, speaking for the first time. "Something's clearly amiss with our friends. Ammarich, you go over, and ask them politely what the problem is."

Ammarich rose a little grumpily and sauntered over to the circle of hawks. The rest of the wolves kept their eyes fixed on him as he spoke with the assembly of birds. Although the pack could hear an animated discussion, they could not make out any words over the distance. Their conversation had come to a halt; the wolves whispered to each other, wondering what the matter might be.

Eventually a troubled-looking Ammarich returned with the two very agitated senior commanders, Lorcan, a northern harrier, and Corvus, a black falcon. When space had been made for the birds to sit among their circle, Ammarich began to speak, very softly and seriously.

"Adarix, brothers. Our friends have received calamitous news. A messenger arrived from Vigmar late in the day. Only just now has she passed on her information to the squadron leaders. I will let Corvus complete the tale."

Corvus and Lorcan looked at each other. The two birds appeared terribly upset. Corvus could barely speak, he was so worked up, and Lorcan was too grief-stricken to even make an attempt to report what had occurred. Adarix and the others waited patiently for the birds to find their voices.

"Lord Adarix," Corvus said finally, on the edge of tears, "the Air Marshal is dead."

"What?" exclaimed more than one of the incredulous wolves. A hubbub of growling, agitated voices ensued. "Aeron-Urd? Impossible! How so? Was he killed in action? Was it an accident?" The dismayed questions came in a jumble from all sides.

Adarix said nothing but clamped his jaws tight and growled under his breath as the uproar continued unabated. "Quiet!" the wolf leader finally snarled. The others fell silent.

"Corvus, repeat to my brothers what you told me," Ammarich said.

"We don't know a lot," the falcon said. "The story, if it's accurate, is difficult to hear and painful to accept. The honor of the hawks and falcons — of all the air defense forces — has been blackened."

"What was the message?" Adarix asked calmly.

"That Aeron-Urd was executed after a trial. He had been charged with treason and then found guilty by a military tribunal of his peers. He's been replaced by a member of the high command to whom we must now report. Little further detail was provided. Apparently the Air Marshal had formed another air corps, which he, along with some others, planned to use to overthrow the Emperor and Empress."

The hubbub broke out anew.

"Was anyone else arrested and charged?" Adarix asked over the increasing din.

"If they were, we haven't been informed about it."

"Anything else?"

"Nothing officially, but the messenger told us what she learned on the way here. Off the record, that is."

"And what was that?"

"The messenger confirmed that Aeron-Urd had indeed formed an air unit reporting directly to him. I gather it was a squadron made up largely of merlins, and its future assignment was unclear. It appears that one member of that group testified against the Air Marshal. None of the squadron's officers are known to us, so I can't attest to anything. I gather that the messenger encountered a few of them after the arrest. The unit was broken up and dispersed after the trial, and that's how she ran into them."

"Is that it?"

"Rumors about Aeron-Urd consorting with opponents of the current regime have been circulated."

"Unbelievable," one of the wolves interjected.

"And yet no one else was arrested," Ammarich pointed out.

"As I said, not to the messenger's knowledge."

"Does that not seem unusual to you?" Adarix asked.

"Perhaps. But such deeds can always be carried out in secret."

"Yes, certainly, but only if there's a good reason to keep them secret. I would not expect that to be the case here."

"What are you saying, my lord?"

"You tell me, Corvus. What's your view of this story?"

The wolves were listening with rapt attention to the exchange. Where was Adarix heading with this?

Corvus hesitated. He looked at Lorcan, who took up where the other had left off. "Lord Adarix, comrades of the wolf pack," the harrier explained, "Corvus has given you the official line, the one that's been communicated to us. But I'll tell you what I think. I've known Aeron-Urd longer than Corvus has. The Air Marshal was my elder by a few years, but we grew up in the same region of Arundati and we trained together. I know him to be a loyal professional soldier. Such a treasonous move on his part would be unthinkable. I do not believe what we've been told."

"Lorcan," Adarix said, almost gently, "I respect your opinion, but are you telling us there are no circumstances under which Aeron-Urd might take such an action?"

"What are you saying, my lord?" Lorcan said, affronted by this apparent slight to Aeron-Urd's reputation.

"I am not saying anything. Just think carefully about my question before responding."

Lorcan looked toward Corvus and then back at the wolf leader. Then, contemplating Adarix's question, he stared into the dying embers for an entire minute, while every other animal present held their breath. At last the harrier raised his head and said, "I can think of no such situation."

Adarix looked around at his band of brothers. "Can no one think of a single reason why Aeron-Urd would take such an action?"

The wolves all avoided one another's eyes or stared at their leader in bewilderment. Finally, out of a shadowed corner, a single voice was raised. "I can."

"Ah, Emrin-Can. Somehow I thought you'd be able to see it. You're the only true politician among us — that is, of course, besides me," the wolf leader said. "Go ahead, enlighten us."

"Aeron-Urd would take such an action if he had no other choice — if the Air Marshal felt threatened and understood that to remain loyal to Vigmar would mean his own death. In other words, he would act out of a need for self-preservation."

"Thank you, Emrin. Perceptive as always."

"So you believe the charges to be fair and appropriate, my lord?" asked Corvus, his feathers totally ruffled.

"I didn't say that. What Emrin is describing is a scenario in which Aeron-Urd — or perhaps any one of us — would act accordingly."

"I still don't believe it," Lorcan declared. "There would have been other options for the Air Marshal, and the unit he created could have had many purposes."

"Such as?" asked Ammarich.

"Personal protection, reserve units for the front lines ... to name just two plausible rationales."

"I grant you that, Lorcan," the wolf admitted.

There was another moment of silence as the fire's embers began to crackle and seemingly reignite. In the evening stillness, an unearthly cry of *kee-aah* was heard from on high. The wolves looked up into the sky.

"One of my cousins. His cry of lament," Corvus said sadly.

They all listened to the mournful call, ears pricked and lost in thought. It was repeated several times before fading off into the distance.

Adarix brought the company back to the here and now. "Lorcan, Corvus," the wolf leader said with a slight bow of his head, "Aeron-Urd and I did not always see eye to eye, but I had the utmost respect for him as a leader and a bird of principle. We wolves share in your mourning and honor his memory." After the briefest of pauses, he added, "All this conjecture is about trying to set the record straight, if one can ever hope to do that. None of us may ever know what really happened. Despite what any of us may think or the personal sorrow we may feel, it's after the fact now. The more important question is, now what? What you conclude the truth of the matter to be is up to you and your fellow officers, but how you respond is of concern to the rest of us."

"You are correct, my lord," Lorcan agreed. "We were in the midst of that very discussion when Ammarich came over to discover what the brouhaha was about."

"What are your options?"

"We can accept the story as it has been relayed to us, consent to the new command structure and carry on fighting with you as if nothing had changed. Or we can reject the story, recognize that we are supporting an unjust regime that has severed its claim upon us, and grasp the fact that those remaining are threatened by a similar fate whenever the opportunity suits Blakfel. If we concur with the second choice, we will walk — or rather, fly — away from this whole sordid business with all due speed."

"I see. And what are the factors that might affect your decision?"

"Our personal loyalty to you, Lord Adarix, for we now have little left to offer the regime in Blakfel. Our sense of duty as soldiers. Our fear of reprisals. Our own individual plans, such as they might be for predators of the sky."

"Do you think there might be a third option?"

"A third option, Lord Adarix?" repeated the harrier, after glancing at the falcon.

"You know, I have half a mind to change our current course," Adarix said with a twinkle in his eyes. "It occurs to me, Lorcan, that we have accomplished enough, done enough harm to the enemy in this part of Aeronbed. I suggest to you, my friends, that we might find a greater purpose in heading back toward the north. And perhaps later on, when we have met with success, we may even find a reason to return to Vigmar. Who knows what surprises might lie in store for us — or what surprises we may yet have for Blakfel. If so, Lorcan, I, for one, would greatly welcome your company and your support in this new direction. So, what say you?"

To say the company was astonished would be an understatement. It took a few moments before anyone fully understood the thrust of Adarix's words. Emrin may have been the first to understand the implications, but the wolfhound was not about to reveal it. Thus it was Ammarich who was the first to speak. "Amen to that, brother," was all the wolf had to say. The remainder of the wolves, always prepared to follow the guidance of their sage eldest brother, simply nodded or growled in approval.

The two birds remained puzzled by the turn of events. The offer had come completely out of the blue, and it took a while for Corvus and Lorcan to fully grasp its possible repercussions. Given the momentous nature of Adarix's suggestion, the falcon and the harrier did not feel they could speak for their fellow officers without further consultation. Accordingly, the birds went back to the roost to undertake a meeting.

While Adarix's invitation was not unwelcome, it still took plenty of intense discussion for the birds to weigh the various issues involved and decide whether or not to cast their lot with the wolf pack. In the end, the squadrons agreed without reservation. To a bird, they took the view that Aeron-Urd, their revered leader, had been cruelly and unjustly dealt with by the authorities in Blakfel. Thus, while Lorcan did not mention it, they had an underlying motivation for agreeing to the offer — revenge. Adarix had provided them with an opportunity they were not about to pass up.

THE UNITED BEARS OF HEIMBORN

The council meeting was in full swing. The bears had gathered in a small hollow, little more than a dip in the ground, surrounded by low knolls. On the other side of the rises, the respective clans were encamped en masse. It was late afternoon and, after a good day's march, they were tired but in good spirits.

"I won't attempt to honey-coat our situation, cousins," Eirwen was saying. "The enemy has a clear purpose. He is fleet of foot and quicker to attack. He is more experienced in the art of warfare and has greater numbers. He is also far more ruthless and vicious than we bears. For our part, we've lost the element of surprise, we are without allies and, having lost the support of Gullhinder's clan, we don't even have the benefit of a united front. We have much to learn about warfare, are venturing into unfamiliar territory, and have no real idea what we want to achieve beyond our survival."

"Why so upbeat, Eirwen? Let's not dwell only on the good news," Vidar interjected with a guffaw. "We can take it, can't we, cousins?"

Eirwen joined in the laughter, relieved to see that the clan chiefs had not lost their sense of humor. They would need it during the tough days ahead. After living amid his own kind for so many months, the polar bear had begun to identify closely with the plight of his Heimborn relations.

"It was not my intention to depress you. We bears are not without our strengths and advantages," Eirwen continued. "Where it comes to combat, we have no ingrained habits, the kind that could lead us astray, as it did the panthers. We are calm and steady. We don't suffer from overconfidence, because we know we have to struggle every day, and that very weakness becomes our strength. Moreover, our great size makes one of us equal to at least two or three of the cats.

"But most important of all, cousins, is that we've had our fill of persecution and humiliation. We know there can be no going back to the old way of life, and that gives us the determination to see this war through to its end. We are fighting for our lives, and for the right to live as equals with all other creatures. They will never understand this resolve, and so they will always underestimate us. This steadfastness will be our strong suit and guide in the weeks and months to come.

"I won't say that right is on our side. That's too easily said, and too simplistic. For that matter, I'm sure the Black Legion believes they are acting as honorably as us. But I do know our cause is just, as equally I know theirs is not. And that is why we shall prevail."

"Well said, cousin," roared Bakman.

"And we have you to guide us," Anat added. "That's worth a thousand legions of panthers!"

Eirwen felt humbled. He was not one for speechifying. In fact, the polar bear felt awkward speaking in such an exaggerated, rousing fashion. Nevertheless, he took the view that the bears needed an occasional pep talk. After so many years they had become accustomed to subservience and indecision; it had become a familiar, comfortable pattern. He could see his cousins' moods swing daily. They needed regular reassurance and cheering on to keep their spirits up and their stomachs fortified for action.

Every now and then Eirwen's mind would turn to Adarix. He would long for the wolves' cohesion and resolve, but just as quickly he would wonder how the wolves would survive when the war was over. What would they — a fighting machine without a fight — do to occupy their minds? Perhaps they'd turn on each other. There was much to be said, Eirwen considered, for the bears' easygoing approach to life. The polar bear just hoped that their fire, once lit, would burn long enough for them to prevail in this great struggle.

Gullhinder's Sethana clan would not budge from Heimborn; to a bear they had remained behind, safely within the confines of their own region. Haefan's Adelgrid clan had agreed to march with the others, but Eirwen could tell that their hearts were not in the struggle; they were present in body but not in spirit. Eirwen knew he had to rely on the others, notably Bakman, Vidar and Aedelborn, all of whom Eirwen believed had enough fighting spirit and common sense to lead their forces into battle, and even to victory. Not to forget Anat, of course, who had taken on Goran-Art's mantle to a degree that had surprised the other clan chiefs.

But, all in all, they were still few in comparison with the hordes of panthers. The bears would need more than fighting power. They had to be better prepared and fight smarter. Ultimately Eirwen decided to leave Haefan and his clan behind to guard the gates of Heimborn. The polar bear didn't want to be caught napping by abandoning the bears' homeland. It needed to be protected just in case Parthanyx returned, and he trusted that the Adelgrids could at least be counted on to defend their own territory.

The rest of the bears, under his command, would move north, toward Manaris and the forces of Vigmar. His aim was either to take Aeronbed's capital by surprise or to join Vigmar's northern army. In the latter case, Eirwen hoped that the superior strength of the combined armies might enable Heimborn to defeat the cats on the battlefield. Failing that, they'd be strong enough to compel the Black Legion to enter into peace negotiations.

But achieving either goal raised two huge questions. How heavily defended was Manaris and where exactly was Vigmar's Army of the North? The bears had no falcons or hawks or speedy land-based allies to scout out nearby or distant territories. Eirwen was aware at least that there were no contingents of panthers nearby, but beyond that, he was unable to obtain much more information. Thus the bears were operating largely in the dark.

It had even crossed Eirwen's mind to search out Adarix and his wolf pack. Now that winter had come to an end, the polar bear was certain they would have returned to the hunt. But where would the wolves be now? He had no idea. When winter set in, the pack had been hiding out somewhere to the south of the bears' present position, opposite to the direction they were marching in.

That was one problem, but the second was worse. The intelligence was as stale as month-old bread. The wolves would have been on the move since winter ended. They could be anywhere by now and, even if nearby, difficult to track and pinpoint. They were wolves after all, skilled in disguising their presence and intentions. It might take months to find them.

Eirwen couldn't waste time and dissipate precious momentum in what was likely to be a fruitless search. Moreover, even if he was able to locate the pack, even more time would be needed to iron out the arrangements between two uncertain and wary allies. So he decided to press on toward the northwest.

The bears of Heimborn, now united, would advance cautiously, gathering information and training as they went, until they were nearer Manaris. At that point they would send scouts further afield. Hopefully they would then learn enough to make an informed decision about what to do next.

For the first few days all went well. They made excellent progress across Aeronbed's central plains, and the bears responded to Eirwen's directions competently and cooperatively. The polar bear was greatly relieved to discover that the panthers were not lying in wait. The reports had turned out to be accurate; the Black Legion had apparently continued northward to take on the lions, capture Manaris and then pursue them ceaselessly.

However, as to where the various groups of big cats were stationed throughout Aeronbed, the bears knew very little. And not only the lions and panthers — what about the others? For Eirwen this lack of good intelligence raised another issue. What would the bears do if they encountered lions rather than panthers? Would the enemy of his enemy become his friend? Or were all the cats of one mind when it came to the status of the bears? Perhaps their recent falling-out would come to a quick end when faced with an aggressive new army from Heimborn.

Eirwen needed to know more about the lions. Asking around, he discovered that Aedelborn had been the last clan chief to personally meet with King Albiorix. The two bears spoke the following day, as the bears continued their advance.

"What can you tell me about the lions, cousin? I was fighting them — and many of their relatives — tooth and nail for several months before I met up with Goran-Art's clan. But never once did I speak to any of them. Most of the time we hit and ran; it was only at the very end that the cats even knew of my existence. It seems foolish now to admit it. Who knows, I might have learned a lot."

Aedelborn scowled. "Cats are cats, Lord Eirwen. What more can one say?"

"Hopefully a lot more than that, Aedelborn. You are Heimborn's senior clan chief. You must have had plenty of opportunities over the years to parlay with them."

The old chief's grimace said much, in particular that he had no wish to think about such matters anymore. Eirwen, however, persisted, and finally the bear began his painful saga.

"You need to understand that, a long time ago, the lions delegated all responsibility for their relationship with Heimborn to the panthers. As a result, in recent years we encountered lions only sporadically. In point of fact, there were only two ceremonial days each year when we were 'permitted' to meet the King and his entourage. A small delegation — escorted by panthers, of course — was paraded to Manaris, where we sat down, exchanged pleasantries and presented Albiorix and some of the other lion elite with gifts, tokens of our subservience and our gratitude for their protection. *Protection*. What a laugh!

"And then, once the grand ceremony was over, we were sent packing back to Heimborn. Well, more like shepherded, I guess, so we bears couldn't interact with and *contaminate* the local population. Frankly, Eirwen, I'm not sure why Albiorix bothered with the ritual. We certainly didn't need or want it." Aedelborn scowled and spat on the ground. "Who knows," he added. "Perhaps the ceremony allowed the lions to maintain some pretense of governance, or maybe it was to absolve their conscience."

"How many went each time?"

"Two clan chiefs were delegated. We used to take turns. As you can guess, it was not an experience any of us welcomed. Last time, I went with Goran-Art. You can well imagine how our cousin seethed throughout the entire affair. I could barely keep him in check."

"And before that?"

"Before that I went with Gullhinder. You see, once I had become the senior clan leader I was expected to attend every time, accompanied by a more junior chief on a rotating basis."

"What can you tell me about Albiorix?"

"A typical lion: proud, haughty, hard-nosed. A cat of little patience and no fool, I'd warrant. Naturally, apart from his set speeches, he didn't have much time for us."

"Was there anyone else that you met or saw, someone you think may be important or with whom we could start a civil dialogue?"

"Sorry, couldn't say really. Those ceremonies weren't what I'd call social affairs. And there was little in the way of chitchat. Not that I sought out conversation, if you know what I mean. The whole business was humiliating. Just wanted to get it over with and make sure Goran-Art didn't blow his top.

"I did meet one of Albiorix's advisors once, named Temorwig, I believe. Big, sturdy fellow. I think he's related to the king in some fashion, although I didn't quite get the connection. Tough as a tree but not as sharp as Albiorix. I suspect he'd be getting on a bit by now.

"Albiorix, I know, has a family. A couple of sons, I believe, no doubt very much engaged in the war with Vigmar. I assume they must be at one front or another; they were rarely present at the events. Oh yes, and he also has a daughter, but I never paid much attention to her."

"Oh? Why not?"

"You know, the fairer sex and all that. Not in the same league. In any event, the lioness is quite a bit younger than her brothers. I think I was introduced to her once in passing, when she was a cub, but I'd barely remember her face now."

"The question is, Aedelborn, can we do business with the lions now that the panthers are at odds with them?"

Marching steadily along, Aedelborn reflected silently for quite a while. Finally he said, "There's no getting around the fact that we bears have suffered equally from all the cats. No one in Aeronbed has been our friend. Perhaps eons ago, but not in my time. I wish I could answer your question more favorably, really I do. But on my part I've never seen any willingness to bend, never heard a word of kindness or received the slightest hint of understanding from any of them, whether lion, panther, tiger, leopard or whatever."

Seeing he had little more to gain from that quarter, Eirwen thanked Aedelborn and dismissed him. The polar bear then called for Anat to come forward, and she was quick to arrive at his side. Eirwen asked the clan chief whether her brother had ever spoken of his meeting with Albiorix.

"By the time Goran-Art returned to Ethanead, he was furious — too angry even to tell me what happened. For days he said nothing, only stalked off into the mountains, where I presume he was stewing and plotting his revenge. You know how hot-blooded my brother was; he rarely kept things inside for long. But in this one case he did. I knew better than to press him. Goran-Art would always come around eventually, so I simply waited."

"In the end did he say anything?"

"Yes. I believe it was having to live through that indignity on their own — just the two of them – that caused him so much torment. In Heimborn we have the company and protection of one another. In Manaris, Aedelborn and Goran-Art had to face the entire court of Aeronbed on their own. I'm sure Aedelborn told you how demeaning the ritual is. The clan chiefs are watched over like prisoners, paraded before Albiorix and forced to submit a tribute, along with whatever 'tax' it's deemed we owe them. Oh yes, naturally everyone observes the niceties and the protocols to save face, but it's clear enough what's going on.

"You know, Eirwen, the lions won't even touch us. They consider bears unclean; they think we might give them diseases. The gifts are not handed from paw to paw but placed on a stone altar. Someone else

— one of the lesser cats — picks them up and takes them to the King. Albiorix never even touches them! All the while, the panthers stare and smirk. Goran-Art said he would never go again unless ... " Anat did not complete the sentence.

They walked on in silence. After a while Eirwen asked, "Unless what?"

"Unless it was with upraised claws and bared teeth. Can you blame him, cousin?"

The message was clear enough, and Eirwen chose not to answer. In the face of such a history and such anger, he hesitated before posing his next question. Still, he was determined to pursue his idea. "Did Goran-Art ever suggest that there might be among the lions some more reasonable ones, some with whom we might work together?"

Anat's scornful look said it all, but her reply was even more derisive. "Surely you're joking, my lord. Haven't you been listening? The lions are no better than the panthers. In fact, I'd argue they're even worse, because they let the panthers do their dirty work for them. Won't even sully their nice clean paws on us *vermin*. Good riddance to the lot of them, I say! So if you're looking for words of comfort and compromise, you've come to the wrong place. Save your energy for battle. The only praise I'm prepared to give any cat is to Parthanyx and his Legion for getting rid of the lions. Justice has been served in at least one quarter."

Eirwen was dismayed by Anat's bitterness; the new clan chief seemed to have wasted little time in taking on her brother's deep-seated sense of injustice. Were things really as bad as all that, or was she just parroting Goran-Art's prejudices and thus honoring his memory? Not that he could really blame Anat; her brother's brutal death had been horrifying.

After what he'd heard and witnessed, the polar bear could not blame either clan chief, or any of Heimborn's inhabitants. After all, he was a latecomer to the villainous treatment meted out by the cats; he hadn't suffered from years of torment and cruelty as they had. So what did he really know? One thing was certain: the clans' distrust of outsiders and abhorrence of the lions made his task of seeking potential allies that much harder.

"I'm sorry if I've brought back unhappy memories," Eirwen began.

"Memories? These thoughts are so fresh in my mind they will never become anything so distant as memories. Every morning I wake up picturing my brother's murder."

Eirwen ignored her retort. "But these are important questions," he said. "The answers will help shape my plans in the days to come. You must understand that I still have much to learn about this world."

"My lord, we are all doing our duty," she replied.

"Duty? Right now your duty is to help me," the polar admonished. "So let me ask one more time, and please think carefully before you respond. Did Goran-Art ever speak even somewhat positively about any creature in Aeronbed?"

Anat did as she was told. For several minutes they walked along in silence, side by side along the dusty, overgrown trail.

Finally and somewhat grudgingly, Anat replied. "Goran-Art spoke of no such creature. However, if you wish to glean any solace from my brother's words, he did mention once that he found the younger generation of lions more curious about us bears than repelled. Hah! If you ask me, it was because their elders hadn't had sufficient time to indoctrinate them."

"Age does not bring to all creatures equal measures of wisdom and understanding," she added after a brief pause. "I'm afraid that's all I can offer, Lord Eirwen."

"Thank you, Anat. I appreciate your candor, and I apologize again if my words have caused you pain."

"It actually feels better to speak of Goran-Art. I miss him less at such moments."

"Then I'm glad to have brought you that small comfort."

Now walking alone with his thoughts, Eirwen wondered how much store he could place in those words. They were second-hand observations from one bear whose opinions were highly suspect, at least to Eirwen's reckoning. Could anyone else among their number provide more balanced and useful advice?

Hunspek, always quick with words and insight, would probably have something to offer. But he was off working with the advance scouts and the few small birds they had available, seeking to expand their knowledge of the surrounding countryside. He would not be available for some days, maybe longer. Somerled had been too frail to come on the trek north, so the elder had stayed behind in Heimborn with Haefan. Would the wise old bear have been able to suggest anything else? If he had the time and opportunity, the polar bear determined to put the question to him.

And then Eirwen remembered what Fridis had told him about Haidar's father. The elder mountain goat had made great efforts to negotiate with the lions to avoid war. If that was true, there had been among the cadre of lions at least one animal who'd been prepared to negotiate with his kingdom's opponents. So at least in the past there had been individuals in Aeronbed with whom one could work. It was a start, something the polar bear could build upon and better than nothing. Eirwen took consolation from that small shred of knowledge.

❧ 53 ❧

A MEETING OF MINDS

E isa and Olwen set off in search of the mysterious light, or at least its source. However, their destination proved to be much farther away than expected. The trek took the rest of that night, as well as the whole of the next day and night.

The panther and lioness arrived as dawn was breaking in the eastern skies. The sun's lemony light was pushing through the treetop canopy, piercing through the branches to the forest floor. A light mist was rising and the glasslike waters of the lake now mirrored the cloudless blue sky above. It was a site of beguiling tranquility and beauty. At any other time the two cats might have been spellbound by the pastoral splendor, but on this day they remained focused and businesslike, paying no heed to such delights.

After completing a hasty reconnoiter to ensure that they were alone and the spot secure, the two cats immediately went to work, searching every likely place for some sign of the light's source. Soon enough they had concluded that they were no further ahead, at least in their attempts to solve the mystery. Although they were certain of the location, not a solitary clue could be found.

Despite their fatigue, Eisa and Olwen prowled the neighborhood for several more hours. They found a number of old animal tracks and scents, but in the end there was nothing of consequence.

"Do you think we've misjudged the location?" the lioness asked, sniffing under a bush.

"On the contrary," the panther responded. "We both know this is the place. Whatever we're looking for is probably right in front of our noses. We're just not seeing it because we don't know what to look for."

"More likely it's too well hidden."

"Perhaps, but let's not forget the possibility that the source of the light may not be fixed. It could already have been moved. By now it might be far away."

"But we didn't see the light move, nor did we see it again after that one huge flare."

Eisa shrugged. "Possibly that's all there was to it."

"A star crashing to earth?" Olwen asked.

"Then we would have heard something and seen some signs around here. But we've come across nothing unusual, right?"

"Right. The place is beautiful enough but also completely ordinary. So I'd argue that the light wasn't natural but rather something created, something magical — perhaps by a wizard! Who knows, Eisa, my father's wizards may still be roaming about the land. They could have headed to these parts and the light was of their making." Olwen began to get excited at the very thought of Mirati's return.

"I suppose it's always possible," Eisa said. "If so, what are they playing at? What are they hoping to achieve?"

"A signal?" the lioness suggested. "For me?"

"Well, you're here, right on cue. But where are they? Why wouldn't they stick around?"

"No idea, I'm afraid," Olwen said, shrugging. "I've come to realize that wizards are mysterious creatures, not normal like the rest of us. No offence to your father, of course."

"None taken."

"Who could possibly hope to read their minds? Perhaps they're still here, Eisa, watching us and not yet ready to show themselves."

The two cats instinctively looked around, checking every possible hiding place.

"If it is Albiorix's wizards, they're keeping well hidden."

"Well, they are wizards, after all. If Mirati and his brothers can't hide from the likes of us, they can't be very good at wizarding, can they."

Eisa laughed. "That might be the case. Unfortunately, we're getting nowhere with this train of thought. We've had a long night's trek and a frustrating search. I'd say it's high time for a good catnap."

Even thinking about sleep caused the two cats to yawn. "I spotted an excellent tree back a bit," Eisa added. "Let's wait there while we think about what to do next."

They made their way to a massive oak tree whose stout branches overhung the lake. The two cats leapt up easily. Lying well hidden among the foliage, they slept off and on as they contemplated what to do. Although disappointed, Eisa and Olwen were not disheartened, for they had been realistic in their expectations. The excursion was only a small detour in their progress northward.

The panther was sleeping soundly when Olwen nudged him awake with a paw. The lioness signaled him to keep quiet. "*Someone's coming,*" she hissed, nodding to indicate the direction.

Listening intently, the panther made out two separate voices getting louder by the second. Every now and then he could distinguish the odd word, but he could not catch the drift of the conversation.

From the cats' vantage point, camouflaged by the leafy branches high above the ground, Eisa and Olwen could listen to everything that was going on while remaining well hidden. Nevertheless they tensed, crouching low, and did not move a muscle. Unfortunately, while they could hear well enough, the leaves prevented them from seeing the new arrivals.

Time and recent experience had taught Eisa and Olwen to be wary. Despite the bucolic surroundings, danger lurked everywhere. The cats had not encountered another creature since they'd left the capital of Aeronbed, and they were loath to confront anyone or act precipitously. Right now, all they had was questions. Were the approaching animals friends, foes or some neutral party? Were they scouts for a much larger force or just a couple of careless travelers? Might they be lost or wounded and need help? Or, just possibly, could these creatures be associated with the light?

Whoever they were, wherever they had come from, the newcomers certainly had no fear of being noticed. They were carrying on a conversation as if chatting comfortably in a cozy den. Eisa and Olwen looked at each other, mystified and greatly curious about the strange turn of events.

At last the words of the strangers became clear as two animals came within hearing range. "Well, I say we must have missed it," the first voice was complaining. "I told you we should've gone to the right at the last turning. In fact, we should be on the other side of this lake, over by those tall reeds."

"Give it a rest, Vulpé," the second creature snapped, clearly annoyed. "I'm telling you, we still haven't come across the right spot. My instincts are quite strong about this."

"Your instincts? Bah! You said it wasn't far and it's taken two whole days to get here. Don't you think my instincts are as good as yours? Certainly my nose is just as good — hah! probably even better. And now that I think about it, Haidar, I'm beginning to pick up some very peculiar scents. Ugh! Most unpleasant ones at that. I don't like it, not at all.

"We should give this place a quick once-over and then beat it. I'm starting to think the light was just a distraction or — even worse — a lure, some kind of trap. You know what I mean. We have to remember why we're here, Haidar, not get sidetracked on some wild goose chase."

"I seem to recall that it was you who pushed for the detour. You insisted on investigating the light while I wanted to carry on."

"I did? Well, that was yesterday. This morning, things look quite different. Look, Haidar, one must be nimble in such matters, always prepared to change course when it's warranted."

"Something has drawn us here, Vulpé. When we first noticed the light, I thought little of it because I was so preoccupied by our mission. But while we were traveling here, I changed my mind. That was no haphazard event. It was a beacon, meant for us."

"Oh, come on, Haidar."

"No, no, I admit that at first I objected, but you were right all along. And now you will find there was a purpose in it."

"As long as it wasn't some trick. I don't want to end my days as some creature's lunch. You know, it could just as easily have been a warning to stay away. It's all in the interpretation."

"I tell you, Vulpé, the light came from a friendly source."

"How can you know that?"

"I just can. It's as simple as that."

The first creature sighed loudly. "That may well be, but remember, the signal could also have drawn someone less friendly. We can't have been the only ones within range around here. No animal could have missed that light."

Eisa and Olwen watched as the new arrivals came into view and then stopped directly beneath the tree. The surprised lioness mouthed a silent question to her partner: *A fox and a mountain goat?*

Eisa did not respond. He was finding the newcomers' conversation especially thought-provoking. These two creatures were not just lost or out for a stroll. There was something special about them, beyond the curious fact that they were not natural companions. And they were on some kind of quest.

The strangers stopped immediately below the cats' vantage point.

"Maybe the light was not such a rare occurrence after all," said the fox.

"I don't know," the goat replied. "But I'm sure it was meant for us."

For several seconds neither animal spoke. The fox sat down and said, "Well, now what, Haidar? You always — "

"Be quiet, Vulpé," the goat interrupted, "and let me think."

The fox yawned. It had been a long night. Taking advantage of the opportunity, he put his head down.

Haidar began prowling slowly around the edge of the lake and in the surrounding bushes, sniffing and prodding at the ground from time to time. After several minutes he returned to the big shade tree.

"Well?" Vulpé asked again, lazily raising his head.

"It's just out of my reach — not physically but in my mind," Haidar replied. He spoke absent-mindedly, more to himself than to the fox. "I have the strongest impressions that all together do not make sense. I know the light was significant. We're supposed to be here. But why?"

"What do you mean by impressions?"

"Perhaps I only mean to say instincts. Sometimes I get these mental pictures of objects or creatures. My father had the same gift, or so I was told."

"Your father?"

"It was my father who traveled extensively in Aeronbed. He met with the lions, or at least one of them. He also had these visions."

Instincts Vulpé could accept, but visions were another matter, entirely outside his ken. "I never knew that," the fox said. "Well, of course, I know nothing about your background."

"Few do. It's a long and unhappy tale. I've only told two or three others about it." The mountain goat lay down beside the fox.

"And that is why Gloton asked you — "

"Outside of Vigmar's forces, I am one of the few in Blakfel who has ever traveled into Aeronbed. More than that, my family has a history of seeking reconciliation with the lions."

Haidar was not sure why he had suddenly chosen to reveal so much to Vulpé. However, once he began to talk, it was like water overflowing a dam — the words just kept coming.

"I see," Vulpé said. "In fact, I begin to understand a great deal. So tell me — "

At that precise moment Olwen and Eisa jumped down from their hiding place.

✲ 54 ✲

THE INTERROGATION

The two cats landed right beside Haidar and Vulpé.

"What the — " the startled mountain goat bleated. He leapt up, followed immediately by the fox.

Normally Olwen would make short work of two such interlopers. However, these were not normal times, and the lioness had heard enough to know she wanted a proper conversation with the strangers. Why were they in her father's kingdom? And what was this talk of reconciliation?

And normally Haidar and Vulpé would have hightailed it out of harm's way, in opposite directions, without a moment's hesitation. But their only goal in Aeronbed was to meet up with the big cats. Despite their initial surprise and fear, the two were more than prepared to stand their ground and confront Eisa and Olwen.

At first the fox and goat stood as if paralyzed, too shocked to do anything. The cats had the advantage of surprise; they were also much more powerful and on their home turf. Nevertheless, Haidar and Vulpé, despite their apprehension, were smart enough to realize that the cats' failure to attack when they had the opportunity indicated a desire to talk rather than to kill.

The two cats were amazed to find such an unlikely pair involved in some sort of mission. Haidar and Vulpé were equally perplexed to encounter a lion and a panther together. The discovery confounded their plans: Haidar had been looking for the lions but Vulpé's intent was to search out the panthers. Both had to be circumspect about what they revealed to each other, as well as to their new acquaintances.

"Greetings, er, strangers," Olwen said, attempting to appear both regal and welcoming. "What brings you to the lands of King Albiorix of Aeronbed?" Given the recent events, she wanted to emphasize the lions' legitimate claim to the kingdom, but she immediately regretted the clumsy phrasing.

Haidar and Vulpé hadn't rehearsed what they would say when they finally ran into representatives of Aeronbed. After a brief hesitation, bowing low, the fox spoke up. "Forgive me, my good lady and good sir, you've caught us unawares. In our surprise we quite lost our power of speech — only temporarily, of course. In time you'll learn that we are accomplished conversationalists — me in particular." He was blathering, he realized. Better quit while he was ahead.

"Sorry," Vulpé apologized again. "These are difficult, er, unusual times, and we humble travelers have to take, er, great care." The fox stopped, wagged his tail — too enthusiastically, he feared — and sat down again.

To his dismay, neither cat responded. Olwen's gaze was unreadable. The panther just stared at him but every now and then he would shift his wary eyes to Haidar as if in warning. Vulpé decided he needed to be more forthcoming.

"My, er, traveling companion and I are on our way from Blakfel to Manaris," the fox went on. "The capital of Aeronbed."

"The name of the capital is well known to us," Olwen said carefully.

"Yes, well, er, of course you would," Vulpé continued. "We have business to conduct with the, ah, authorities,"

"What sort of business?" the lioness asked.

"Not the sort of business you can reveal to everyone you run into," Vulpé countered, a little more sharply than he intended.

"Perhaps if we introduced ourselves ... " interjected Haidar, hoping to smooth things over.

"An excellent idea," Olwen said, leaving it to the two intruders to start.

"My name is Haidar," said the mountain goat. "And my, er, associate, is called Vulpé."

"Haidar? An unusual name for a mountain goat, is it not?"

"I have been told that, my lady," Haidar replied noncommittally. "More than once."

"In fact, I'd say it's more fit for a lion," she said almost accusingly, as if the goat had stolen his name from a more worthy creature.

Haidar sighed deeply. "It's a long story, one that I would be happy to relate to you in the fullness of time. That is, if I knew to whom we are speaking. On that score, you now have the advantage over us."

"I beg your pardon, I have forgotten my manners. I go by the name of Olwen, and this is Lieutenant Eisa."

The fox and goat did a double take, and Vulpé quickly got the picture. Though Eisa had a rank, Olwen was doing all the talking, so she must have a more exalted position. Certainly she had an air of authority that could not be denied. It was most curious: a lioness and a panther together in the far eastern reaches of the kingdom. It didn't add up.

Eisa, meanwhile, glanced at Olwen, wondering why the Princess hadn't revealed her status. What had she to fear from these two outsiders?

"I presume you know you have traveled well into Aeronbed proper," Olwen continued. "Vigmar is a long way behind you."

Vulpé and Haidar looked at each other. The two cats were certainly not making their task easy. Nevertheless, Haidar remained undaunted. At least the interrogation had begun in a civil manner. In the midst of this terrible war, that fact alone was encouraging. Perhaps by some miracle they had managed to meet one (or two) of the few creatures with whom they might actually find common ground.

Vulpé knew nothing of Haidar's family history, but the mountain goat had always known that his unusual name had potential to gain him entry — or at least a hearing — where others would be immediately denied. It was clearly time to make the most of it. "Perhaps, my lady, it might help if I told you my tale."

"Go ahead then," Olwen replied.

"I suggest that we all get comfortable," Haidar said. "This may take a while."

As Vulpé looked on with undisguised astonishment, Haidar began to trace the story of his past.

55

HAIDAR'S STORY

"The name I was given at birth was Cernus. Although Cernus is, without a doubt, a right and proper name for a mountain goat, when I heard the story of my late father, it seemed only right and proper to change it to Haidar.

"I will be completely open with you. My station in life is modest; I am nothing more than a lowly servant in the castle of Blakfel. Yes, I see you are surprised. We are your enemy, are we not? Yet here we are, wandering about in your land and now talking freely with you about our mission. By all rights, you should already be at our throats. But these are strange times, and things are as they must be. I know my friend Vulpé, here, would behave in a similar fashion."

Although the surprised fox was quick to nod in agreement, speaking the truth was far from his forte. Vulpé was appalled by what he was hearing. The mountain goat was speaking without pretense, guile or any effort to deceive. Haidar was about to tell the two cats everything — maybe even more than the fox himself knew about his companion. Should he intervene? His curiosity piqued, he decided to see how the tale played out. Somehow the situation might still work in his favor.

The goat had admitted to being from the enemy camp, and in the direct employ of the hated Emperor and Empress. The two cats reacted instinctively. Despite their attempts to play it cool, they growled quietly, their eyes narrowing and their tails twitching. But this creature was clearly no ordinary goat and, as he had already observed, these were not ordinary times. In truth, who *was* their real enemy?

Haidar hesitated, realizing he had to let his words sink in.

"Go on. We're all ears," Olwen said after she'd calmed down.

"As I was saying, I work in the castle. I hold neither fancy title nor exalted status, but my family's position was not always so diminished. My father was a diplomat, an adviser of the previous Emperor. This would have been before your time, for I can see you are both young in years. My father was dedicated to the cause of peace between Vigmar and Aeronbed. He always fought for understanding and tolerance among all animals.

"However, in Blakfel's court he faced many who were opposed to that view. They thought him a naive fool and they conspired against him." He sighed. "Perhaps that's the nature of court life. Perhaps, after all, things are not much different in Manaris, or in any other court, for that matter."

Eisa and Olwen already knew from their own experiences that the goat spoke the truth. But they said nothing as Haidar continued with his story.

"Possibly my father was naive, but I can assure you he was not a fool. He was simply out of step with his times, for the prevailing mood in the Empire had moved on. Not enough members of the court shared his views, and many of those opposed to him sought war as an answer to all life's problems. War has always been the simple solution, however harsh the results for the common herd.

"My father could not fight them all, though he tried long and hard to do so. He still had influence with the Emperor, and he made as much use of that advantage as possible. But he stood in their way, and they were determined to eliminate him."

Haidar paused, swallowed hard and glanced up to the sky. The afternoon was moving on, the shadows increasing, the forest glade hushed. None of the others spoke. The goat was sharing deeply personal memories; they were not about to interrupt him.

"At the time," Haidar went on, "Vigmar was disputing several matters with Aeronbed. I needn't explain to worldly animals such as you that such a state of affairs is normal — to be expected, even — in relations between friends or rivals. Differences arise over territory, relationships, possessions — you name it. We do not communicate the same way with each other and misunderstandings occur. Some of us may be more hot-blooded and intemperate than others.

"Calmer and more reasonable creatures hope arguments can be settled, whether easily or with effort, and the pecking order observed. They seek to prevent the disputing parties from coming to blows, then to open combat and finally to all-out war. It's a continual struggle to practice such forbearance, is it not? My father was one of those who are capable of understanding the views of others, seeking conciliation and finding common ground. His words of advice at that time were crucial to preserving peace between the two neighbors.

"Even before this time, Vigmar had been at odds with Aeronbed over a territorial claim. Hostilities simmered, and every now and then skirmishes would occur and sometimes loss of life resulted. But more often than not, both sides worked out an accommodation and let things be. I don't remember now who was claiming what or who already held the piece of land, or even how big it was.

"Was one side more in the right, more virtuous or correct than the other? Who among us can judge? Standing here before you, I will not claim that we in Blakfel are better in our ways than you in Manaris. All I can attest is that the creatures of Vigmar are a mix of the warlike and the peace-loving, the noble and the mean-spirited, and I know in my heart that Aeronbed is exactly the same. Can either of you, in all good faith, disagree with me?"

It might hurt Olwen and Eisa to admit it, but they could not. They knew Haidar's assertion to be as undeniable as the morning sunrise. The two cats shook their heads.

Haidar took up his story once more. "My father had a nose for which creatures were bellicose and to be avoided, and which were more amenable to talking things over. He knew with whom one could reach an agreement, cut a deal or even construct a lasting peace. He was prepared to negotiate wherever and whenever the other side was willing. With great patience he won the trust of those in authority in Aeronbed — at least, some of them — and he opened doors that had previously been shut to Vigmar.

"But while he was away, his enemies — a younger generation mainly, more hawkish and aggressive — created suspicion in the Emperor's mind. They said my father was ambitious for his own sake, that he was betraying Vigmar and selling out to Aeronbed. He had been gone a long while, conducting negotiations near Manaris, time enough to sow the seeds of doubt. When he finally returned from those lengthy talks, he was met with distrust and shunned by the majority of those in power. My father was unable to convince the Emperor of his good intentions or explain to him what he had achieved. However, he did not give up, persevering even against those odds.

"Tensions between Vigmar and Aeronbed continued to escalate. The war faction exaggerated every minor incident and constantly railed against Aeronbed. Meanwhile, my father kept trying to smooth things over and promote compromise. Things got worse and worse. My father's few remaining allies began to desert him, for they could not withstand the abuse being heaped upon them. The prevailing views of the Empire were against them: the mood was for war. Those against it were painted as weak and cowardly. It was a painful time.

"My father had a confidant in Aeronbed, a young lion (so I was told) with whom he kept in regular contact, even as matters deteriorated. As time went on, it became more and more difficult to communicate with him. The court began to see as treasonous my father's attempts to keep that last channel open, and they were considered a threat to the war faction. Although things were a little better in Manaris, I gather, similar challenges existed there. Every dispute led to another, and those who favored war were gaining in strength.

"My father and his trusted counterpart kept looking for some solution that would break the impasse, or at least keep war in check. He was forced to exchange information with this cat through secret means, through intermediaries whom he could trust to pass on messages, and by holding meetings in secret places along the border.

His enemies suspected him and sought to find out how and where he was operating.

"I don't know who was responsible or how they managed it, but I do know that somehow both the meeting places and the channels for messages were discovered. By that point his enemies in Blakfel had determined that my father was the primary obstacle to what they wanted. He still had some influence, however slight, with the Emperor — perhaps nothing more than his words of caution and his calm manner — but it kept open warfare from breaking out. At least, I like to think so. But, as I've said, his opponents saw war with Aeronbed as the answer to their problems. In my opinion, my father was the only source of light keeping the darkness from taking hold."

"What happened then?" asked Vulpé, as eager as the others to know how it all turned out.

"I'm not really sure. Either my father's secret route through the mountains was somehow discovered or he was betrayed. Whatever the case, he was followed to the rendezvous point. I don't know if his last planned meeting ever took place. He was, in any event, horribly murdered. To make matters worse — if that's possible — my father's death was used as propaganda against Aeronbed. Its soldiers were blamed for killing a 'great patriot' of Vigmar. The inevitable calls for vengeance followed quickly enough. Ultimately his death set off the chain of events that led to Aeronbed becoming Vigmar's 'vile enemy,' one to be conquered at all costs. So his rivals killed two birds with one stone. With one blow they removed the main obstacle to their aims and created the perfect reason to start a war. They must have relished the irony.

"Over time, much of this history has been forgotten. Of course, it happened many years ago, and most of those involved were killed in battle or, now too old to fight, have been put out to pasture. Naturally the real villains were smart enough never to go near a battlefield. They were more than happy to see everyone else die for their *just cause*. A new generation holds the positions of power now, and we are still paying the price for that foolishness."

"*Foolishness* seems hardly the word for it," Eisa said.

"You're right, Lieutenant," sighed the goat. "*Evildoing* would be far more appropriate."

Darkness had fallen now. It seemed as if the forest, now quiet as a tomb, had been listening to the sad tale with equal attention.

"A war has a way of wiping out the stories of those who oppose popular movements," Haidar added. "Thankfully, a few stalwarts can be found to keep the memories alive, at least in their hearts. And when the opportunity comes along, they can share those memories with anyone who cares to listen." It was a self-serving observation, but the others did not condemn the goat for it.

"What was your father's name?" Eisa asked.

"Parvash," Haidar answered.

The lion and panther exchanged glances.

"Does the name mean anything to you?" the goat asked. "Either of you?"

The goat looked from one cat to the other, hopes rising.

"No," Olwen said. "Sorry."

"'Fraid not," Eisa added. "Of course, those events happened a long time ago."

"One curious thing, though," Haidar said, a little more upbeat now. "Some years after my father's death, I received a parcel, a small, square object wrapped in rough cloth. When I opened it, I found a small painting of my father and a lion on a mountain ledge. Accompanying the picture was a dedication to my father from that very cat.

"Somehow my father's contact — whose name, I was told, was Haidar — must have figured out how to get it to me. I often thought about that picture. When I managed to put the elements together — the story, how it all happened, the consequences — I decided to dedicate my life to making things right. I also changed my name, with my mother's permission, from Cernus to Haidar, in memory of that noble animal, for he too risked much by trying to do the right thing. I'm sure my father would have approved.

"I never heard anything more of this cat. Naturally, with the ongoing hostility and constant recourse to fighting, I've not been in a position to seek him out. The whole thing has been a tragedy, but — irony of ironies — out of this misfortune I have now been given an opportunity to make things right. Vulpé and I have been tasked with making peace between Aeronbed and Vigmar. It's all I've ever sought to do.

"I can only imagine that my namesake died long ago. Perhaps he and my father met again in another, more peaceful world. But I have often asked myself, what if he had a son or daughter who was filled with a motivation equal to mine?"

When Haidar had finished his tale on this more optimistic note, Vulpé could only ask himself: *What now? What do I do? What do I say?* He hoped the cats wouldn't think to ask about the role he played in Blakfel. Could he trust Haidar to keep quiet about it?

Eisa, meanwhile, turned to the lioness. His glance said: *Does any part of this amazing tale make sense or sound at all familiar?* Olwen's expression, however, gave nothing away.

The forest glade remained silent. Only the sound of the wind, pushing its way through the treetops, could be heard.

56

EXPLANATIONS

W as Haidar speaking the truth? Could the mountain goat even separate fact from fiction? Perhaps he was simply repeating some old family lore, told and retold to comfort him in moments of unhappiness and loneliness?

The cry of a distant bird sounded in the woods beyond the lake, breaking the stillness. Olwen seemed lost in a trance. Unbeknownst to the others, she was thinking back to the past — not as far back as Haidar's tale, but to her own early years, much as the goat had looked back to his.

At long last the lioness seemed to wake from her reverie. "I believe what you say is true," she said. "The story is familiar to me. Of course, I've only heard the version from our side of the mountains. I never imagined I would meet someone who was actually connected with it, friend or enemy. Years back, my father told me about the efforts to seek peace. It happened a long time ago, I think, and I can barely remember the details. It may even have been one of my father's uncles who acted as the go-between. Was he named Haidar? Really, I don't recall."

Olwen had posed this last remark to herself. She shrugged in reply and then carried on. "It's possible. But I never met the animal in question. He died well before I was born."

"One of your uncles?" Haidar and Eisa asked simultaneously.

"Er, yes. I mean, no. One of my father's uncles, my great-uncle," Olwen answered, appearing to notice them for the first time.

"If I may be so bold, my lady," Haidar said, "who are you exactly?"

"It's about time I acknowledged my station in life," Olwen replied. "You need to know the playing field you're treading on. I am Princess Olwen, only daughter of King Albiorix."

It was Vulpé and Haidar's turn to stare in astonishment. However, being well-versed in court protocol, they recovered quickly. The pair immediately rose and bowed low. Olwen, after so many days on the run, was well beyond such formalities. She barely acknowledged their efforts.

Straightening up, Haidar spoke once more. "Forgive me, Princess, but now I am quite perplexed. If I may be so bold a second time, why are you two on your own, without company or entourage and, to all appearances, wandering about in the borderlands? Do you not have an important role to play somewhere else? Are Vigmar and Aeronbed not at war?"

"We four are well met," Olwen said, laughing wryly. "Perhaps we are like lost souls, searching for ... " The lioness's voice trailed off, but then she remembered herself. "You have spoken openly and honestly; I respect that. Something tells me Eisa and I were meant to join up with you. But before we head down that path, we need to tell you about what's happening in Aeronbed. Since you left Vigmar, much has changed, and not all for the better."

She turned to Eisa. He then described in detail how the two friends had come to be at that very spot.

When the panther had finished his long tale, Haidar spoke up. "I want to make sure I truly understand you, sir. Do you mean to say that Aeronbed is now ruled by the panthers — the Black Legion — and not by the lions?"

"I fear it is true. King Albiorix has retreated to the far north of the country with the remnants of his armies, or so Princess Olwen and I have been led to understand. Of the south we know nothing. We are, to put it bluntly, in a state of civil war."

"But the war with Vigmar continues?" asked Vulpé.

"As far as we know, that too is the case. As you can understand, our contact with the outside world has been virtually non-existent. Even this news is several days old, perhaps even older."

While Haidar was dismayed by this turn of events, Vulpé was delighted, although he of course revealed nothing outwardly. While the mountain goat regarded the lions as natural and inevitable intermediaries, the fox knew otherwise. The Empress's scheme had always been to work out an arrangement with the panthers. Now, given the rapid ascendency of the Legion, such a deal would be much more meaningful. Vulpé's route of approach was now clear; he had the answer to his dilemma. But could he deliver the entire kingdom to Vigmar on his own?

"If the Legion remains in the field," the fox asked Eisa, "who then commands in Manaris? That is to say, who is making the decisions?"

"The panthers' Grand Council and one Baron — I mean, *Archduke* Rithild, who has taken charge. Why do you ask?"

"Just trying to improve my understanding of the lay of the land, Lieutenant — complete my education, as it were. And you said, did you not, that the capital is three or four days' quick march from here?"

"I did not say so, but yes, that would be a fair approximation."

Eisa eyed Vulpé suspiciously, doubting that those were innocent questions. He asked the fox upon whose authority they had risked so much by venturing into Aeronbed.

"Upon the highest authority, Lieutenant," the fox declared rather pompously. "That's all I can say. Regrettably, I am not at liberty to divulge further details. For the safety of those involved, let me just add that we are empowered to contract an agreement with the powers that be in Aeronbed and to seek every assurance that it will be upheld, no matter what follows. I'm sure you understand the necessity of keeping mum on such matters. Even the trees have ears."

Eisa wondered whether he should press the point, but let it go. Instead the panther took another tack. "Yet you do not find the story of your companion instructive? Look what befell his kin. Are you so sure you stand on firm ground?"

The suggestion took him aback; it was something Vulpé had never considered. Might he return home to find everything had changed in his absence? The more the fox thought about it, the more he realized that anything could happen. No one and nothing could be trusted. But yet, the fox told himself, if he returned with a deal, surely that would make all the difference. Haidar's father had had nothing like that to offer.

"I am more than confident in my position, Lieutenant," Vulpé replied after a few moments of reflection.

"You're too late in any case," Olwen interjected. "King Albiorix is in the north, under attack and in no position to parlay with the likes of anyone, let alone you two."

Vulpé carefully considered what to say before responding. "My commission is to seek peace," the fox said noncommittally. "I must pursue it, notwithstanding the situation."

Meanwhile, Haidar was not really listening to this exchange, totally lost in thought as he considered his options. There seemed to him no point in continuing. The lions were defeated and on the run. Was King Albiorix even alive? If not, right in front of him stood the most senior member of the lions of Aeronbed, and the lioness seemed more than willing to entertain conversations about peace.

However, Olwen ruled no one, so what would be the point? It was a shame. The goat felt he could have dealt with the lions, but Eisa's story of the ruthless coup d'état had convinced him that he could never seek out the panthers as partners. Haidar was tormented by this turn of events. *Another opportunity gone to waste* was all he could bitterly conclude.

"That mysterious light," Vulpé said out of the blue. "Did you find out anything about it?"

The question brought the others back to the present. Their shared disclosures had made them forget the reason for the unusual happenstance of their meeting.

"No, nothing at all," Eisa replied flatly.

"And you?" asked Olwen.

"The same, I'm afraid," Vulpé answered, honestly this time. "I thought we might have misjudged its location, but Haidar convinced me this is the right place. Still, I'm not so sure."

"No, Haidar is correct. This was the spot, or very near to it," Olwen declared. "I readily confess I've never seen anything like that burst of light."

"Nor us. Like a bolt of lightning that went on and on instead of disappearing in a flash, right?"

"Yes, though less like lightning coming down from the sky. More like a very powerful lantern pointed up at it. And it got brighter over time, not the other way around."

"And we all saw it?"

"No mistake about that, and apparently from different directions. It was definitely not an illusion."

"Eisa, does such a light foreshadow anything?" asked Olwen.

The panther seemed puzzled. "I don't know, Princess. Or at least if it does, I can't recall," he replied. "Let me think about it a while."

Reminded of their original purpose, the four creatures decided to return to their searching. But they pursued the task in a half-hearted fashion, already convinced that the source of whatever they had witnessed was long gone. And of course their results matched their expectations: they found nothing new.

Nevertheless, while they searched, the participants took advantage of the opportunity to think about what they had learned that day. Eisa and Olwen had become aware that someone of importance in Vigmar was seeking an end to the interminable conflict. That news was useful and all to the good, but what could they do with such knowledge in their current, unempowered state? Perhaps it was just information to store away for another day.

Haidar saw no point in pursuing the quest. Seeking out the lions in the north was too dangerous; he and the fox would be forced to cover unknown ground. And in Manaris they would not find a like-minded intermediary with whom they could discuss mutually acceptable terms. In the goat's view, the state of affairs in Aeronbed had become too confused and volatile; better to let it play out. But all was not lost. If he bided his time, Haidar could at least hope for another reversal of fortune. The civil war was far from over; the lions could still return to power.

The mountain goat was less than keen on returning to Blakfel. He had been rather enjoying his time away from Vigmar, even if forced to escort the annoying and secretive Vulpé. With failure now looming, what would the future hold for him back at the castle? At best it would mean going back to the same old thing: playing cat-and-mouse with the powers that be, making no progress in life, continuing to serve in the kitchen — in sum, nothing more than a reprise of his father's futile efforts. Even worse, those same authorities in Blakfel might decide to punish his failure severely (not a rare occurrence).

But if the goat could not go back or move forward, what option was left? As he thought about his quandary, he glanced over at the lion and panther. Had those two been sent to him for a purpose?

Vulpé had the easiest time deciding what to do. Panthers and lions were all alike to him. He just had to do the Empress's bidding. As for his traveling companion, Vulpé now knew Haidar's whole story: the goat was a friend of the lions, through and through. The fox didn't need him to meet with the panthers; in fact, his name might even present a liability. And in any event, he was far too emotional about the whole thing. Haidar wouldn't be able to hide his distaste for the bellicose black cats.

To top things off, Vulpé had managed to work out the way to Aeronbed's capital, more or less, and how long it should take him to get there. He could steal away at night and be long gone before the others realized it.

57

THE MEANING OF LIGHT

L ater on, the four animals sat huddled together beneath the tree where they had first encountered each other. Eisa returned to the question the lioness had posed many hours earlier. "You asked about the meaning of light in prophecy," he began. "Of course, we don't know if what we saw was a sign of things to come. Unlike — "

The panther, suddenly uncomfortable about revealing the lioness's story to strangers, shifted course. "I've remembered something my father told me. He said that light, especially a very bright light like this one was, is related to enlightenment and intuition. I think all four of us experienced an overwhelming impulse to travel here, whether we wanted to or not. So we did, and now we've learned much as a result. Perhaps it was not what we expected, but it was something important to us.

"Light is an omen signifying good fortune or the end of a difficult period. Let's hope that's true, for the poor creatures of these lands have suffered enough. Of course, light can also be seen as casting out the darkness of night or of ignorance and evil. Somehow we saw a small slice of truth and goodness in this land of shadows. Unfortunately, the light did not last long. Quite the opposite — it was over in a flash.

"Hopefully it's a signal of better days to come. We just don't know when. Who knows, maybe it will show itself again tonight and we shall see it at close quarters this time."

It was an exciting idea — a chance to witness the amazing burst of light again. Perhaps the first signal had been an invitation, one that they'd readily accepted. Now their faith might be rewarded by an even greater display of pyrotechnics. The thought comforted them. Even Vulpé wondered whether he should stay the night in case he got to see the wondrous light again.

"Now, if it was a beacon and not just a light," Eisa was saying, "it can be seen as either an invitation or a warning."

"So which is it?" asked Vulpé.

"Well, there's the rub," Eisa said. "We just don't know."

"So either we've been invited to stay or we've been warned to keep away," Vulpé said. "Not much help there, I'd say,"

The panther laughed; he was used to such cynical reactions. "That may be the case, but all our instincts told us to come, did they not?"

"True, very true," Haidar agreed.

"But we poor souls are easily fooled by the gods, or spirits, or what have you," countered Vulpé. "We could have been deceived into coming here."

"Do you really think so?" Olwen demanded.

"Isn't it true they play with us? Aren't we nothing more than their pathetic pawns?"

The goat jumped in. "In this case, all four of us felt exactly the same. I agree with the Lieutenant."

"Is there anything else, Eisa?" Olwen asked.

"One more thing. If the light was cast by fire, it would reflect a need for rebirth and cleansing, for breaking free from past prejudices and old ways of thinking. In sum, we are in a position to create something new. It's like the power of the day and the awakening of the sun, which frees us from the night through every waking hour."

"So that's all to the good, then," said the practical fox.

"Yes, most of what the light could signify is very positive," the panther agreed. "Of course, we don't know for sure if the light was an omen. We are just supposing."

"If the light returns tonight, I'll definitely take it as a good omen," the fox declared. "We four, having the presence of mind to make the trek here, will be blessed by good fortune in the days to come. I, for one, am looking forward to a real display of power."

The others silently contemplated the idea of the light and their good fortune. At that moment, as if to punctuate those thoughts, dawn arrived, flooding the lakeside with a gorgeous yellow glow.

"And if not," continued the fox, blinking, "we've lost nothing but a day of hunting and a night of sleep."

"Do you think the light will come again?" Olwen asked Eisa.

The panther shrugged. "Your guess is as good as mine, Princess. But since we're here, we might as well wait."

As there was little more to add, the animals let the matter rest. All four were of like mind: even though the chance seemed slim, none wanted to miss the opportunity. The pleasure the light had brought was great indeed.

Vulpé realized that his plan for a nighttime flit would have to be postponed for a whole day, and even until very early the next morning, when the other three would be sound asleep after their long night's vigil. He intended to get as much sleep as possible in the following hours.

❦

THEY HAD PLANNED TO TAKE TURNS STANDING WATCH. HOWEVER, IN THEIR eagerness to witness the light again, all four stayed awake, more than happy to maintain their expectant vigil. No one wanted to chance missing anything of what might occur.

The moon rose; its faint glow broke through the evening mists to shine down on the quartet for several hours. Much to their collective disappointment, however, nothing else happened. Aside from that silver crescent and its accompanying stars, darkness reigned supreme over their little world.

Soon enough, fatigue overtook excitement. Each animal curled up and went to sleep exactly where they had been standing watch. Each, that is, but Vulpé. The fox had arranged to be the final sentinel; he could then slip away unseen if nothing came to pass. After a good hour, the first faint shimmer of dawn was appearing, and the fox came to the conclusion that further waiting would be in vain. The others were sleeping like youngsters after a long play session of play; a quiet departure would never be easier.

The fox's only (small) regret was taking leave of grumpy Haidar, whom Vulpé had come to respect and even like, in some strange way. However, the fox's sense of duty to his mistress and the importance of the mission trumped everything else, certainly any personal feelings. Vulpé had always assumed his path would eventually diverge from Haidar's. Now was as good a time as any: the way to Manaris was clear and he no longer needed the goat's guidance.

Vulpé wondered idly what would become of Haidar, whether he'd be safe with those two powerful cats. The fox suspected — hoped, even — that they'd let him go, after which the mountain goat would likely choose to return to Blakfel. Now that the panthers were clearly in control of Aeronbed, what else could the poor creature do?

The fox stole away, leaving the others without a backward glance. He suspected they wouldn't pursue him, but he still took care not to direct his first steps toward Manaris. Rather, Vulpé headed north, planning a circuitous route to throw the others off track, just in case. Only much later would he begin to veer west toward Aeronbed's capital.

58

GOING THEIR SEPARATE WAYS

B y the time Vulpé's exhausted companions had thrown off the heavy cloak of sleep, the sun had been up for several hours. It had already taken its usual place in the east, just above the highest treetops. However, the trio could see little of its light, for the red-streaked sky was dark with huge, billowing clouds that seemed to reach up to the distant heavens.

Noting the absence of the fox, Haidar suggested that Vulpé might be wandering about, still faithfully maintaining his watch or searching for the source of the magic light. However, when he could not be found, they were forced to conclude that he'd given them the slip. The cats' first inclination was to suspect both Vulpé and Haidar of lying, colluding to allow the former time to flee in pursuit of some villainous scheme. The mountain goat's obvious puzzlement forced the panther and the lioness to admit that the idea made little sense. Vulpé had clearly deceived everyone.

"I'm not really surprised," Eisa declared. "I suspected the fox from the very beginning. He asked too many questions about the Black Legion and Manaris."

"He did?" the perplexed mountain goat said. "I hadn't noticed."

"You were too caught up in your family memories. Anyone could see the fox for what he is — no friend of yours."

Haidar, frowning deeply, was too dismayed at the thought to say anything.

"But I do wonder why he left you behind. He must trust in our merciful instincts," continued Eisa, half teasing.

"We should go after him," the lioness growled. She cared more about what the fox might be up to and less about his motives. "A scoundrel like Vulpé would betray our presence to the first Legion soldiers he comes across."

Eisa, however, was quick to disagree. "The pursuit would be no easy task. We'd have to search a vast territory."

"Then the sooner we get started, the better."

"Don't forget, Princess, Vulpé has several hours' head start and will certainly be covering his tracks. Even worse, he'll be heading toward Manaris. That's the last place you and I want to go."

"You're convinced he's on his way to Manaris?"

"Given what Haidar has told us, I do. Of course, Vulpé might not make it to the capital. He doesn't know the territory west of here. He may get sidetracked or lose his way. He might run into creatures who are less easygoing and quicker to condemn than we are. Not everyone is willing to stop and merely question a stranger. If you ask me, I'll bet the fox doesn't live long enough to tell his tale to anyone."

"What if he does?"

"All right, let's say Vulpé reaches Manaris unharmed. Well, that's where his problems will really begin. I wouldn't want to be negotiating with Rithild. The fox will be biting off far more than he can chew if he faces that old schemer. Let's look at the possibilities. He might refuse to meet with Vulpé and order his execution before the poor fellow gets to say a word. Or he might reject the fox's overtures and send him packing. With luck, Vulpé might survive to get home, but he'll have nothing to show for his efforts.

"Then again, if Rithild does agree to negotiate, he'll run circles around Vulpé. Any resulting accord will be so full of clever words, tricks and nuances as to be meaningless. Remember, I know that cat better than anyone. He can fool even the most brilliant of opponents. At the end of the day, even if Vulpé succeeds, the accord will not be worth the parchment it's written on. The fox will return to Vigmar in disgrace and failure. In sum, Princess, let's not underestimate the challenges he is facing."

"What you say only adds to my worry. Under duress, the fox could happily give us up, either to curry favor and get what he seeks or to escape death. I say again, we should go after him. And the longer we stand here deliberating, the greater the distance we have to make up."

"What if the story of a treaty is false?" Eisa countered. "Haidar might be only the first in a line of unwitting dupes. Maybe Vulpé is just a spy for Vigmar, trying to find out what he can about Aeronbed's state of affairs. Maybe he's already pursuing another mission or has gone off in some other direction. Or perhaps he found out what he needed from us and is already returning to Blakfel.

"You see, Olwen, we're faced with too many unknowns. Maybe none of it matters; maybe it all does. Whatever the case, though, I'm sure you're right about Vulpé being prepared to give us up. So I agree that getting out of this place as fast as possible would be our wisest course of action. But let's not chase after the fox or retrace our steps back to Manaris."

The two cats retreated into frustrated silence as they tried to work through Vulpé's motives and possible moves.

Haidar was greatly put out by Vulpé's deception. As he listened to the back-and-forth between the cats, the goat's mind had returned to his original discussion with Gloton about the mission. Who was really behind the scheme? Had the wolverine been speaking on his own authority or was it on behalf of some creature (or creatures) higher in the pecking order? The list of those who ranked higher than him was limited: just the Emperor, the Empress and a few senior military officers. Gloton had assured Haidar that, if they were successful, he and Vulpé would have unqualified support on their return to Vigmar.

Haidar had never completely trusted either Gloton or Vulpé, on that point or any other. Quite the contrary, the goat was certain they'd shared only a small fragment of the whole truth. Still, seeking a peace treaty seemed too elaborate a cover story to weave just to gather information on the enemy. Perhaps the truth was even worse. Was it possible they'd never expected him to succeed, that this operation was simply a feint meant to confuse the enemy?

Haidar's misgivings, until now held in check, began to grow rapidly. Perhaps he was just a naive pawn in Gloton's game. If so, what about Vulpé? Was the fox mixed up in the scheme as well or was he too a victim of deception? Had he really gone on to Manaris or, having found out about the Black Legion's success, had he decided to play it safe and return home? No, the goat concluded. Even Eisa had noticed Vulpé's insistent questions; the fox was indeed pursuing his goal in Manaris. It must be the real thing — but what exactly was it all about?

"I'd like to make a suggestion," the mountain goat interjected into the silence.

The two cats, who had almost forgotten about Haidar, looked at him questioningly.

"Since hearing the news of King Albiorix's overthrow, I'd been of two minds about what to do next. You know how much this mission means to me. *Means to me* — hah! That doesn't even come near the whole truth. It's been my life's dream! And I was so confident of achieving success this time. Once again it seems that the cause of peace has been torn from my grasp." The goat pawed at the ground in frustration.

"But I did not come here with my eyes closed," he went on. "Not at all. You wondered, Lieutenant, why Vulpé was prepared to abandon me so readily, and you were right in saying the fox is no friend of mine. But the truth is even more damning. Vulpé works for the Empress, Dona Morana. I'd never met the creature before we set off on this cursed mission. I was conscripted — after many attempts at persuasion and appealing to my better instincts — to help Vulpé get safely through the mountain passes and into Aeronbed.

"I'm guessing he now feels confident about reaching the capital on his own, and he may well be right. The only surprise is that he's prepared to throw in his lot with the Legion. I assure you, Princess, I had no inkling of his plans. I'd always assumed we'd be talking with members of your family. As you say, Lieutenant, I was too preoccupied to pay attention to what Vulpé was really after. I've been careless; I admit it.

"Still, I could hardly have stopped the fox from leaving anytime he wanted. It's impossible for one lone animal to keep watch every hour of the day and night. And I've got to acknowledge that Vulpé is no fool. I may not agree with him, but at least he's got someone to negotiate with — your kin, Lieutenant Eisa. That's a lot more than I can claim."

"You had a suggestion to make," said the panther flatly. He didn't appreciate being reminded about his family.

"Sorry. The point is, once you told me the King has been pushed out of Manaris, the only thing I was certain about was that my mission has come to an abrupt end. I would never negotiate with the Black Legion. So I've got two options. The first is to return home; the second is to find a way to stay here with you two.

"That first choice is clear-cut. I know the way back and I don't believe you'll hold me here against my will. Will I be held to account for returning with nothing to show for my efforts? Well, if my real role was nothing more than helping Vulpé get this far, I've achieved that. I may not like it, but there it is. As for remaining here with you two, I'm not so sure you'd welcome my company or what purpose I could serve by staying here in Aeronbed."

The goat looked at the two cats, hoping for some word or gesture to indicate that they'd be thrilled to have his company. They said nothing one way or the other, so Haidar carried on. "As I listened to your conversation, a third possibility occurred to me. You see, standing before me in the absence of King Albiorix is the legitimate successor to his throne, the true ruler of Aeronbed, Princess — well, possibly now Queen — Olwen. Of course, only if the King is not in a position to fulfill his royal duties."

After a brief pause to let that idea sink in, Haidar carried on. "Do you understand what I'm saying? Could I not return to Vigmar and advise them that I — alone, without Vulpé — have negotiated a treaty with the successor to Albiorix?"

Olwen's head rose and her eyes glistened. She straightened her back and puffed out her chest at the mere thought of being Queen. Eisa, meanwhile, gave no indication what he thought.

"I know that word will eventually reach Vigmar about the Legion's successful attack on Manaris and its taking control of the Kingdom," continued Haidar. "In time, of course, that report will be confirmed. But until then, there will be a period of uncertainty about the true state of affairs here. No one will be absolutely sure what's going on. As long as I'm the only one who returns to Vigmar and no one can contest my version of events — at least with any assuredness — I will remain the sole authority on what has taken place here. That period of grace would give you two time to accomplish what you have to do."

"I'm sorry, Haidar," the panther said quickly. "What you suggest is simply fantastical. It may seem harsh to say so, but Olwen rules nothing and no one. Except me, of course."

Olwen, however, already a queen in her own mind and not so easily swayed, took a different tack. "Vigmar has no knowledge of that fact, Eisa, at least not yet. And how could they know what power I have if the fox does not return safely? As you've already noted, his chances of meeting with failure or death are high."

"I'll concede that, Princess, but then what?"

"Then we lions would have the support of Vigmar to crush the Legion. Not the other way around."

It sounded all too simple, and it was. "It would never stand up to scrutiny. In fact, it would fall apart as soon as Vigmar asked where our forces are."

"Can we not bluff? Even if the pretense survived only a little while, it would still work in our favor."

"How?"

"It would give us time."

"Time to do what?"

"Time to meet up with what's left of my father's forces, to join with him in the struggle to reclaim Aeronbed."

"And do you trust Vigmar? What will they be up to in the meantime? Gaining strength and position, I'll warrant. Moreover, what will the Legion be doing while we're trying to meet up with your family?"

Olwen's enthusiasm began to wane. "At least it gives us something to do," the lioness responded weakly. "And a bit of an advantage, even if only temporarily."

"And how much better is that than continuing with our original plan to head north?"

"At least my father won't have to fight on two fronts."

"We know very little about Albiorix's actual situation. I wouldn't dare try to speculate on how the struggle is going."

Olwen was forced into silence, frustrated by her companion's constant questioning, for which she had no really good responses. The lioness knew that their original plan to find the remnants of Albiorix's army had hardly been thought out, but at least it relied on their own skills to make it work, no one else's. Pretending to be the rightful queen of Aeronbed and signing a treaty would be another matter, one that would be much more difficult to pull off. And perhaps the idea of such a treaty might anger Albiorix; in truth, the lioness had no notion of her father's views on the matter.

Eisa now turned his attention to the mountain goat. "As for you, Haidar, you'd be taking on quite a risk."

"Would it be any greater a risk than what I bear now?"

"Certainly a greater risk than if you return home and simply admit defeat."

"You have no idea what life is like in Blakfel."

"You're right, I can't speak to that. But I can imagine what might happen to you if Vulpé manages to return to Blakfel and expose the truth of the situation."

Haidar considered the implications. But after all he'd been through, the goat was not easily cowed or discouraged. "Like you, Lieutenant, I too trust in signs and portends," he said, ignoring the question. "No chance encounter between creatures is trivial. On the contrary, it is meant to happen, no matter how random and insignificant it may appear to be at first. And consequences, for better or worse, flow from each encounter. I can leave here today and, like you two, wander around aimlessly in the wilderness. Sorry, no offence meant.

"Or I can trust that our meeting here is of great significance and will ultimately lead to some momentous conclusion — well, at least something more than giving Vulpé a leg up. So I can choose to take a stand. My choice to risk it would be no less worthy than the one my father took, and, hopefully, more successful. If I should fail, I can only say that an honorable death is better than a shameful life. As soldiers, you both know that."

The cats were impressed by Haidar's passion. However, Eisa was still concerned about the practicalities of making the goat's plan work. The panther wondered what would be involved in pursuing it, for the scheme was at best vague and at worst foolhardy and dangerous. Beyond pretending that the lions had agreed to some sort of treaty with Vigmar and thus bringing to a halt the Empire's current campaign, he could not see their way further.

Despite his doubts, Eisa was prepared to give the goat's proposal its full due. The panther sat quietly, trying to work through everything needed to make it work. Meanwhile, the eager Olwen had jumped to her feet and was pacing back and forth. The lioness wanted to get on with it, whatever *it* was.

Amid the twittering of birds and the buzzing of insects on this surprisingly warm morning, Eisa caught a distant rumble of thunder. He glanced skyward and sniffed the humid air. The hairs on his back began to rise. "We must put off further talk about Haidar's idea. There's a storm approaching," the panther said hurriedly, rising to all fours. "This place is far too exposed for safety. We need to find a more sheltered spot."

Olwen and Haidar were content to follow the panther's lead. "We came across nothing better on our way here," the lioness said. "What about you, Haidar? Did you spot any possible refuge?"

Haidar had, but in their rush toward the mysterious light, he and Vulpé had not taken the time to explore it. The spot was some distance away, toward the southeast.

Retracing Haidar's steps back toward the mountains took the three creatures a good hour, even at a fast pace. With little difficulty they found what Haidar had noticed: a deep cut in an outcropping of rock at the base of a steep cliff. Although by no means a perfect shelter, it would provide the trio with a comfortable, well-hidden sanctuary from the impending storm.

The cats and the mountain goat alternated napping and keeping watch. Accompanied by the deepening rumbles of the approaching thunder, they pondered what to do next.

59

HEADING NORTH

T he wolf pack made good time heading back north, as if it were being prodded and pulled by a demanding but invisible claw. However, the pressure to make good speed did not stem merely from some inner drive. Believing that the pack had squandered precious time on an unjustifiable, if not frivolous, excursion, Adarix was now anxious to make up for the lost time and waste of energy. As a result, the wolf commander gave his pack and the accompanying hawks little rest during their forced march.

Fortunately, the raptors' ability to act as advance scouts meant that the wolves had little need to worry about unforeseen traps or potential misadventures. Since lying low to avoid the enemy was no longer required, the pack was able to proceed as if it had already discovered prey and was moving in for the kill. Soon the wolves were back in familiar territory, the deep valley separating the land of Heimborn from the extensive mountain ranges that divided Aeronbed and Vigmar.

At one of their rare rest stops, Ammarich was making his rounds, checking on his younger brothers, when he came across Adarix sitting by himself on the crest of a small knoll. The pack's commander appeared lost in thought as he gazed up at the still-white peaks lying off to the west. Ammarich sat down beside his brother but, respecting the other's need for quiet, said nothing.

"Do you have any idea what lies beyond those mountains?" Adarix asked after a while.

Ammarich shook his head. He knew what — or rather, whom — Adarix was thinking about.

"It seems curious to me now," Adarix continued, "that we never gave much thought to what kind of creatures live on the other side."

"If I recall the moment well, my lord, we had rather a lot to chew on," his older brother replied. "I hardly need tell you, of all creatures, that professional warriors enjoy few moments for idle speculation."

Adarix ignored the dig and pressed on. "So you know nothing about this region?"

Ammarich shook his head.

"I know we wolves generally care little for such particulars," his brother persisted. "I just thought that, in your travels, you might have picked up something about the place."

"Afraid not, brother. I just assumed we'd find more of those blasted cats, like the ones we ran into last winter." The older wolf glanced toward the distant range. "I'll bet those slopes are crawling with all kinds of them." Then he shrugged. "Still, such differences mean little to me. They all die the same."

Ammarich turned back to Adarix. "Since we arrived in Aeronbed, all we've come across is cats," he said. "Nothing but cats. What makes you think it's any different over there?"

"I don't know, just a hunch. I've been thinking about it more since we moved into this valley. Seeing those mountains every day, you know, gives one ideas."

Ammarich understood everything without being told, but he had no desire to talk about it. "Perhaps one of the others might know," he suggested.

"You think so?"

Ammarich didn't really believe that, but, remembering Adarix's torment over the death of Eirwen, he was prepared to indulge his brother. "I don't rightly know. None of the pack will have any idea, that's for sure. Possibly the hawks — they travel much further afield than we do. Corvus? Lorcan? Maybe even Emrin-Can. That dog never fails to surprise us."

"Send the three of them to me, why don't you."

Although the sentence was couched as a request rather than a command, to Ammarich it amounted to a brushoff. It was all the more surprising because he had expected (or at least hoped) Adarix would shrug off his suggestion as not being worth the bother and not pursue it further. Now the older wolf felt duty-bound to voice his objections.

"Don't we have more important questions to worry about, Adarix? For example, where are the enemy's troops? We've been marching for days now and not seen a single one of those wretched beasts. Doesn't that little fact give you greater pause for concern?"

He jumped up and began to stalk about. "Who knows, maybe the war has ended and they forgot to inform us." Although Adarix opened his mouth to respond, Ammarich was in full flight. "But if the war is still being fought, why have the cats left the battlefield? And if so, where did they go? Perhaps our feathered friends have missed some important clues and we're walking into a trap. Really, doesn't this nothingness disturb you at all?"

The wolf commander growled at him. "Do not forget who commands here, Ammarich. I did not bring the pack this far and with such success to ignore my instincts at this — or any other — moment. I can see, hear and smell just as well as you. And my sixth sense is as finely honed as yours, if not more."

His brother, however, was not so easily put off. "Well, then, my lord, how do you account for the enemy's absence?"

"I don't account for it."

"What do you mean?"

"I don't have an answer. Life is full of mysteries, Ammarich, and many take a while to resolve. You, of all my brothers, understand that. Just think back to Utgard."

His brother said nothing, but to the elder wolf those words rang true. How could he, of all the members of the pack, forget such a place?

"Whatever the case," Adarix continued, "I have absolute faith in the keen eyesight of the hawks and falcons. The cats can't hide so well that they'll escape our friends' vigilance."

"As long as you're not contemplating some wild goose chase."

"I am merely wondering what lies beyond those mountains. Is it so much to ask?"

"Of course not. It's the answer — and where that answer may lead us — that worries me."

"Always the worrier, Ammarich."

"My worrying has usually served me — all of us — well."

"Aye, I grant you that, brother."

"Let's not beat around the bush, Adarix. I know what this is about."

"You do? So you're a mind-reader now?"

"It doesn't take much mind-reading to know what ails you."

"Really?"

"The fate of Lord Eirwen."

Adarix said nothing. Instinctively he looked back toward the craggy mountain slopes.

"So it is true," Ammarich continued.

"Listen, my brother — my friend, I thank you for your concern. But do not worry. Yes, the events of the past year still weigh heavily upon me, and I cannot help but think often about what occurred. But Eirwen's death does not cloud my judgment. The call of duty stirs within me every day. And that duty — and my loyalty — begins and ends with the pack. I know why we are here and I will see you all through to the end, whatever it might be."

Although Ammarich was not completely mollified, he respected his brother's wishes. He went off to look for the three he'd named, leaving his leader staring at the sheer cliffs and craggy outcroppings of the not-so-distant mountains for a sign of ... something. What exactly it was, neither wolf knew.

The others arrived in due course and were questioned in turn, but none of the three could offer further enlightenment. As far as Corvus and Lorcan were concerned, the land beyond the mountains was isolated; it was crossed by no flight or migratory paths and was far enough from their homeland to be uncharted territory — in essence, a wasteland. The two birds never had cause to travel in those parts, so they had no personal knowledge of the area.

For his part, Emrin, a keen student of Vigmar's history, had a vague idea that creatures different from the big cats called it home, or at least they had once upon a time. But the wolfhound could not add more to that limited information. Still, being curious about all things, he was more than willing to give exploring it a try. He'd do anything, in fact, for a new adventure.

Adarix was not prepared to go that far; he did not want to lose the valuable dog to a journey of such duration. However, the wolf leader felt he could safely let one of the birds go and explore for a day or so. The trail before the wolves presented few obstacles and seemed almost morbidly quiet; the pack's travel north should be secure for the time being. He asked Lorcan and Corvus to dispatch one of their more experienced birds, who would reunite with the pack a few days hence where the valley opened up to meet Aeronbed's central plains.

Feeling equally confident about the lack of immediate danger, Lorcan decided to take up the challenge himself. As Adarix watched him depart, the harrier called out a farewell from the air, then rose higher and flew west until he was little more than a speck in the sky. The pack quickly turned its attention back to the advance northward. Within minutes the remaining birds had taken flight and the wolves were on the march once more.

While each member of the pack was experiencing the usual range of anxiety, hope, doubt, ambitions and expectations, the wolf leader alone carried an additional burden. Although Adarix's body was on the trail, his ears, eyes and nose attuned to what lay ahead, his mind remained with Lorcan and those ever-present mountains. He imagined himself flying over that unknown world far beyond his purview, gazing down. What new creatures might be below? What new secrets might be uncovered?

Although Adarix would never admit it to another creature, for some months now — well after he had publicly mourned the loss of Eirwen — he had begun to suffer recurring nightmares about the bear's death. In those dreams, the wolf and the polar bear were clambering up that same treacherous mountain trail. However, this time the enemy forces did not pursue or surround them; instead the two animals were alone, struggling ever upward to reach a place of safety. The wolf would be in the lead as Eirwen stretched out a paw to him, seeking help with the ascent, but Adarix would turn his back on the bear and leave him to his fate. At that precise moment Adarix would wake up, full of anguish and despair. That was not the way the polar bear had died, not at all. Why had he dreamed it so?

The wolf leader was troubled by this insistent vision, by the very fact that he dreamed it, and even more by how it inevitably ended. Adarix was not one to dwell on the past; his creed was to learn from his few mistakes and move ever forward. Why was this different? Yes, he had doubted and falsely accused the bear, but he'd also held back from acting on his suspicions. Indeed, he could reassure himself that in the end he'd done nothing inappropriate or wrong.

Still, feelings of guilt continued to plague Adarix, and he was certain the nightmares were evidence of that guilt. Was this, he wondered, what encountering a true and honorable creature meant? Could even one's own thoughts be held to account, not just the actions they led to?

60

QUESTIONS

As Adarix had suspected, the way forward offered no surprises. Indeed, the lack of threat was now so pervasive that he had difficulty keeping the wolves focused and alert for potential dangers. He ordered Ammarich to devise some war games in order to keep the wolves' edge sharp and their mood resolute.

At last the trail wound its way into the heartland of Aeronbed and the mountains of Heimborn began to recede from view; the pack now faced the kingdom's wide-open plains. The wolves and hawks stopped to make camp and await Lorcan's return. It was a well-needed rest before setting out into what was foreign territory for the wolf pack.

While the others waited — patiently or impatiently, depending on their temperament — Corvus flew off toward the mountains to see if he could find his friend and fellow officer. The black falcon, anxious about Lorcan's flight into the unknown, was keen to check on his whereabouts. If necessary, he could also offer assistance.

Meanwhile, the absence of enemy forces continued to worry the wolf pack. The mystery had begun to weigh upon them all, not just its leaders.

"I don't understand it," Asteel said to Ammarich. "A year ago we were fighting tooth and nail around here, dodging patrols left, right and center. Now the country's as empty as my nephew's head."

"I agree, brother — and not just about your nephew. At first I thought it might be some kind of strategic withdrawal. But even so, wouldn't you leave some troops in place to keep track of enemy movements? But — nothing! Not even those horrible buzzards." The wolf looked skyward. "It just doesn't make sense."

"I was saying to Alberic yesterday that our forces in the north must be so successful that every available unit of cats has been called to the front," Asteel said. "And then I remembered it's old Nashorn leading the fray up there, so that can't be the answer."

Both wolves laughed. "I was joking with Adarix the other day," Ammarich said, "suggesting the war might be over. Now, well, I'm not so sure …" The older wolf's voice trailed off.

"Pity we've been out of touch with Vigmar since we moved north. There's no way of finding out."

"Unfortunately it was the only way to maintain secrecy. Even Lorcan and Corvus have broken off contact with their old mates."

"Still, if the war is over, you would expect some occupying forces to show up, even this far south."

"Maybe not. It all depends on the timing. Some of the lions could be fighting some sort of rearguard action."

"If so, where are they?"

Emrin-Can came up to the two wolves as they were chewing over the puzzling state of affairs. "Here's our smart young friend," Asteel said. "The wolfhound usually has all the answers. What do you think, Emrin?"

"About what, my good sirs?" replied the good-natured dog.

"About the absence of the enemy," Asteel said.

Emrin flopped down, looked around and paused to think. "Usually the simplest answer is the right one," the big dog said finally.

"And what would that be?" Ammarich asked.

"The lions had no need to be here, so they left to go where they were needed."

"And where would that be?"

"Well, it certainly wasn't south or we would've met them already.

And not east to Vigmar or west over that mountain range, so that leaves only the north."

"Why not east? Perhaps they've invaded Vigmar."

"Not with our forces crawling over much of this kingdom. And the mountains in this region are too difficult to cross. If it were possible, we would have come that way into Aeronbed instead of making that great trek to the south."

"And why not west?"

"Because Aeronbed's enemies do not lie there. What would be the point?"

"Could the war be over?" Asteel suggested. "And we missed the big battle?"

"Hah! Doubt it. Even as removed as we are now, we'd have seen or sensed something. No, I'd say nothing's changed."

The two wolves contemplated this notion. The wolfhound's logic seemed sensible enough, and in any event, they had no information to counter it.

"There's only one answer," Emrin said. "The lions went north."

"All right then, how far north?"

"Now that question, cousins, I can't answer. But I can say, given the lack of fresh scents, it's been some time since the cats were around here. The trail's gone completely cold."

"You'd think they'd leave some troops behind," Asteel persisted.

"Unless Aeronbed is much weaker than we thought."

"If you're right, Emrin," Ammarich said, "I'd say there's nothing left to do but press on and finish them off."

Just then the trio heard a high-pitched cry and then a howl. One of the camp's sentries had spotted the returning birds. All eyes turned toward the southern sky, and all talk ceased.

61

WHAT LORCAN FOUND

Those few who knew why Lorcan had been away assembled to hear what the harrier had to report. Adarix signaled for quiet.

"I won't bore you with all the details of my trip through the mountains," Lorcan began, "save to say it's much more difficult than it looks to find a way in and out, even for a bird of my flying abilities and strength. The slopes are steep and unstable and the wind currents treacherous and unpredictable; few passes permit passage through to the other side. In sum, those mountains provide an almost impervious barricade that acts as a natural fortification, like the castle at Blakfel. I can understand now why so little has been heard about what lies beyond them.

"In terms of vegetation, it's not so different from what we've found here, but access for you wolves would be demanding, as the forests and thickets are denser and more threatening. Of course, eventually I did manage to find a route through to the other side, but following it was difficult. Out here, you know, one can see far and wide when you're up in the air. There, however, the terrain is broken up by many deep valleys and hidden ravines; clearings and open spaces are few and far between.

"So you will understand, Lord Adarix, when I admit that I flew over only this end of the region. The land is vast, a country unto itself. In fact, it seemed to go on forever; I couldn't see to the other end of it. It would take a bird many days, probably weeks, to explore the whole place, even one who knew it well. To try to explain the place would be like the proverbial blind cat trying to describe an elephant. If the creature can only feel one small part, he will get the whole picture wrong. I fear, my lord, that may well be the case with me."

"No matter, Lorcan," the wolf commander replied. "Carry on with your tale."

"When I first flew over the mountains, I had to alternate between flying low and high to see as much as I could, to put together a comprehensive picture. Regrettably, I saw no creatures, neither cats nor any other animal. Nevertheless, I had the distinct impression that I was being observed the whole time I was there, by someone too well hidden for me to spot. You know how, when things are too quiet, it doesn't feel right. Of course I heard the usual subtle forest sounds, the quiet buzzes and chirps of a hot midsummer day, but it should have been noisier. It was like the place was devoid of life — or being kept under wraps."

"You tried several locations, of course," Adarix said.

"Absolutely. I flew back and forth over several enclaves without noticing anything different. I would have liked to investigate further, for failure does not sit well with me. But I knew I had only so much time, especially if the return here was going to be as difficult as getting in." Lorcan paused to straighten a few ruffled feathers. Everyone waited impatiently, all eyes and ears focused on the harrier.

"Go on," Adarix prompted.

"Knowing I couldn't return with empty claws, I flew down to one spot that seemed more promising than the others. It appeared to be some kind of encampment, an open area surrounded by high, steep cliffs, and carefully concealed from unwelcome visitors whether from land or the air. When I landed, I could tell right away that the spot was too neat and tidy, too carefully maintained to be natural. So what was it?

"The more I searched around, the more I could tell the place had been recently inhabited. There were several caves around the open area. I asked myself, 'Do I dare explore inside?' Those sorts of caves are not meant for birds like us; they're too deep and dark for our liking. My eyes are good for many things — pursuing prey, for example — but penetrating the nooks and crannies of caves? Not so much. Still, knowing that guessing would not suffice, I braced myself and went inside. Let me tell you, Lord Adarix, the experience was pretty unnerving, especially because I still had that sense of being watched."

"Get on with it, Lorcan," said Adarix, somewhat irritated by the bird's color commentary.

The harrier, however, was in no hurry to get to the point. "As I said, it was clear that whoever lived there was very skilled at covering their tracks. I had already noted a sharp cleft in the rock that concealed an entry into the camp. Honestly, you'd never know from the outside that it existed. More than that, there was no trace of animal tracks in or out.

"After some hesitation, I chose one of the larger caves and went in. It was higher up the cliffside than the others and appeared to be grander. Don't ask me how I concluded that, my friends. I can't explain. It just did. Like the ground below, the cave and its entrance had been swept clean. However, despite the neatness, I did find two things. The first was the tracks of big cats — several of them, but only in the cave itself. I would say they'd been searching for something, or someone. But whoever they were looking for had already left and had been careful not to leave a trace."

"So some animal had been living there?" Ammarich asked. "That is to say, before the cats' arrival?"

"More than one animal. Plenty, in fact, given how many caves there were."

"Perhaps the cats were searching for one of their own," Ammarich said.

"I doubt it," the harrier replied.

"Why?" Adarix asked.

"Because I saw no signs of that, my lord."

"You said you found two things," Adarix said after a brief pause.

"The second was farther back in the cave, carved into the rock wall — an inscription. I almost missed it. The cats certainly did. They'd given up too easily; I could see their prints did not go that far back in the cave. Some instinct must have driven me to look there. The inscription read, 'In memory of my brother and leader. I will never forget. Justice will be done.'"

For a few moments the wolves contemplated the words. No one spoke.

"That's it?" Adarix said, finally breaking the silence.

"That's it."

"Anything else of consequence?" the wolf leader asked.

"Only that leaving the territory proved to be difficult, as I expected. The entry and exit points are almost impossible to see, even from the air. The place is a magnificent stronghold. Or, I suppose, it could be a prison. Such walls can keep creatures in as well as they keep others out."

"A most thoughtful observation. My thanks for your efforts, your detailed report and especially your courage," said Adarix, who was as generous in his praise as he was demanding of obedience. Turning to the others, the wolf asked, "What say you to all that you've heard?"

"Difficult enough to decipher, and impossible to be certain about its full meaning," Ammarich said carefully. "Except for one thing: there must be another party involved in these struggles, one we've not heard talk of before."

"Or perhaps two other parties," Emrin remarked. "One of whom has suffered a great personal loss and feels a deep sense of grievance."

"And seeks revenge," added Adarix for good measure.

"Sounds like someone we should get to know," Ammarich said.

"But where can those creatures have gone? They've disappeared like phantoms," Corvus said.

"Not to mention the cats," Ammarich reminded them. "They too have disappeared."

"Perhaps a battle between the two sides has already taken place," Adarix suggested.

"If so, then who won?" asked Corvus.

"If the cats had won, there'd be signs of carnage and destruction."

"Perhaps Lorcan didn't find the battle site," Asteel suggested.

"You can't easily hide a battlefield. Lorcan would have come across some signs of turmoil, and certainly more than a few carcasses," Adarix said. "I'd say one side is still on the run."

"Or the cats are still on the hunt," Ammarich added.

"Pity we don't have more time to check it out," Emrin said.

"We may yet. This discovery could be important, brothers," Adarix said. "We now know we have potential allies."

"But what kind?" Asteel asked, laughing. "They could be weasels for all we know."

"It's unfortunate they're so skilled at hiding," Ammarich observed. "We may never find them."

"Perhaps they'll find us first," Emrin said.

"If so, let's hope they conclude that we're friends and not enemies."

"If that's the case, we have one thing going for us," Emrin added.

"And what's that, cousin?" asked Asteel.

"We're not cats."

"Amen to that," said Ammarich.

62

THE PANTHERS IN
ASCENDANCE

Archduke Rithild purred with sheer delight, reveling in his recent rise to the very pinnacle of Aeronbed's power structure. The contented cat was enjoying his triumph — and digesting a fine lunch — by taking a stately afternoon stroll through the castle's serene gardens. As he sauntered along the well-trimmed pathways, he was accompanied by a number of council members, political advisers and assorted court minions, all ready to offer unsolicited (and often uninformed) advice or to respond to his every beck and call.

To a cat, the panthers were basking in the warm sunshine and enjoying the delectable spring air. Hints of a bountiful summer to come were visible to every nose and eye. Yes, without a doubt, everything was right with their world. It was a particularly happy troop that occupied the sumptuous residence of the former King of Aeronbed.

"Ah, this is more like it," one particularly sleek panther sighed contentedly. He stooped to sniff an early-blooming rose and then swatted carelessly at an overly adventurous bee. "I do declare, cousins, Manaris has never suited us so well."

"Well said, Zlatan," added a second. "And the Council's gathering place is a great deal grander now."

"Absolutely," Zlatan agreed. "A far cry from that crowded dump where we used to hold our meetings. There wasn't room enough there to swing a — "

"Oh, I don't know," another interjected with a loud laugh. "I rather miss the grubby lane, the wretched hour, the secret knock, the cozy surroundings as we sat cheek by jowl ... "

The panthers all joined in the communal mirth.

"Now I see why Albiorix kept us at such a distance," Zlatan declared. "If we'd known how wonderful his palace was, we'd have overthrown the old rogue long ago."

More laughter ensued.

"I hate to dispel your jovial mood, cousins," Rithild said, "but self-congratulation is hardly called for in the circumstances. Don't forget, we owe our good fortune not to our personal efforts but to the unrestrained enthusiasm of my nephew Parthanyx."

"That may well be," Rashtad, one of the more senior councilors, replied. "And naturally my cousins and I will be delighted to offer Parthanyx our thanks at the very next opportunity. But I ask you, Archduke, who sits in this fine castle and graces Albiorix's grand table? We do." The cat laughed long and hard, and once again the others joined in.

"Aye, but remember, we all sup here at Parthanyx's pleasure."

"Hold on now, Rithild, let's keep things in perspective," Rashtad said, a little more forcefully. "Parthanyx is only a regional commander who was lucky that all eyes were focused east, toward Vigmar. I dare say things would have been greatly different in an equal contest. From what I hear — "

"I'd be very careful about repeating ill-informed opinions," replied the Archduke. "Parthanyx is no ordinary general. Albiorix hangs on by a mere thread, like a spider caught in his own trap. No more lives left for that old cat, I'll warrant. He'll be history before the summer is out, and Parthanyx will return to Manaris in triumph to take the reins of power. And where will the Council be supping then?"

"Before Parthanyx returns to us in *triumph*, he'll have to wrestle those demons Don Grimezel and Dona Morana to the ground," Rashtad declared. "That won't be an easy task."

Several murmurs of assent could be heard from the assembled group.

"Anyway, Archduke," Rashtad carried on, "when the time comes, surely we — that is, you — can control him. The Council has the collective wisdom of many years and the political insight necessary to maintain order and control in Aeronbed. Governing a country is far different from commanding troops in the field. We all know that."

"Yes, but does Parthanyx know that?" Zlatan asked.

Silence reigned as they all looked at one another.

"Parthanyx is young. He'll come to understand," one of the council members declared finally. He gestured to the Archduke. "Rithild will bring him to heel."

Rithild just grunted. The new leader of Aeronbed was not as confident as the others about controlling his nephew. However, he was not about to reveal his doubts to these self-serving hacks, sycophants, petty bureaucrats and latecomers.

The cats began to pair off as they meandered around the pleasant courtyard. There was little for them to do, and even less to worry about, in these fair-weather days. With the fighting far enough away in the north and east and in the paws of a capable general, a sense of comfortable security prevailed among these politicians and party faithful.

Zlatan picked up his pace to walk alongside Rithild. After a few minutes of silence, he touched the other gently on his shoulder. "You know, Archduke," the panther said, almost sighing absent-mindedly, "I was just thinking back to the days before our ascendancy. Already it feels like such a long time ago."

Rithild nodded, not bothering to respond, although he felt exactly the same as Zlatan. The old days were more like a bad dream, one he could barely recall in the light of this new, perfect era.

The other cat, not dissuaded by Rithild's silence, added, "I was wondering what happened to your young acolyte. What was his name?"

"Who are you talking about, Zlatan?" Rithild said curtly. "I recall no one."

"Surely you remember. What *was* his name? Eisum. Eiser? No, not that. Yes, yes — Eisa! Wasn't it Eisa? A young lieutenant."

"You must be mistaken, Zlatan, No one of that name ever worked for me."

"Are you sure, Archduke? I could have sworn — "

"Absolutely not," Rithild interjected. He picked up his pace as he tried to move away from Zlatan.

"No, no, it's all coming back to me now," Zlatan said. He sped up as he tried to keep level with the Archduke. "Eisa was the son of Kalishin," he continued, "of the house of Dariah — "

Through an impressive archway that marked the entry to the gardens, a sturdy young panther entered the enclosure, catching the Archduke's eye and thus interrupting Zlatan in mid-sentence. The newcomer, a stranger to this group of hangers-on, began to make his way directly toward Rithild. All heads turned to follow the cat's progress as he stepped lightly but smartly along the intersecting paths.

The other panthers' small talk ceased. Even Zlatan made no further attempts to pursue Eisa's whereabouts. Rithild was immensely grateful for the interruption. The last thing the Archduke wanted was to be reminded of his former lieutenant, the only panther who could attest to his past double-dealing.

When the newcomer had arrived before Rithild, he bowed low and held out a document.

"What's this?" said one of the more curious onlookers. Laughing, he came over to join Rithild and Zlatan. "Another self-promoting missive from our noble Parthanyx, announcing his latest one-sided victory?" The other panthers began to chortle and hoot as one.

Rithild, however, expressed no amusement. He read the note silently while the others looked on expectantly. A puzzled look came over the Archduke's usually inscrutable face.

"Now, Archduke," demanded Rashtad, "don't keep us in suspense."

"The message is not from Parthanyx, or anyone on the front lines. It's from the captain of the Palace Guard."

"How boring," drawled a courtier. He turned to his neighbor to pick up where their chat had left off.

"What possible news could he have?" another said derisively.

"Isn't it time for lunch?" a panther named Antakama asked. "You there! Soldier! Bring us some food and drink," he commanded of the new arrival.

"We just ate, you wretched glutton," declared Dughyl scornfully, garnering a round of laughs from his friends.

"I don't care. I'm peckish again," Antakama responded, rubbing his stomach.

"Quiet, all of you!" Rithild ordered. "It's a most unusual message."

"We're all ears, Archduke," purred one of the new councilors. "Literally panting for the news!" The others laughed at his little witticism.

"An envoy has come from afar," Rithild said flatly.

Groans all around. "Is that all? Send him away, Archduke," Zlatan said. "We've better things to do than listen to impertinent emissaries asking for favors."

"Yes, it's time to eat," Antakama pouted. "And I must be fed." This produced more groans and chortling.

"Just because we control the spoils of war," Zlatan said, ignoring Antakama, "doesn't mean we have to give them away so easily."

"There are no details on what the envoy seeks," Rithild went on, ignoring the complaints. "It's a red fox, of all creatures. The wretch won't even say who he represents."

"Let a vile fox in here? To sully our beautiful palace?" Rashtad groaned. "Next thing you know, we'll have to invite the bears in!"

The panthers laughed again, all save Rithild.

"So what's it all about, my lord?" asked Zlatan, when the laughter had subsided.

"Even that's not so clear. The fox wouldn't give any information to the Guard."

"Bah! Kill him. Have the guards execute the villain right on the spot!" Rashtad exclaimed. "I don't know why they bother us with these trifling matters."

"Let's get back to lunch," Antakama persisted. "Or is it teatime already?" Some of the panthers groaned anew.

"Silence, you idiots!" thundered Rithild. "Let me think."

"Well, he's either a brave fox or a foolhardy one," ventured one of the more high-spirited panthers, daring to ignore the Archduke's command.

"You know what they say about those rascals," added Dughyl. "The expression 'crazy like a fox' doesn't come from nowhere. I'd be careful, Rithild. Just send him packing."

"And let's get back to eating!" Antakama said.

"Quiet!" Rithild snarled again, fixing his colleagues with a particularly savage glare. This time they took him seriously.

No wonder Parthanyx took matters into his own paws, Rithild thought as he tried to get his mind around the fox's outlandish request. *How did the Council become so full of buffoons and surrounded by such layabouts? They'll all have to go, as soon as Parthanyx gets back. Especially Zlatan — he remembers too much for his own good. We need young, vigorous, up-and-coming fighters, not old dilettantes and ne'er-do-wells like this lot. Power has already corrupted them.*

Seeking to remove himself from his oafish peers, Rithild motioned to the messenger to accompany him to a quieter corner of the garden. As they walked, the Archduke quietly asked, "The fox said nothing else?"

"No, sir."

They continued in silence for a few more paces.

"Shall I send in the captain of the Guard?" asked the messenger.

"Yes, do."

Rithild paced back and forth impatiently while the Council members and palace officials looked on from a distance. The captain of the Guard trotted in, accompanied by the messenger, and quickly revealed what little he knew.

"My lord Archduke, at first I just dismissed the creature, for he appeared to be nothing but a grubby lowlife, unfit for your company. Faced with my wrath, he did as he was ordered. That is to say, he left the way he arrived, helped along by my front paw for good measure. But the wretch returned in the blink of an eye, like an unwelcome flea. So I sent him packing once more, this time with a really good swat."

The captain paused to demonstrate his prodigious talent for swatting lesser creatures. Rithild stayed back out of harm's way.

"Would you believe it, the fox was completely undeterred. Again the creature came back. I assure you, my lord, I threatened him in more ways than one, but the wretch was most insistent. He would not take no for an answer. In normal times I would not have troubled you, sir. I would have dealt with him on my own — you know what I mean. But these are not normal times.

"I asked the fellow the nature of his business. The impudent villain said he would provide details only to you. I asked him on whose authority he presented himself. He replied that, apart from your good self, Archduke, he came from the highest authority in the land. I pushed the fox hard, but he would not elaborate. He kept maintaining that the matter is of the utmost urgency, and that the future of Aeronbed rests with the message he has to deliver to you."

"Hmm. Do you think the creature mad, Captain, or possibly dangerous?"

"No, my lord. He's pretty ragged and dirty, and completely bushed. I'd say the fox has been traveling for many days straight through and with little rest. By now he won't have the strength to hurt a fly. But of course looks can be deceiving. I'd keep a close eye on him, I would. If you wish, sir, I can stay nearby, just in case."

"So, Captain, if he is not mad, you take him for an honest fellow?"

"Who can tell for certain these days?" replied the captain, shrugging. "But there's something remarkable about the creature, I'll say that much. Despite being worn out, the fox has a confident air about him. I warrant he's no charlatan and that he speaks the truth — what little he's revealed of it, of course."

"I thank you for your good judgment, Captain. You speak well and plainly — better than many around here." Rithild glowered at the surrounding company, although none of them bothered to take note. "Go now. The Council will retire to the King's Great Hall. Bring the creature to us there, and do stand near when you return. Let's see what this fox has to offer us."

63

AN AUDACIOUS CUSTOMER

After the captain of the Guard had departed, Rithild ordered the other panthers to gather round. "Fellow councilors, we have a visitor from afar, apparently with an offer to consider. Well, we shall see for ourselves. Mark him carefully, cousins, but keep your counsel until we have finished. What the creature has to propose we can discuss among ourselves, later and in private."

The other panthers nodded or mumbled their assent, and the assembly quickly moved indoors and took up their assigned positions in the Great Hall, forming a large half-circle with Rithild at the very center.

With little delay, the captain returned with the disheveled Vulpé. After introducing the fox to the Archduke, the panther stepped back, just a little apart from the council members and their assorted advisors — close enough to intervene but not so close as to be intimidating.

Vulpé, meanwhile, looked around at the horde of cats with his bright, beady eyes. Despite the fox's motley appearance, he seemed invigorated and confident. Keeping his focus on Rithild, he bowed low to the entire company and sat down. The other panthers kept their distance, nodding their heads slightly but carefully in return. In such times, an ambitious official or courtier never knew with whom he might be dealing; he would not wish to give offense right off the bat, at least not without good reason.

No one uttered a word. Then the Captain spoke up. "Archduke, this messenger — "

"Not a messenger, Captain. An envoy," Vulpé corrected loudly, without taking his eyes off Rithild.

Still no one spoke. Nothing could be heard but the panting of a large pack of savage predators.

"I have the honor of addressing Baron Rithild, ruler of Aeronbed, do I not," Vulpé added, more by way of a statement than a question.

"Archduke Rithild, to be precise," responded the panther stiffly. "And, to be absolutely clear, I rule in the name of Parthanyx of Heimborn."

The fox raised his eyebrows slightly, licked his lips and stroked his whiskers. The panther had been forthright in his reply, but Vulpé chose not to respond to the clarification.

"And you, sir," Rithild continued. "Pray tell us who you might be and whom you serve."

Since stealing away from Haidar, Olwen and Eisa, Vulpé had had a few days to contemplate how he would embark on this challenging conversation. However, the fox also knew he would have mere moments to weigh up the situation and the nature of the creature with whom he would have to bargain. The one thing he had not expected was the need to tussle with an entire company of panthers.

The ferocious-looking beasts seemed prepared to eat him for dinner at the merest ill-considered wag of his tail. To a cat they were all as dark and cruel-looking as Eisa. Still, the fox kept reminding himself, the Lieutenant had turned out to be not nearly as menacing as he'd first appeared. The thought comforted Vulpé and reminded him not to make the mistake of judging cats on appearance alone.

Vulpé took the view that his encounters with the Empress would serve him well in a situation like this one. The fox had learned to be a quick study of the imperial donkey's moods, to flatter her when required or to obfuscate the issues when necessary. Nevertheless, he had always dealt with the Empress one to one. Here, having to contend with a whole host of potential skeptics and critics, he felt the ground to be much less secure. Should he simply ignore the other council members or try to bring all of them into the orbit of his argument? Should he be bold or restrained? Should he act haughty or humble? Should he be completely truthful or hold something back?

It seemed to Vulpé that everywhere he went he met creatures with titles. Obviously it mattered, so the fox decided he had better give himself one. Since no one in this court could doubt or question him, anything would do. Still, it had better sound good. A name from Vigmar's folklore suddenly came to him.

"My name is Vulpé, my lord, Count Vulpé of Ajatar," declared the fox boldly. "I serve the Emperor and Empress of Vigmar."

That got the assembled panthers going. Vulpé heard several low growls and snarls, plus some not so subdued ones. More than a few outraged mutterings immediately ensued; back hairs rose and one panther even assumed an attack position. The big cats all glared as one; if looks could kill, Vulpé would have died on the spot.

The fox guessed that they would have torn him apart had they not been so disciplined. Nevertheless, he was equally sure some of the panthers were already salivating and unsheathing their claws for what was to come. He noticed one particularly hungry-looking one. *Probably missed the call for lunch*, Vulpé thought idly. He tried to exude an unruffled serenity, but inside he was quaking. He hoped desperately that none of the panthers could notice his shaking legs.

Rithild, however, ever the consummate politician, revealed not one whit of reaction, save for the slightest hint of surprise. Without even bothering to look around the half-circle, the Archduke held up a huge paw for quiet.

Vulpé was struck by the simplicity of the gesture — and how immense that paw was. Rithild looked much bigger and tougher than the rest of them; Eisa seemed but a youngster in comparison.

The Archduke had a commanding presence. His signal worked immediately; the muttering and growls stopped and the room became quiet once again. Even the hungry-looking one sat back down.

"You're a brave creature, Count, to venture so far from your home and to speak so boldly."

"In the name of peace, the brave will venture far, my lord." Vulpé smiled inwardly. He liked that one; it had a quotable ring to it. Haidar couldn't have done better.

Rithild, however, was not impressed. "Peace you say, Count Vulpé? Peace, while our armies are tearing themselves to bits? Peace, when the armies of Vigmar roam at will throughout this fair kingdom? Peace, when so many of our noble heroes lie dead, mourned by kith and kin? Your suggestion, Count, demonstrates enormous effrontery."

The cats appreciated the eloquent rejoinder, although Vulpé wasn't quite sure what *effrontery* meant. A few panthers began to lick their lips, no doubt in expectation of what was to come.

The fox, however, was by no means finished. "It is as you say, Archduke. These are cruel times. That is precisely why I have traveled so far and risked so much. Is it not time our armies ended this terror and destruction? Is it not time to reach some kind of accommodation for the sake of our many suffering citizens?"

"Perhaps. Or perhaps it is something else again. Your sudden appearance here might suggest that the Emperor and Empress have something to fear, now that Vigmar must face the mighty tide of panthers sweeping over Aeronbed. It's only a matter of time before that tide becomes a flood and we submerge Vigmar in the process." Some of the panthers hissed in delight at the image.

"Nicely said, my lord," Vulpé countered. "But didn't you just admit that the armies of Vigmar occupy much of this fair kingdom? Frankly, I doubt that a single soldier of Aeronbed has managed to set foot in Vigmar. Not with one claw or hoof, to my reckoning."

The panthers didn't like being reminded of that fact. More snarling and cursing ensued.

"That failure, sir," Rithild spat, "is nothing more than a legacy of the lions' corrupt regime. Albiorix and his like are gone from this court, snd they're on their last legs in the north of this land. Time is on our side, Count Vulpé, on the side of the panthers. Vigmar has yet to see the full might of the Black Legion. When their teeth and claws — "

"I beg your pardon, my lord," interjected the fox. "I did not come here to compare respective fighting abilities or zones of occupation. I came here to speak of peace. For the sake of argument, let's say things are as you contend. If so, then what do either of us have to look forward to? More years of brutal warfare between us; much loss of life among the young, the weak and the old; the destruction and waste of a generation of animals. Surely no one wants that."

"I might ask you the same question. It was not Aeronbed that invaded Vigmar, but the other way around."

"Let's ignore the origins of this war, which started long before our days. Let's talk rather of bringing an end to it."

"All right, let's do that. What have the Emperor and Empress got in mind? What offer can they make to compensate Aeronbed for its many losses?"

"Both parties have suffered."

"But only one, it appears to me, has come forward with a peace offering. The other — that's us, let me remind you — is quite content with the status quo."

The fox began to grasp that Rithild was not going to be a pushover. The negotiation was going to require some deft handling.

"Really?" Vulpé said. "Really? You are truly content with the status quo?"

Rithild cocked his head, puzzled by the fox's challenge. The other panthers had been watching the exchange like onlookers at a very competitive tennis match. All of a sudden, it looked as if their favorite might have misplayed.

"Speak plainly, Ajutar. Why should we not be content?" the panther leader asked, gamely swatting the ball high into the air.

Vulpé smiled broadly. He got to his feet and began to stroll around the room, looking at each panther one by one as if contemplating his own dinner menu. He liked turning the tables, creating a bit of consternation.

"You do know what you're facing, do you not, Archduke? Or are you merely playing a game, showing a bit of false bravado? Well, perhaps I might do the same if I were standing in your place. After all, what would I have to lose?"

"The only thing anyone's going to lose around here is your head!" cried out an impetuous panther from the back.

Vulpé's smile grew even wider. Rithild growled a loud, "Quiet!"

"I do apologize, my good sirs, if I have caused anxiety," declared the fox. "Some things just have to be brought out into the open. So that we're all singing from the same songbook, so to speak."

No one spoke. No one knew what Vulpé meant or where he would go next.

"Perhaps my news comes as a surprise to you. Perhaps I've overestimated your intelligence network. You see, Archduke, not only do I serve the Emperor and Empress, I am Vigmar's chief of internal security. Nothing gets by me; I know and see everything. That's why they asked me to meet with you. No other animal is as well suited as I am, because no one knows as much as I do." It was only a half-truth, but it was better than no truth at all. And, given the uneasy exchange of glances among the panthers, it seemed to have done the trick.

"Yet Their Majesties can afford to lose you?" Rithild countered valiantly. "You might, sir, never return. In times of war, accidents and missteps can occur at every turn."

"No one is irreplaceable; I am but one of many. Their Majesties have entrusted this important mission to me and I have willingly accepted their trust. If I fail — for whatever reason — someone will follow after me. However, of course, my death will not be forgotten." A veiled threat — the fox liked that.

"You were about to explain exactly what it is we are facing, Count."

"You know, of course, about the fierce fighting going on in the northern part of Aeronbed."

"Of course. Yet another stalemate."

Vulpé shrugged as if unwilling to dispute such a conclusion. "And I suppose I need not tell you about our southern and central armies, which by now should be approaching the heartland of Aeronbed."

The fox noticed a few looks of surprise and discomfort. He'd swatted the ball into an awkward corner. That was good — the news had come as a surprise to some. Still, Rithild himself gave nothing away, and no one else responded. The mutterings had stopped.

"And naturally you know about the army of lions still active in the eastern reaches of central Aeronbed."

A smash hit.

"What?" the astonished Archduke snarled. Rithild could not hide his surprise. The ball had gone right past him.

There was, of course, no truth in Vulpé's statement; he was simply extrapolating from his meeting with Princess Olwen. It was quite an extrapolation — from one lioness and one panther to an entire army — but Rithild and the Council could not know that.

"That's not possible. How do you come by this information?" the Archduke demanded.

"I have just traveled through those parts to get here. I saw them with my own eyes." Again, a half-truth was better than no truth at all.

"How many?"

"I cannot rightly say. I'm sure I did not see them all."

Vulpé was beginning to enjoy his encounter with the panthers. They could not refute what he was saying, for they had not one whit of knowledge to the contrary. Several of them moved off to a corner to confer privately.

"You see, Archduke, despite your recent victory, your continued existence here in Manaris is still precarious. You live on the cusp of a tiger's tooth, if I may employ that expression. You can only fall one way or the other."

The fox had their undivided attention. It was time to go in for the kill. "However ... " He paused for effect while they all gazed eagerly at him.

"However," Vulpé repeated slowly, "I have come to Manaris neither to threaten nor to coerce you. Let us speak no further of such dreadful matters. I have come only to offer you, the Black Legion, an honorable peace, one between two worthy adversaries. An accord that has much to provide both parties. All can be victors now. That is how life can be for us as we move forward together."

The fox stopped and sat down. Rithild, meanwhile, needed time to think. The panther could go either way, ordering the fox's immediate execution or stalling for time. The news about the lions had come as an embarrassing surprise; he had been caught unawares and heads would roll. In due course he'd find some poor wretch to blame. The name Zlatan came to mind.

The Archduke was not a hundred percent convinced by what he'd just heard. But he had to admit that the fox was brave, cool-headed and adept at negotiation. No animal in its right mind would have done what he had done: marched into the enemy camp armed only with words. Unless, of course, the creature was telling the truth and as sure of his ground as Count Vulpé appeared to be. Yes, there was definitely something to the story; the fox could not be written off as a fool or crazed. Nevertheless, the substance of his words had to be tested.

"I'm prepared to hear your terms, Vulpé," declared Rithild. "But remember, as I stated earlier, I rule in the name of General Parthanyx. My nephew will need to be made aware of the specific conditions and what Vigmar has to offer us. He will decide on our course of action, not me."

"When you've heard me out, Archduke, the benefits of what Vigmar proposes will be more than apparent," the fox replied benignly. "The agreement will not be hard to sell to the General."

64

NEGOTIATING PEACE

Rithild had been surprised by the news Vulpé had presented to the panthers' Grand Council. If a previously unknown army of lions was on the move in central Aeronbed, that was truly alarming.

The fox had seemed confident of his facts, but appearances could be deceiving. The Archduke had met many charmers during his career, sly characters who at the end of the day turned out to have far more style than substance, more wit than wisdom. Perhaps the fox was lying, or perhaps he was telling the truth but had misread what he'd witnessed. If the story was accurate, however, the military situation had become much more complicated, even, as Vulpé had put it, unquestionably precarious. Rithild blamed Parthanyx. Why had the young fool not kept some troops in reserve to protect their flanks?

However, the panther leader was not going to take the fox's word for it; he would have his subordinates check out the story. That would also allow him to play for time, giving him an opportunity to reflect on Vulpé's offer at leisure. The Archduke saw no harm in listening to the details. In any event, the Council would have to confer with Parthanyx, and that could take days, possibly weeks, to achieve — more than long enough to confirm the veracity of the fox's tale.

Rithild had offered food and a bed to Vulpé, who, judging from his haggard appearance, had been traveling for some days and eaten little during that time. After all, at least on the surface of things, the fox seemed to be telling the truth. Vulpé had gladly accepted the panther's hospitality. He knew that the negotiations were only beginning, and he would need all his strength in the days to come.

The delay gave Rithild time to consult the others. "Councilors, cousins, what say you?" the panther asked after Vulpé had left their company. "Do we have an honest fox with a valid offer or do we have a charlatan who has set out to fool us?"

"If he's lying, he's a smooth one all right," Rashtad said. "And if he's telling the truth, we'd best take a hard look at the terms he's offering."

"It makes no sense to me. If the military situation favors Vigmar that much, why bother to sue for peace?" Zlatan argued. "If they're so sure of things, why not just let the war continue its course?"

"They've just caught us at a weak moment," Dughyl said. "We're fighting among ourselves, cat against cat. When the lions are defeated by our superior fighting ability, the natural supremacy of the Legion will be reclaimed. I say we give the fox the heave-ho."

"But do we have enough time to defeat them?" Rashtad countered. "We are winning, of course, but it's not over yet. And if the fox is telling the truth, the lions have forces no one reckoned on."

"Bah! Parthanyx has Albiorix on the run. That mangy lion and his brethren will be extinct before we know it," Antakama said. "And then the General will return to deal with the riffraff."

"Who would accept anything a fox has to offer? Their reputation for thievery and trickery precedes him," added another. "I say we have nothing to do with the villain. Hah! I'd happily parlay with a bear before trusting this count."

"You would, would you?" Zlatan growled. "Then you're more of a fool than you look."

"Colleagues, please. Let's keep things civil," Rithild exclaimed over the ensuing din. "I see we have the usual consensus — that is to say, none at all. Still, you do raise a valid point, Councilor Zlatan. Why are they making this offer if the situation favors Vigmar so greatly? In my view, we need to hear this fellow out. Specifically, what are his actual terms? And the fox will have to answer all our questions. We'll meet with the Count again after dinner. So look sharp and keep your wits about you."

"About time. I'm starving!" said Antakama, racing for the heavily laden table.

Rithild rolled his eyes skyward and made a mental note: *another good-for-nothing the Legion can well do without.*

WHEN THE APPOINTED HOUR ARRIVED, VULPÉ HAD RESTED AND EATEN AND cleaned himself up. The fox felt better than he had in weeks.

This time Vigmar's emissary was escorted into a small but elegant meeting room, where he now faced a much reduced contingent of panthers. Clearly the Archduke had decided to dispense with some of the lesser lights of the Grand Council.

The panthers were arrayed around one half of a large circular wooden table, with Rithild in the middle. One lone empty seat, directly facing him, was clearly reserved for the fox. The chair was lower than all the rest, forcing Vulpé to look up at the cats. This was obviously meant to place him at a disadvantage, especially as he was already smaller than the panthers. But it had the opposite effect on the fox; he saw their need to play such games as an indication of weakness.

"So, Count, let's get down to business," Rithild said, almost jovially. The Archduke had already concluded that he had little to lose and much to gain from the interchange. Since all the risk lay with Vulpé, he might as well enjoy himself. The panther leader had already ordered a small force to check out Vulpé's story; hopefully they would report back before the negotiations ended. He had few troops to spare, but Vulpé's information was too important to leave unchecked.

"However," Rithild continued, "before you provide us with the details of the offer, one of my more astute colleagues has raised the question of why. Why, if the military situation favors Vigmar so much, would your emperor and empress want to talk about peace? And before you reply, let me add an observation from past experience: this sort of move is hardly in keeping with Don Grimezel's nature."

"My lord, you raise an excellent question, and I congratulate your estimable colleague for his insight. At this moment I can only say by way of response that all will become clear when I have revealed the outlines of the treaty Vigmar proposes."

"So be it. The Council is prepared to wait. Nevertheless, I have another question. How can you, Count Vulpé of Ajatar, assure us that you are indeed who you claim to be? How will you convince us that you are not some clever, fast-talking rogue, an imposter with schemes that we have yet to figure out? And I must add, sir, if that is indeed the case, we shall assuredly figure out those schemes, and you will be the sorrier for it."

Vulpé was unfazed by Rithild's challenge. It was, in fact, the one question he could answer completely honestly. "A second excellent question, Archduke," he responded forthrightly. "And I'm glad you have raised it now, so I can clearly establish my credentials before we begin. Let there be no mistake about it, I represent Their Imperial Highnesses and come with their blessing and instructions. What I have to offer does not have to be approved by any other intermediary, does not have to be vetted by any committee of elders, and does not need to be signed off by any council. You have my guarantee that any agreement I take back from this table will be the final word. There will be no reneging, double-dealing or counter-proposals."

Rithild was impressed by the fox's direct, clear-cut response, but the panther was not done yet. "Yes, yes, we understand and appreciate that, Count. But you have as yet given us no proof that you are their true representative."

"My lord, I was just getting to that point," Vulpé said grandly. He jumped up onto his chair and whipped out from a concealed pouch a gold amulet, its mark unique to the imperial family of Vigmar and Arundati. With a meaningful glance, he reverently laid this gleaming object on the table before the startled Rithild.

The panther picked up the amulet, examined it carefully, and then placed it back on the table. It was no common object, and no common creature would be carrying it. Clearly the Count of Ajatar was exactly who he said he was.

"Well, my lord?" Vulpé said, with no small degree of satisfaction.

"Count, you appear to be a creature of your word. We shall doubt you no further."

One of the other panthers leaned over and whispered in Rithild's ear. The Archduke waved him away with a dismissive paw.

"What is it, Lord Rithild?" the fox asked blithely. "Does one of the councilors still have a lingering concern?"

"It is nothing."

"No, I insist," replied Vulpé. "I would not want anyone to have doubts about me."

"In that case, Count, my colleague wishes to be assured that you have have not stolen the object from someone else, perhaps the real emissary." Rithild looked a trifle embarrassed.

"Not a problem, my lord. It's a fair question," the unruffled Vulpé said. "I admit that foxes have a somewhat disreputable reputation. But let me assure all of you here, the stories about my family have been grossly exaggerated. We foxes have been unfairly maligned for many years, and reputations are hard to live down — or up to, for that matter. Ask any animal. Ask Aeronbed's former ruler, the so-called king of beasts. Where is he now?" He saw a few nods and smiles of acknowledgment around the table.

"In answer to your colleague's inquiry," continued the fox, "no, I did not steal the talisman. Can I prove it? Yes, as a matter of fact, I can. There is a way to open the amulet that would never be known to any thief. If you give it back to me, my lord, I shall open it and reveal what lies inside."

Rithild gave back the amulet. While the curious panthers looked on, Vulpé performed the intricate maneuver necessary to open it. The amulet was delicately hinged on one side, and the two halves opened up to reveal an engraved emblem representing Vigmar's imperial family. There could be no doubt as to its origins. Further, the talisman contained a note that referred to Vulpé by name and kind. There could be no doubt at all about his authority to possess it.

The panthers peered closely at the amulet, hesitant to touch it. "Magnificent, and most ingenious," Rithild said.

"Is it not?" Vulpé added, greatly satisfied at the response.

Nods all around.

"This is my gift to you," the fox declared grandly.

"What?" exclaimed the startled Rithild. "No, Count, I could not accept it."

"On the contrary," Vulpé said. "It was given to me by the Empress herself for a purpose. As it has now served that purpose, I make a present of it to you, my lord. You would oblige me greatly by accepting it." The fox had craftily positioned the panther so that he could not reject the gift, and now Vulpé was owed something in return.

The panther chief, not taking the fox seriously, had not planned for such an eventuality and had no gift to give in return. The Archduke cursed himself for failing to think ahead. He could only own up to it as best he could. "Count Vulpé, your generosity embarrasses me, for I have nothing of such value to offer you. Your visit was so unexpected. But before you leave, my good sir, perhaps we can provide you with some modest tokens to take back to Her Highness."

Vulpé bowed low in acknowledgment, smiling to himself.

"Now let's return to our business," Rithild added abruptly.

By the end of the evening, when their negotiations were finished, Rithild was forced to admit, at least to himself, that the fox had proposed a most appealing alliance. No one could ever have expected something of such a nature from Vigmar. It came with so few risks that Rithild considered accepting it on his own authority, without even referring it to Parthanyx. Possibly, just possibly, the Archduke might also reap personal gain; if it was successful, the prestige and stature of the treaty's co-signer would rise to exalted levels. Should he dare?

Still, despite everything, the wary panther needed to be absolutely certain about the military situation. Rithild wanted to hear back from the scouts he'd sent out to test the truth of the fox's story. The outline of the treaty had been completed swiftly, for it was simplicity itself, but now that the talks had ended, there was no reason for delay. The Count was eager to be on his way back to Vigmar.

Rithild was forced to defer Vulpé's departure by proposing a state dinner in his honor for the next evening. The invitation, he hoped, would allow another day or so to pass before Vulpé would be in a position to leave, providing the panther with precious time to consult again with the Council and to hear back from his scouts.

For added assurance and to speed up communications, Rithild dispatched yet another panther unit, this time swift messengers, to meet up with the first group. Everything now depended on what he heard from them.

65

THE STORM

The odd trio of animals — tawny lioness, black panther and white mountain goat — crouched down, huddling together in the deepest recess of their meager hideout. They felt and heard the approaching storm long before they could see it.

First came an increasing buildup of oppressive heat and humidity that left the three wilted and breathless. Then distant murmurs and angry growls were added, growing ever louder, deeper, longer and closer. The trio felt as if they were surrounded by an entire army of outraged beasts, all grumbling and snarling in unison. The resounding roars gradually evolved into rolling explosions of thunder that seemed to rise from the very bowels of the earth, shattering the still air and causing the ground to shake. But those were just the preamble to the main event. Next came the abrupt cracks and crashes of sheet lightning that illuminated the darkened sky from horizon to horizon.

Immediately outside the cave, things remained strangely calm. The storm was still some distance away and seemed in no hurry to arrive. However, given its prelude, the three knew that when the downpour finally arrived, it was going to be harsh and violent.

The storm crept up on the animals like a fox out to steal the eggs of an innocent chicken. A gentle, elusive breeze, just imperceptible inside the cave, began to waft about them. At first it brought relief from the oppressive heat, but soon enough the gusts picked up in both tempo and turbulence, increasing the sense of menace. It was clear that the tempest had reached their doorstep. Even as the three companions arrived at that miserable conclusion, the storm's fury flung itself upon them without mercy. The wind coiled around them like venomous snakes, tossing dust, leaves and twigs deep into every corner. Even sheltered by the cave, they could not escape its onslaught.

Despite the furious assault, the ever-curious Olwen dared to crawl over to the cave entrance to see what was happening. She was just in time to see several small tornados pass by, flinging heavy tree branches in their wake. The lioness ducked instinctively, covering her head with her paws. Then, blinking through the driving grit, she peeked through her claws to see the last remnants of blue sky disappearing in the distance, enveloped by an ominous black shroud. As the thick clouds began to pile up overhead, Olwen slunk back into the depths of the cave.

The temperature dropped steeply and swiftly. The two big cats shivered despite their thick coats, and Haidar retreated even further into the cave. The three animals knew they were about to experience something far worse than a normal summer thunderstorm. Something was amiss, something lay in wait for them, and the winds were just the beginning.

At first the rain appeared to be holding itself in check, as if waiting for word from on high before the deluge could start. The blustery gusts intensified from mere windstorm to unrelenting gale. And then, with one more mighty crash of thunder, the agonizing tension was broken and torrents of water were unleashed. The thunderstorm was right above the mountain slope, and apparently happy to stay there a while. Its clamor battered their ears and the cascading rain washed over and down the mountainside, forcing its way into the cave entrance.

Fast-flowing rivulets became torrents that took advantage of every crevice and gully; before long there were rivers where none had existed before. Following the paths of least resistance, they spewed into the valley below, carrying off everything in their path. One of those rivers found its way into the cave, creating a multitude of small pools in the lower areas, which then connected to form one vast pond that covered the entire floor. The cats tiptoed further and further back to join Haidar, and all three sought higher spots to avoid getting drenched. Olwen and Eisa huddled together on a small ledge, while Haidar looked on forlornly from his own perch a short distance away.

The explosions of noise were excruciating, the winds pierced into the very rear of the cave, and the rain came down in unrelenting torrents. None of them had ever experienced a storm of such intensity. The cats, usually so courageous, were petrified, flinching with every flash and crash. The mountain goat was more fatalistic. Perhaps his end had come; he might as well give himself up to whatever form of death would come his way.

66

HAIDAR FOLLOWS A CALL

A ll storms, even the most violent and pitiless, must eventually blow themselves out, move on to torment other poor creatures, or simply dissipate when they've exhausted their seemingly boundless energy. By the time this storm had run its course, the two big cats were sound asleep, exhausted by the chaos and the tension of avoiding the threatening waters.

But Haidar remained wide awake, observing what was happening beyond the narrow cave mouth as best he could. Once the storm had quieted down, the mountain goat got up and stepped nimbly through the newly created lake, using rocky outcroppings where he could to avoid stepping in the chilly water. Reaching the cave entrance, he stopped to gaze out at the forested valley beyond. Night had fallen, but the land, washed clean by the heavy downpour, was bright under a full moon.

Normally after such an onslaught of wind and rain, Haidar's mood would lift with the clearing skies. So why, the goat asked himself, did he feel as if the storm had not wholly passed? Was the tempest an omen, a warning of greater dangers lying ahead, yet to be confronted? He shook his shaggy head to clear away the pervading sense of menace. But that did not help, and he wondered whether Eisa and Olwen felt similarly troubled.

Something — someone? — was calling to him, drawing him out of the cave. He looked back at his two companions, but both were sound asleep. Should he wake them? No, the call was to him alone. Whatever or whoever was waiting for him in the forest gloom, he needed to discover on his own. Haidar knew it made little sense for him to go off by himself. The panther and lioness were far more powerful than he; they offered protection from possible aggressors. The call, however, was too strong. He could not withstand its lure.

Although some might label such behavior foolhardy, his need for an answer, plus an underlying spirit of adventure, overcame the mountain goat's normal sense of caution. It occurred to Haidar that he must have inherited that trait from his father. But in a hostile world, boldness has its limits, and Haidar's emerging loyalty to Eisa and Olwen made him reluctant to stray far. The goat told himself he'd just take a quick look around, staying within hailing distance of the cave. Given the state of the other two, he was sure he'd return long before they awoke; they'd never even know he'd been out.

The winds at his back were brisk and a new set of heavy clouds was sweeping in. Already the sky was darkening as he set off. He scampered down the slope, heading toward the southwest. No rational reason dictated his choice of direction; only his instincts led him on.

Picking his way through the debris strewn about by the gale, Haidar hopped lightly through several newly created streams that still cascaded down the mountain. He then worked his way into the thick forest. The goat could still hear the distant throbbing of thunder, even though the storm had long since passed by. Was a new tempest brewing on the other side of the mountain, or was he still hearing the previous storm as it continued to speed across the land? Or was it something else again?

Several large trees had fallen in the storm. Limbs lay haphazardly everywhere, obstructing his descent. The trails had disappeared altogether under water or newly fallen brush. The way ahead was tricky at best, impassable at worst. The distant rumblings continued, but his immediate surroundings remained eerily quiet.

Hearing not a single bird call, the goat concluded that the region's feathered creatures had been blown far away. The frogs and insects, which were equally quiet, had probably taken shelter in the newly created pools and did not yet dare show their heads. Occasionally a damaged branch would fall to the ground with a thud or an unnerving crash. The only other sounds Haidar could hear were those distant, almost musical rumblings.

The goat had to scramble under and around the mangled trees, slide down steep, mud-slicked slopes and shove his way through dense underbrush. Sometimes he was forced to take a wide detour in order to maintain his direction, a compass bearing determined by some inner voice. Drawn as he was by whatever was calling him, it was not long before Haidar forgot he had only been going to take a "quick look around" and then return to the cave.

He lost track of time; he even lost track of his route. The low murmur of thunder kept him company; it seemed to have become more constant and regular, almost chant-like. There was something about its music that entranced him. As he pursued his course, Haidar began to realize it was that very sound that was calling to him, impelling him forward. It was the source of the melody that he was actually trying to find.

The mountain goat finally realized that he was hearing not thunder but something else — something he had never heard before, something both pleasing and threatening at the same time. Every now and then Haidar would stop to question what he was doing, to ask himself why he did not turn back to seek out his two companions. He could not answer those questions, and he continued on notwithstanding.

Eventually the chant became easier to make out, and the goat concluded that he was getting near its source. Although Haidar was certain it lay close by — maybe just ahead — the view and his way were blocked by so many fallen branches and broken brush that he was forced to circle around until he found a gap in the undergrowth. This took some time, but in due course he was able to find a barely visible accessible path along which he could struggle. The goat, trying to keep as quiet as possible, fought his way step by step through the prickly brambles and heavy scrub.

All of a sudden he came upon a sharp ridge that fell away abruptly on the other side. He stumbled, caught himself just in time and pulled back. When he could focus on the view beyond, Haidar realized he was standing on a partially concealed lookout over a small, sheltered valley. Down below, he could see an immense band of animals sitting in a large circle facing inward. Because of the deep shadows, he could not make out what kind of animals they were, but he could definitely hear them. They were chanting in unison, in such deep voices that all together they sounded much like the ominous rolling thunder of earlier in the day.

Haidar recalled his sense of foreboding, his sense that something more was afoot than just a storm, as terrifying as that had been. Was this it? Who were these animals and why were they singing like one being? More to the point, why were they here, and were they friend or foe?

The goat could not pick up any scents. Moreover, since his eyesight was not the best among the world's creatures and night had already closed in, clarifying who they were would be an impossible task. Should he risk getting closer? Or, now that he'd learned the important fact of their existence, should he retreat and go back for Eisa and Olwen? As a trio, they commanded far more strength and authority than he could alone, but could Haidar hope to find his way back to this place? What if the strange animals departed before he returned? What tremendous opportunity might he miss? Or, looking at things from the opposite perspective, what danger might he avoid?

Uncertain what to do and well aware of the stakes involved, Haidar hesitated for several minutes, hunching down in the undergrowth. Finally he concluded that something had drawn him, and only him, to this very place. His instincts had told him — pushed him, even — to search out these animals. He could not turn back now; he would go down to meet them.

Just as the mountain goat arrived at his momentous decision, he heard harsh voices and felt heavy paws land on his shoulders. Haidar had been so mesmerized by his discovery that he had ignored the likelihood of guards posted to keep out interlopers or threats to their safety — intruders like him. Before he knew it, he was being roughly dragged down to the hollow below.

67

AN ENCOUNTER WITH
STRANGERS

The chanting stopped immediately and all eyes turned toward Haidar. None of them looked at all welcoming.

"What have we here?" a deep, menacing voice growled out of the darkness.

"We caught this villain up above," one of the sentries said, not really answering the question. "On the ridge, watching us." One sentry maintained a firm grasp on Haidar's neck, while the other held on to his hind end. The goat had no hope of escape.

"A spy!" someone else said.

"Not much of a spy," another said with a laugh. "He got himself caught soon enough."

"Well, we don't know how long he's been up there, do we," the first voice said.

"Or if there are more of them about," one of the sentries added.

Silence reigned over the gathering as they digested that disquieting thought.

"Did you — " the original questioner began.

"Of course," the sentry interrupted curtly. "We've been scouring the perimeter ever since we found him. You never know."

Haidar thought it best to say as little as possible, at least until he had heard more and knew where he stood. His captors were pushing down his head, strong paws holding him carefully. Their scent was unfamiliar; the mountain goat still couldn't figure out who or what they were.

Someone prodded him roughly, claws digging painfully into his flank. Haidar grimaced but did not speak.

"What should we do with him?" asked the sentry.

"Depends on how much he's heard."

"No," the first replied. "It depends on how useful he might be."

"How so, comrade?"

"He may be able to tell us more about these parts, about who is out here looking for us and what we need to watch out for."

"I doubt he'll tell us anything."

"Oh, you'd be surprised how much a creature will reveal — under a little duress, that is." The speaker, evidently the leader, snorted, and no one said anything to contradict him.

For a several seconds a deathly quiet ruled the little hollow. Haidar breathed slowly, trying to remain calm, waiting.

After a while, another ventured, "Perhaps he doesn't understand our language."

"Or perhaps he's got no tongue."

"Well, then, he wouldn't make much of a spy, would he," said the chief inquisitor, chuckling. "Can't understand us and has no tongue." Others joined in the laughter.

A calmer voice spoke for the first time. "Perhaps we should send our spy back to the main camp. Do we really have time to deal with a prisoner? We're moving out first thing in the morning."

"True enough," replied their chief. "That miserable storm set us back a good day."

"Not to worry, cousin. It will have set our enemies back on their heels just the same as for us. Hah! No one could have escaped such fury! Every creature hereabouts will have run for cover."

"Luckily we were well sheltered down here. Little harm done," agreed the sensible voice. "Others, more exposed? Well, I feel sorry for those poor fools."

"Whatever the case, friend or foe, everyone's probably sloshing about tonight in a bloody bog."

They all went quiet, apparently lost in their memories of the violent downpour.

"What can he know about us anyway?" one of them asked finally. "There's not much to tell."

"Really, you surprise me, Est—," the first started to say, then caught his mistake. "No, sorry, no names. You see how easy it is, comrades? We forget ourselves and then start to use our real names. The point is, our spy knows where we are and how many we are. Perhaps he's already figured out what direction we're going in as well. Still, I imagine he doesn't know our purpose, who we are and how many lie in wait behind us — until we start saying more. So let's keep our guard up."

"Perhaps he's not a spy at all," suggested the voice of reason. "Just some lost creature wandering about in the storm, someone who heard our chant and was curious to know who we were."

"I told you we should have kept quiet," another voice interjected.

"Shut up, the both of you. Our songs are important to us. You all know that."

"You surprise me, you really do. How could you forget we're at war? No innocent animal would be wandering about in these parts, certainly not now. He has to have some purpose, and I warrant it's not a good one!"

"Unless it's peace," Haidar finally dared to say, as clearly as he could from his almost prone position.

A jumble of voices ensued.

"What did the fellow say?"

"At last the scoundrel speaks."

"So he has understood everything. I knew it."

"I told you we shouldn't have sung."

"Shut up, all of you!" commanded their leader. The other animals became still. "You'd better explain yourself, spy, while you still have the ability to talk."

"It would be better if I could look at you," Haidar said. "At least then I would know my audience."

"So you can try to fool us with your lies," the first sentry said, "and have an easier time shaping your deceit."

"I have no foe in this war," Haidar bleated. "To me, all creatures are friends."

"*Friends!*" snarled one of his captors. "Bah! You can't be our friend and a friend of — "

"Bring the spy into the light," the voice in charge commanded.

Pushed and pulled once more, Haidar staggered forward until he was facing the most senior of the creatures, or at least the one who gave the most commands.

"So you say you are our friend. Convince us then, *friend*. What seek you in these parts? And how was it that we found you spying on us? Friends do not spy on friends, at least not to my reckoning."

At last Haidar could make out the animals that had captured him. The mountain goat was more than a little unnerved by the sight. He believed he was as open-minded as any creature, and he'd always maintained (at least to anyone who cared to listen) that he was more tolerant than anyone he'd ever come across. Haidar was accustomed to the notion of dealing with the big cats, first the lions and now, since meeting Eisa, even the panthers. But this was a different matter. He was now facing the most unexpected of creatures — heavily built, powerful, and much larger than any cat he'd ever met. Bears!

The mountain goat had come across only one bear in his life: Lord Eirwen. Their encounter had been brief and had taken place a long time ago, a world away from where he now stood. But he remembered feeling unnerved by the great white beast. Despite what Fridis might say about her always courteous friend, Haidar had never been quite sure about Eirwen, neither completely trusting him nor understanding his purpose in Vigmar. And now, arrayed before him, stood a whole host of such creatures. They were not white like Eirwen but various shades of black and brown, and not exactly of the same size and shape but, to Haidar's mind, every bit as fierce and frightening. The goat felt like the proverbial fish out of water, or at least well out of his depth.

"Well, *friend*, you're awfully quiet now," the bear said with a smirk. "Nothing more to say?"

"My lord — " Haidar managed to utter.

But the bear cut him short. "I am not your lord. I am nobody's lord. We're all cousins or comrades here. Let's get that straight, for starters."

The goat decided he'd better avoid the issue altogether. "I hail from Vigmar," he said abruptly. "And I have been sent here on a mission to bring about peace between Vigmar and Aeronbed."

That sent all the bears into paroxysms of laughter. Astonished, Haidar didn't know how to deal with their reaction, so he retreated once more into silence. He might have expected many responses — surprise, distrust, curiosity, wonder, even hope — but derisive laughter was not on the list.

After a few moments, failing any other response from the bears, Haidar dared to venture forth again. "You surprise me, er, comrades. You find the notion of peace a trifle, a mere matter of amusement? If so, perhaps you know little enough of war and suffering."

It was the wrong thing to say. The laughter died as quickly as it began. One of the bears growled, rose up on his hind legs and stepped forward menacingly. As if in pain, he howled, "*You*, goat, know *nothing* of us and the suffering we have borne!"

Others joined in with a chorus of angry cries and snarls. Haidar shrank back as best he could, though still held tightly. The sentry would have ripped out his throat if their leader had not intervened.

"Well, you've certainly touched a raw nerve with your fine speech," declared the chief. "Perhaps ignorance is your excuse, but some of my cousins will not let that insult pass so easily." The bear stopped as if to consider the options. "You're lucky I'm so easygoing. Otherwise I would let my cousin finish you off here and now, and we'd go happily about our business."

"Enough talk, comrade. It's getting late," said another. "Once this donkey of a goat has finished with his insults, I imagine he'll want to regale us with a long, self-serving tale about his miserable life. Well, I, for one, don't have the time or the heart to hear him out. We must decide what to do with him — right now."

"Hmmm. I fear my cousin is right, friend goat," the chief bear mused. "What should we do with you?"

Haidar dared to open his mouth but was silenced by a quick cuff to the head. Fortunately goats have thick skulls, so the blow did little more than hurt his dignity. Still, he got the message: further protest or attempting an explanation would serve him little this night.

"This is a most curious business, comrades," concluded the group's leader. "It's not every day a mountain goat wanders into our midst. If it were a panther or a lion — well, then, our course would be clear. But creatures exist that are not clearly on one side or the other in this conflict. Our so-called friend speaks of peace between Vigmar and Aeronbed. Perhaps he's been wandering in these woods for so long that he doesn't know we care little about such matters. What is Vigmar to us? Nothing. What is peace to us? Just another word to disguise intimidation and oppression."

The chief signaled to two of the bears. "Take this miserable wretch to the base camp. Perhaps they'll have time to hear him out and put him to good use. And mind where you go — it's treacherous out there. There are pockets of water and quicksand everywhere, especially where you least expect it. Friend, for your sake I hope you're telling the truth. You'll find that our tempers are as short as our time."

Haidar was whisked away as quickly and as roughly as when he'd first been brought to the encampment.

68

HAIDAR DISAPPEARS

Eisa and Olwen looked down at the dark forest into which Haidar had so recently disappeared. The sun had just risen over the steep mountain peaks behind them, the sky as colorful as the day before. The welcome rays had already begun to warm their still damp fur.

Like the two cats, the drenched land around them was slowly recovering. Mist rose gently from the pools of water remaining in the depressions below and on irregular outcroppings of the rocky slopes above. To their left, a stream cascaded in a series of small waterfalls, its origins a mystery. The still dripping trees beyond were basking in the golden glow of a new day.

The lioness and the panther sat quietly side by side, resting on a high jutting rock just beyond the quickly receding shadow cast by the mountain, apparently lost in contemplation. A welcoming morning, blissful fragrances and the gentle sounds of the newly created stream may have greeted them, but their thoughts were far from tranquil.

"Where could that miserable goat have gone?" Olwen growled, her piercing eyes scanning the forest. "And what mischief could he possibly be up to?"

"Who can say?" the equally frustrated panther replied. "I trusted

Haidar. The goat seemed an honest enough creature, and unlike the fox, he appeared to truly believe what he was saying. But first one and then the other vanishes, which inevitably leads me to suspect some plot is afoot. Were they sent to waylay us until confederates could arrive to finish us off? Was it a clever plan foiled by the storm? And then I begin to doubt my instincts. Could they be so off-kilter?"

"We've become sloppy," the lioness said. "We let our guard down. One of us should always keep watch. We forgot that we can trust no one else."

"True enough. But we were not ourselves yesterday. Was it not a most unusual day? Did you not feel it?"

"Of course. A storm of such magnitude? Who would not be out of sorts? I'll not forget it as long as I live."

"Ah yes, the storm. But I wasn't talking about the weather. Didn't you sense something else out of the ordinary? It wasn't just the rain and wind gnawing at our minds."

"You mean, beyond the light?"

"Yes. And perhaps that feeling also affected Haidar."

"Are you suggesting that explains what happened to the goat?"

"Possibly. I wish I knew, and I wish he'd trusted us more."

"What makes you say that?"

"Haidar wasn't telling us everything."

"The fox was certainly keeping secrets. I wonder what his game really was."

They were both silent for a while as they digested these notions.

"Now what?" the lioness interjected suddenly.

"Only two choices. Continue on our way or go after him."

"Go after him? Haidar?" Olwen snarled. "Why?"

"Because if the goat is our enemy, he knows too much," Eisa said flatly. "And if he's our friend, he has put himself in harm's way."

"Yesterday you argued against pursuing the fox."

"But this is different."

"Different? How?"

"I can't explain, Olwen. It just is."

The lioness growled quietly. "Seriously, Eisa, don't you think we should pursue our original plan to head north? Is that not our only hope of survival?"

"It's certainly the safest, most logical path. In fact, I can't muster a single argument against the idea."

"Well, then?"

"So why do my instincts push me in another direction? You see, I do believe there was something in what Haidar said."

"The goat said many things. Which in particular?"

"That any encounter between creatures is significant. Maybe we don't understand what it means at the time, but the point is, we can't abandon Haidar now."

Olwen groaned. "First you say you doubt the goat. Now you say you can't leave him to his fate. You can't have it both ways, Eisa. Which is it to be?"

The panther laughed. "You're right, of course, I have to decide. Do I go with my doubts or my instincts?"

The two sat in silence for a long time, contemplating the choice.

"You do know what lies in that direction?" the lioness asked, gesturing straight ahead.

"Yes, I do. If we travel far enough, we'll likely run into creatures who will kill me on sight."

"And not just you. I doubt the Black Legion loves me any better. But it's not our fate we're talking about. It's the dangers facing the goat, or those that the goat will create for us."

"My kinfolk will take Haidar for one of the enemy. He's a stranger and it's a time of war. The goat will not survive an encounter with the Legion."

"Perhaps our new friend Haidar is but the vanguard of a race of grumpy, malevolent mountain goats opposed to everyone."

They both laughed at the outlandish idea, which served to ease the tension.

"Do you trust me, Olwen?"

"I do, Eisa. Completely."

"Then I say we must go after Haidar."

The lioness remained silent for several more moments, then asked, "Do you know which way to go?"

"My instincts tell me straight ahead, down there. I'm convinced that's where he went." Eisa pointed southwest, into the depths of the dark forest lying at the base of the mountain. "As likely as anything we're walking into a hornets' nest," he added.

"We can escape from hornets; they're just protecting their turf. But four-legged creatures bent on killing us? That'll be far worse."

"I won't force you into going," Eisa said.

The lioness was surprised by his suggestion. "We can't part now. Our paths have been intertwined since first we met."

This pleased the panther, although he said nothing in return. Without further delay, Eisa rose and began to descend the slope, leaping gracefully from rock to rock. The lioness followed immediately behind.

69

PURSUING HAIDAR

The storm had left its path of destruction everywhere. The lioness and panther struggled through the thick forest. It wasn't long before they had picked up the goat's scent and noticed several clumps of his hair where he'd passed through more confined areas. The two cats began to speculate about what might have spurred on the goat.

"Were you suggesting," Olwen asked, "that Haidar was being pushed by the same feeling that's driving you?"

"The more I think about it, the more certain I am. Especially given his brooding nature. I just wish he'd waited to talk to us. After all, Haidar is only a goat, with few means of defense or attack."

"He may not have teeth and claws like us, but mountain goats are nimble on their feet and awfully hard-headed — in more ways than one."

"True enough," the panther said, laughing. "I'd forgotten about his horns."

The pair lapsed into silence as they struggled forward. At length they leapt up onto the fallen trunk of a gigantic old tree that bridged a deep gully full of muddy water.

"If the goat was driven by the same force, what's happened to him now?" the puzzled panther asked as he crept along the trunk to the other side. He spoke as much to himself as to the lioness.

"Is it possible that Haidar's returned to the cave?" Olwen asked.

"If so, he'd be using the path he took on his way out, the same one we're on. I can only hope he's still searching for what's spurring him on, and that we're only a short way behind him."

They considered the latter highly unlikely. The only conclusion the pair could draw was that some misadventure had prevented the goat from returning. Were they on a doomed rescue mission? Would they find Haidar's body, too late to help? Or worse, were they about to fall prey to the same fate? Perhaps, Olwen considered, Eisa was confusing instinct with the lure of a spider's web, and a trap lay in wait for all three of them.

The two cats reached the end of the makeshift bridge and jumped down to the ground. They were soon forced to scramble over a host of branches and smaller trees felled by the massive trunk.

"Do you remember the rumbling we heard after the storm ended?" Olwen asked after a while.

"Yes."

"I don't hear it anymore."

"So?"

"We heard it for quite a while, on and on, as if the storm was still going."

"I understand, but what of it?"

"The rumbling has disappeared."

"I still don't get your point."

"What if it was not the noise of the receding storm but something completely different?"

"What else could it have been?"

"That's the point I'm trying to make," Olwen said rather curtly, a little annoyed that the panther was so slow to grasp her meaning. "Let's try to work out what else that noise could have been."

The panther groaned. It sounded like a stupid game to him, a waste of energy. Olwen, on the other hand, thought her companion was being exasperatingly dim.

"It was just the storm moving away to the west," declared Eisa.

"Now, as it's no longer within range, we can't hear it anymore. End of story."

"But what if that assumption is wrong? What if it was something else, something much different?"

"For example?"

"For example, what if it was the thing — whatever that thing is — that's drawing you on? You keep saying you feel this irresistible pull. You call it instinct, but perhaps there's wizardry in the air."

"But what could the sound be?"

"Something supernatural. Or something animal-made that you and I have never heard before."

The panther had simply assumed it was the storm moving off, but then he had fallen asleep listening to it. When he'd woken many hours later, the rumbling had ended. He hadn't given it any more thought. "Let's assume that's true. What then? How does that affect our plan?"

"If it was animal-made, at very least we must keep up our guard at all times."

"And," the lioness continued, before the panther could comment that the point was pretty obvious, "and if the sound was unrelated to the storm and now has stopped, perhaps Haidar was the cause of its stopping."

"Or whoever was making the sound," responded Eisa, now getting into the game, "had to go into hiding to avoid being discovered."

"Yes, also possible."

"Do you realize how loud that rumbling must have been? We could hear it quite a way away, even back in the cave. It would mean that whoever or whatever made the sound was huge, or that quite a few creatures were involved."

"Or the source was a lot closer than we imagined."

"In either case, it's a rather unnerving thought. As you said, we must take extra care."

"Or avoid searching out its source altogether."

The panther had reached a small clearing. He stopped in his tracks and turned back to look at the lioness. "I thought you trusted me," Eisa said. "*Completely.*"

"I do. It's just, back then, I hadn't considered the possibility that we might be walking into a trap."

"All right, what would you rather do?"

Olwen hadn't expected that. The lioness had presumed Eisa would play his usual trick of making up more arguments to counter whatever idea she proposed. Now, confronted with the responsibility of making the choice, she wasn't so sure she wanted to back out. Indeed, if a scruffy old mountain goat had dared to make such an exploration, two powerful cats should be more than able to take care of themselves.

"No, no," Olwen replied, her tone far from certain. "Let's carry on. We've already come quite a way as it is."

"Not exactly a vote of confidence," the panther said grudgingly. "Still, I'll take what I can get."

They carried on, tiptoeing though the soggy terrain as best they could, following the signs of Haidar's progress: broken branches, trodden grass, hoofprints in still soft mud, more tufts of hair caught on thorns. Finally they found their way to the place where the mountain goat had been captured and dragged away.

"It's clear to me what happened," said Eisa. "You see — "

"It would be obvious to any cat," interrupted Olwen. "Haidar discovered some bears, watched them, and was captured, then taken away."

"But not killed. There are no signs of death, no scent of blood. That's important: these were merciful bears. Or, more likely, they lacked the authority to kill a stranger. At least, not right away."

"Bears. So far north?"

They bounded down to the encampment. The bears, of course, had moved on, but not without leaving signs of their recent presence.

"You see, all around here?" the panther pointed out. "I saw plenty of this in Heimborn. Their tracks are clear."

"At least Haidar's still alive," Olwen said, gesturing at the goat's hoofprints.

"It looks like they took him along with them."

"Who would want a prisoner in such times as these?"

"I see the unit was heading north," Eisa said. "However, they are few in number, too few to be out here by themselves. So I can only assume they are part of a larger group. I suppose Haidar was sent back to the main body for questioning. That's what I would do in their position."

"Drawing on your vast military experience, Lieutenant?" Olwen said.

Eisa laughed. "Well, then, Princess, what would you do?"

"I'd say you're forgetting another possible scenario."

"I am?"

"You've been assuming Haidar was taken prisoner. What if the goat was actually one of them? What if his amazing tale of seeking peace held no truth at all? He could just have been meeting up with them at this prearranged spot — and reporting on our hiding place."

The panther was taken aback. Although at first he was inclined to reject the possibility, he had to accept that Olwen could well be right. They had no proof one way or the other. "Do you really think it's possible?" he asked after a few moments.

Olwen thought carefully before replying. "Honestly, no," she said. "Haidar does not seem that sort of creature. And Vulpé's behavior seemed to surprise him even more than it did us. No, I believe the goat was playing it straight. Still, it is possible, and we'd be wrong not to think about what that would mean."

"You were right to suggest it. Better to consider the implications while we still can."

The cats stopped to rest and work through the impact of Haidar's potential treachery. However, it was but a half-hearted exercise. Time weighed heavily on them, and both felt anxious to get moving.

"Further south it is," concluded the lioness with a sigh. "So be it. We should find Haidar's trail easily enough. At least the wet ground makes tracking easy."

"Into the bears' den, as it were."

"They'll not welcome either of us. I don't need to tell you, Eisa — "

"Yes, yes, I know. We'll need to keep our eyes open." He almost laughed.

"Not just our eyes, but our claws as well."

70

SEARCHING FOR LIONS

The shadows lengthened as the afternoon sun began to recede in the western skies. A day after the tremendous storm, a couple of panther units were on duty in the open plains and high hill country far to the east of Aeronbed's capital.

"Tell me again, Vlad, what are we looking for?" asked one of the soldiers.

"One day, Estrog, you really will be the death of me. Or the both of us, for that matter. Don't you remember the Sergeant's orders?"

"Todog? He didn't tell me anything. No one ever tells me anything. They always assume I'll figure it out on my own somehow. Did they tell you?"

"Todog told me. And you were standing right beside me when he did, you idiot! Where is your mind at?" Vlad looked searchingly at his companion for several seconds, as if hoping to discover the answer. When Estrog did not reply, his companion shook his head sadly. "We're looking for lions, you dimwit," the panther said.

Estrog sighed deeply. "Oh yes, now I remember." He sat down and scratched at an annoying flea.

"This is beginning to remind me of that ridiculous escapade in Heimborn," the other cat said.

"Don't remind me, Vlad. What a screw-up that was."

"Let's look on the bright side, Estrog. It may have got us demoted, but at least we were sent to the home front. And believe you me, mate, it's a lot safer here than fighting up north. You'd think we planned the whole thing, it worked out so well." Vlad laughed, somewhat bitterly.

"Except that here we are again, back in the thick of it."

"Just a little reconnaissance mission. We're only looking for some sign of lions."

"In these parts?"

"I know, it's hardly likely. That's why it's such a great assignment. Couldn't believe they were asking for volunteers. I grabbed it in a second, I did." Vlad laughed again, more happily this time.

"But how far do we search?"

"They only gave us a few days. You can only go so far in such a short time, right?"

"We've seen nothing at all. Any lion in these parts would have to be off his nut!"

"Crazy or not, if they're here, we have to report them."

"We've got nothing at all to go on."

"Except what that wretched fox said. It beats me how the higher-ups could be so taken in by such a con. I saw through him as soon as he showed up. What a scam! I would have sent the scoundrel packing, I would."

"I thought the fox turned out to be the real thing."

"We'll see, Estrog, we'll see. Early days yet. That's why we're out here searching. To see if he was telling the truth."

A loud voice rang out. "You two, quit your gabbing and get on with it."

"Yes, sir," they replied together. "Yes, Todog."

Vlad added in a mutter, "What a grouch! Can't even get a short nap without some higher-up barking orders."

"Todog hasn't been in a good mood since Heimborn. I suppose he'd rather be on the front lines with the others."

"The bloke doesn't appreciate the favor we did him. Safe and sound in Manaris, soft bedding, regular eats, the occasional jaunt to the countryside? Can't complain, eh, Estrog?"

"I suppose you're right, Vlad," said the other with a sigh.

"Course I'm right."

Estrog said nothing.

"Oh well, we'd better get on with it," his partner declared. "I reckon tonight should be the last of it. Then it's back home to our cozy beds. Let's head to that forest over to the southeast. I'd hide out there — that is, if I were a lion."

"But you're not, Vlad."

"You amaze me, Estrog. You really do."

LITTLE DID THE TWO PANTHERS KNOW IT, BUT THEY WERE BEING CAREFULLY observed.

"Do you see those two?" said the large brown bear. "A right pair of stupid ones."

"Lucky for them we don't want to give away our position by killing them," responded his companion.

"But they're walking directly toward us. They'll be right on top of the lookout within minutes."

"I reckon they'll walk right by without even noticing. I'll bet those two couldn't find a crazed beaver if it landed on their heads."

"What can they possibly be doing out here? There's not nearly enough of them to fight us."

"I warrant they're looking for something — or someone. Maybe not even us."

TWO MORE HIDDEN SETS OF EYES WERE PEERING OUT AT THE SAME SCENE.

"I don't believe it," Eisa declared in a whisper.

"What?" Olwen replied.

"It's not possible!"

"Tell me, what?"

"You see those two panthers over there? They were the guards when I was a prisoner back at Heimborn. Those louts I told you about, remember? This is amazing. Here, of all places!"

"Do you think they're still looking for you?"

"Not after all this time. Surely I'm not that important. They've got some new bone to chew on, I guess."

"Some more approaching on the left, Eisa."

"Where? Oh yes, I see. I think, Princess, my old friends are getting a little too close for comfort."

"Let's move on."

The lioness glanced toward the setting sun. "Yes, but let's wait a bit. We should have more shade in a couple of minutes. Shouldn't be long now."

The lioness and the panther waited until the moment to depart seemed particularly auspicious. Then they rose stealthily and crept away from their vantage point. Unfortunately, to make good their escape, they had to cross a sunlit glade. Even more unfortunately, their path was taking them directly toward the waiting bears.

"PSST, COMRADE. TWO MORE CATS COMING FROM THE OTHER DIRECTION. I don't like this. There may be more out there than we think."

"Agreed, cousin. Back up as quickly and quietly as you can. Let's move."

AT THAT PRECISE MOMENT, JUST AS THE LIONESS WAS APPROACHING THE sunlit area, Olwen smelled the bears. The hair on her back rose straight up. She growled ferociously and leapt instinctively into the air, across the glade and into the shadows on the other side. Eisa, following immediately behind, copied her without a second thought. When they landed, they found the bears had vanished. But it was enough.

"ESTROG, DID YOU SEE THAT?"

Vlad pointed at the clearing and hunkered down in the tall grass. Estrog crouched similarly, hugging the ground with all his might. They looked at each other.

"What do you think, mate?" Estrog said.

"Definitely. One lion, maybe two. One light-colored and the other dark."

"One or two? I'd say a lot more than that. Four or more! Maybe an entire patrol! Must be a forward unit. And I'll bet there's even more nearby. Blazes, Vlad, that cursed fox was telling the truth!"

"I told you the creature was on the level, didn't I? We'd better get out of here and let Todog know what we've seen. This bloody place isn't safe at all."

Without further ado, the two panthers raced away to report to their superior.

"We saw a whole pack of lions, Sarge," Vlad said, barely containing his excitement. "Crossing over by the far woods. Tough to say how many, but my guess would be several units."

Todog was no fool. He knew the pair, knew them well enough to doubt their every word. "Show me."

Moving through the grasses as furtively as possible, they led Todog over to where they'd been stationed. Vlad pointed to the glade, where the sunlight was now fast disappearing.

"I don't see anything," Todog growled.

"You'd hardly expect lions to wait around for you, eh, Sergeant?"

Todog didn't appreciate Vlad's tone, but what he was saying was true enough. "You're certain?"

"Yes, sir. As plain as night follows day."

"You both saw them?"

"Yes, Todog," the panthers answered in unison.

"You're sure about it?" Todog persisted. "If you two have messed up again, you'll be on night duty forever."

"I'd swear to it, Sergeant," Estrog said. "On my mother's grave."

"Your mother's still alive," grunted Todog.

"Whatever. Go down there and check yourself if you don't believe us. You'll see their tracks soon enough. Anyway, can't you smell lion in the air?"

Todog was a brave cat but he wasn't about to place himself in harm's way without real need. The other two were not the brightest of soldiers; however, in this instance they seemed pretty confident, and they had no reason to lie. If they'd spotted a few lions there could well be more, far more than his small troop could fight off. Todog sniffed the air — yes, absolutely, there was a definite scent of lion. But how many he couldn't be certain. Nevertheless, it was enough evidence for him.

The Sergeant knew that Archduke Rithild wanted news of any lion sightings as quickly as possible. In their few days out, none of the patrols had witnessed anything. Todog saw this development as a chance for vindication, a way to redeem himself for past failures. Success meant a chance to return to the front lines, to where the real action was, and where the panther felt he truly belonged.

Moreover, the first to get word back to Manaris would be well rewarded. Better him than one of the other patrol leaders. Thus, the Sergeant concluded, he had to move fast; if necessary, he could always fudge things later.

Todog looked back and forth between the clearing and his two miserable underlings — several times, in fact, as if that might make a difference to his judgment. It didn't, but the panther did conclude he'd seen and smelled enough. He'd make the report himself.

"All right, let's get out of here. They've already sent a messenger from Manaris to speed things along," Todog declared. "At least now we'll have some worthwhile news to give him."

71

FRIDIS UNDER DURESS

Fridis was on her way to find Raicho. She had, of course, started her trek westward primarily in search of Haidar. But Fridis now realized that goal had been wildly optimistic. Looking for a single creature — or even a couple of them — in this vast and difficult terrain was like trying to locate one particular pinecone in a whole forest. The duck, torn between her curiosity about the jewels and a lingering anxiety that Haidar required her assistance, was also bedeviled by the fact that she had no idea where to find either the mountain goat or the falcon.

Haidar, she guessed, had to be wandering about somewhere in that part of Aeronbed, but the goat was not alone, and where exactly he was going remained a mystery. As for Raicho, Aeron-Urd had told her the peregrine falcon was on the front lines, although he had been pretty vague about the exact location.

Fridis was smart enough to know she couldn't go flying around aimlessly searching for her former companion's new squadron. Not only was it dangerous, such an effort could take a lifetime. The duck needed more information than what the Air Marshal had given her. Failing that, she would have to use her brain and work from what she already knew from her time in Vigmar.

The war was being fought throughout Aeronbed, from one end of the kingdom to the other. She knew the falcon hadn't been sent to the north and, given the lack of information about the whereabouts of the southern army, a posting there would be highly unlikely. Raicho had to be stationed in the central region, probably due south of where she was now flying. At least the front lines were on the same side of the mountains dividing the two countries, so she wouldn't have to re-cross that challenging terrain.

Recalling reports about a narrow valley that opened onto wide plains, Fridis concluded that she could simply fly down the valley and over those plains. There she would find the falcon or one of his fellow officers, or at least some creature that might help. How hard could it be, after all? Luck favored the bold: it was no time to be timid. And really, what other option did she have? Vigmar held nothing for her; she might as well enjoy herself in Aeronbed.

And so, having worked out her rather simplistic approach, Fridis flew toward the southeast, noting as she went the puzzling absence of signs of life below. She was about a week into her renewed journey when the winds began to pick up sharply around midday. Before too long, the threatening skies were rapidly gaining on her.

At first Fridis tried to outfly the impending storm, but soon enough the thick, heavy clouds closed in around her, bringing driving rain, confusing winds and encroaching darkness. Buffeted and thrown about this way and that, the duck was being pushed dramatically off course.

When the lightning and torrents of rain became too intense, Fridis was forced to land and seek shelter. Under an immense, swaying pine tree in the middle of a seemingly endless forest, she crouched down below the low-hanging branches, letting the raindrops roll off her back and onto the sopping ground. Fridis was drenched — everything was drenched — but since she was safe and unharmed, the duck decided there was nothing for it but to sleep until the fury of the storm had passed.

By the time she awoke, the rain and winds had subsided and a warming sun was high in the sky. Tendrils of mist wafted about as the saturated soil and vegetation slowly dried in the heat of the new day.

The little duck shook off any lingering drops, preened her feathers and then flew up into the clearing skies to figure out where she'd ended up.

Once she was up in the air, the surrounding countryside made no sense to her. Fridis was completely disoriented. In front of her, where she thought she'd find open prairie, were the beginnings of yet another extensive mountain range. To her dismay, the highlands seemed to go on forever. And behind her, where she expected to see mountains, the duck found plains instead. Her one constant point of orientation, the sun, was not where it should have been, at least not to her way of thinking. Had she been wrong about the lay of the land, or had she simply become totally confused in the storm?

The more Fridis tried to figure things out, the more muddled she became. She was not used to this kind of confusion. Had she simply flown in a circle and ended up where she'd started the day before? Or had she been blown so far off her course that she'd actually covered a vast distance, traveling far beyond where she expected to be? Fridis was horribly lost and had no bearings to help her set a new flight path.

Baffled, the duck flew around in ever-widening circles, trying to find some familiar landmark. Eventually she gave up and accepted that she would have to adopt a new role as intrepid explorer in unknown territory. Which way to go? She didn't want to fly over the mountains, so it was either to the left or right. At least, she told herself, there were only two choices.

Too bad there's no ice wall to peck at, Fridis thought, recalling what had first led her into this amazing adventure. That thought set her mind floating on a river of memories, although not all of them were happy. What had she learned from those experiences? At this point it didn't seem like much at all. More often than not she'd simply fallen from one adventure into another, without much foresight or planning. Now here she was back where she'd begun: alone and friendless, but this time not by choice.

Although frustrated by this turn of events, the duck could not be brought low for long. She didn't consider the situation serious enough to use the magic stones. She would have to deal with her predicament by simply carrying on.

Choosing her path was a matter of letting her instincts guide her. If she had been blown too far to the south or west (which seemed the most likely scenario), all she had to do was chart a reverse course. So Fridis turned east and began to fly along the edge of the mountains, hoping they would guide her back to where she'd left off. After a day's flying, however, the mountains began to meander (if mountains can be said to meander) in a distinctly southeasterly direction. The duck was forced to make another choice: part from their comforting presence or head further south than she would like. Fridis knew she'd eventually have to fly south, but she was not yet ready to take so bold a step.

After a good night of rest, Fridis left the foothills and continued due east, into the open plains country. It was early in the morning; the air was fresh and the winds fair. The duck was flying high towards the sun, which was blinding in its intensity. She had not gone far when she sensed danger.

Fridis may have learned only a little since arriving in that strange world, but her encounter with Blakfel's guardian hawks had engrained one piece of wisdom into her very being: when attacked from above, veer off sharply and make for cover immediately. The duck put her wings together and dropped like a stone, letting gravity speed her descent; she was flying faster than she'd ever flown before. Of course, terror and an instinct for self-preservation helped immeasurably. She heard a whoosh as something whizzed past her tailfeathers, missing by mere inches.

A hundred thoughts flashed through her mind, and a range of emotions — self-criticism, doubt, curiosity, bravado and, eventually, regret. Fridis had seen no creatures of any kind for days, not since leaving the welcoming Sesteros clan. At first she'd simply wondered about the absence of both friend and foe. But then, once accustomed to it, she'd ceased to keep a proper watch. The duck blamed herself for being so nonchalant about the dangers.

The assailant had flown at her from the direction of the sun, so the bird clearly knew how to attack. Yet it had missed. Were her skills improving or was the other unskilled or young and not well practiced? Since the bird had swept by so quickly, she'd only a vague inkling of its kind. Her mind had been focused on survival and escape, on seeking safety on the ground.

What would the hunter do next? Would it strike again or search out new prey? Was it alone? If it had accomplices, how long could she fend them off? Suddenly overwhelmed by anger, she wished she possessed a sharp beak and talons of her own to strike back. Fridis found herself regretting her independent streak; it had left her alone, without allies or friends, both of whom she sorely needed at that precise moment.

Fridis swooped and dropped, using every defensive measure she could devise. If the predator intended to attack again, it was certainly taking its time. The ground rushed up to meet her. The duck focused on making sure she didn't injure herself as she careered into the depths of the forest below. She just missed a few partially fallen tree trunks, then continued on until well hidden by the dense foliage.

So, she was no longer alone. More to the point, she was no longer in a world where she was relatively safe. The duck hunkered down, curled herself into a tight ball and waited, motionless as a statue. She'd remain there until the coast was clear.

After several hours, Fridis guessed her assailant must have left the scene to search for other prey. Of course, down below the trees she was well hidden; an attacker wouldn't see her at all. Nevertheless, Fridis was equally handicapped. She was safe but trapped, unable to spot her enemy. When could she risk flying again? How could she continue her search with the constant threat of attack lingering over her?

Slowly, bit by bit, Fridis emerged from her sanctuary. She hopped up onto an exposed rock, then onto a wide branch, then to another, more slender one and so on, moving ever higher, hoping to gain a vantage point where she could see the skies above her. It was not easy, especially as she had to move slowly and her webbed feet were not made for gripping wood slippery with moss.

When she had made it as high as she could safely go, Fridis poked her head through the greenery, scanning the horizon. At last she could make out something, but it was not a welcome sight: not one but three birds, all circling high overhead off to the east. They were not flying lazily but rather making use of the warm updrafts — as birds with great wingspans like to do — to float upward. Being so far off, they looked to Fridis more like angry insects, swooping, darting and almost stopping dead in mid-flight. It would have been a curious, even entertaining spectacle if they had not been trying to kill her. For the moment, at least, they seemed more preoccupied with each other than with her existence.

The three birds began to head in her direction, resuming their wide circling movements. Once in a while, one or two would dive to take a closer look at the ground, while the third would stay on high, evidently for a wider view of what was occurring and watching out for potential enemies. Once or twice the three passed right overhead. Fridis tucked herself in tightly, trying to stay as hidden as possible.

Apparently spotting nothing in the dense forest canopy, the birds turned their flight path toward the west. Still, for some time Fridis dared not move, just in case they returned. Finally, after several more minutes, she poked out her sleek head for a good look upward. She could see nothing; the trio had given up and flown off in search of other victims.

Who were they, the duck wondered, and why were three such predators flying about together in this vast, empty region? There had been something familiar about the birds, but she hadn't taken even two seconds to hope they might be friendly. Hiding had been her one and only priority.

Should she continue on in the same direction or head for safer ground? But where was safer ground? The duck had not one but three enemies to worry about, and no allies nearby to offer help. The odds were almost insurmountable; how long could she ward off her pursuers? Not long, she knew. Concluding that a quick getaway was the only available option, and putting the farthest distance between herself and her enemy the smartest thing to do, she would go east. Only this time she would pay much closer attention to the skies around her.

This time Fridis flew lower, as close to the treetops as she dared, in case an escape should prove necessary. The duck resumed her earlier route due east, trying to maintain a flight path over well-treed terrain. Unfortunately, the further east she flew, the more open rangeland she encountered. The mountains to the south, with their dense forests, began to fade from view.

Suddenly Fridis heard an unfamiliar cry, a *kee-aah*, followed by one she had heard, a high-pitched *kreee*. She had been spotted again. The duck tried to dive, roll, bob and weave all at the same time, anything to confuse the attackers. But she was certain they would easily figure out where she would seek refuge, and in this open rangeland, such places were few and far between.

In her desperation, Fridis was forced into a brave but risky strategy. Instead of dropping to the ground, as they would be expecting, she spun around and flew right up at her attackers. She hoped the tactic would surprise and confuse them, or at least give them pause to think. They might just miss again.

Fridis continued upward, flapping her wings as hard and fast as she could, ascending as quickly as a duck could manage. After a few seconds, however, she realized it had been a stupid idea. Her speed could not come close to the others' rate of descent. She had simply made herself an easy, open target! All she could think of now was her impending doom.

72

GOOD NEWS AND BAD

The duck's three opponents were still some distance overhead, now obscured by the midday sun. Despite her misgivings, it occurred to Fridis that her plan must be working — the birds had failed to attack. However, just as this comforting thought struck her, she knew without a doubt that one of the three had changed its flight path to begin an inexorable, deadly dive.

She braced herself, preparing to take evasive action, perhaps a subtle change of direction or another spin move. However, nothing happened: the attacker did not attack. Instead, to the duck's surprise, her assailant flew right past at a safe distance, turned beneath her and then came up right up alongside.

Somewhat out of breath, the approaching bird called out to her. "Princess Fridis!"

Fridis could have dropped out of the sky from sheer astonishment. "What? Who?" she quacked in turn, her attention still divided among the three predators. And then, leveling off from her upward course, she twisted her head to look at the bird, which was now on her other side, opposite the sun. "Lorcan!" she cried out in amazement. "Is it really you?"

"Yes, and Corvus is flying above us."

Fridis glanced upward, and the black falcon dipped his wings in greeting. The duck was lost for words — although not for long. "I, I don't really understand what's going on," she said. "But one thing's for sure, I can't tell you how happy I am to see you both."

The harrier understood completely. All four birds flew down to an open area amid a grove of trees.

"It appears we hawks are destined to keep meeting up with you in most, er, unexpected ways," Lorcan declared. "At least this time no injury resulted." The harrier looked over to the third in their small company. "My apologies, Princess. Let me introduce Tulkinar, one of our newer recruits."

The red-shouldered hawk, looking awkward, bowed stiffly.

"Tulkinar is not to blame for what occurred earlier. He joined the squadron months after you left Blakfel," Lorcan continued. "So he did not know you and simply acted instinctively when he caught sight of you from afar. To be honest, even Corvus and I weren't certain it was you."

"You're the last bird I expected to see in Aeronbed," Corvus added. "In this neck of the woods especially. Fortunately, we're delighted to say, Tulkinar missed."

"Our new recruit needs more training," Lorcan said. "Either that or you've learned some excellent countermoves since we last attacked — I mean, that is, since you first arrived in Vigmar. I assure you, Princess, Tulkinar got quite a talking to after that first foray."

"And we've been searching for you ever since we figured it out," added the black falcon.

Tulkinar looked embarrassed, but Fridis laughed, as much in relief as enjoyment. "The Air Marshal would have been greatly amused by this happy turn — or should I say *re*turn — of events," Fridis said. "How is my old friend, by the way? I've been gone for so long now. I feared for Aeron-Urd's health when last I caught up with him, and I've thought about him often ever since."

Dismayed, Lorcan and Corvus looked at each other, then gazed down at their talons.

Tulkinar was simply bewildered. Seeking to fill the silence, the young hawk began to speak. "Lady Fridis, I apologize profusely for my attack, and can only thank the gods of the sky I did not succeed. One assault on a royal guest was terrible enough; two would have been unforgivable. I can only be grateful the Air Marshal was not here to witness it. I was trained by Aeron-Urd himself, and had the utmost respect for him."

"Had?" Fridis asked.

"Yes, I'm afraid so," admitted Corvus. "It was a cruel blow."

"Killed in battle?" Fridis asked.

"Far worse," the falcon replied.

"What could be worse than that?"

"Killed by treachery."

The duck was aghast. "When did this happen?"

Lorcan told her. The news staggered Fridis. The timing coincided with her last thoughts of Aeron-Urd. The duck had feared some evil or wrongdoing had befallen the gyrfalcon, and she'd hoped that employing the gemstones on his behalf would save his life. They had not, and now she knew the stones were not all-powerful. Or, Fridis wondered, perhaps she had already used up their available power.

Her happiness at meeting up with the hawks was mitigated by the knowledge that her dear friend was dead. Indeed, the realization that the jewels had not worked was nothing in comparison to the reality of losing Aeron-Urd. Fridis remembered his melancholy mood when last they'd met. Sadness — about the Air Marshal's unfair fate, about her inability to help him, about her failure to be there when he needed her most, and finally about the loss to his loyal officers — overwhelmed the duck. First Eirwen, now Aeron-Urd. Was she destined to lose all her dearest friends?

The birds told her as much as they knew about the gyrfalcon's final days on earth, although, since they had not spoken to any witnesses, what they could explain was limited. Lorcan also recounted what had transpired since then: the decision by Field Marshal Adarix to change his route, the search the wolf commander had asked the harrier to undertake of the mysterious land to the west, and how that effort had ultimately led to their present meeting.

"Perhaps it was fated," the falcon went on. "We were not supposed to be here, but the storm delayed our advance. The way forward was so waterlogged and dangerous that Adarix, curious about what Lorcan had already found, commanded the three of us to return to these parts to explore further. We were on our way back when we ran across you. Honestly, Princess, I'd say the chances of such a meeting were one in a million."

"Life follows strange paths, does it not," Fridis replied. "Frankly, Corvus, it never fails to amaze me."

73

A RESPITE OF SORTS

The four birds flew on to the wolves' encampment.

Unlike Eirwen, since their first encounter on the open plains of Vigmar, the duck had spent little time with the pack. As a result, Fridis had never come to know the wolves and learn to appreciate their ways as Eirwen had. Nonetheless, she held no prejudice against any of them and was anticipating reconnecting with the pack, Alberic in particular.

The duck was welcomed enthusiastically. Perhaps the excitement stemmed from admiration for her independent and spirited nature, or perhaps from her apparent opposition to Vigmar's status quo and her well-known friendship with Aeron-Urd. Of course the duck had also been the closest companion and confidante of Eirwen, who'd sacrificed his life for the wolves so they could carry on their struggle. All those factors served to endear her to these professional warriors who were now rejecting the Empire's sway.

In this world, meetings with former comrades usually presented an opportunity for rejoicing, and this unexpected encounter was no exception. For Fridis, though, the celebration was muted. The news of Aeron-Urd's execution had greatly saddened the duck, and it had also created doubt in her mind about both the gems' power and her chosen path.

The others, of course, had no knowledge of her futile effort to save the Air Marshal's life or how that failure tormented her. Fridis felt responsible for his death and could not understand her lack of success. Had the stones failed to work because she had mishandled them, or was their power reduced by great distances? Could she have asked for the wrong outcome? Or were their powers limited in ways she had yet to comprehend? Indeed, what other mysteries about the gems had she yet to expose? And if the stones' power had simply run its course, was there any point to her self-imposed mission to find Raicho and unravel the mystery of their history? All these questions — and the implications of each — weighed upon the duck, despite her pleasure at being back among creatures she knew.

While Fridis had longed for company, she also wanted to properly mourn Aeron-Urd's death. But she did not know how or where to go to express her sorrow, and the rapid pace of events was interrupting her thoughts and preoccupying her mind.

Notwithstanding the duck's personal concerns, the reunion created an opportunity for the entire assembly to reminisce and reflect. They had not laid eyes on each other for more than a year, and there was much news to share. Naturally Fridis longed to hear the exact details of Eirwen's death, and even though Adarix was less than keen to relive the event, for her he did so. The wolf commander was much more willing to talk about fighting the big cats of Aeronbed, and his decision to ignore the instructions from Blakfel and reverse the pack's course.

The hawks and falcons retold what they knew about Aeron-Urd and their decision to join up with the wolf pack. Fridis, for her part, spoke of the events in Blakfel, her ministering to the injured and sick, her time with Aeron-Urd and Raicho in the south, the mysterious mission of Vulpé and Haidar, and her own travels and explorations. Still, the duck felt uncomfortable about discussing her expulsion from Vigmar, and she remained silent about the purpose of her trip into deepest Aeronbed, hoping to avoid any mention of the gems.

All this telling of tales took the better part of the day's celebrations. While Adarix would normally be anxious to return to the trek, the wolf commander recognized that this unexpected opportunity provided a rare moment for his loyal followers to relax and recoup. Another day of rest would also allow the saturated trails to dry. The march north could easily wait.

It was only late in the afternoon that Adarix's thoughts turned to the mysterious region Corvus and Lorcan had been exploring for a second time. After all the merry-making, the wolf commander was feeling especially relaxed and jovial. Turning to the falcon and harrier, he asked, "What more did you two discover on your latest foray? Beyond, of course, our lovely Princess."

Fridis would have blushed if a duck could do so.

Lorcan answered first. "You'll recall, my lord, that I had a strong sense of being watched the first time I went there. So I said to Corvus and Tulkinar, 'Let's surprise these fellows, maybe even catch them napping.' We went back to the spot where I found the cat tracks and the inscription, but this time we took great care, flying as low and silently as possible through the tighter passes, keeping out of sight."

"What inscription was that?" interrupted Fridis, her detecting instincts immediately on high alert.

For the duck's benefit, Lorcan recapped his discoveries from the earlier trip. Fridis peppered the harrier with questions. "Intriguing. Are you sure it was new, not some ancient marking?"

"Oh, yes, very sure. It was freshly done, all right. You could tell by how the ground had been cleared around the writing. I'd say it was only weeks or months old."

"So some great injustice was recently perpetrated in this land."

"Yes. I reckon it was related to what took place in the camp."

"But why go to such an extent to hide one's tracks?"

"Exactly my question. It seemed like an immense bother."

"And yet it worked. You felt as if you were under surveillance, but you could find no one."

"I give them credit for their skills, whoever they are."

"I suppose if you're on the run from a far stronger adversary, the fewer signs you leave behind, the more confused the adversary is likely to be."

"What surprises me," Adarix interposed, "is that we know of no such group of creatures — that is, ones with such a bone to pick with the cats."

"Or with so much to fear," added Corvus.

"Perhaps they were bears," Fridis suggested.

The others looked at the duck in astonishment. None was more surprised than Adarix. "Why bears, of all creatures?" he said.

Fridis paused. She had hoped to avoid mentioning the gems, but in her curiosity over the puzzle, she had forgotten. How much should she tell them?

"No doubt everyone here knows about the fabulous mines in the Misken Mountains," she said. "But have any of you heard the story of the magical gemstones?"

"Ach, the jewels — that old story!" Adarix declared. "I've no time for such fairytales."

"Yet the story has deep roots in our wolf history," Ammarich added quickly.

"Ah, there's our wise old scholar speaking. He's remembered his early lessons, unlike the rest of us," Adarix said, laughing. Some of the other wolves joined in.

"Laugh as you wish, brother. Of course such legends seem amazing to us now. And, since everyone likes a great story — the greater, the better — doubtless they've been exaggerated out of all proportion over the years. Still, they are usually grounded in some truth."

"What do you remember of the tale?" Fridis asked innocently. The others had apparently forgotten that the discussion had begun with her question.

The older wolf sat back and scratched an ear before responding. Like Adarix, he was enjoying the party. "Well, let's see if I can get it straight. It's not often we sit around like this anymore, and it's certainly been a long time since I've heard the story told. Ah, yes, it's coming back to me. It was the badger's find, a local by the name of Achimi, I believe. He had partners, but I can't recall their names. Of course, no wolves were involved at that point; if they had been, I would certainly have remembered. Hah! Even the slowest of my brothers would have made sure to memorize the details where wolves were concerned!"

Ammarich laughed cheerfully and carried on. "Achimi had already discovered the world's richest mine. The badger was wealthy beyond belief, and then to top it off, he found these unusual gems while digging around one day in his caves. They were unusual in that they were not rough but already cut, polished and contained in leather bags. Clearly some other creature had left them there.

"But that's just the beginning of it. As the story goes — and I'm shortening my tale because it would take far too long to tell — the badger almost came to a quick end that very same day. But the gems saved his life. They had magical powers, you see; they could do the bidding of whoever possessed them. Naturally, Achimi had no idea about that at first. The badger was alone. He had fallen inside a cavern and could not move; he was going to starve to death. Not knowing what to do, he prayed for help. I'm not certain which of the stones he used, but that's a minor detail. Whatever the case, help arrived. Just like that, in the wag of a tail, he was transported outside to safety.

"You can well imagine what followed. Achimi, being no fool, quickly realized the value of what he now possessed. He kept the gems a secret for a while. Well, I guess, who wouldn't? Eventually, however, he revealed his good fortune to the others. I gather they used the stones as they pleased, no doubt to enrich the partnership further, until one fine day the gems were stolen. One of the partners was to blame. Humph, no accounting for friends, I suppose, even during that golden era."

Adarix laughed at that last observation.

Fridis piped up. "The three partners were a falcon, a leopard and a bear."

The wolf commander's laughter stopped abruptly. He stared at the duck but said nothing.

Ammarich was not so quiet. "So you've been learning a thing or two about our history, Lady Fridis."

"Well, you know, in my off hours and on my travels," the duck replied.

"Let me guess," Ammarich went on. "You've had the lecture from Señor Piro."

"What?" she quacked, unable to contain her surprise. "How — "

"That old badger's claim is well-known. His tune is a familiar one to us wolves," Ammarich answered, all smiles.

"But how do you know of Achimi? The Misken Mountains are an awfully long way away from your hunting grounds."

Ammarich nodded in the direction of Adarix. "Our chief has his strengths, and naturally I defer to him on almost everything. But it is the role of the pack's eldest brother to keep alive the wolves' noble lore and history. Adarix is our commander in all matters military and strategic; he is our leader. But it's my job to gather what I can about our past, both good and evil, and pass on those stories to the younger generation — those who are prepared to listen, that is. Hah! You know the younger generation; few have ears for such boring subjects. All they think about is fun and games! And Adarix is no help. As you can see, unlike me, he cares little for the old legends."

"Not that little," Adarix responded.

"I stand corrected. He does care, more than a little." Once more Ammarich laughed easily.

"But you still haven't answered my question," Fridis persisted.

"Nor you mine, Princess," Ammarich countered.

Fridis was not used to being questioned, and she still wanted to keep her counsel on this matter. But having already revealed to the others her trip to the southern mountains of Arundati, she thought it safe to acknowledge that she had met Misken's former mine manager. "Yes, you're absolutely right. Piro gave us the whole tour, and afterward over dinner he told me the story of that famous discovery."

"But did he tell you the whole story?"

"The whole story? I don't know. Really, how could I? That was the first I'd ever heard anyone speak of the gems."

"Well, for example, did he tell you how the stones got there in the first place? And who the rightful owners were?"

"Er, no, he didn't. He said no one knew."

"Perhaps the badger was right, as no one can really say for sure. But I suspect Piro omitted that part on purpose. You see, according to our lore, Lady Fridis, the wolves are the rightful owners, and it was they who placed the stones there for safekeeping."

Now everyone was listening carefully, even Adarix.

"What?" quacked Fridis again. Once again, right under her very bill was a source of information she would easily have overlooked.

Ammarich laughed sourly. "As I suspected, this information comes as news to you. That doesn't surprise me, of course. The badgers have always tried to claim ownership of the gems, never acknowledging other creatures' prior rights. Well, I guess that's fair enough. Perhaps we wolves would do the same if the tables were turned. Though I'd like to think we have a stronger sense of honor."

"Why would the wolves hide the stones there, of all places?" asked Fridis.

"What better place to hide gems than among other gems? It's like hiding one tree in a forest."

"But why there, in Misken? It's an awfully long way away."

"Don't forget, we met here in Aeronbed by chance, Lady Fridis. War brings us here, not choice. And wolves — in fact, all creatures — were not so confined to one or another region as they are now. Wolves of all colors and types used to roam through Vigmar and Arundati in the old days."

"But why hide them at all?"

"The jewels were powerful and, I'm told, could have been used for good or evil. They were too precious — or too dangerous — for any pack to leave lying about above ground."

"Of course, the idea of keeping them safe makes great sense. But depositing them in the depths of the Misken Mountains hardly seems to have worked. There they were, left alone all those many years. How did that happen?"

"A most astute observation, my lady. History has it that the wolves agreed to act as guardians of the stones on behalf of all creatures. Seven members of only one clan — the most senior wolf clan — were in the know about the gems' exact whereabouts. The other clans, recognizing the stones' importance and the heavy responsibility those seven shouldered, accepted that arrangement. They only vaguely knew where the stones were.

"But, in return, it was accepted that the keepers would never use the power for themselves. Only the chiefs of all the clans would have the right to use that power, and, of course, only for good. It was up to the clan of the keepers to decide whether the rationale was just and necessary. As you can imagine, the stones were rarely used."

"I still don't understand what happened."

Ammarich sighed. "No one does for sure. The accord broke down, and over time the knowledge of their location was lost. But when word leaked out about that scoundrel Achimi rediscovering the gems, the wolves made several attempts to recover them. Of course, Achimi was no fool; he knew their value was boundless. He and his partners kept them well hidden and protected, from rightful owners and false claimants alike. And you've seen the mountains — they're almost impenetrable. Sad to say, we wolves met with no success. And then somehow fate intervened: the jewels disappeared again. They've never been seen since, though stories persist to this day as to what happened. Perhaps, Lady Fridis, you've heard some of them in your travels."

The duck, ignoring Ammarich's implied question, asked one of her own. "But didn't the kings of Vigmar get hold of the three stones?"

"Three stones? Piro didn't tell you?" The wolf smiled sardonically.

"Tell me what?" What more surprises were in store?

"There were not three jewels, but four."

"What?" Fridis could hardly believe this new twist. "Piro even told me that Achimi wished there were four instead of three, so they could have been distributed evenly among the four partners."

"Hah! Piro's a great storyteller; I'll give the badger his due. That would be just the kind of clever embellishment he would add. Makes the whole tale more convincing, don't you think? Of course, it's possible Piro might have been testing you, to see how much you already knew. Tell me, Princess, what did he call the gems?"

"Call them?"

"What name did the badger give the stones? All such precious objects have a name."

"Piro just called them the Misken gemstones. Is that not right?"

"Hah! It would certainly serve his purposes by enhancing the badgers' claim to ownership. But no, it is not right. They are properly called the Stones of Blakvul."

"The Stones of Blakvul," the duck repeated, half lost in thought. "So what happened to the fourth one?"

"I've no idea." The wolf shrugged. "I've always assumed the gems are still together, hidden away somewhere, waiting for the rightful owner to rediscover — and claim — them."

"Which, I take it, is one of you."

Ammarich smiled again. "To be precise, Lady Fridis, as the eldest brother of the Tasandik clan, the first and foremost clan of wolves in all these lands, it would be me."

74

THE HAWKS' DISCOVERY

"Now you know why my brother is so taken up with our ancient history," Adarix said. "Although," the wolf leader added, "as with many other great myths that promise fortune, he's unlikely to live long enough to see the day it comes true." He laughed at his little jibe. The pack joined in, such good-natured kidding being their way.

"This look backward, however fascinating, has taken us quite a way from my original question," Adarix continued. "I was asking Fridis why she believed this neighboring land might be populated by bears."

Fridis, her thoughts now consumed by the lore of the gemstones, was abruptly pulled back to the present day. Since the duck did not want to reveal that she was on the trail of the thief (or thieves), she tried to keep her answer as vague as possible. "It was something I picked up on my way back from Misken," she managed to explain. "One of Achimi's partners was a bear named Merithu."

"That's right," Ammarich said. "You mentioned him earlier. It was a brown bear, if I recall correctly."

"Yes, that's what I heard," agreed Fridis. "I was also told the bears have no allegiance to any other creatures and keep to themselves. And they are not normally found in Vigmar or Arundati but come from

Aeronbed. So, putting two and two together — their secretiveness and lack of allegiance — a mountain retreat might be the perfect place for them. And that might account for your not knowing what lay beyond these mountains."

Adarix took a few moments to digest this idea. Was it possible? Why not? If so, what could it mean? The wolf was not really sure what he was searching for, or how relevant it was to learn that this land, so shrouded in mystery, could be inhabited by bears. The only thing Adarix knew was that the tragic death of Eirwen continued to disturb his peace of mind, and something needed to be put right. But how much more time and resources could he devote to investigating these troubling notions? War demanded total commitment of body and mind. Personal grieving — if that's what it was — must wait. He'd be the first of any pack member to remind a brother of his higher duty.

Adarix turned back to Lorcan and Corvus, leaving Fridis to her own reflections — on Piro and Ammarich, truth and lies, claims and counterclaims.

"Lady Fridis may be correct. But we have no way of confirming it, unless you two discovered something new. So, to pick up where we left off, you were flying low and carefully into this land — this *possible* land of the bears."

"Yes, exactly," Lorcan answered. "We decided to start at the same encampment. I hoped the inhabitants had returned and gotten careless, or that we'd catch them by surprise. Humph, no such luck, I'm afraid."

Corvus picked up the story. "Yes, not a single sign. And this time we explored each cave and went further afield. Fortunately, because there were three of us we were able to cover more ground. Still, we didn't have a lot of time and, as Lorcan reported earlier, the whole place is both a maze and a fortress at the same time. It's hard to see anything even on a clear day. And in this instance we ran into a lot of mist — lingering around the slopes after the storm, you understand. It made our — "

"Go on, go on," Adarix interjected, impatient with the lengthy preamble.

Corvus got the message. "It was Tulkinar who discovered it. You carry on, Lieutenant."

"Yes, sir," the hawk said, somewhat surprised at being thrust onto center stage. He stepped forward into the circle. "I had flown over what appeared to be a rock slide. But something about it didn't seem right: too neat and tidy, if you know what I mean. So I flew in for a closer look. After a couple of passes, I concluded it had been deliberately created. Not natural, you see, but animal-made. By some pretty big and powerful creatures or, if not, some pretty clever ones.

"Still, it was by no means obvious who was responsible. I thought about this for a while and then I asked myself, why would any creature do this? What would be the point? Then it struck me — I was at the top of the slide. I had to see its result to know the answer. So I flew down to the base of the mountain. And that's where I found it, or rather, them."

"Them?" Adarix said.

"A large contingent of panthers. All dead, crushed by the rocks or killed in the fall. I'd say they were taken completely by surprise. An absolute massacre, and not a single member of the other side seems to have been killed in the effort. Given the state of the carcasses, I'd say it happened some weeks ago, maybe even longer."

No one spoke as the assembly took in this shocking information. Adarix's mind worked feverishly. What did it all add up to?

"Sir, do you want us to explore — " Lorcan began.

Adarix held up a paw for silence. "No," he said after a while. "You've done more than enough. Excellent reconnaissance work. I thank all three of you."

Adarix directed his next comments to the pack. "We've learned enough to make one important conclusion. There's now another army in the field, whose power and intentions we must take into account. They are evidently clever, strong and well led. Most important, they fight against the cats. The question is, are they friends of ours by default, or are they just out for themselves, and therefore enemies of everyone else? Finally, where are they now?"

"Perhaps they're just holing up somewhere," suggested Emrin. "Hiding from the inevitable retribution."

"Would you do that?" Ammarich asked.

"I don't know," replied the wolfhound. "I'm not sure how their minds work. I suppose it would depend on the situation and their strength."

"On both counts we know too little," Adarix said. "We can't safely judge the matter either way."

"So once again we ask you, sir," Corvus interjected. "Do you want us to explore further?"

Adarix reflected before responding. "No," he declared finally. "I'm tempted, I really am. But we've stopped here long enough. Although we've learned a great deal, it might take a lot longer to learn only a little more. We can't afford further delay."

Adarix jumped up, once again the resolute pack commander. "Brothers, cousins of the land and sky — and you too, Lady Fridis — we must prepare ourselves for departure. We have made the most of our well-earned respite, but now we must continue our advance. Soon we shall meet the forces of Aeronbed, and when we do, we will strike a blow to their heart and win this war — if not for Vigmar, then for ourselves."

The wolves cheered lustily at their leader's call to action and began to ready themselves. Adarix called upon Ammarich, Alberic and Emrin to plan the pack's movements over the next few days.

Fridis was greatly troubled by everything she'd heard. It appeared that the situation in Vigmar was far more complex, and loyalties far more confused, than ever before. Could anyone possibly explain to her what this war was all about? And by falling in with Adarix and his wolves, where did she now stand in the whole affair?

75

SOME SURPRISES FOR THE BEARS

"A messenger has arrived, Lord Eirwen," intoned the stout black bear. "From Vidar. An urgent matter requiring your immediate attention."

"Yet another message, yet another urgent matter," Eirwen muttered under his breath, irritated at being disturbed. It seemed as if every question, no matter how trivial, had to be referred up the line. He sighed wearily. "These commanders need to take some responsibility, to stand on their own feet. How will they possibly cope when we come face to face with an army of well-trained and determined cats?"

The optimism created by the bears' early success had long since dissipated, and the hard grind ahead loomed in the polar bear's mind. Eirwen was feeling the strain of command, and the wretched storm had not helped his mood. Many of the trails had become waterlogged or filled with debris; as a result, the army's progress north had slowed virtually to a halt while the bears labored to restore safe passage. It seemed to Eirwen that he was spending entire days wrestling with a myriad of petty administrative matters rather than getting on with it. Whatever *it* was — advancing on the cats, occupying territory, winning the war, to name only three possibilities — not one seemed to be happening, at least according to his reckoning.

The polar bear looked up to face Bakman. "Can't Vidar deal with it on her own?" he groused.

"This one, I think not. I've already been briefed on the gist of the message. Really, it's a story you have to hear for yourself."

Although exhausted, Eirwen was also curious. Bakman did his best to push away mundane requests and usually dealt with problems from his more apprehensive subordinates on his own. Eirwen respected his judgment in such matters. "All right, show the messenger in. But tell him to be brief."

A modest temporary structure had been constructed for the bears' commander-in-chief. There Eirwen could hold meetings and get some sleep with a degree of privacy. It was the only privilege he would accept; otherwise he put up with the hardships the other bears were forced to deal with every day.

The hours had passed slowly as the bears worked to clear the trail. It was now early evening; the sun was beginning to set but the lifeless air was still warm. After the onslaught of rain and wind, the weather had turned around completely. The sunshine, which had begun to dry the sodden terrain, had been the one small respite in an onerous day.

As the cautious bears had moved slowly out of Heimborn and onto the plains of Aeronbed, Eirwen and Bakman had become the de facto decision-makers on strategy and tactics. The polar bear had chosen Bakman, out of all the clan chiefs, because the latter not only shared his enthusiasm for the great cause they had taken on but also had turned out to be especially calm and efficient. The others had been relegated to junior commanders.

While this new, streamlined decision-making process pleased some of the clan chiefs, it had irritated others, especially those further down the chain of command. Eirwen ignored both the satisfied and the malcontents; caring about neither compliments nor criticism, he had even less time to worry about offending their leaders. The polar bear had needed to improve how decisions were made and how orders were carried out. His attempts to counter discontent by delegating more tasks had somehow failed to take hold. Moving away from the bears' traditional consensus-building approach had been much more challenging than Eirwen had expected.

The messenger arrived and waited for permission to speak. Eirwen was so tired he had actually closed his eyes and begun to nod off. Suddenly he opened them, startling the young bear. "Well?"

"Sir, there's quite an upset in Vidar's forward camp."

Eirwen stopped him. "Can't the Commander deal with it?"

"No, sir."

Eirwen sighed. "All right, carry on," he said. "And keep to the point."

"Yes, sir. A prisoner was brought into the camp, captured while apparently spying on the advance scouts."

"Unusual, but haven't we put in place rules to deal with spies?"

"Yes, sir, but this particular creature says he knows you."

"Knows me?"

"Yes, sir."

"I doubt it. I'm not known in this part of the world, except of course among the bears. What kind of creature is it?"

"It's a goat — a shaggy white goat, to be specific. With sharp black horns."

"Don't they all have horns?" Eirwen said, sighing. "I don't know any goats. Have Vidar deal with him as she thinks best."

"Excuse me, sir. That's only the beginning of the message."

"There's more to tell? I told you to get to the point."

To his credit, the messenger held his ground. "I'm keeping it as brief as possible, sir. The sequence of events is relevant."

Eirwen sighed again, more audibly. "All right, continue," he said. "Wait, what name does this goat have?"

"We don't know as yet."

"A name would clearly help, especially if the creature says he knows me. Why has Vidar not yet found out his name?"

"She was in the process of doing that, my lord. You understand, sir, we've met few other creatures in this part of the world. Well, to be accurate, this is the first time we've come across anyone. So that was curious enough, but to find one that claimed to know you was something else again. And then what happened next — well, that was truly astounding! And I hasten to add, my lord, because this meeting was so unusual, the goat's questioning was the center of attention.

Everyone was focused on the intruder when some should have been watching elsewhere."

Eirwen groaned. "Your instructions were to keep the story succinct. I fear I'm going to like the next part of this message even less than the beginning. Before you say another word, go ask Bakman to come in. He'd better hear the whole thing so it doesn't have to be repeated."

Once the other bear had shown up, Eirwen directed the messenger to continue.

The messenger took a breath and carried on. "Vidar was standing there, attempting to question the goat, when a huge disturbance was heard at one side of our encampment. All of a sudden, with a single bound, a panther and a lion leapt into the very middle of everything, landing on either side of the goat. As I said, someone should have been paying attention. It was an unpardonable lapse of security."

"That will be for me to judge, not you. And then what happened?"

Eirwen no longer felt like nodding off, for his entire attention was now focused on the incredible tale. Bakman, his eyes wide, was listening with equal amazement. Both, however, were trying to appear calm and collected.

"Well, sir, everything and nothing. The two cats growled, roared, spat, bared their fangs and stood by this goat as if to defend him with their very lives. But, to our surprise, they didn't attack any of us. We just stood there dumbstruck — I mean, that is to say, Vidar ordered us to stand fast. Of course our company outnumbered the three by great odds; we would have gone in, in the blink of an eye, if we'd been ordered. Might have lost a few, but that's what war's all about, is it not."

"Indeed it is. So why did Vidar tell you to hold off?"

"It was because the goat said he knew you, and they appeared to be allied with him. It made no sense at all; the situation was simply beyond our experience. Commander Vidar thought you'd want to know, if not intervene directly."

"But I know no creature of that sort in Aeronbed. How would anyone besides the bear clans even know I'm here? And certainly no lion or panther can claim to be a friend of mine. What did this goat do then? Did you witness all this personally?"

"I did, sir. First off, his reaction to the cats' arrival was even more curious. He'd clearly no idea they were about to intervene. At first he didn't react at all. I'd say he didn't know what to do — stunned, as it were. Certainly as stunned as the rest of us. Then, as the cats seemed about to go on the attack, it appeared he was trying to restrain them. If they were a gang of cutthroats, it was a curious one. I would say they were more at odds with each other than with us. Of course, a goat is a breed apart; he doesn't have the powers the cats or we bears have. Perhaps that's all he could do."

"Bakman, what do you make of this story?"

"Never heard the like before, my lord. But, of course, conducting a war is new to me. I imagine you've come across many such curious incidents."

Eirwen sighed again; there was no getting around it. "I'd better take charge," he declared. "Stay here, Bakman. You're in command while I'm up front. And keep your guard up. Put everyone on alert; this may not be an isolated incident. Possibly it's only the beginning of a very clever maneuver on the part of the cats, meant to draw our attention from an attack from some other quarter."

Eirwen went off with the messenger. It did not take the two bears long to reach the clan's encampment, and they met up with Vidar just outside it.

"Sorry to trouble you, Lord Eirwen. Matters like this one are well beyond my ken."

"Mine too. You have nothing to apologize for, Vidar. Everything's secure now?"

"Yes, my lord. I've doubled the perimeter watch. No one can enter unannounced and those three cannot escape — although escape seems to be the last thing on their minds. Should they turn on us, we have them greatly outnumbered."

"Well done. Take me to them."

Dusk had surrendered to nightfall by the time Eirwen arrived in the camp. The silhouettes of the three strangers stood out against the large fire burning brightly behind them. Surrounding the trio, an army of watchful eyes was riveted on them.

The polar bear strode around to the other side of the fire in order to see the three creatures more clearly. Some of the bears made way for him, stepping back into the shadows. From his new vantage point, Eirwen could see the savage eyes and cruel teeth of the cats, but the head of the goat was lowered and he could not make out the creature. The two cats followed his progress with their gaze, boldly turning their heads to watch him.

Once he'd found a good spot, Eirwen rose up on his hind legs, towering over everyone else. Vidar and some of her senior officers took their places behind him to accentuate their dominance of the situation.

Eirwen called out in a loud, gruff voice, "Who is the creature who claims to know me?"

The polar bear's size and demeanor must have seemed particularly intimidating, for the lion and panther appeared to lose some of their aggressive attitude. They looked from the bear to Haidar with more than a little curiosity as the goat raised his head in greeting. His long hair was matted with thorns and other debris, his beautiful ivory coat stained with mud. Still, to Eirwen there was something oddly familiar about the creature, though it was only a vague memory from a distant past life.

The goat spoke up. "Lord Eirwen Northlander," he said.

It was a name the polar bear had not heard in a long time. "I am he," replied Eirwen loudly. "And who are you?"

"Do you not remember me, my lord? I am Haidar, from Blackfel Castle."

For several moments Eirwen was at a loss for words. No one else spoke, everyone waiting for the bear to respond. A great deal was at stake.

"Haidar?"

"Yes, Haidar, my lord. The friend of Princess Fridis."

When he heard the duck's name, Eirwen's throat constricted and tears came to his eyes. Since his fall from the mountain and his rescue and new life among the bears of Heimborn, Eirwen had given little thought to his former life. He had been too preoccupied — first by the effort of getting better, then by the bears' desire for a hero, and finally by taking on that role and the responsibilities that came with it. That process had been a blessing, but it had come with a cost: he was no longer the easygoing polar bear of old.

Tired and frustrated by the challenge of corralling the bears into an effective army, Eirwen had grown increasingly irritable. The demands of leadership were weighing heavily upon him. Going to war had been much harder than he had anticipated. Being so preoccupied, he had not given much thought to how his disappearance would have been received back in Vigmar. Certainly he thought he might be missed, but he'd also assumed that everyone would carry on their lives without him and eventually he'd be forgotten. Suddenly and unexpectedly, Eirwen was being confronted by his former life, in the shape of one creature and the dear memory of another. He was surprised at the depth of his own reaction.

Could this really be the same goat? Here of all places, and with such unlikely and unwelcome companions as these two creatures, despised enemies of Heimborn and Vigmar? Eirwen knew Haidar more through his friendship with Fridis than through any personal connection. He had been more than a little taken aback by the greeting, but could this mountain goat be an imposter or a charlatan? The polar bear needed to be certain.

"You've caught me by surprise, Haidar, to say the very least. How did you know I was here?"

"My lord, through no great act of brilliance or magic. As I was being brought here, I overheard one of your comrades mention your name. I was as surprised then as you now find yourself. Back in Blakfel, of course, we considered you long dead."

"Dead? How so?"

"The wolf pack reported it many months later. You were swept off a cliff, last seen, I believe, battling valiantly with two mountain lions." The goat looked uneasily at Olwen.

The story seemed genuine, and the voice and scent were familiar. Eirwen saw no reason to doubt the goat. "The report of my passing, I'm pleased to say, was a tad premature," the bear responded dryly. "I suppose it was an understandable mistake. However, as you can see, it was far from accurate. I have my cousins here to thank for that. I did take quite a tumble, and my excellent recovery was due entirely to them. Without their care, the outcome would have been very different.

"Listen, Haidar, I accept that you are truly who you say you are. However, now we have a more challenging problem. As far as I know, you are not an enemy of Heimborn. Nevertheless, you've arrived with two, er, friends who are much less welcome. You all will have to explain yourselves, and it had better be an explanation worthy of your most illustrious ancestors. Otherwise, your lives will be worth no more than the hind foot of a wolverine."

As the mountain goat opened his mouth to reply, Eirwen stopped him. "Before you say anything, Haidar, you should know that Fridis often spoke well of you. I probably know only a small portion of what kind of creature you are, but, because of Fridis, I am predisposed in your favor. I therefore want to believe you.

"Nevertheless, my good feelings may not be sufficient to save you. They do not account for your presence in a war zone, apparently supporting the enemies of both Vigmar and Heimborn. You're a long way from the castle kitchen now, Haidar, and I need to understand plainly what is going on."

76

MORE SURPRISES

"My story will sound unbelievable," said the mountain goat, "but I swear it's the entire truth, and my fellow travelers here can at least vouch for the latter part. You will have to hear me out, I'm afraid; hear the whole saga as it unfolded. Since it is such a long story, I suggest we all sit down, stretch our legs and get more comfortable. Otherwise our backs will begin to ache and you will curse me for not getting to the point."

Haidar's confidence surprised Eirwen. It hardly seemed justified, given the goat's predicament. Still, the polar bear saw the logic of his suggestion. As long as the guards kept a close eye on things, he was more than willing to let down his guard. He indicated his agreement but signaled Vidar to ensure that the watch maintained their vigilance and regular patrols of the perimeter. This surprising encounter could still, he considered, be a trick to put the bears at ease while enemy troops surrounded the camp.

As Eirwen contemplated these possibilities, Haidar began his story.

"First, my lord, let me introduce my, er, traveling companions: Princess Olwen of Aeronbed on my right and Lieutenant Eisa on my left."

The two cats bowed somewhat stiffly, while much muttering and low growls could be heard from the assembled bears. An officer in the hated panther military and the daughter of the King of Aeronbed — what a combination!

"I won't say you are welcome, Princess and Lieutenant," Eirwen replied. "Although I will acknowledge your rank, and your courage in standing by our mutual friend when you clearly had no need to."

Olwen and Eisa bowed their heads slightly, accepting the praise, but said nothing more.

Eirwen signaled to Haidar to begin, and the latter launched directly into his tale. The goat began with Gloton's request for his help, moved to the journey through the borderlands into Aeronbed, delved into sighting the mysterious light and meeting the two cats, detoured to Vulpé's disappearance, climaxed with the storm that had besieged everyone in the region, and finished with the mysterious rumbling that had drawn him to the bear clan, where he had been seized and brought to this place. Olwen and Eisa confirmed with nods the part of the saga that had begun with the sighting of the light.

Haidar's tale took some time to recount, but it was so intriguing that no one lost interest or nodded off, despite the late hour. When the telling had ended, the mountain goat added the story of his father and his own long-standing quest for peace, as an explanation of why he had agreed to embark on the seemingly mad enterprise.

When the goat had finished, everyone turned toward Eirwen as if awaiting his judgment. For a few moments the bear simply looked at the three prisoners. Then he asked, "Can you prove any of this?"

Without any hesitation, the goat answered, "No, my lord, I cannot. The part about my father I told to the Princess, but of course I could have been telling lies even then. And if we were to come across Vulpé, I'm not so sure I would trust the word of that fox. So I rest my case on my account, such as it is."

"Let me put aside any response for the present," Eirwen said, "and turn to your two accomplices. Perhaps they can explain why they were wandering about alone in these parts while their forces are engaged elsewhere. Are *you* the spies, rather than Haidar, scoundrels who have conned our simple friend into protecting your skins? Or perhaps you are deserters, on the run from your own troops. What do you two have to say in your defense?"

Neither Olwen nor Eisa had expected such a turn of events, or to be called upon to defend their actions and presence in the region. They had jumped into the action out of a straightforward desire to help their companion; the cats had seen the potential for a fight, but not for a grilling like this. Should they simply tell the truth? Though their story might be less compelling than Haidar's, it was just as hard to believe. Who should go first? Where to begin? Knowing their lives depended on their next words, they hesitated, once again looking to each other for guidance.

Before they could say anything, Haidar spoke up. "My lord, I object to your use of the word *accomplices*. It makes them appear guilty even before they can speak in their own defense."

"Are you now their advocate, Haidar, as well as their friend?"

"I had not intended to act in such a capacity, but if I can assist my two young friends, I am more than happy to do so. They could have been well away from here by now, so they clearly sacrificed their freedom to save me. I owe them that much at least."

"This is not a court of law. We are an army on the march, or at least we were until the storm slowed our progress. And now we are trying to find grains of truth amid the chaff of fine speeches. In the end, I — and only I — will decide where the truth lies and where it does not. I assure you, Haidar, I will dispense justice quickly and fairly. So consult your clients and let's get on with it. Time is pressing on us like the unhappy weight of a cat's paw."

It was an ill-chosen image, and a most unwelcome choice of words for Eisa and Olwen, reminding them of where things stood. Their lives depended not just on what they had to say but also upon the quality of mercy that Eirwen chose to dispense.

"We shall take only a few moments, my lord."

Eisa leaned over and whispered to Haidar, "What kind of a creature is this white bear? I have not seen his like before."

"Eirwen's sudden appearance in Vigmar was as surprising as it is here. He and his friend Fridis simply turned up one day. They were discovered by the wolf pack, wandering about the grassy plains south of Blakfel. They announced themselves as royal visitors from the Far North, he the King of the Great White Lands and Fridis a lady of his court.

"They were introduced to the Emperor, and without much ado Don Grimezel announced that Lord Eirwen was to be his new champion. He appointed him commander of Vigmar's forces in the ensuing campaign against Aeronbed. Eirwen accepted the charge, came up with plans and led the invasion. As I said, he was given up for dead, but as you can see for yourselves, the bear is very much alive.

"I admit I know Eirwen only through other eyes. However, I can say a great deal more about his friend Fridis, who I came to know and like."

"Is this Fridis a bear like him?" asked Eisa.

"No, she's a duck. It was an unlikely pairing, but they seemed very attached to each other."

"Would that she were here to speak on your behalf," said Olwen.

"If wishes were horses ... "

"What would you suggest we do?" Eisa asked. "However limited your knowledge of his background, you clearly know him better than we do."

"I cannot say whether the others will influence his decision, but I believe Eirwen to be an honorable creature, a bear of his word. I have heard no evil spoken of him, and his companion thought most highly and fondly of him. Having said this, I can see that his temper has changed somewhat for the worse. The mantle of power, I suspect, is wearing upon him."

"Therefore ... ?"

"Therefore I believe he will not make up his mind about you beforehand. This is no show trial after which you will be summarily condemned to death. He will attend to your words and he will give you a fair hearing. So say everything in your defense; do not hold back. But do not taunt or anger him with your words. And do not give the rest of them any weapon to use against you."

Olwen's eyes narrowed. "What do you mean by that?" she asked.

"If you have ever committed any, er, ill-advised acts against these bears, do not speak of them."

Eirwen's gruff voice brought a halt to their brief conference. "Your clients have had enough time, Haidar. Let's get on with it."

"I believe we are ready to begin, my lord." And then, turning to the two cats, the goat asked which of the two would begin. Eisa chose to speak first.

The panther began by following the goat's advice. "First, let me say, my lord, that neither Princess Olwen nor I have never harmed any inhabitant of Heimborn. Whatever atrocities the Black Legion has committed, we had nothing to do with them."

That assertion generated several threatening growls and snarls. A couple of large brown bears even rose angrily from where they were resting. Eirwen held up a paw, commanding silence. When things had calmed down, he said, "Let me stop you there, Lieutenant. You two may be individually blameless, but the cats have subjected Heimborn to subjugation and torment for generations. My cousins here will find it hard to understand the difference between your own actions and those of your brothers and sisters."

Again muttering resulted, but this time of assent. A few bears were moved to cry out, "Hear, hear!"

"I understand, my lord," the panther responded quickly, "although I trust neither of us will be held to account for the actions of an entire species of cat. I will not defend my panther kin. Indeed, I utterly condemn them and their repugnant acts." Eisa paused briefly, then went on. "You may choose to think those are the words of a false friend or that they come cheaply. You may argue that I'm disavowing my brothers simply because I face retribution from those whom we used to oppress — just trying to save my own skin. I can see how it would be easy to think so."

The bears had no difficulty agreeing with that statement. The panther saw many nodding heads and hardened expressions around the fire, which was now growing low.

"But this isn't the first time I've faced such a trial. Only weeks ago my cousins — good comrades, I thought — brought me before a supposed court of law and speedily condemned me to death. Now here I am, facing yet another trial. I will no doubt go down in history as the only creature to be tried by both sides in this bloody mess. I can only hope that your justice is fairer than that of my kin."

"A most surprising admission, Lieutenant. We are anxious to hear more of it."

"You must first hear my preamble, my lord: how it came to be that I was in this part of the world in the first place."

The polar bear gestured to the panther to proceed.

Eisa drew a large breath and went on to describe his work for Rithild, his attempts to connect with Parthanyx and the others, his revulsion at what he heard from them, his brief service with the Black Legion, his missing of the debacle of the rock slide, the resulting suspicion and trial, and his escape and subsequent meeting with Olwen. His story was as interesting to his audience as Haidar's, perhaps even more so, since it concerned the bears directly. It was the first time any of them had heard the now famous victory of the rockslide told from the panthers' viewpoint — and it pleased them mightily.

Eisa, taking into account Haidar's warning, spoke as honestly as he dared and with suitable modesty. While the panther did not mention Rithild's advice to ingratiate himself with the bears if he had no other option, he did not try to avoid the hard truths about the panthers' cruelty — and of course he had not perpetrated any of the foul deeds himself. Finally, whatever his personal prejudices against the bears might be, Eisa knew this moment was not a time to dwell on them. He acquitted himself well in the proceedings, as well as any cat so ill-placed could have done.

Olwen's performance, surprisingly, was another matter. As a mere lieutenant, Eisa's subordinate role had given him a chance to learn how to read an audience, to understand when he must please his masters and to practice acting in an "appropriate" manner. However, as a princess and the daughter of a doting father, Olwen had had no such opportunity. On the contrary, she'd been accustomed to everyone else doing her bidding all the time. Thus, when the tables were turned —when she was forced to sit at the servants' end — she did not know how to behave. Consequently, Olwen's tone was condescending and she was unwilling to account for her behavior.

The lioness did corroborate as much of Eisa's story as she could: her discovery and the saving of his life. She argued that her prior role commanding troops in the north meant that she had battled only against Vigmar and had never really encountered the bears. So the lioness too could maintain that she'd never perpetrated a single evil act against a bear.

Olwen could have noted that she was now on the run because the panthers had overthrown the established order of lions. In essence she had been brought low; she was now an outcast without a shred of power. Such an acknowledgment might have provoked a shred of sympathy among the bears, who could easily relate to being powerless, but Olwen could not bring herself to speak of those matters. The situation was simply too humiliating to admit to, even though the bears of Heimborn, of all the creatures in Aeronbed, would have been the very first to understand the notion of humiliation.

77

DELIBERATIONS

When everything had been said, Eirwen went off to consult with Bakman — and only Bakman — on what to do next. The polar bear knew that emotions ran high among the bears when it came to panthers. It had been expected, although never stated categorically, that little mercy would be shown to the hated creatures, whether encountered in battle or otherwise. In brief, they would be quickly dispatched. However, no one had imagined a scenario like the one that was presently unfolding.

It was important to think through the matter calmly and rationally, not to make matters worse by hasty overreaction. Eirwen also wished to avoid the inevitable lengthy, rambunctious debating session, with a host of inflamed bears arguing for one outcome or another. However, his attempt to settle the fate of the two cats in a careful fashion failed miserably.

While Eirwen and Bakman were still deliberating, Anat barged into their meeting place, insisting on seeing them before any decision could be made. The clan chief did not wait to be invited to voice an opinion. "You must recognize that I — the bear who has suffered more than anyone else here — I should have a say in their punishment."

"Really? And why is that, Anat?" Eirwen said coolly.

"Isn't it obvious? Do I need to explain myself? Do I have to reopen those painful wounds here and now for your benefit? Parthanyx killed my brother, did he not? You know it — you witnessed the foul deed."

"Parthanyx does not sit before us," Eirwen reminded her.

"Any many others have suffered similarly," Bakman added. "You are far from the only one with dreadful memories."

"Of course, of course. But I am here now, standing in front of you. Let's just say, cousins, that I speak for those who have been wronged by the panthers."

"And you believe you understand best how all your cousins feel?" Eirwen asked.

"Oh, indeed I do," the bear replied vehemently.

"And I'm sure you're determined to tell us," Eirwen said.

"There can be only one verdict for their crimes — death!" Anat growled, ignoring the polar bear's sarcasm. "Kill the both of them, before it's too late."

"And what crimes might those be?"

"Oppression, murder, genocide — take your pick."

"But neither cat admits to having committed any despicable acts."

"In an era of tyranny there are no innocent bystanders! These two may have no blood on their claws, but others carried out the deeds for them. *All* cats share in the guilt, no matter what role one may play. The lioness is a member of Aeronbed's ruling family. The panther admits to serving with the Black Legion's forces — inside our homeland, no less. Surely those two facts alone make her responsible and him complicit."

"The panther has explained what occurred. The lioness was fighting in the north, not against us. We have no evidence of any crime."

"And you believe them?"

"Their stories sound credible to me."

"Whatever. It's of little consequence to me where they were or what they did. I say again, the whole tribe of cats is guilty of every crime against us. There can be no exceptions."

"I don't agree with you, Anat."

"Then, my lord, you are a fool. A bigger fool than ever I would have imagined."

"You forget your place, Anat," Bakman said.

Eirwen was appalled by Anat's accusation. He knew she had strong feelings — and with good reason — but her manner was out of order. Still, he tried to remain composed and methodical in his response. Two of them losing their tempers would not improve matters. "We have no witnesses to support any charge. One of those three is accused of spying, the other two of supporting him. But even that first allegation lacks evidence, let alone proof."

"Bah! I care not a fig about the mountain goat. Let him go. I'm only condemning the cats. We must set an example, send a clear message to our enemies that we will be as harsh and ruthless as, as ... "

"As they are?" Eirwen added calmly.

Anat tried another tack. "Lord Eirwen, are we not at war?"

"Yes, we are, and these three are prisoners of war and entitled to certain rights."

"Rights! Are you mad? Look how the cats treated Heimborn!"

"Is this how you want the bears to present themselves, as no better than the Black Legion? That would give us nothing to offer Aeronbed. If all we can do is emulate a gang of thugs and killers, then we might as well be done with it. I, for one, want no part of a war that replaces one group of tyrants with another."

"We're better than that. We would never sink to their level."

"I couldn't agree more. And so we must begin — and end — our journey with that honorable commitment. It is the only way we can win, the only way we can command respect."

For a moment, Anat stood open-mouthed. Then the furious bear, obviously seeing no hope of success, jumped up and rushed off.

Eirwen, equally angry, hesitated only briefly, then rose and called after her, "Don't worry, Anat. In the days to come I'm sure you'll have plenty of opportunity to satisfy your bloodlust." He regretted his outburst immediately. But if Anat heard him, she ignored his words.

"Well, Bakman?" Eirwen asked in the momentary silence that followed.

"I think I can guess your thoughts, my lord."

"I'm sure you can. Although I wasn't certain about my decision before Anat showed up, I am now. Those two cats have committed no crime that I can see, certainly no crime worthy of such punishment. At the same time, we cannot rightly let them go. They are our prisoners, after all, even if because of their own foolishness and naive sense of honor."

"But we have no capacity or resources to watch over prisoners."

"Just one more thing we have to work out. They won't be the only prisoners we'll have to worry about in the days to come." The black bear's doubtful look provoked a further observation from Eirwen. "I know this may seem hard to fathom right now, Bakman, but, well before this struggle is over, those two cats may prove to be of great value to us."

Worry now erased the doubt on Bakman's face. "I don't see — " he began.

Interrupting whatever objection his confidant was about to voice, Eirwen added, "We'd better announce my verdict immediately — before Anat starts stirring up trouble."

The two bears started back down the trail to Vidar's forward camp. "Are you certain about your decision?" Bakman asked.

"No. It's just the best I can come up with under the circumstances. Sometimes I wish I could enjoy the comfort of Anat's certainty."

"Don't forget that her conviction is born from great sorrow. The two are inevitably related."

At first Eirwen kept walking, without a grunt or word by way of reply. Finally he said, "I understand that Anat is not alone, far from it. Her grief is honest, her anger is not out of line, and her views are held by a great many of Heimborn's bears. In sum, I understand why she has taken this position. I just don't think it's the best solution or the right thing to do."

"I concur. But this won't be the last of it. You'll need to bring her around sooner or later. With Gullhinder standing apart and Haefan's minimal effort, we cannot afford any more leaving the alliance."

"Understood, Bakman. Thank you."

Without further conversation the two bears made their way back to the center of Vidar's camp. Although it had been a long and difficult night, Eirwen took comfort in the fact that, at very least, the enemy's forces hadn't turned up to add to the challenge of sorting things out.

Rays of morning light were beginning to penetrate the overhanging branches, flooding the campsite with the welcome brilliance of dawn. Upon arriving, they found that the fire had died down, leaving only some smoldering white ashes. Some of the exhausted bears had taken the opportunity to rest, but most were still maintaining a vigilant and nervous watch. The three interlopers had remained where they were, seated to one side of the firepit, alert to what was going on.

Word had got out that Eirwen was on the move, and some of the other clan leaders had turned up to observe the results. Noticing them, Eirwen growled to Bakman, "This is not a performance. Why are they not back with their units? When I announce my decision, I don't want any commotion or signs of dissent. We must show these cats that we are as one on this matter. Call over the commanders so I can speak with them first in private. Then I want you to return to base camp right away. Someone needs to keep on top of things back there."

Some unpleasant snarling and grumbling ensued when Eirwen announced his judgment. Nevertheless, they accepted his decision, although grudgingly. The polar bear still had enough authority to be assured of that comfort.

Anat, however, was not to be seen. She'd evidently guessed which way the wind was blowing and, not wanting to hang around to witness the cats' gloating reaction, had decided to remain apart from the others. Eirwen was not sure whether her absence was a good or a bad thing. While Anat would have no second opportunity to restate her opposition and counter-arguments, equally he would have no chance to elaborate on his rationale and win some understanding of its merits.

❧ 78 ❧

THINKING ABOUT THE BEARS

While Eirwen deliberated their fates, Haidar, Eisa and Olwen waited patiently for the verdict, catnapping or studying the surrounding bears with an almost detached air of fatalism combined with curiosity. Bears were still a relatively new species for each of them.

"They're not quite what I expected," the panther said. "Especially their leader."

"My thoughts exactly," agreed Olwen. "Of course, until now I'd only seen bears from afar or heard idle chatter about them from some of my cousins. In my younger days, if you ever encountered a bear it was a novelty at best. At worst they were alien creatures to be regarded with great suspicion. This white bear, however, does not appear to be particularly malevolent or cruel. A serious and no-nonsense commander, yes, but not evil. Unless, of course, he's a master of deceit."

"I would never take Eirwen to be deceitful," said Haidar. "I may not have trusted him initially, but that was my error, not his doing. I simply misjudged him. If nothing else, the bear was always honest in his dealings with me."

"Don't beat yourself up about your initial reaction," the lioness declared. "When all is said and done, they are still bears. They will always be pretty rough around the edges. And since they don't have the finer, more sophisticated qualities of us cats, you can't really expect much."

Eisa and Haidar did not know how to respond to that.

"If it weren't for Lord Eirwen," Olwen continued, "this band of cutthroats would have killed us long ago."

"That's more or less what I would have expected before tonight," the panther said. "But their professional manner has surprised me. In all honesty, Princess, what would we have done if the tables had been turned?"

"I try not to think about such things. Right now it's all about survival."

Facing death as they still were, Eisa didn't feel like arguing the point with Olwen. However, his friend's comments troubled him. The panther remained silent as he reflected on her take on the bears. Haidar too kept his counsel, gazing off into the distance.

"Tell me again, why did we come after Haidar?" Olwen asked Eisa after a while, as if the goat were not sitting there beside them. Her eyes were carefully following the movements of one of the clan chiefs.

Eisa sighed. "The reason is lost to me now. It seemed like a good idea at the time. In truth, it was the only idea that came to me. I think I was drawn to this place just like Haidar was. Perhaps I sensed that he needed our help."

"Don't think I don't appreciate it," the mountain goat said. "Few creatures in this world would have risked so much."

"That's because excessive stupidity killed off most of those naive types," Olwen snapped. "Consequently there's very few of them left to boast about their generous sacrifice."

"Really, Olwen, what other option did we have?" Eisa asked, ignoring the slight.

"I could name two or three. And none of them would have resulted in our being condemned to a swift execution."

"You really think it will come to that?"

"Have you seen the way they've been looking at us?"

"Wouldn't you be just as contemptuous if the positions were reversed?"

"The bears hate us. So be it; I couldn't care less. They're nothing but ignorant pests. Up till now I've never given the creatures much thought, so I can't really get worked up about them one way or the other. Unless, of course, they attempt to kill me. Then my anger will know no bounds, and they'll be the sorrier for it."

Eisa took no notice of her threat. "My point is," the panther retorted angrily, "we would condemn them to death just as easily as they might condemn us. No, actually — much more easily."

"I suppose you're right. But that doesn't make me feel any better."

The panther suddenly laughed, his anger dissipating as quickly as it had risen. "If it's any consolation, as an expert in being condemned to death, I can tell you it's not really so bad."

"You're in a good mood, considering your — our — position."

"Don't forget I've already been in this exact same predicament. And I've come to the conclusion that one can always find a way out of it."

"I hope you're right, Eisa." The lioness sighed. "This is still a new experience for me."

"Just think of poor Haidar," the panther said. "Goats aren't blessed with as many lives as we cats."

Haidar's throat constricted and he swallowed hard.

"You should be all right," Olwen said to the goat. "I think your old friend is going to want to keep you around, even if it's only for a bit of reminiscing. And of course, let's not forget that the mountain goats are one of the neutral parties in this age-old conflict — neither fish nor fowl, as it were. That should keep you alive. In fact, Haidar, you may have found a new — and much safer — life than you'd have hanging about with us."

"Except that my mission wasn't to bring about peace with the bears. It was with the cats. So, ironically, I need you more than I need them."

"Kind of you to say so, but we weren't much help before and we're even less now."

"Maybe," Haidar replied. "Still, as the Lieutenant says, the game isn't over yet. Not by any means. Anything — "

"If it is to be death," Eisa said, interrupting him, "we must meet our end steadfastly and heroically. It must be an honorable death."

"That sounds like something a panther would come up with," Olwen groaned. "Didn't you just say one can always find a way out?"

"Of course, but I also have to steel myself for the alternative."

"Suit yourself," responded the lioness. "As for me, I'm a long way from using up my nine lives. If death is to be the verdict, I'm more than ready to fight my way out. If we both go for it, one of us might escape and live to tell the tale."

"They're coming back," interrupted Haidar. "It looks like our wait is over. Oh dear, Eirwen looks pretty serious. In fact, they all look pretty solemn. I'd say it's not a good sign."

The worried trio sat nervously, the cats' tails flicking back and forth, while Eirwen appeared to be consulting further with some of his comrades. Finally, the polar bear, accompanied by a phalanx of severe-looking clan chiefs, moved to stand opposite them.

Everyone was now awake, attentive and on high alert. For a few moments no one said a word as Eirwen seemed to weigh his options further. Somewhere off in the distance, Haidar could hear the raucous chatter of birds, but in the small sheltered grove, all ears and eyes were focused completely on the unfolding drama.

THE VERDICT AND ITS
AFTERMATH

The captives were now ordered to stand. Eirwen sat down and began to speak. The polar bear was not about to waste words; there was little preamble and no ceremony to his pronouncement.

"Haidar, Princess, Lieutenant, you have been charged with spying or being accomplices to spying. You claim you are not guilty. Have you anything further to say before I announce my decision?"

The three animals glanced quickly at one another. Eirwen had already given them plenty of time to explain their actions and their presence in that part of the world; there was nothing more to add, no protests worth making. All three shook their heads. As they were doing so, several shadows passed rapidly over the campsite and then vanished; no one on the ground bothered to give them a thought.

"In that case," Eirwen was saying, "let's proceed." After hesitating only briefly, the white bear continued with his pronouncement. "Haidar, given that you have not played an active role in this conflict, that you have not opposed the bear alliance, that you are involved in a mission of peace, and that no real evidence has been brought against you, I find you not guilty. You are free to go. That is, once you and I have had an opportunity to speak further."

The relieved mountain goat bowed low but said nothing.

"As for Princess Olwen and Lieutenant Eisa, since no evidence has been brought against either of you, and you can be accused only of coming to the aid of a party who has been judged innocent, I determine that you as well are not guilty of the charges. In addition, since no creature here is in a position to accuse you of other, individual crimes, no further charges will be made."

Eirwen paused to let his words sink in. The two cats, who had been unconsciously holding their breath, exhaled sighs of relief.

"Unfortunately, because we are in a state of war with your kind, neither of you can be released," the polar bear continued. "Princess Olwen and Lieutenant Eisa, you will remain prisoners of war until we can determine what to do with you, or until the war comes to an end, one way or another."

The two cats were impressed by the logic and fairness of Eirwen's decision. They had expected worse, and doubtless they would have received a great deal less leniency from their own kind. Indeed, Eisa knew that for a fact. What kind of creature was this strange white bear?

Since Olwen and Eisa had been deemed innocent but not granted liberty, they would remain stuck in a limbo-like state. Prisoners of war — what did that mean? And how long would it last? As they began to reflect on the implications of Eirwen's decision, a curious thing happened. Well, in fact, three curious things, the first just after the white bear rendered his judgment.

A young black bear had rushed onto the scene and now approached Eirwen. It was as if Haidar, Eisa and Olwen had become spectators at a play. What was about to unfold? As Eirwen leaned down, the newcomer whispered in his ear. At first he barely reacted, neither showing excitement nor losing his composure. However, when he apparently grasped the gist of the message, Eirwen glared furiously at the prisoners, and at Haidar in particular. The two cats turned to stare at the goat, but he could only return a look of confused discomfort.

As if a button had suddenly been pushed and a great clockwork engine set in motion, everyone began to move. Commands were shouted, repeated down the line and then passed on to smaller units.

Bears began to scurry this way and that. Entire squads disappeared into the surrounding woods and new ones arrived to replace them.

For a moment, it seemed to the three captives that no one was paying any attention to them. Olwen, quick off the mark as usual, whispered to the panther, "Look, Eisa, something's happened. I'd say they're under attack. We should make a break for it while we can. This confusion won't last forever."

Eisa, however, would not budge. "What for? We have no country, no friends, no fine principles to preserve. We've nothing to stand up for and defend, nowhere to go and no role to play. And if we succeeded, we'd only end up being on the run from yet another party to this conflict. At least here we're safe. In time we can figure out what to do."

"You may have nothing, Eisa, but I do. I have family and something to fight for — and you can be part of it. We can go up north, find the King and what remains of our army. And then — "

"Be honest, Olwen. You know that the possibility of finding your father and kinfolk was nothing more than a faint hope. We'd have to cross so much territory, so many enemy lines. At best our chances were slim. I've got a completely different idea."

The lioness did not appreciate the lecture, or being interrupted. She glared at the panther, who simply ignored the look.

"Rithild counseled me," Eisa continued, "that if I ever found myself in such a position, to make myself useful to the bears. That is, pretend to change sides. The Baron may have been misleading me, but perhaps there's a grain or two of sense in his advice. I know you'll think the idea is crazy, and half of me would agree with you. However, the other half is asking, *Why not?*"

The two were speaking frantically in hushed tones as the activity around them reached a fever pitch. Olwen's reaction to the panther's idea was as he had predicted: she was horrified. It was so preposterous and repugnant to her that the lioness couldn't think of a thing to say.

The three captives had been left completely alone, but the window for escape was closing as quickly as it had opened. Several burly bears were moving toward them, with the clear aim of leading them away to some sort of confinement.

However, at that very instant Eisa and Olwen witnessed the second curious event. More shadows crossed over the encampment, and something darted low — a bird of some kind. At first, in the noise and confusion, no one had taken any notice of the silhouettes against the sky, but when the mystery bird dived over the camp, several pairs of eyes shot upward. It was too late. The bird was gone in a flash and no one had time to identify it.

As the unknown birds began calling to each other, Eisa and Olwen were being pushed, prodded and hurried away through the woods, with Haidar in tow. The two cats glanced back, and what they observed was the third striking oddity to occur.

While the entire army of bears appeared to be rushing about in all directions, Eirwen seemed to have stopped paying attention to what that was going on. He was walking back toward the center of the campsite, to where the three captives had been sitting, and he looked as if he didn't have a care in the world.

While the companies of bears orbited around him like so many planets speeding about the sun, Eirwen rose onto his hind legs and simply stood there at his full height, his front legs raised and his deep black eyes looking up at the blue sky. The full light of the morning sun glistened off his great white head. It was a glorious spectacle — the polar bear was a figure of absolute calm in the midst of chaos.

❧ 80 ❧

THE FINAL SURPRISE

T he breathless young bear who had shown up so unexpectedly just after Eirwen announced his verdict had been a messenger from Bakman. She had travelled so quickly to get there that she could not speak at first. When she was finally able to spit out the message, it contained the news that Eirwen feared most: enemy forces were on their doorstep.

He knew the bears were ill prepared for a real set-to, but Eirwen could take consolation in the fact that at least some units had remained appropriately vigilant. Patrols from the rearmost clan unit had heard the approaching forces and had quickly alerted their company commanders. Since they had not yet caught sight of the newcomers, they were not able to describe who or how many were closing in.

However, forewarned is forearmed, and being on the defensive is much easier than taking the offensive. According to the messenger, Bakman had told the clan chiefs to dig in and prepare for an attack, then he'd sent as many reinforcements as he could to the rear. Eirwen's presence was requested immediately.

As soon as the polar bear understood the seriousness of the situation, he took a long, hard look at Haidar. So the goat had been fooling him after all. It was just as Eirwen had feared: while the bears were preoccupied with that little charade, that stupid sideshow, the main event was taking place elsewhere. He considered killing Haidar on the spot, but he was far too busy taking charge of things to deal with the betrayal immediately.

Eirwen called together the clan leaders who were present, briefed them quickly on what little he knew and gave them their orders.

"Aedelborn needs assistance," the polar bear said to Vidar. "Can you spare any units to go to the rear?"

"What about our front line, my lord? What if a second attack occurs here?"

"We don't hold the high ground here. However, the perimeter is well guarded and we have excellent protection from the upper ridge. Post more troops up there and send out some scouts, first, to see what — if anything — is in front of us, and second, to ensure we have a safe path for retreat in case we have need of it."

Although Vidar seemed rather unsettled by the thought of retreat, she signaled her understanding and went off to give instructions.

Eirwen was about to head back to the main camp when the shadows reappeared and the unknown bird swooped down. The bears had been so preoccupied with their strategizing that at first they failed to notice the silhouettes above. When they did look up, they just missed seeing the bird dive and then soar away. It was then that the bears realized the enemy — at least its accompanying air power — was already upon them.

Eirwen gave immediate directions to the others, and the bears ran off to take up defensive positions. Battles were invariably like that — surprise, muddle, chaos and confusion more the norm than certainty and order — but this one had barely begun. Things were not looking good.

The birds were calling to one another. Amid the pandemonium, Eirwen heard their cries. He stopped and then slowly moved out of the deep shadow of the tall pine trees and into the sunlight, which shone down brightly on the exposed central area of rock and grass. Then he stood up on his hind legs, raised his paws, palms up, and directed his eyes skyward.

The flurry of activity continued. Contingents of bears moved into place and frantic orders were being hastily repeated up and down the line. The only ones watching Eirwen were Eisa, Olwen and Haidar, captivated by what they were witnessing, and their guards, who had stopped prodding the captives so they too could watch.

The two cats saw first the shadows and then the birds themselves, circling high overhead in asymmetrical loops. The birds were too high to make out what kind they were, but low enough to reveal that they were large and predatory. After a time, a single bird broke away from the group and began a slow, careful descent. It landed right at Eirwen's feet. None of the bears thought to attack it; perhaps they had no idea how. The other birds kept their distance, still flying high.

Yet more amazing developments, thought Eisa and Olwen. *What could possibly happen next?* As if to answer their question, the bird bowed, spoke briefly to the great white bear, and flew up to alight on Eirwen's outstretched palm. Shortly thereafter it took off again to join its comrades.

When Eirwen turned to face the watching animals, he was no longer that fatigued, worried bear. He was transformed, radiating energy and delight. A glow seemed to emanate from him, making the bright sunlight seem pale and washed out in comparison. Eisa and Olwen saw him call out to one of the clan chiefs with a new set of orders. In the blink of an owl's eye, all action ceased; the troops were ordered to stand down.

Eirwen marched past the three prisoners without saying a word. But suddenly the bear stopped in his tracks, turned and motioned for Haidar to walk along with him, leaving the perplexed cats and their guards to follow in their wake. The little troop continued on in this fashion until they arrived at the base camp, where Bakman greeted Eirwen with a questioning look. Eirwen gave his deputy more instructions and then retreated alone into his temporary shelter.

Slowly the clan chiefs began to show up, arriving singly or in pairs, until all of them were assembled — that is, all except Aedelborn. When they had arrayed themselves in a semicircle facing south, Bakman went into Eirwen's shelter to summon their leader. The polar bear emerged, looking no less refreshed and energized. The other bears were struck by his new vigor and enthusiasm.

"Cousins," the polar bear began, "this is a momentous day. We are not under attack. Far from it, we — "

Eirwen was interrupted by a loud roar and a commotion in the dense forest behind him. As he turned to face the noise, from out of the thick bush lumbered a slightly disheveled and very unsettled Aedelborn. Despite all the racket, the clan chief was alone. Eirwen hugged the confused bear, who indicated with a motion of his head that others were behind him. As they turned to await the visitors, the other clan chiefs looked on with increasing curiosity.

Out of the dense, dark woods and over some low brambles leapt an immense fanged creature. Some of the bears instinctively rose to defend their ground or even counterattack, but Eirwen was faster. He rushed over and tackled the creature himself. Just then, more of the creatures leapt into view.

The bears were not sure what to do and stopped short. Eirwen and the creature were rolling over and over, growling and roaring. Then they broke apart and stood facing each other. And then came the most curious thing yet witnessed by Eisa and Olwen. The two combatants simply collapsed on the ground, convulsing with laughter.

"Eirwen!" said the unknown creature. "I cannot believe my eyes!"

"Adarix," replied Eirwen, "I have so longed for this day, I cannot tell you how much."

"How? What?" they both said in unison, then laughed again.

"You and I have much to talk about," said Eirwen. "It will take us many days and nights, my friend. But first I must explain you to my very surprised cousins."

"Yes, you must, my lord. However, there is still one more surprise before we break off to talk. I beg you, Eirwen, look up in the sky."

"I see Corvus, Lorcan and the others. They brought me the news of your presence."

"Look more closely, Eirwen," commanded the wolf.

The polar bear did as he was bidden. Among the falcons and hawks was one bird of different shape and measure, a bird that was now descending toward him. At first Eirwen thought his eyes were deceiving him, but then he knew it to be true.

"Fridis!" the polar bear roared with delight. The duck flew in circles around him, her joy equal to his. Then she landed and they hugged each other as closely as a bird and a bear can, too emotional and teary-eyed for words.

"This bear has no end of strange friends," Eisa said to Olwen.

"And you haven't even gotten to know the duck yet," Haidar added. Then he headed toward the happy pair, calling out loudly, "Princess!"

"Yes?" Fridis and Olwen responded in unison. The lioness and the eider duck looked at each other in amazement. Haidar and Eirwen simply laughed.

Soon the small clearing was full of wolves leaping joyously about in celebration of the reunion. The bears and the two big cats looked on with ever-increasing astonishment amid the rejoicing and catching up with old friends and comrades.

THERE WAS INDEED MUCH TO TELL, BOTH GOOD AND BAD. AND DESPITE THE undisputed joy of their reunion, Eirwen had much to account for. His failure to contact his old comrades over the previous months — and Fridis in particular — had left them in the dark about the fact that he was still alive. His excuses were accepted and he was forgiven, but his friends made known to him, in no uncertain terms, what his apparent death had meant to them. Notwithstanding his very justifiable reasons, the polar bear now felt ashamed of his negligent behavior. Still, his friends did not dwell on the issue; they were far too happy to waste time complaining. They were also brimming over with news and stories. Their long and fascinating tales, with twists and turns both amusing and sad, took many hours to relate.

After a couple of days and nights of intense conversation and enthusiastic celebration, Fridis and Eirwen found time to steal off by themselves. The two companions were once again able to enjoy a precious moment of peace together, sitting and contemplating the stars above. Only now, with no observers present, did the duck feel she could speak completely freely.

Fridis first asked Eirwen whether he had managed to maintain possession of his gemstone during the fall down the mountain and his rescue by the bears. The polar bear replied that, amazingly enough, he had; fortunately the pouch had been securely tied around his neck. However, he had not used the stone since, at least purposefully. Fridis was comforted to know that, between them, they still possessed the three magic gems.

The duck went on to relate what she had told no one else in any great detail: her surprising conversation with Señor Piro; her decision to pursue the trail of and the truth about the magical stones; her meeting with the Sesteros family; Raicho's key role as family historian; and finally Ammarich's astonishing claim of ownership and his revelation that a fourth gemstone existed. That fourth stone still lay undiscovered somewhere, and Fridis was determined to continue her investigation until she found it.

After the duck had finished her story with that fervently expressed intention, Eirwen hesitated before responding.

"I know what you're thinking," Fridis said. "There's a war on. It's not safe for a poor little creature like me to go flying off all alone. I've no chance of success. I should — "

The duck had been in full flight, her dander already up, when the bear held up both paws to silence her. "You're right, of course. You've more than proved you know how to take care of yourself. However, you are also my friend, and it's natural that I worry about your safety. I don't need to tell you that danger lurks everywhere."

"Especially in Blakfel," she reminded him pointedly.

"Yes." The bear sighed. "I admit I was wrong about your staying behind. That turned out to be the most dangerous place of all for you. You're far better off here with me — with us."

Eirwen smiled broadly and then laughed. "Haven't I always said that you make a great detective? If anyone can work out this puzzle and find the missing gemstone, Fridis, it will be you."

EPILOGUE

Vulpé sat down, right in the middle of the last crossroad he'd encounter before leaving the Kingdom of Aeronbed. Before him lay the narrow, precipitous trail that would take him up through the mountains into Vigmar. Behind him was the main road back to Manaris, while to his left and right wound a rough footpath that ran parallel to the vast mountain range dividing the warring neighbors.

The trip from Manaris had so far unfolded without incident. Vulpé had just bid goodbye to his protectors, a small company of panthers that had guided him to the intersection. The fox turned to watch the swaying tails of the big black cats as they began their long return trek to the capital. He kept his eyes fixed on them until they were mere specks on the distant horizon. Their orders had been to take him safely to this particular crossroads, which was considerably north of the route Haidar had chosen to enter Aeronbed.

The cats, going on Vulpé's story — later bolstered by the erroneous report that packs of lions were roaming the lands west of the capital — had chosen this longer and much more tortuous northerly route. The irony was not lost on Vulpé. His fabricated story had now resulted in increased discomfort for him and a delay of several weeks in his return to Vigmar. Unfortunately he had not been able to convince the panthers otherwise and was forced to go along with their plan.

Still, it was but a small price to pay, for the fox's meeting with the panther leaders had been wildly successful. Vulpé would arrive home in Blakfel triumphant, with the signed peace treaty in his paw — just somewhat later than he'd originally planned. And on his return Vulpé would lay claim to the title he'd made up when he met Rithild in Manaris. He'd become the Count of Ajatar in reality, with all the rewards and trappings that came with noble rank. It was, the fox considered, the least that he deserved.

The panthers had now disappeared and the fox was completely alone. It was midday; the sun warmed his back as he listened to the wind whistling through the grasses of the high plains. The challenging route into the mountains directly ahead climbed sharply, while the track toward the south looked tempting as it fell gracefully away into sheltered forested valleys.

Vulpé was inclined to ignore the advice of the panthers, for he knew that only one lion actually roamed these parts: Princess Olwen. How the fools had managed to exaggerate a single lioness into an entire pride or two was beyond him. Unless, of course, Olwen had been wrong about her family's whereabouts or had been lying to him all along. After all, in such difficult times, who could tell an honest creature from a dishonest one?

Was the risk worth it? The fox was tormented by a rare moment of indecision. He could remember the meandering route Haidar had taken with him, at least well enough. All he had to do was get back to where they'd met Olwen and Eisa, and he would be home free, more or less. However, in the ensuing weeks much could have happened. He had no way of knowing what new obstacles or dangers might lie in that region.

The way forward was new to him and hazardous enough, but according to the panthers it was well concealed and easy to follow. Vulpé thought about it some more, and even began trotting south to see how it felt. No, it didn't feel right. After a few hundred paces the fox returned to the crossroads.

Vulpé could not take the risk. He'd accomplished so much, it was best not to tempt fate with a late, rash choice. He would opt for the surer route. He shook himself from nose to tail tip to clear away any remaining indecision.

Firmly resolved, Vulpé marched straight toward the mountains as fast as any determined red fox could manage. He did not look back again.

AFTERWORD

The tale of the Ravenstones began with a lonely bear on a northern ice floe in search of adventure. It wasn't long before our hero found allies, a duck and a raven. And then his path took him to places he'd never imagined, dangers he'd never expected and challenges that pushed him to his limits. And that turned out to be just the beginning.

When I finished books One and Two of *The Ravenstones*, I reached two conclusions. First, the story of the magic stones and the many characters involved had barely begun, and it would require several more volumes to reach the appropriate conclusion. Second, to do justice to the entire story and give every character its due, I needed to tell it from more than one perspective. To do so required switching to the viewpoint of the "enemy," the big cats of Aeronbed. There was another tale to tell there, one that was separate and apart from — but inevitably intertwined with — the fate of Eirwen and Fridis.

In my acknowledgments for Book One of this series, I listed the many, many folks who directly or indirectly helped my writing and publishing process. For this third (and all the following) volumes, I could easily repeat the exercise and leave it at that, for I shall always be in their debt. However, since completing that pleasant task of thanking others, I have come across texts that bring new meaning to what I've written, ones that I feel are worth adding to give more depth and significance to my own words.

I started writing the *Ravenstones* series (which was not its original title) many years ago. My first purpose was limited: I wanted to create engaging characters, ones about whom readers cared and wondered what would happen to next, and made them want to know the final outcome. In so doing, I aimed to weave a storyline that provided characters with depth and color, surprises, the odd twist and turn, an appropriate amount of danger, risks and rewards, and an eventual happy ending.

Of course the story evolved, and so did the characters. Things became much more complicated, and so the saga took much longer to tell than originally conceived — seven volumes, in fact. (And if my energy and the public's enthusiasm hold up, I'll finish a prequel and a sequel.) *The Ravenstones* is much more than a story of adventure, mystery, personal growth and heroic quest. I've also tried to deal with themes that I hope resonate with the reader, including prejudice, faith and friendship, to name but three.

This is but Book Three. If you've enjoyed things so far, you've got a lot more to look forward to in the months and years to come.

— December 2020

PREVIEW OF BOOK FOUR

Book Four of *The Ravenstones*, *Gains and Losses*, will soon be available on Amazon. An excerpt begins on the next page. For more information, visit **www.theravenstones.ca**.

BOOK FOUR
GAINS AND LOSSES

AMMARICH'S OBSERVATIONS

"What do you think they're talking about?" Ammarich asked.

The unexpected question took Asteel by surprise. Duty bound, he raised his head just a tad, focusing his eyes and ears on the objects of the enquiry.

The two wolves were lying low, crouched down amidst clumps of bunchgrass and well-shaded by a stand of willows. Until this moment they'd remained as motionless as statues or, more to the point, as predators intently focused on unwary prey. In this instance, however, their gaze was aimed not at potential dinner or threatening adversary, but rather at two comrades: Eirwen, the great white bear, and his friend Fridis, the dappled eider duck. The pair were sitting some ways off, on a small open hillock, engrossed in conversation, one the wolves could not overhear, no matter how hard they tried.

The sightline had been perfectly chosen, offering the watchers a clear view not just of the bear and duck but also the open grasslands beyond. Even farther, in fact: all the way to the vast snow-tipped mountain range that separated the Kingdom of Aeronbed from the Empire of Vigmar. It was late afternoon on a calm and untroubled summer day; a wisp of a breeze blew gently off the plains toward them.

"You hear me, brother?" Ammarich said, impatient for a response. He spoke a little more sharply now and with greater urgency. "What do you think?" But even as he repeated his query, the older wolf was not sure why he was being so persistent. It was a rhetorical question at best, and he could hardly expect Asteel to have the slightest notion.

His brother continued to stare straight ahead, sphinxlike. Neither twitch of muscle nor blink of eyelid revealed that he'd even heard the question. After a long while, without the slightest movement of his head, Asteel's eyes caught those of Ammarich. His look betrayed just enough contempt to say, *Why are you bothering to ask me this? Do you think I'm stupid?*

"I know, I know," Ammarich acknowledged, sighing. "It was a pointless question. Forget I even asked."

Asteel, however, wouldn't let the matter drop. "Why are we here, brother?" he groused. "Our friends are neither lost nor in need of protection. Haven't we better things to do with our time?"

A large family of quails strolled across the trail leading down from their vantage point. They stooped to feed on whatever they could find, apparently oblivious to the nearby wolves. The chubby birds reminded Asteel that not only was he irritated by the useless spying endeavor, he was also starving. As if on cue, his stomach rumbled and he began to salivate. Adding to his discontent, Ammarich seemed completely indifferent to both the birds' presence and his own bodily needs.

As his brother deigned to answer, Asteel repeated his objections, adding some growls for reinforcement.

Ammarich sighed again. "Has it never occurred to you," the wolf said at last, "that the sudden appearance of Eirwen and Fridis was unprecedented, even extraordinary? One day the pair did not exist, the next they were among us, traipsing across the plains as if they'd been in the Empire for a lifetime. It was uncommon strange, if you ask me."

"*Unprecedented*? *Uncommon strange*?" Asteel repeated, laughing. "Your vocabulary, Ammarich — it's growing by leaps and bounds!" With an outstretched paw, he pushed his brother in the shoulder.

The wolf's gesture was affectionate but when he spoke next his tone became more serious. "You couldn't be bothered to answer my question, Ammarich, but let me try to reply to yours" — Asteel glanced back toward the duck and bear — "although I'm sure my response will hardly satisfy you. To put it most simply, I try not to trouble myself with matters that don't concern me.

"I *could* make it my business to follow strange scents down dead-end trails, but what would be the point? We wolves need our sleep and fresh minds for more important things — like my missed lunch, for example."

Ammarich tried to object, but his younger brother, on a roll now, could not be stopped. "And I'd put it to you that we have a war to win and real foes to defeat. Do you list Erwin and Fridis among our many enemies? I doubt it. Quite the contrary, they've proven themselves as stout and true as any ally — both of them."

When Ammarich opened his mouth to speak, Asteel held him off again. "Nevertheless, if you're really so worried, why not put the matter to Adarix? Or, better yet, to Alberic. Our young brother was the first to spot the pair, was he not?"

"Aye, Alberic was the first, and I did ask him. Actually, he agrees with me. He too found their arrival curious. At the time, both Adarix and Alberic had questions for the pair. The bear and duck were full of great stories but, at day's end, there was no meat on that bone. Nothing of substance; no facts to back anything up.

"Adarix would have interrogated them further, and fully intended to do so. But with the turn of events that followed their arrival at Blakfel, any questions about their origin — and so many others — were forgotten. Before you could blink an eye, Eirwen was our new lord and commander. I need hardly say, no one cared about such concerns after that."

Asteel grunted. "That's not how I remember things."

"What?"

"You heard me."

"So how *do* you remember it?"

"Of course, what you say is true enough, and I can't quarrel with your account. But that was just the beginning. You forgot to mention what happened next."

"And that was?"

Asteel snorted. Was his brother playing him for a fool? "Adarix's intention to kill Lord Eirwen and your own counsel against the idea. How could you forget that small detail? We were all sitting outside Utgard, as I recall. Night was falling, and Alberic was with Eirwen."

"Much has happened since then."

"Nothing that would cause an honorable wolf to distrust the white bear."

Ammarich chose not to respond.

"So, which one is it, brother?" Asteel pressed. "A faulty memory or renewed doubts?"

"Renewed doubts," Ammarich replied flatly.

"I see."

They turned back to keeping watch. The bear and the duck were still talking quietly, paying them no heed.

"So you never spoke to Adarix?" Asteel asked after a short while. "One on one, that is, about your, er, worries?"

"No, I did not. What was the point? Eirwen was presumed dead and Adarix had to live with the guilt. Guilt ... Hah! I wish I *had* talked to him, for it is too late now."

The two wolves lapsed into silence once again, their eyes fixed on Eirwen and Fridis, as if the simple act of watching might produce an answer to Ammarich's concerns.

At length Asteel asked, "So you intend to reopen the matter?"

Ammarich did not answer right away. What *was* his purpose, after all? Of course he recalled Adarix's plan to do away with Eirwen before they entered Utgard. But that scheme had withered away, like grapes on the vine after an early frost. Once the pack had made its way through the strange forest, any talk of such killing ceased.

During the fighting season in Aeronbed, the opportunity to ask Adarix about the pair had never arisen. Later on, Eirwen's apparent death had served to upend his brother's confidence and cement his shame about misjudging the bear. Even worse, Eirwen's startling resurrection had elevated him into some kind of demigod while simultaneously reducing the stature of the wolf commander.

In sum, Adarix had ceased to be the all-powerful leader of old. No longer to be feared, the wolf commander had become little more than the bear's acolyte. To say that Ammarich found the new order of things disturbing would have been a huge understatement.

The duck's behavior had also begun to trouble the wolf, especially her fascination with the Blakvul jewels and their history. Fridis had no right to poke her nose into such matters: not only was the duck a stranger to Vigmar, she was certainly no wolf. Curiosity? Yes, that would be appropriate, for every creature has a right to be curious. However, anything to do with those jewels — past, present or future — was the prerogative of the eldest brother of the Tasandik clan.

No matter who else might claim them, the magic stones remained the property of the wolf pack, and Ammarich alone was their lawful guardian. The only snag was that, over time, the gems had been well and truly lost: no one knew where they were. At least, that was the generally accepted wisdom among Vigmar's creatures — those who cared about such matters, that is.

Once Fridis had revealed her interest in the gemstones, Ammarich's curiosity about the duck and the bear had increased exponentially. The wolf took to weighing up everything he had heard or witnessed since the two strangers arrived, trying to make sense of it all.

Quite reasonably, everyone was currently focused on the next moves in the struggle. During a war, no one cared to waste time on myths and ancient history. Up to now, even Ammarich, who, as the eldest Tasandik brother, took the history of the jewels as his particular domain, had paid little attention to their whereabouts. But Fridis's meddling had begun to whet Ammarich's appetite for knowledge. His appetite and suspicions had grown apace.

The armies were now at rest while greater minds determined the path ahead. As a senior member of the brotherhood, Ammarich should have been part of those sessions. His darker thoughts took him elsewhere, however. Making his excuses, he went off by himself, a respite that allowed those thoughts to simmer and his former neglect to dissipate. All that was left behind was the evil sludge of an idea, one that obscured his better instincts.

What had occurred since Eirwen and Fridis first arrived on the scene? First, the Emperor's sudden and unwarranted decision to make

Eirwen the empire's new champion. Second, the duck's miraculous recovery from near death — or at least, that was how he'd heard the story. Third, Eirwen's sorcerer-like ability to get through the impassable barrier surrounding Utgard. Even Ammarich had witnessed that event, and the magic light it had generated, although from a distance.

In the euphoria that followed the pack's entry into the forest and the sweetness of life inside, none of the other wolves had thought about the incident again. They'd become like cubs, giving little consideration to anything but their immediate pleasure. That is, all except Ammarich. Why had he not felt that wonderful bliss? At the time his explanation seemed reasonable enough: for the pack to make its way through the forest safely and unhindered, someone had to hold on to the gift of reason. Otherwise, the whole lot — wolves, wolfhound and bear — would still be in Utgard today, wandering around aimlessly, never to be heard of again in the outside world.

But that was then. Now Ammarich felt differently. While a clear answer still eluded him, the wolf had started to wonder whether he was destined for some other, greater purpose. Although the eldest Tasandik brother, he had relinquished his natural place as pack leader, happy to accord it to Adarix, the second-born.

Adarix was best cut out for the role. No one disputed that fact. His fighting skills and commanding presence were renowned; indeed, in the annals of wolfkind no other example of such dominance existed.

The wolf leader could not be bested in one-on-one combat. Ammarich recognized that reality, and knew instinctively not to pick a fight he could never win. He had accepted his place in the pack without complaint, understanding that its strength and success were of prime importance. He loved his brother. In fact, he loved all his brothers. And he was comfortable — more than comfortable — in his role as the respected wise counselor and keeper of the family lore.

Ammarich took all his responsibilities seriously. Where others might accept things blindly or with little consideration, he would think through every implication. But since his many cousins considered Fridis and Eirwen as good, thoughtful, noble creatures, even beyond reproach, he could not share his concerns. He would take it upon himself to consider the consequences for the pack if his fears proved to be true.

Something — or rather someone — was nudging him, intruding on his thoughts. In his reverie he had forgotten about the goings on in front. Asteel was poking him in the shoulder. "They're making a move," his brother said under his breath.

Eirwen and Fridis had begun to meander away, towards the distant mountains. The bear was gesturing to the south and saying something to the little duck. The wolf, greatly frustrated by his inability to make out their words, knew that it was in moments like this — when creatures are completely relaxed — truths were usually revealed.

"Do you think we can get any closer?" Ammarich asked, indicating a point further down the slope.

"Doubt it," answered his brother. "If we dare move a paw from here, the game will be up. As it is, we were lucky to find such a sheltered spot; anywhere else would leave us completely exposed."

Asteel had soured on the whole business. The hours were creeping by, he was stiff from inactivity and hunger was gnawing away at his mood. Little more would be gained from perpetuating the charade. "I'm going back to camp," the wolf declared suddenly. "I'm so hungry, I could eat a — " He stopped in mid-sentence. "Isn't there a feast planned for tonight? Why don't you come along. I'll save a place for you, brother."

At first, it seemed as if Ammarich had not heard him. The older wolf kept staring into the distance, following the movements of his quarry. Then, shaking himself, he came back to the present. "Perhaps," he said. "You go on. I'll stay a while yet."

For several seconds Asteel weighed up a few pithy ripostes. At last, he simply shrugged and, without another word, edged backwards into the bushes, so as not to reveal his brother's presence.

Ammarich kept observing Eirwen and Fridis until the sun had sunk low in the sky. When the encroaching shadows enshrouded the bear and the duck, the wolf concluded there was nothing to be gained from maintaining his vigil. He had watched and pondered enough for one day.

Just as his brother had done, Ammarich retreated into the bushes and back to the welcoming society of the wolf pack.

FROM THE AUTHOR

Thank you for reading the third volume of The Ravenstones. I hope you enjoyed the book and are keen to explore the rest of the series. Book Four, *Gains and Losses*, will be released in early 2021. Book Five, *Death and Life*, is scheduled to be released later in 2021.

If you have a moment and are so inclined, please leave a review of *Olwen and Eisa* (or the earlier books) on Amazon and/or Goodreads. And don't forget to tell other fantasy readers what you liked about it and/or the series. I am grateful to any reader who takes the time to do so.

I can be reached via the *Ravenstones* website, **theravenstones.ca**, if you wish to provide further comments or ask any questions.

— C.S. Watts

ABOUT THE AUTHOR

During a distinguished career in government, C.S. Watts has worked for and advised three Prime Ministers, two Premiers and a slew of Ministers on a wide variety of topics, including foreign affairs, intergovernmental relations, economic development and governmental reform.

In his thirty-five years of service across Canada, in Washington and London, the author served as a diplomat, negotiator, speechwriter and gifted policy advisor, whose cool head and penmanship were always in demand. He has now turned his ability to render extreme complexity not only into readable and accessible memoranda, but also into highly engaging prose to the world of fiction.

X ⓕ ⓘ

THE RAVENSTONES SERIES